A POTTER'S TALE

DAVE DAVIS

STORY MERCHANT BOOKS
LOS ANGELES
2019

ISBN: 978-1970157048

Story Merchant Books
400 S. Burnside Avenue #11B
Los Angeles, CA 90036

www.storymerchantbooks.com

Cover art & interior design by IndieDesignz.com

PROLOGUE

It's time, don't you think, for you to get to know me? I know you after all. It's odd of me to permit an imbalance in our relationship.

My apologies.

I know this about you: you're made from the dust of my stars, from my protons and electrons, my molecules and muscles; my neutrons pass through you like ghost bullets, leaving no trace; my suns warm you; my planets support you, though you're less than grateful. You treat your gifts—and each other for that matter—with less respect than I'd like. I'm sure you've heard that you're created in my image—passionate and apathetic, loving and cruel, generous and selfish. All-powerful and impotent. The perfectionist and the sloppy builder.

Yes, just like me.

But I realize there are impediments to your knowledge of me.

The first is what to call me. It's true I have no name, or many. The unpronounceable *Jahweh* for example, the arrogance of I-am-who-I-am. Or Father, raising the specter of my gender, a laughable but understandable worry; humans are so—what's the exact word here?—*invested* in gender and sex. Or God. You may call me any of those, or none. Or you may use the name I prefer—the Potter, with a capital *P*, please.

Then there are questions about my nature. Am I, for example, singular or plural? Singular like Jehovah or Allah. Or plural like those raunchy Greek gods in their virtual heavenly reality show? Or like the Norse gods playing in

Scandinavian splendor? Or like the Mayan's Heart of Sky and Feathered Serpent and their crew? We'll learn more about the Mayans shortly.

Then there's the question of my person, not the flesh-and-blood type (another silly issue), but how to address me. Am I the first person, I? Am I the third person, He/She?

The truth is I am all persons, even the second, you. Created in my image, you may recall.

Perhaps we focus too much on these things. In the end (there's always an end, just as there's always a beginning) what matters is the story, not the name.

I like the beginning of the story, where it's always the same. When I hold it tightly in my hand—the tiniest, densest grain of matter and energy conceivable, the remnant of my last attempt. I like it when I open my hand to release it into the vacuum of timespace, exploding it, creating it. Scientists describe this movement as sudden, though without the usual benchmarks of time or matter to gauge it, "suddenness" is rather meaningless, don't you agree?

I like to watch it unfold, sculpted by me like a potter, at least at the outset. I like the anticipation, thinking that perhaps this time it will be *right*. I like the waiting, unpressured by limits or accountability. In some ways, it's like the story itself, unfolding, writing itself. If I appear too critical, too much the perfectionist, you see, I am blessed and cursed with an abundance of time and space, of expectation and hope, even grains. Oh, and stories, perhaps especially stories.

I should tell you a secret. Of it all—the creation, the unfolding, the mystery about who or what I am, the ending—I do like the stories the best. The Potter's tale.

SECTION I

THE MISCHIEF OF PLANETS

1

PALENQUE, YUCATAN PENINSULA, 1932 A.D.

He thought she was stupid.

Some spoiled daughter of a university big shot. A lightweight poseur, a faux-intellectual who thought a summer spent in an archeological ruin would be just the ticket to get her into graduate school. And she wore those distracting, tight-fitting clothes. Everyone else, in an effort to minimize the sweaty heat of the jungle, wore loose-fitting trousers and tops. Not her.

He was simultaneously annoyed and stimulated by her. He believed she'd never contribute anything to this particular archeological expedition, perhaps to anything archeological.

Alberto Ruz Lhulier had never been so was wrong.

"Professor?" she'd asked, in that irritating, young-person way, a rising, almost-question capping the one word. "Pro-fess-*er*!?"

It was early, an attempt to dodge the intense heat of the day at the top of the Temple of Inscriptions. By noon it would be almost *unbearable*, like an oven.

"Look at this! All the temple floor stones are perfectly smooth, except here. D'you see?" She was excited, breathless from causes other than the climb to the top of the temple. She was also right: the uppermost chamber of the temple—rising almost ten stories above the jungle—had recently been cleared. "See over here?" She pointed to the center of the floor. "The pattern is different. I noticed it yesterday, so I came here early and I walked around it, until I…" The parade of 'I's' stopped suddenly, caught in her excitement. She bent down, stretching her tight jeans.

For once, his eyes were focused elsewhere, watching her trace several carefully placed holes in the smoothed floor of the stone, each filled with round plugs the size of a small tree branch. Smoothed over by generations of sandals and the broom of time, they were hardly visible.

"Do you see?" she said, more exclamation than question. "Those are holes bored into the stone, plugged. This is a trapdoor, a doorway! I bet there's a stairway built in underneath, maybe leading to a tomb! Who knows?"

He had some difficulty hiding his excitement. Before him, in a matter of seconds, Anna-Louise was transformed from a stupid young girl interested only in adventure (and one young crew member who had taken her fancy) into an intuitive, intelligent woman.

Later, he would call the unearthing of the tomb of Pakal the Great the most important find of the twentieth century in the Americas.

He was wrong again.

What was *under* the tomb, *that* was the discovery of the century. Perhaps of the millennium. Perhaps ever.

2

WASHPO. WASHINGTON DC. MONDAY MORNING

His mother used to sing to him, *"Not too fat, not too thin, just as nice as Gunga Din. Not too short, not too tall, just the right size overall. Not too ugly, not too handsome, he's perfect and then some. Not too dumb, not too bright, her little boy is just right."*

Thirty years later, the song reveals some predictive power. Noah is somewhat less than striking and an inch or two short of tall. If he's slightly thinner than his mother would have wished, that was the product of a careful, non-indulgent nature she herself modeled. And if she was wrong about his brightness, how could she have known what he would become? Or *who* he'd become. She's been gone for years, the gift of breast cancer; she can be easily forgiven.

In the cosmos of the white room, Noah is the sole living object, a microbe in the universe. He adds the only color to the picture. Not his skin—he's pretty much a text-book Caucasian with English roots, tanned from a summer sun that lasts far into the fall and winter. No, it's his checked brown and blue shirt, his tan pants that call our eyes to him. Oh, and his *Where's Waldo?* socks.

The white room is a proud advertisement for the Color of the Year defined by the designers of Bezos 1 Plaza. Less *Cape Cod Cloud* or *Inuit Sunset* (as retinally orgasmic as they might have been), more knock-your-eyes-out, mom-put-a-ton-of-bleach-in-the-laundry white. Williams-Sherman's *Snow* in the hallways, *Pale Ecru* on the walls. This is an aggressive white pushing its way into corners and erasing lines and shadows. It blurs the shapes of things, as though an iridescent fog has squeezed through the pores of the building. Erich describes the white as a canvas on which deaths, births, wars, and rising tides can be painted. And the fires of course.

The white is relieved by little flecks of color on the walls. Sepia-touched century posters are framed in (you guessed it) white. A beigey-tan, taupey-brown floral design not found anywhere in nature but which by some miracle finds its way to the carpet makers of the District.

In the early morning light of the bleached room, Noah is the picture of pleasant, silent contemplation. But appearances are the thieves of reality: if we were to put our hand over his heart, we'd feel it pounding—110, 120 beats a minute. More, perhaps. We'd watch his hand move to a small pendant resting on his chest, rubbing it like an alcoholic uses his medallion. We'd touch his brow and feel the sweat on our palms.

He is an insomniac of sizable, even clinical, proportions.

Most nights it gnaws at him, memories like tiny rats chewing on his feet and legs, on the inside of his thighs, but mostly on his brain. It strikes like a schoolyard bully, slamming his overweight body into Noah's. Insomnia, the tyrant, destroys the peace of a dreamless, smiling sleep, leaving in its path a dark-morning awakening, a mild unpleasantness congealing into the anxiety of the day. On its worst days, it is a bottomless well of regret, days in which Noah becomes a heart-rushing, sweating whirlpool of thought.

He derives some comfort in the few gifts of insomnia. It's propelled him (that and an unusual mind) out of high school at an early age and into an accelerated program in math, physics and chemistry at Georgetown, into medical school and residency. And then, fueled by events, ambition and a kind of hungry curiosity, into journalism. The insomnia, and the mental machine behind it, are like rafts, floating him to WashPO as the Lead Health and Science Reporter.

The largest newsgathering agency in North America, WashPO is a juggernaut assembly plant, taking facts, figures, data and information, reordering and synthesizing them, producing easily digestible and above all, *accessible* (the current buzzword from WashPO's communication staffers) news. And then disseminating that news by any of the WashPO channels—websites, Twitter-feeds, email blasts, TV-streaming, video/podcasts. Despite the alimentary analogy of plugging data in at one end and churning news out at the other, it holds great interest for him. Like a giant vessel, it holds the story on these pages.

Noah would caution us not to be too impressed by his title. "Leads" exist in pretty much any domain, created at the drop of a hat or an email. A long string of them are already at work in Gardening and Pollution, Geology and Petrochemicals, Inter-personal Relations, Congressional Affairs, the last attracting rude remarks like metal filings to magnets. Let's not forget Cooking and Eating Out. Noah had a little thing with the Eating Out Lead for a while; they had fun with her title.

But it takes more than leads to move the wheels in the news-industrial-information complex: it also takes collaboration between the individual curiosities and minds. A straight storyline is one thing, say a new scientific discovery like a gene identified in the almost-constant quest to diminish the impact of autism or Alzheimer's, medical bookends of the early mid-century. But, a bifold story? Alzheimer's linked to pollutants, for example. Or the trifecta? Alzheimer's plus unwanted chemicals plus unethical corporate behavior? Better still. And those highly multifaceted stories, their angles glistening like light on a diamond? Those are the best, Erich always says.

Erich is WashPO's editor in chief. Erich Fulweider.

Erich occupies a small frame, perpetually bent forward as though thrusting itself into the jaws of the news lion. He plunges into meetings as though driven by a strange inquisitive appetite, asking, "Who? What? Where?" in a voice pitched just below dog-ear level. It emerges from a point just south of his salt-and-pepper moustache, like nails on chalkboard. Erich sees the world as a giant living-breathing *Facebook*. Noah is never sure: is Erich the nephew of the current mayor or the one before him (the one in prison)? Is he the cousin of someone in Congress? It's of little importance; Erich name-drops like Johnny Appleseed spreads apple seeds.

There's also a more polished Erich who loves to hold monthly, we're-all-one-family sessions in which he describes the WashPO World. Staff members gather in the lobby while Erich appears on the third-floor balcony like the pope, blessing his flock. He grabs his little hand-held (Noah and his friends make jokes about Erich's little hand held; all men are little boys inside), telling them, "We are *the* information platform. News services in every part of the world *need* our information!"

For the most part, he's right. Ever since the early part of the century when the social media king bought the *Post*, moving it from pulp to digital, from

Washington to the World. It's when you get him alone on an elevator or in the hallway (rare occurrences; he has his own special elevator to whisk him to a little white-on-white aerie) that Erich's internal dismissiveness makes itself visible. If you're one of his hundred employees, that is. If you're a member of the board, or a congressman, or the president, your fate is sealed: you'll have a kiss planted on your ass.

He's not, however, totally without merit. He has introduced several innovations to WashPO ("inn-oh-*vay*-shuns." Try it. There, right through your nose. Perfect).

One of them is teams. Erich believes that reporters need to collaborate not just within their own field—crime, say—but across them. History plus Science. Business plus Ethics. To grease that process, there are random seat assignments, stirred into the meaningless acronym stew of WashPO. Once a week, reporters are directed to different workspaces, getting RSA'd elsewhere. And finally, if a team finds a really big story (an RBS—now you're getting it), they're assigned rooms. (Yes! *A room!*)

Noah is almost the only person at Bezos 1, the WashPO headquarters, cheating dawn by a few minutes, and beating Hernando, the green-shirted security guard, by a few minutes more. Hernando sits on a raised dais in the three-story atrium of Bezos 1, his grin often the first and the most welcome sight that greets Noah every day. Hernando is a refugee from Colombia, happy to be anywhere but his war-raped, overheated country.

In the white-white newsroom, Noah focuses on the warmth of the coffee in his right hand, reaching with his left to touch the carved talisman that hangs around his neck. His fingers begin to scroll through his e-screen, gliding over stories, focusing, *focusing* on the silvery slippery feel of the semi-glass on his fingertip. Focusing on the edges of symbols carved into the pendant, a reminder of the Taliban. He feels the sweat drying on his back, a shivered conquering of PTSD, another gift from Afghanistan.

News stories, the talisman, and the slippery feel of the e-glass: they're working, holding back the storm, at least temporarily.

Noah pushes his way past Headlines of the Day, cataloguing last night's tornadoes, products of the ever-rising sea and overheated globe; a new typhoon (Armando, the first of the season) hammering the Philippines; the most recent terrorist attack. And more.

NASA reports no evidence of life forms beyond Earth despite six decades of work; extra-terrestrial intelligence (ETI) efforts defunded by Congress. White House announces youngest-ever junior science award winner. Charter schools continue to grow; recent stats show excellence in math & science. CERN researchers claim Higgs boson (the so-called "God Particle") is proof of parallel universes. Gates-Clinton Foundation to move the Third International Congress on Advancing Science from fire-ravaged Sydney to Melbourne. Homeless camps now in every state, some holding thousands. Dark Energy trumps Dark Matter: astrophysicists claim expanding universe is proof. Mayan ruins hold new clues about a vanished civilization, archeologists say.

In the scrolling world of stories, the last headline stands out. It's accompanied by a picture of a teenage African American girl, tall for her age, with incredible dark eyes, a surprising black jade. She is standing beside a poster of Mayan temples, a *city* of temples. Above it, in the rounded balloon letters kids like to use, the words, "THE COLLAPSE OF THE MAYAN CIVILIZATION: CHAOS, CLIMATE OR SELF-CAUSED?" The caption reads, "Fourteen year old wins national science prize."

Touching his talisman again, Noah thinks, *random, unrelated stories*. Movements in a pinball machine. He is wrong. Like Alberto Ruz Lhulier almost a century before, he misses the undercurrent of purpose in a sea of randomness.

Worse, Noah stands on a thin ice-pond of memory, a poor protector from what's to come.

3

PALENQUE. YUCATAN PENINSULA.1935 A.D.

Alberto Ruz Lhullier was wrong about other things, too. He thought there'd be only a few steps leading down to a tomb, that they'd make their discoveries later that summer.

That was three years ago.

The stairs were so packed with debris that uncovering each one consumed several days' work, removing the stones and rubble; loading it into heavy burlap sacks; taking them cautiously down the steep, sun-baked, once-red exterior stairs of the temple; sifting through the rubble like gold panners from the last century.

The creators of the internal stairs had established a narrow landing half way down, aligned the stairs perfectly, and then filled the space with rubble so carefully that it hardly deserved the name: less debris perhaps, more a barrier, dissuading visitors, even well-intended ones.

Ruz Lhulier was as determined as the tomb-builders. Guided possibly by the ghost of ancient architects, his surveyors indicated that, for every meter ascending from the main floor of the plaza, there was an equal distance downward into the base. Slowly, methodically, like patient archeologists unwrapping a mummy, he and his crew released each step from its bondage. Finally, on an early June morning, with the rubble cleared, they reached the tomb.

It offered four separate and quite distinct gifts, like the four corners of the world.

The first gifts were pictures. Pictograms and glyphs filled every inch of the walls and ceiling of the tomb—pictures portraying the conquests of a famous king, his shield carved and painted; portraits of his court and wives; images of tributes owed to him, slaughtered pigs, gold, jewelry, treasure; pictures painted in magenta, in scarlet, in mahogany, in the color of blood. Portraits of the king himself, the *ahoub*, whom the temple celebrated. He was Pakal, more formally *K'inich Janaab Pakal*. Born in 603 A.D., dead eighty years later after a reign of 68 years. Modern scholars place Pakal as the greatest king of Palenque, perhaps of the Maya, unusual for his desire to end war. A king whose reign marked the height of Mayan culture and of Mayan peace.

And whose death marked the slow disintegration of their civilization.

The second gift was an antechamber to the tomb, oddly barren. A few cups and urns. Three wooden stools, an overturned table carved with symbols representing amity and friendship, but broken in two as though smashed by a giant's hand. Two small obsidian blades, vaguely disturbing. And the bones of several individuals—men, the bone specialist said. They found no remnants of distinguishing clothing or decoration, no feathers, no leather skirts or belts, no jewelry. Servants sacrificing their lives for their ruler, they concluded, a common occurrence in the tombs of the great—proof that they'd found a tomb of the great *ahoub*.

Ruz Lhulier, Anna-Louise and their colleagues were mistaken about them too.

Standing at a triangular doorway the height of a tall man, the barrier and debris now almost totally cleared, Alberto Ruz Lhulier thanked the workers who'd labored to make this possible, one in particular, nodding to Anna-Louise. They moved the final wall of stone and dirt leading from the antechamber to the tomb itself, revealing its contents, unseen by humans for a thousand years. Breaking through a triangular door on one side of the antechamber, this was the third gift, awing them as much as Carnarvon's opening King Tut's tomb years before.

Their flashlights gave them only glimpses of the tomb, one jigsaw piece at a time. Fragments of rich Mayan red-orange on the walls. Glowing, calcified deposits in the walls and ceiling. Vases, goblets, clothing, eating utensils, bowls, objects that the tomb's occupant would need in his next journey, like the contents of a suitcase. Stalactites and stalagmites, rock-hard icicles and skinny towers of calcified water, glistening. Stalagmites like candles, as though illuminating the dark tomb.

A massive sarcophagus almost filled the space, covered by a giant's carved stone slab, sculpted in baroque detail. An icon of the Maya to this day, the sarcophagus lid revealed a reclining god-king ascending into a heaven oddly divided into two—one side mirrored almost perfectly by the other, the shape of an ancient tree occupying much of the space. Years later some would say the picture represented a sort of spaceship, that objects around the king were heavenly bodies.

They were partly right.

They believed the discovery to be unparalleled, the greatest discovery of the twentieth century.

They were mostly wrong.

Despite the grandeur of the crypt, the massive stone slab and its mirrored world, a more important discovery lay in the room, easily missed.

A space had been created beneath the king's sarcophagus, elevated about the width of a man's hand by eight heavy stone legs. Almost by accident, months later, it was where graduate students found a codex—a bark-paper book, its leaves painted white, filled with prophecy. It was the fourth gift.

Years later, after the excitement of the discovery had passed, scholars would decide it was *this* finding that was the purpose of the extensive debris.

What message could a book carry that one would bury it in this fashion?

What events had led to its creation?

4

WASHPO. WASHINGTON DC. MONDAY MORNING

The ice-pond of memory wears a thin crust. As he finger-scrolls though the news of the day, Noah takes a greased slide into a sudden, heart-pounding depression, a chest-tightening, heart-racing plunge into cold water.

"Here I am again," it whispers to him, its voice more frightening than Lucifer's. *"I am the simultaneously huge and tiny black hole of PTSD."*

If you ask, Noah will likely say it started in Afghanistan, after his transition from medicine to journalism, when he worked with Reporters Without Borders. The truth is—reporters really have truth as their only currency—it began much earlier. Afghanistan was only the door to the black hole.

Noah was posted as an imbedded reporter, assigned to Helmand Province, south and west of Kabul, at the end of the third decade of the sad love-hate triangle between the US government, the Afghani people and the American military. The sport of war had created hundreds of facts: thousands of Americans, allied forces and Afghanis killed over thirty years, double that number returned with physical wounds, maybe four times that number with invisible ones. Sometimes the invisible wounds are more traumatic and life-threatening.

Noah has one of them.

The facts of his PTSD flash in front of him like some time-lapse photographic display; they've worn a large pathway in his brain. It begins with Noah's translator, an affable, earnest, compact man named Mohammet, imbedding himself in Noah's work, earning his trust. After several weeks, Mohammet developed a story that he had heard about a dozen or so children hiding in a nearby cave, hungry and cold, needing to be brought out and cared for, freed from the Taliban. Noah had come to trust Mohammet, proceeded to convince the platoon commander that sending a task force into the cave made sense and would "save the kids." It was not an easy chore, the convincing. The task force itself, led by the commander, with four of Noah's friends plus Mohammet and himself, entered the dark, cold cave intent on saving children only to be met by Kalashnikov-sprayed bullets, treachery and no children. Or, as Noah calls it later, the same Noah who never swears, "A fucking ambush."

It's here that the rapidly moving screen shots slow down, almost stopping. As Noah hit the ground, ducking, he pulled Mohammet into the protection of his body. Mohammet was whimpering, clinging to Noah like a life raft, murmuring words in Arabic, a prayer possibly, but for what? His life? Their death? He heard Mohammet chant, "This is him! This is him!" Words repeated in Noah's nightmares years later. Seconds later, Noah saw who Mohammet was talking to.

The fighter loomed above Noah, basketball player-tall, dressed as a fashionable Pashtun, pointing a rifle at Noah's head. With the cold morning sun brightening the cave, Noah could see two other fighters on the ground, a small maroon-red lake slowly formed between their heads, fed by the two streams. The fighter's foot was heavy on Noah's neck, holding him; his rifle could have kept him there forever. And then in an instant, the shooter's left shoulder exploded. He spit blood, copious amounts, surprising, running like a small bright red waterfall, down the dirt tan of his long dress, onto the gray sand and stones. The fighter had been shot by one of his friends, BJ, his last dying effort.

Noah has a strange memory of what came next, replayed a thousand times in the theater of his mind. As the Pashtun fell to his knees, he reached into his pocket, retrieving a knife carved in exquisite detail. *Probably bone*, Noah thought, going to the place minds go to protect themselves. Noah struggled against the fighter's foot, the foot that still pressed his neck into the stony, gray ground.

There was a strangeness in the bedlam, though: the knife was not meant to kill him. The fighter used it to free a small pendant around his own neck, offering it to Noah. "You take, you take," he mouthed, nodding, an almost friendly gesture from the man who only moments before had killed Noah's friends and colleague-soldiers. Nodding, offering, gesturing, then dying. Noah reached up, holding a rounded piece of carved stone the size of a nickel in his hand, a leather thong attached. Stunned, beyond hearing and belief, he received it like some kind of an offering, tucking it into a pocket.

In the early morning, a little band of six had entered the cave, a small troop celebrating the folly of trust. By lunch, all but one of them had been killed, their breakfasts of instant oatmeal and fear still undigested in their stomachs. Mohammet had died in a burst of fire, anticipating virgins and praise from the Prophet. There were no children there—just adults, all but one dead. And no rewards.

As for Mohammet? His name wasn't Mohammet.

It was Judas.

And the name of the little operation? It wasn't Save the Children; it was Betrayal, a theme in Noah's story, perhaps in all stories.

From his own personal memory of hell, Noah has kept two things.

First, the talisman, which acquires greater significance in the days still hidden from you: in some ways it lies at the heart of our story. Second, a new friend, someone that, like the smell of a decaying body, has yet to leave him.

This second gift found him in Afghanistan—storms of insomnia that invaded his night hours, along with the heart-pounding, gut-cramping pain of PTSD. Within days, he had become anorexic then finally, virtually catatonic. "You was like some zombie, man," Hank, his bunk mate, said. "You was totally out of it, you know, hadn't eaten in two days. I had to carry you to the medi-tent." And he did, like he carried bales of hay every fall for his father.

They took Noah to one of several post-trauma camps, this one just north of Helsinki. There, in a facility that held a hundred or more semi-survivors in one-story, red brick buildings that looked like well-off farmers' houses, some slowly got better.

Noah's nurse-therapist was Aija, a woman who bore the high cheek bones, round Slavic face and reluctant smile of the Finn and the compassion of a saint. And who wore a surprisingly distracting mini-skirt. They met in a room painted the color of bile, a small window high on the wall.

"Anyone would feel guilt here, perhaps survivor guilt, Noah. What you have just described? It is a terrible thing to happen to anyone." Saint Aija shared this sentiment, or variations on it, when Noah was with her. She described her weapon: "Understanding, Noah. It is one way to conquer these feelings, perhaps the only way."

"You're right I feel guilty. I *am* guilty!" Noah erupted, angry at himself of course, not at Aija, the woman with the tiny skirt and enormous compassion. "I led those guys into a trap. I talked them into going!"

Noah wanted to keep returning to Mohammet, to keep beating himself up, but she pushed further. "Do you often feel guilty?" she repeated quietly. "Do you feel responsible?"

Yes.

Early on, Noah had learned to identify himself as the cause of most things. No, *identify* is too bland: for him it would be *blamed*. Blamed himself for the Afghani killings (it's why Noah has carried the talisman with him for years, a reminder of his faults). Blamed himself for any errors in his experiences as a doctor. Blamed himself for the breakup with Deborah, the love of his life.

Aija steered the conversation into a ninety-degree turn. "Tell me about Mohammet, Noah," the insistent voice.

"I trusted him, you know, *trusted* him," Noah whispered, riding a wail of self-pity. Tears flowed, the first, the early water of healing.

"So, on top of feeling guilty, it sounds as though *you* feel betrayed, too," Aija said, quietly, so quietly one could choose not to hear.

"I know you feel this guilt, Noah. We will need to talk about it, but what you said about Mohammet made me think you see him as *betraying* you. It makes me wonder if you've ever had that experience before." Her mini-skirt crept up her thigh.

"You mean in a war?" from Mr. Facts-as-currency.

"I mean more generally. Have you ever been," now very softly, "betrayed?"

How could she know? The ground opened in front of him, dropping him into the middle of his love affair with Deborah. How his best friend, Pete, with his black dick and his blacker heart, had fucked her, had fucked with his life. How could she know?

There, in the small therapy room with the hideous bile green walls, with

Aija's legs crossed demurely below her impossibly short skirt, with the anemic Finnish sunlight streaming through the tiny, high window, Noah was suddenly, vulnerably, naked.

They worked through it, Aija and Noah, ploughing fields of superficial details and harder but bitter, deeper feelings and meanings, the fuel of a million therapy sessions, all part of the military medical record, duly detailed and locked in some electronic Guantanamo.

There were things probably not in that record, too, pleasant things, like the every other evening smoke-saunas, with other patients, once even with Aija, unnerving but comical. There were Skype-calls from Hank, helping elevate his mood, propelling him to recovery. There were regular calls from his mother. Years later, Noah recalled less pleasant memories, digging them up from some dark garden with only the fragile spade of memory. These occurred spontaneously, often in dreams—sessions with someone he could only describe as military intelligence, shaved head at the sides and a close-cropped buzz on the top, all bulk and no smile. Not in Finland, though: they were sometime *before* Helsinki, before Aija and his therapy. Before the smoke saunas. And they were somewhere else. In a house, maybe.

At the end of sixteen weeks in Finland, the result of his and Aija's getting-it-all-out sessions, the PTSD shrunk and Noah grew. As for Pete and Deborah? Be patient.

Ten years later, Noah can still hear Aija's voice down the corridor of time, tangible as a choir: "When you start to feel this way, find something else to do or think about to distract yourself, like taking that small—how would you say this?—talisman? Yes, the little pendant. Take it, feel it, push the memories back into the rubbing stone."

Always the good student, that's what Noah has learned to do. He even hears the words—"poosh," for example—in her Finnish-English, like a mantra.

Like a prayer.

5

PALENQUE, YUCATAN PENINSULA, 683 A.D.

The Scribes, just ahead of A'Ciliz in a long parade of Mayan priests and princes, were arguing about who should lead them. A'Ciliz, towering above them, distant as a star, was less interested in the how and what of the procession, or even of the great peace accord. His mind asked *Why?*

Four forces had brought them to this point in the history of the Maya, five if you looked closely enough. Pakal the Great had called them the pillars of change.

First, there was the death of several kings who had thrived on war as though it were food and they were gluttons. They'd ruled cities to the south—Copan, Yaxchatlan, Tikal, others. Their sons, in the ways of children, turned against their parents' beliefs; they were tired of war, hungry for peace, a different kind of food.

Energized by the loss of the war-kings trade became a second giant force for peace. Trade routes carved into the jungle and across the plains had grown plentiful and—more importantly—lucrative. Carried along by the swollen rivers of trade was prosperity, allowing the chief merchants of the city-states to argue convincingly against war. It was hard to trade with people who hated you, or worse, they said (hiding their sarcasm behind a merchant's smile) whom you'd killed.

Many of those arguing for peace were the voices of women, the third great force for change. Tired of losing sons and husbands, tired of the pain of childbirth only to feel the greater pain of loss as they saw their sons die on battlefields, they refused to be silent.

Change needed a fourth element, a leader, in this case Pakal. Charismatic, full of the will and the means to unite the Maya under a common banner. So powerful that a city was built by and for him, its strengths matching his. Only he could bring the kings and rulers of warring city-states together for days of celebrations, for the signing of a peace accord.

Peace, Pakal said, was a necessary tool for progress, an innovative concept for the Maya. Convinced in his heart of the importance of harmony among his people's city-states, he labored tirelessly to bring the other kings to the table, all to occur in Palenque during this week.

It was a huge congregation—a cascade of dinners and luncheons, of hunting parties, of music and dance entertainment from many of the nation-states. A sexual orgy using temple-virgins from conquered city-states not part of the peace pact, an activity in which eunuched astronomer-priests—their testicles long ago thrown to the crocodile resident in the temple-pools—could not participate. The kings had also brought their entourages of wives and children, attendants and scribes, swelling the population of Palenque, the seams of the city bulging like a dress made for a thin woman but worn by her obese cousin. Along with them came the stragglers and prostitutes, the pick-pockets and hangers-on. If nothing else, they came to watch so many kings in dialogue, not fighting; no one in living memory had seen such a thing.

And there were the serious discussions—decisions to be made about boundaries, about crops, about trade. Each required the heaven-guided efforts of A'Ciliz and his colleagues, blessings by the priests, prayers before and after the proceedings.

Despite enormous tensions and anxiety ahead of time, it had gone well. Even A'Ciliz, still held captive by an inner dread, smiled as each successive meeting and decision passed with little hint of rancor. Goodwill floated like incense in the air.

There was a final force for change, the fifth pillar, invisible to all but a few—the document which A'Ciliz held close to his chest, tightly, like a precious object. In future years it would be labeled the Palenque Codex. Today it held no name for A'Ciliz, only dread. Crafted from white-painted bark, the length and width of his long forearm, it sat as though it were a strange, sleeping, malevolent child.

How to interpret what the child held? How to explain it to the kings waiting for him at the top of the temple?

He clutched it closer, a pointed sword against his chest.

At first, he had thought it a mistake.

For years, he and his mentor, Nantua, had plotted the rise and fall of the planets, stars and the moons, much as their predecessors had done for centuries. Like them however, they kept highly accurate records—pages of white-bark notations and drawings, painstakingly detailed. They'd introduced new technologies, built or carved new, precise tools, created better recording methods. Nantua was an especially skilled artist, his records of the night sky as accurate as a modern photograph and his small stone carvings, formed tiny replicas of constellations. They'd employed precisely crafted narrow temple wall-slits and openings elaborate to track the movement of the gods in the heavens, especially the manner in which the god-planets crossed constellations. They discovered the concept of parallax, using two points to determine an object's distance. For A'Ciliz, the Temple of Inscriptions was one of them; the other was a village a day's walk away.

Their work yielded new measurements and discoveries, each year more precise than the last. It was in the planet we call Venus that they noticed the change first. Venus, the morning star, was a planet important to the Mayan people, especially to its astronomers and mathematicians; it danced with the sun. Every year, at the same time in the spring, Venus crossed the path of the Mayan's most sacred night-sky constellation, the Seven Gods. In the days when there was no light pollution, more easily seen, the Seven Gods reflected the Mayan belief in the creation of Earth.

Though more difficult for you to see as you pollute the night sky with your own light, it is still visible. You call it the Pleiades or the Seven Sisters, a constellation of stars I created for you. It is not just a random set of stars to which your imagination—another of my gifts—gives a name; it is a true portal, a gateway.

"Nantua," A'Ciliz said to the older man early in the still-dark Palenque morning, "This troubles me." He had taken great care to note the moment at which Venus crossed the path of the Seven Gods.

They were huddled over the white-bark pages of records—years of them—stacked in front of them. Dozens of candles were spread around the room.

Nantua brought several bark-pages closer, taking care not to spill wax on the pages or to set them on fire. The warm early morning seemed full of dread as a small, painful ball grew in A'Ciliz's stomach.

They had plotted Venus' movements for decades, careful to erase any doubt. Over time, Venus crossed the path of the constellation slightly earlier each year, meaning that this planet, this *god*, was sliding inexorably towards them, moving. Perhaps, they wondered, were the other planets (they had found five in total) also moving?

Nantua nodded. It was his way not to say anything without thought. Instead, he eyed the younger man with the pale affection of the eunuch.

"*Ah-Chicum-Ek* is one thing, A'Ciliz," Nantua responded, using Venus' Mayan name. "But I have made similar observations. I have recorded and re-recorded the circuits of the planets a dozen times. Like you, I thought I was in error and kept the idea to myself, thinking not to furrow your brow. Look here," he said, pointing to two charts, pulling one from the floor, "Mars did not align precisely with the dawn of the first spring day as it has in the past. And this," he said, as he reached for older birch bark documents, relieved that he could finally share a secret fear, "matches what our ancestor wrote *katuns*, many centuries ago. Their drawings are more primitive than ours, but still…." His voice trailed off as A'Ciliz nodded quickly, equally excited.

"I have also noted the same thing in other planets. I made a related notation myself last year, but in Saturn, rising over the west. And I have confirmed the finding using two points of reference. Here, look!"

The two men bent their heads over the graphs and notations, the planetary maps, the pictures of the horizon, candle light projecting their flickering, hunched shadows on the walls of the temple. How could it be that two, no, perhaps three planets, appeared earlier with each passing year? That their distances, measured by parallax and precise timing, seemed to be slightly closer? In particular, that Venus appeared to cross the Seven Gods slightly earlier each year. The Seven Gods represented the ancient stories of origins of the Mayan people and perhaps more. By dawn, they asked their scribes for even earlier charts and noticed the same thing—not as well recorded nor as accurate, but leading them down the same path.

The near planets were moving closer.

Their work, always a source of energy and pride, became all-consuming, as much a part of their everyday labor as their air or food. Early on, they agreed to speak to no one about their findings. Revealing the movement too soon, especially without proof, might cause fear, possibly panic, not an end to be desired. And so they toiled, plotting through the night over months and years, Nantua sketching carefully, transferring some of his work—that of the Seven Gods especially—to stone. Even through his final illness, when Nantua spent painful nights propped up in his cot in the temple-observatory, they continued to compare and measure. And to talk.

On one still night, awaiting the dawn and Nantua's demise, watching the Seven Gods, they heard a child cry, its mother walking behind the temple, attempting to calm the baby. "Do you ever wonder," the older man asked, "what your life would have been like if you had not become an astronomer-priest? Perhaps married and had children? Your drawings, even your small carvings, are exquisite. Your sketches have even been accepted by the King for his tomb. You are such a talented artist and sculptor; you could easily have been a famous scribe."

"Occasionally I do wonder, master," came the answer. "Our life, it strikes me, is like a tree, beginning at its trunk, nourished by the roots of our parents and their forebears. And at each point in our life we can only take one of many branches, can we not? And, I have not on the whole regretted my choice," A'Ciliz said at length.

"And I too," said Nantua, knowing his end was close. "I would have not known you for example. I have valued our friendship greatly. But why," he asked, "is it not possible to see that we can take *both* branches, perhaps many." It was an important question—important for A'Ciliz, both astronomer and scribe, for you, for the universe.

Sadly, the question was lost in the aftermath of Nantua's death. Through the rise of Palenque, through the early peace-building years, A'Ciliz slaved only to prove, then diligently document, his discoveries: the nearing Venus, the movements of the other planets, and a mystery he could only guess at.

Finally, he was ready to present his case to the king.

Obtaining a private audience with Pakal was no easy matter.

It was not that A'Ciliz did not see the king regularly. He was often called on to consult the stars for signs of the gods' blessings or luck, especially when the king engaged in battle (a thing of the past for the most part) or increasingly as he cajoled the other kings to share his dream of peace. But on those occasions, Pakal was surrounded by dozens of other priests, lieutenants, generals, merchants. To find him alone, to tell him about this finding without alarming him, that would take time and cunning.

He knew this about Pakal. Of his four wives, he favored the third and youngest, spending an evening or two each week, often a full night, in her company. He was as alone there as at any other time in his week. Her house lay near the entrance gate surrounded by guards, but the king himself was alone with her, to roar like a jaguar when he penetrated her. Knowing that the king was often sated of her favors by late evening, A'Ciliz arranged to meet this wife, explaining his problem. It was best of course after his seed was spent; it would be dangerous to interrupt him beforehand. Perhaps, A'Ciliz suggested, she could take the king to the garden afterwards to wait for them? She agreed.

Lovemaking mellowed Pakal.

Despite A'Ciliz's fears, the king appeared pleasantly surprised to see the priest at such an hour, not at all, as A'Ciliz feared, angry. Since A'Ciliz knew little of the ways of men, he could not understand how the king's unruly, charismatic, often-angry character could be so becalmed, so much unlike the jaguar whose sign he ruled under.

"You surprise me, A'Ciliz," Pakal said, pulling his wife's cloak around her bare shoulders, keeping them from the cool night air. Clad only in a thin gown, her breasts were just visible in the thin cloth. He yawned, stretched his legs and back, leaning against a jacaranda tree, just now in the earliest bloom of spring. "We see each together almost daily, yet you choose to interrupt a man when he is with his wife? This must be serious indeed." Incredibly, he smiled.

"It is, sire," A'Ciliz said, his knees scraping the stones of the small garden, nervous now that he, after years of work, could reveal his findings to Pakal. Pakal, who had beaten or cajoled most of the kings of the Yucatan. Pakal, who was on his way to a vaunted peace accord. Pakal, whose temperament was as unpredictable as the weather. How was he to tell him?

He took a deep breath, plunging, like a morning swim in a cold high-mountain lake, into his story. He shared his and Nantua's findings and their growing certainty.

After two hours of questions—*Was he certain? Was it all planets? What of the sun? What did A'Ciliz think might happen?*—and a slow dawning understanding, that the king came to a conclusion. He drew himself upright, straightening his strong back, previously bent over the documents that A'Ciliz had brought, processing his options. There was a long pause, disturbed by only the jungle's night sounds. Somewhere a monkey screeched.

"I realize that you believe this, priest, and that you have shown me proof. I also realize that only the gods have control over this movement of the planets. But, in my experience, one does not—what is the right word here?—*waste* a problem. Instead, one *uses* it." He paused for emphasis, as politicians have learned to do over millennia, gathering his energy around him like a cloak, "We shall employ this as one employs a knife. Priest, I do not know if the world will end in a *katun* or a million years, but we shall engage this, this *document*"—he pointed to the Codex leaves in front of him, strewn on the pavement of his wife's courtyard—"to tell the kings that they must cease their warring. We shall say that the gods have leaned in to see us better, like angry parents concerned about the fighting of their children. I have no doubt they will bow to me!" His wife stirred then, turning her body so that her breasts rubbed against him, a small wordless chastising. The gesture had its desired effect, another sign of the potency of women.

His arrogance shrunk. "I apologize. They would bow to the *shared* message of peace, the peace of Palenque, turning the world towards a culture of reconciliation. If the kings needed proof that this was the right path, this is it, this document, the work of many years for you and others. If we are right that these are gods and they do in fact watch us, we will say, 'They will turn away from us when we have found peace; the planets will resume their normal course.' If we are wrong, it does not matter. We must be convincing. *You* must be convincing."

All that A'Ciliz had feared—that Pakal would be angry or frightened, that he might punish A'Ciliz for bearing the news, that he would (who knew what else?)—failed to materialize. They were dark clouds on the horizon of A'Ciliz's imagination, now vanished. In some ways however, what was left was worse: A'Ciliz was now the father of this document. He was the one to convince the other kings, all in order that the tide be turned back, the planets returned to their usual, unthreatening orbit.

There was a problem however, as large as the sun. He neither believed in gods nor in their ability to turn the tide.

And he believed that the end would come, not in many millennia, but in one. Although his mind used *katuns* and the other complex mathematical tools of his people, he had calculated a date that we record as A.D. 2012. If he was off by two or three *katuns,* a small matter in calculating the movements of planets, we can forgive him.

6

WASHPO. WASHINGTON DC. MONDAY MORNING

Noah continues to act the role of relaxed reporter, his long legs stretched out in front of him. He slouches in the office chair, finding his own personalized newsfeeds, scrolling through them, discovering an early semblance of control. The tactile process drives away the negative thoughts, partly at least.

In the journey of self-discovery others might call healing, he has found one thing that eases the deep, frightening black hole of PTSD. The focus on doing something, *anything* physical, rubbing the tiny stone around his neck, concentrating on the little e-screen, allowing the little storm of guilt and self-pity to pass through him as if they were neutrons, or ghosts, with no ability to touch or harm him. Certainly with less pain than they had years before. He uses it as a form of reassurance. *You see? You survived this, didn't you?*

He has. Noah remembers Aija's words, and even, with a smile that never reaches his lips, her short skirt. He uses memories as others build muscles. He remembers what his mother said when he had a problems, "Dear, don't worry, the universe is unfolding as it should."

Noah can be forgiven if the irony in her words escapes him.

By the time others start to arrive, he is calm. The self-loathing devolves into tiny waves of self-pity, then vanishes like a bad dream. People around him help the process, and Monday's group is especially large. There are easily thirty people, some of whom he knows well, some not so much. One young woman not at all.

They open their laptops and e-screens, play with their iPhones. This day's huddle is a mix of Health & Science (Noah), Crime (Gerry Watts, trying to make eye contact with Sydney, and failing), Political Affairs (Naomi Zaltser) and two dozen or so representing everything from International Relations to Recycling. Junior staffers, seniors, leads and others. Coworkers, colleagues, friends, occasional lovers, competitors.

Noah is lucky today, one of the perks of being first: somebody new to the team chooses the seat beside him. She is safe for the moment; Gerry hasn't spied her yet.

Among the accomplishments of his life, Noah has graduated in medicine, was a resident at Georgetown-Med Star. He recalls Monday morning case rounds, possibly not much different than what he sees in front of him today. Officially called hand-offs, they allowed the weekend or night team to pass on their cases and patient problems to the next. The rounds permitted something that few would think possible—solutions in health and illness that were not medical. In the journey of his life, this insight became a stream, then a river, leading Noah to quit medicine, perhaps more accurately the *practice* of medicine.

The group is led by Sydney, the head story-writer, the deputy Editor-in-Chief, a hundred pound bird humming with ambition, a tiny lion tamer in the multi-ring circus of WashPO. She moves to occupy the center of the eleventh floor meeting room, a space almost totally surrounded by glass, white boards and flat-screens fixed to the ceiling, a constantly-circulating bath of news feeds.

Noah thinks, *You could write a book called Stories about Sydney.* Skinny, athletic, marathoning Sydney, ten years older than Noah, driven by the news, her tongue as sharp as a surgeon's scalpel. Relentless when she was on a story, constantly in communication (she had two mobile devices, one most likely implanted in her ear). The marathoner wheels a white board into the center of the room, moving effortlessly, waving her Easy-Erase marker like a lion-tamer's whip, saying, with no introduction, "What are you working on, folks?"

Five hands punch the air, a small fraction of the group. Not Noah's however; he watches Sydney's high end jeans, imagining the body parts they wrap, in full-on daydreaming mode. Noah's genitals begin to respond. He is not entirely himself yet, does not even like her.

Sydney grants a tiny head-nod that says *Okay* when she hears a single-themed story. She does not pursue them. She tells the lions, "The beauty of stories are at the margins, their interesting boundaries. The interaction between lasers and surgery, between electricity and heart movements, most importantly, the intersection of stories with people. Understand?" It's a non-question question.

It is why she's the deputy EIC.

"There's news from UCSF about heart-cloning, Sydney." This from Roxanne, equally driven, an older version of the first-hand-up kid in high school nobody liked. Hair-in-a-bun. Birkenstock shoes her mother bought for her as a Hanukkah gift years ago. Pointedly ignoring Noah, she says, "There's this teenager with a congenital heart defect. They took cells from his mother's heart, cloned them, grew them into a functioning heart in less than three months."

"We'll go with that one," Sydney says, writing fast but neatly, an Arial or Calibri gene at work. "I like it. It has a person at the center, and a strong science angle. Do you want Noah on this one?" the lion-tamer asks from her white-board perch.

"Oh no." Rochelle shakes her head, throwing a little *See? Who needs you?* smile in Noah's direction. "I have two cardiologists, an immunologist and transplant surgeon all on top of this. They're *practicing*."

Perfect, Noah thinks, smiling his brightest, unblinking. *Screw you, Rochelle*.

There are more stories like this: a new prosthetic hip that will never wear out; an outbreak of whooping cough caused by parents not wanting to immunize their kids, putting hundreds of others at risk. Many stories about the effects of global warming—so ubiquitous they're no longer news. Finally, the hour almost behind them, Sydney says, "How about something from the new girl?"

The newbie is Katherine Chien-Forest, the exotic Asian more reflected in her name than her looks, though her eyes convey some of the East. She is the young woman beside Noah.

She stands, pulling her chair back, reaching her just-over-five feet. The men in the room, Gerry especially, notices her compact, athletic body, her short-cropped black hair, her oval face, as attractive as a model's. The women notice her outward calm, her professionalism; they see a competitor. Noah sees something else entirely—a small geographic area of blush, creeping from her neck into her jaw, a sign of—what?

"Good morning, everybody," she says, "I'm Kate." Several of the team encourage her to talk about herself (not Sydney, even more business-than-usual that day, perhaps pre-occupied), "Well, okay, about me. I graduated in social work and law from the UofT." She pauses, noticing *no comprendo* stares. There are dozens of U of T's, from Texas to Toledo. She gets it.

"Oh, that's the University of Toronto. I worked with the *Globe and Mail* for five years, probably the closest to WashPO in Canada, and specialized in social justice and equity, their health implications like access, equity in healthcare, outcomes research?" Her statements have an uptick at the end.

She doesn't tell them that she's an award-winning reporter, was actively recruited. "I've done a little freelance since, some on-line blogs, some on-air, and......I'm glad to be here."

She shrugs then, a bare lifting of her shoulders, and smiles. There is a hint of Canada in her voice. She says *proe*-gress instead of *prah*-gress. Noah can almost see the Mounties riding up behind her.

And for reasons a bit obscure to him, he is almost himself again.

Katherine Chien-Forest also has a news story, on day one at that; ambition runs high in her. It's about a teenager recently awarded the President's Science Prize for her work on the collapse of the Mayan civilization.

Noah plunges into the conversation. "I know a little bit about that story, Syd," he says, his voice rising like some grade schooler's. He makes several around him smile. He smiles too, this time directly at the young woman by his side.

"Good," Syd says, her words as sharp as a paper cut. "You guys work on it together. Show her the ropes, how she uploads stories. Like that." Noah was glad; he wants to suggest it himself.

"The girl," says Kate not looking at a note, "is DiShannia Johns."

"She's fourteen. She's been winning science fairs and projects since she was ten, first in the District, then regionally, now nationally. This year her principal put her name up for the President's Junior Science Achievement award. She got it." Kate smiles. Was she pleased she got the lion-tamer's attention? Several others begin to grin, the virus of the smile. "In fact, she's at the White House today and the National Academy tomorrow. And just last week she was awarded the Clinton-Gates International Prize for Young Scientists—$50,000, plus travel to speak at the International Science Congress in Australia. That's like winning the Nobel Peace Prize at twelve." The reference is to Malala, the young woman who fought for children's education in Nigeria years earlier, shot for her pains by the Taliban, the youngest-ever recipient of the Nobel.

"Her research is in," her voice says, *get this,* "the disappearance of the Mayan culture over a thousand years ago. The paper that won the president's award is termed *A Vanished Civilization; the mystery of the Mayan people.* But what's really remarkable about this kid is how poor her background is. Raised by a single mom, in Southeast DC, above a bar. And she's a brittle diabetic. Her principal says she's one of the brightest people he's had the privilege to know." She checks her notes, "He said 'privilege' like he meant it."

There are nods around the room, like a small wave, though everyone has their assignments and are making notes. "Brittle, how?" Sydney asks, her head rising from the seduction of her cell phone, bringing them all back.

"Apparently she was diagnosed two years ago. The principal said they can't keep her blood sugar in control. One day it's way up, the next day it's too low, causing mood swings, tiredness."

"Typical teenager," from Naomi, the perennial cynic.

"Not really, no, that's the last thing you'd call her," from Kate. "The principal says her mom swears she's conscientious about her diet and insulin, has a pretty consistent exercise and rest pattern, though she doesn't sleep much."

"*Not* a typical teenager," someone says, laughing.

Suddenly, Syd the marathoner checks the time, puts her phone down, claps her hands, and sums up the assignments. The Georgetown flood damage from the latest Potomac rise, the result of lousy construction and rising tides caused by Hurricane Pete, reaching Pennsylvania. The recent fires in Virginia. Congressional refusal to fund global warming reduction strategies. A political scandal involving the Democratic candidate for Congress (sexting; the guy actually held up a photo, saying, "This is not my penis—this one's *way* too small!") Rochelle's assignment, bless her heart, is to Skype her California upmarket MDs. And more.

Finally, Syd says, "Noah, you and, um, the new person—you guys go see the over-achieving teen, would you? Go visit the school? There's some pretty interesting human interest stuff here, maybe slant it to her diabetes, her background. Maybe there's a Mayan connection to our Hispanic cultural push this month. Got it?" A final non-question.

The Metro entrance plunges as deep into the earth as a mine shaft.

Kate and Noah enter it, their journey interrupted by a small posse of homeless, sleeping at the top of the escalator, one of them stretching his arm out from a prone position, trying to grab Noah's ankle, an aggressive, low-level attempt at panhandling. They are identical to the homeless family outside the WashPO building. Noah steps on the escalator first, a confident Metro-rider. Kate, a bit more hesitant, steps in behind him. They are at eye level as they read Walt Whitman's words carved in the stone above them, *I remember them all…*the dead and dying of the Civil War.

She surprises him. "Are you okay?" she asks, her eyes flashing briefly in the vanishing sun. He notices the green flecks caught in the hazel.

The words open a giant chasm for Noah.

She hesitates, then clarifies, "You seemed pretty pre-occupied in the huddle. I was just wondering, if, you know, if you were going through something….." losing steam in the sentence, the slight blush reaching beyond her jawline this time, telegraphing doubt about whether this is a polite inquiry or overstepping.

"What do you mean, okay?" Noah replies, hating that someone would spot this blemish on his carefully crafted, carefree exterior—as artificial as alliteration. She presses on, gently persistent, "Back there in the huddle you looked, I don't know, troubled. Sorry, maybe I shouldn't say anything." Her blush fades.

And for reasons he can't name, the same reasons that operated minutes before, Noah feels comfortable. Opening the door to his PTSD—even exploring its margins—is unfamiliar to him, but this person feels safe. *Talking about stuff isn't part of the XY chromosome deal,* he tells people. Normally he'd dig a little personal moat around himself.

Instead, he says, "I'm okay now, but"—how much to let the moat drain?— "you're pretty perceptive. The truth is I was having a bad morning. Old stuff, I guess." He doesn't open the door the whole way; all of us, Kate included, have to wait. She has her own moat.

Finally, reaching the bottom of the escalator, unaware he's doing so, he lets out a long breath. It's amazing what a single breath can hold. Twenty years, for example. A *katun.* Memories. Some of them painful.

7

N STREET NW. WASHINGTON. DC. MONDAY MORNING

I t's strange how a years of memory can be recalled in a second, a spark igniting a fire. Noah is quiet as they leave the Metro, letting Kate figure out their directions on her iPhone.

Nearly twenty years before, when he was nineteen, Noah met Deborah. It was freshman year, the year of opportunity. To this day, Deborah dances in the ballroom of his heart.

It was like a cornucopia compared to his living-at-home: new people, the profs, campus life, the courses, the women, no longer girls. The freedom. The general drug use, the Viagra-cocaine-hash-fueled parties, the beer (the national university lubricant) and of course the sex, both unwanted and well, wanted.

In the first week, Noah and dozens of his classmates were at a Welcome-to-the-Frosh party, meant to connect the newcomers to their new life. The house that hosted the little frosh-slash-upperclassmen get-togethers was in one of the uncountable two century-old Georgetown classics—lots of rooms off a main entry hall, a giant wide stair case dividing the entry hall neatly into two, a newel post the size of a man's head carved with the university crest. The rooms were marked *Arts, General Science, Engineering, Pre-law, Pre-health & Medicine*, others. Noah searched for anybody he might know, from high school, from local biking contests (his one high school sport). It was a strange scavenger hunt.

Up the wide stairs, he found a sign that pointed to his home, the *Math-Phys-Chem* room. It was a dark-paneled space, probably someone's library in early days. The door was wide open, a skinny black guy blocking it. "Hey buddy, you sure you want to go in there? That's the Asperger party," he said. *Cocky bugger*, Noah thought. The man was smiling, teasing Noah. "Don't look like you'd fit in."

Noah laughed at the guy, or maybe more at the Asperger's reference, thinking alcohol was working its magic on the guy. Going around the guy, Noah stepped across the threshold, entering another world.

A *Guess Who I Am?* game met him, direct from happy land of bridal showers. Noah joked that he thought the ice breaker would be something nerdy but fun, like *Name three famous living astrophysicists you'd invite to dinner*. He was wrong. It was this: when freshmen arrived, upperclassmen (and women) pinned a note on their backs marked with a famous dead person's name. The task was to chat somebody up, get them to give you *Yes* or *No* answers to questions about their back-name. I*s it a he or she? Is she a physicist? A mathematician?* Noah liked the game: later he wondered, only half seriously, whether it was the beginning of his reporter life. After a few minutes, he found someone to talk to, the most attractive person in the room, though, to be fair, there was little competition.

Deborah was a mocha Mona Lisa; he didn't find out who he was until later.

Is there love at first sight? Noah would say *Yes.*

He was at the bar when he first saw her. She was talking with three upperclassmen clustered around her (Asperger's or not, they could spot a tall beauty), all a little shorter, all kind of preening, one bouncing on his tip-toes to look down her front. As he looked at her, their eyes connected. She mouthed, *Save me*. Or at least that's what he thought. The eye contact? That was real.

He *knew*—in the certainty given only to nineteen year old boy-men—that there was something special about the beautiful woman across the room. He bought two beer tickets; if she didn't need one, he'd drink both.

When he brought one to her, he said, "You look thirsty."

Her nod, whether from relief at being freed from the tedium of the Asperger conversation, or from thirst, was all he needed. At six feet, this woman could look him right in the eye. And did. Soon the crowd, such as it was, thinned, and they got to important things like her real name, what courses she had signed up for, and one important, intimate question, "Do you want to know who you are?"

She turned so that he could see her back. He said, turning her around, "You're known for your smile."

"Like this?" channeling Bozo-the-Clown, all teeth. Perfect white teeth against her dark skin, he noticed.

"No, more like this," he said, reaching out, taking the soft margins of her lips, pulling them down and out very slightly, so that the smile was more modest, gentler and, well, less toothy. And more like Mona herself, a form of face-sculpting. And he smelled her, something like lemons and fresh linen. They say smells are the strongest memory. On the escalator ascending from the mine shaft of the DuPont Circle Metro, on the walk on N Street to Eastern Market School, he remembers all of it—the smile, the soundless *"Save me!"* the eye contact, the lips, all of it—like it was yesterday.

The accordion of time.

And thought to himself then how much he wanted to kiss those soft, apricot-colored lips. Noah did, surprising himself. He drew back an inch or two and was about to say something like, *"Sorry, didn't mean to offend you!"* apology of the late adolescent. She kissed him back, though—hard, opening her mouth enough that their tongues could get acquainted.

Oh Sweet Jesus, he thought. Love at first sight, or at least lust at first kiss.

Noah was Richard Nixon, it turned out.

He walked her home that night, the evening full of promise and stars. "Thanks for saving me back there," she said. "Do you do that a lot?"

"Save women? Yes. I do it all the time. It's my job. I left my cape back at home tonight."

"I'd like to see you with your cape," she said, grinning, those perfect white teeth again, against her red lips. "Maybe *without* your cape, too," hinting that she had more in mind. And then she kissed him again, harder than before, their tongues getting better acquainted. Their lower bodies too.

There were walks and coffee dates at first, then dinners in her little apartment, easier when her roommate left for the weekend. The dancing to music they both liked, or made themselves. The slide from dancing upright to dancing horizontally.

Noah believed, at least for months, that they were truly one person. How he would carry on silent conversations with her when she wasn't around. How he would see something, a Georgetown cupcake say, and think, *would she want this?* How he'd see her in class, or across the street heading into the Phys-Chem Block and his heart would race. And finally how, her roommate finally getting the hint, Deborah suggested he move in. Twenty minutes later, he did. Okay, maybe thirty minutes.

They had a year like that. Finding something in a market or a garage sale, a simple basket purchased at the DuPont Sunday market, their big purchase of the day, costing all of two dollars. He watched her move it from one place to another in their little living room, finally finding a spot beside the old fireplace, then placing some dried flowers in it, one by one, like they were little children.

And, apart from their physical and emotional lives, they had other things, things of the mind, in common. They were both math-physics majors, both in their first year, both on scholarships. The first year was packed with an array of physics and chemistry subspecialties. Deborah aced astrophysics. Noah did well on exams and in class, but his mind was elsewhere—on her for example. They'd be studying, lying on the couch in the living room with their laptops, and their thoughts would suddenly turn elsewhere. Before you could say *Neils Bohr*, they'd be making love. *Nerd Sex*, they called it. Just as much fun as the regular kind, Noah used to say.

The goal of the first year was to help students figure out what branch of physics they might like to pursue. Noah had a problem though: his marks displayed a highly developed math aptitude, but his heart was in health and biology, a career in medicine becoming clearer with each passing week. In the midst of the physics courses, their daily lives and even the sex, he put those thoughts on hold, hiding them from Deborah. It was a mistake.

Secrets are almost always mistakes, at least the keeping of them.

And then, as things happen, Noah and Deborah became three.

Not however, in the usual way.

8

N STREET NW. EASTERN MARKET CHARTER SCHOOL. WASHINGTON. DC. LATE MONDAY MORNING

From the moment they emerge from the Dupont Metro station, things appear *wrong* to Noah, as though a door has opened to another, parallel, threatening dimension. It's not that they are lost, or late, or that the too-hot sun has dimmed, but the bricks of the old buildings appear blurred, the sidewalks less than straight, possibly the product of the sun-shimmer on the hot streets. The feeling resides in the pit of his stomach.

It starts with another group of homeless, lying as though in wait for Noah and Kate at the top of the Metro station, huddling under decaying gray blankets, crawling with lice and worse. They smell like grease and dirt, of poverty and despair. One of the men, the closest to him, grabs his ankle in the same aggressive, low-level gesture Noah encountered minutes before. Noah looks at him directly—how many homeless do you pass and ignore?—and for a moment thinks it's the same man he saw at the Metro entrance minutes before. He has the same overgrown scoops of filthy fingernails, wild beard, and half-pony tail. This time his arm is extended and Noah sees, tattooed on the man's forearm, *The Fiery Collapse!*

There's no way it's the same guy. He can't be in two places at once, he thinks. His factual mind outvotes his observational powers.

Their ten minute walk is hot, lightened by alternating sides of the street, staying beneath the trees as much as possible, trying to avoid the sun. It seems closer today.

Approaching the Eastern Market School (officially the Eastern Market Charter School, a Proud Member of the Rose Network) conjures images from Kate's past, unpleasant ones. Her constant striving to be first in classes just like this building holds; the mental machinery she developed to learn, to succeed, be rewarded; the hope, never realized, that this would gain recognition in her family.

Outwardly, the building is a standard, three story red-brick structure built in the mid-late last century. To Kate and Noah, it presents a distorted picture, as though seen through a flawed lens. It offers several dissonances. For one thing, it's nowhere near the Eastern Market. It's perched on a tiny hill overlooking Georgetown and the Rock Creek Parkway. In the unforgiving sun, it looks almost alone in century-old isolation. And another dissonance: the security, even for an urban school in the early-mid twenty-first century, seems excessive. In the days when the NRA still rules, when the Occupy Wall Street movement of the homeless and poor has metastasized to schools and libraries—even then—the door guards, the window-bars and the extended security operation at the front door assume an almost-military presence.

This is one of a chain of charter schools supported by several Fortune 500s, all with the purpose of grooming kids to go into sci-tech industry jobs, like those in the booming aerospace and petrochemical worlds. There is a discrepancy here too: on top of the wealth/poverty divide is an increasing educated/uneducated gap.

The third dissonance is physical. The school is an old building built in the last century, its red brick exterior raising the expectation of long linoleum-lined hallways painted schoolroom-gray, thirty foot square classrooms and rows of lockers. The reality surprises. Inside are brand-new, high-end flat screens and TV walls, computers and tablets, videoconferencing technologies. A giant open space is divided vertically by muscular pillars supporting an atrium skylight and horizontally by wide, Plexiglas-lined balconies holding open classrooms that overlook the main floor.

For those of you who like to count, there is a fourth dissonance. Every school on the planet has noise as a common, pervasive element. Music. Laughing. Talking. Shouting, the result of friendly and not-so-friendly shoving. Teacher noises. Band practices. Coaches shouting and encouraging.

But this school is unusually, even eerily, quiet.

Once they are screened and wanded, once their credentials are examined, once Kate's put her past memories back where they belong, they notice a giant five by twelve banner in the school's atrium, marking the recent success of one of its family. In the friendly, peculiar, puffy writing of children, the banner almost screams (it would be the only noise in the place), *Eastern Market Rose School Network student wins FIRST PRIZE in the presidential science contest!!*

And beside it, also hanging from a second story glass balcony, a more professional poster advertises the *Gates-Clinton Foundation International Conference on Advancing Science; Science at the* **Edge** *of Discovery.* "Edge" is in bright orange italics, leaning forward, hinting at the future. A dozen or so faceless humanoids peer over a chasm into an unknown future, an image which has the power to haunt dreams. *In Melbourne,* the poster says. Noah remembers scrolling through the day's news this morning and reading that the conference had been moved there because of the devastating Sydney fires. But that was this morning—*how did it get to be on this poster so fast?* And beside *it,* a smaller, quieter announcement, highlighting DiShannia's speech to the National Academy of Science conference tomorrow. *Live and web-cast,* it says, in multiple colors. The topic? *The History and Future of the Universe: a Mayan Story.*

Below these signs on the atrium floor sits a large, standing corkboard, its squeaking wheels carrying it across gym and auditorium floors for generations, hosting children's artwork and posters. It also carries the air of an archeological treasure, like something preserved in a museum. In this modern, high-tech space it is nearly prehistoric, another dissonance. On it are tacked or stapled multiple colored pages, each listing a question with answers below them, neatly arranged in columns and rows. A tiny piece of tape sticks uselessly from one of them.

A small clutch of teachers and some older students stand beside this poster. The group swallows the newcomers, and then—as though others were instant-messaged when they arrive—swells as dozens of other kids join it. The little group resembles the staff of any middle school in America, perhaps elsewhere. Miss Hair-in-a-bun, no different than twenty other last-century school teachers, wearing sensible flat brown shoes, possibly Birkenstock like Roxanne's. A hippy sort of teacher, long graying hair drawn in a ponytail. "Science," he says to Kate, shaking her hand for a moment longer than is necessary. A youngish blonde woman makes Noah think, *Where were* you *when I went to school?* A chubby, unkempt guy, the math teacher. A handful of older kids, of every color of the rainbow, of every orientation. A few of the students are in cultural attire; it's *Celebrate our Heritage Day.* One grinning teenager in a long, brown-and-white striped robe and voluminous blouse is from war-ravaged Rawanda.

The principal, Mr. McIntye, is bald, his stomach overflowing his too-low, too-tight belt, is distinguished by a partially tucked-in white shirt and a tie that warrants legal action. They never do learn his first name; perhaps principals lose them when they take on the role. And last, a different person stands at the rear of the group. Short sleeved white shirt, navy slacks. The product of many hours in a fitness center, he is called Nick, introducing himself as the chief operating officer. On shaking his hand and thinking about how he'll write this encounter up, Noah fights the urge to describe him as *"A man from Brussels, six foot four and full of muscles."* Noah is a fan of seventies music. Noah settles on this question, "What's the role of a chief operating officer in a school?" He receives no answer.

DiShannia, the one person they have come to see, is not there. She is still at CNN, in interviews, preparing for her visit to the White House.

Ponytail, the science teacher, is Cor Van der Vries, proud of DiShannia. "She did this with very little help from me, you know. She got re-used poster board"—possibly explaining the little piece of scotch tape—"and worked out the content of each page. These also from the basis of her talk to the National Academy of Sciences meeting tomorrow." A southern drawl slows his speech.

A born teacher, he describes the poster, an orchestra leader using his hands to highlight features of the story. "Every one of the colored pages here raises a question. This first sheet," he points to the top green page, "tells what we know about the Mayan people and the collapse of their civilization, mostly in what we call Mexico today. Archeologists say it occurred around the end of the seventh or eighth century A.D. The Maya were a very advanced civilization, just like the Romans or Egyptians. They'd developed a real *sophisticated* understanding of astronomy and mathematics and of time keeping. Unfortunately, their written works were mostly destroyed by the Catholic Church in the fifteen hundreds."

A question from one of the kids, short and overweight, trying to impress. His name tag reads, "*Amir.*" Answering it, Van der Vies says, "Good question. We're not sure why the priests destroyed the records of the Mayan civilization. Maybe a lack of appreciation for their culture. Maybe they were horrified by some of the Mayan rituals." He stops, not wanting to upset the younger children who had gathered around the poster, striking a balance—too much information versus not enough, fear versus ignorance, a theme in our story.

"We *do* know that the Mayans had developed an elaborate society over a thousand years to about 700-900 A.D. Then," *they-en,* "over a period of fifty years, their civilization fell apart, their cities were abandoned, the people vanished into the jungle. *Here,*" he points to each of the lower pages in peach or pink, "DiShannia has explored possible reasons behind the collapse. Climate change. Over-farming. Population explosion. Political upheaval. War, infectious disease, a crop failure. And here's a final section I find really interesting, called '*An ancient mass suicide?*' She draws on the example of Jonestown." Jonestown and mass suicide are provinces in the same country. It is possible that the Maya resided there, too.

The magnet continues to draw, pulling in a few older students. "Then over here, she lays out why these theories don't really work. She did some *spectacular* research here, by the way. And here," he points to the bottom blue panels, "are her conclusions. Pretty impressive, I'd say." One of the children has a coughing spell, the only sound in the atrium.

Mr. McIntyre, checking his phone, has a text from Di Shannia: she's been delayed again, a small problem at CNN. Kate senses empty space and decides to fill it; she is an expert reporter, driven to fill every minute.

"Could we go somewhere just to talk about the school? About DiShannia? Maybe get a little more back-history on her? Could we use one of the smaller rooms?" The answers are all, "*Yes.*" They form a little posse of the teaching and administrative staff, five of them, leaving the students below. As they make their way up the open, Plexiglas/aluminum-clad stairs Noah notices something.

The stillness in the school, as though the walls are padded in an invisible cotton sponge, is beyond quiet. The kids drift back to their classes, like small sea animals, noiseless as the ocean they swim in. Most of the kids fall immediately to their e-screens, passing their hands over them to start them, even the younger ones, without obvious direction; they appear to *need* no direction. As Noah climbs the stairs, he watches a teacher and student interact directly below him.

He pauses as the youngish blonde woman pulls her chair over to a student who appears to be struggling. He is flipping back and forth between pages on his screen, puzzling over what might be a math equation. Now near the top of the stairs, Noah watches as she and the boy begin to—what's the right word here?—converse. The student asks her a question about the equation. She explains, reassures, nods, points out something on a page. He demonstrates what she has just shown him, showing her his e-screen re-working of the equation. She indicates that he is good, a thumbs-up. *Fine. You've got it. Good for you.*

All without any words spoken, not out loud at least.

And then, the thing that squeezes his stomach, enters his dreams. She turns as she leaves the boy and looks directly at Noah, unsmiling, holding his gaze until he turns at the top of the stairs and joins Kate and the others. There is no way the teacher could have known he was there.

The conference room combines lunchroom functionality with pictures of the kids, a wall-calendar full of school celebrations, student achievements, a school flag.

Nick drops the room temperature. Sitting apart from the group as though judging it, arms folded over a testosterone-sculpted chest. Dismissing the chill, picking up on the refrain of "Kids Who've Made Us Proud!" on one of the walls, Kate asks, "Can you tell us about the other award-winners?" *Aboot*, again. They do: one boy had won the tri-state spelling contest; another got to the national finals in math. Two girls created an after school program for other inner-city latch-key children. "What about her?" Kate points to a picture of a little blonde pixie with braids, maybe eleven.

"Oh," he says, dropping his voice, "she's no longer with us." His face registers the sort of surprise politicians display when asked a question they're not prepared to answer. That kills most conversation for a moment; they are trapped in the silence, an uncomfortable, cold blanket.

Kate warms the room, asking each of the staff what they feel about the school, how it affects them, how they see their role as teacher in a new world of education, what makes them *happiest* about their day. She mines the hour of waiting, even getting Nick to smile a little, discarding some of his COO chippiness.

Noah parks himself across the room from Kate in order to observe her, a needless supervisory task. Her interview skills are so well developed that he can let his mind drift, prodded by the common, compulsive attachment to an iPhone, the source of all breaking news. As he scrolls through his news feeds, he isn't disappointed: death rates from global warming continuing to rise (*The Lancet*, old news, really); staggering environmental refugee numbers, adding to the political refugees; another bill in Congress, stalled by two parties unable to compromise. And then, tired of the old news, he becomes restless. As much as he enjoys watching Kate, he begins to walk around the room. He looks at the class pictures, especially a few pictures of kids on one wall called *Heroes*.

And not just any heroes; these are "Wilcox Heroes." The plaque above them reads, "*We are grateful for the generosity of Major General Edwin G. Wilcox for the creation of these awards, recognizing our highest achievers.*"

They are framed-smiling faces arrayed in parade-like order, from 1990, the first award, to last year's recipient. Some, the later ones, he recognizes—two young women, an Indo-American, the blonde pixie and one young black man. Something flips a memory-switch in Noah's mind—the large gap in the front of the boy's teeth, a not-quite-a-smile hiding braces in one of the girls. His stomach turns when he makes the connection. He does a quick, one-finger search on his iPhone, confirming what his stomach tells him. Each of these children has been killed—two by drive-by shootings, one in a "Tragic Drowning in the Potomac." He finds a piece from the *Post* dated three years before, the mother saying, "He hated the water! Why would he be even near the Potomac?" Sadly, teenage deaths are commonplace events in any American city, but these creep beyond the boundaries of the expected into the range of the suspicious. "Creep" is the right word; his reporter's antennae are up.

He leaves the Wall of Heroes to hear Kate say, "This all seems very expensive— the building, the use of flat screen TVs everywhere, the laboratories, the computers. How can you afford all this?"

She receives an expected, stock answer from the principal, "Good question. We have multiple sources of funding, some large corporate grants from those companies, you know Google and all, who really like our 'product.' We do receive some state and city grants, and we have wealthy donors, and of course our registration fees, and," an afterthought, "some federal dollars too." He flushes suddenly, a tiny crimson tide invading his cheeks. The last few words slide out like an embarrassed fart. It's clearly not part of the stock message prepared by corporate headquarters.

"Well, a very small amount of federal support, I should say; we're obliged not to have you report on that." He looks at the COO the entire time; Nick is clearly not happy with the federal slip-of-the tongue. Noah feels even more of the chill, another dissonant note.

Abruptly, there is a small commotion in the hall, and a brief knock on the door—the school administrative assistant bringing DiShannia to the room.

DiShannia Johnson Johns.

She is not at all what they expect.

9

PALENQUE, YUCATAN PENINSULA, 683 A.D.

In many ways the procession was like an unruly organism, perhaps an alligator or a fat, restless anaconda. At last, it gathered itself, Pakal at the head, the visiting, lesser kings and their courts behind, the dignitaries and wealthy of Palenque and those of the visiting city-states behind them. Following them, the priests, the physicians and sorcerers of the realm. And the scribes of course. And finally, the last in the long train, A'Ciliz himself, towering above them all. This day, in the great peace procession, A'Ciliz looked at the scribes who had joined him, many holding documents supporting his own. One of them in particular moved closer—Hibiscus, the senior scribe who worked most closely with him on creating the night drawings now that Nantua was gone. Hibiscus smiled at him, sympathy filling his eyes, reassuring the priest; he knew of A'Ciliz's doubts about the document.

The march began, its music swelling, the drumbeats of the musicians louder, a slow metronome to match the feet of the hundreds of those who marched. At first slowly, then more rapidly, moving across the entrance plaza, around the palace, across the newly-named southern Peace Plaza. Finally pausing before the wide giant stairs to the Temple of Inscriptions, before beginning the long climb to the top.

Crossing the plaza, even in the sweltering wet heat, was one thing. Climbing the temple stairs were entirely another: they were steep and high, not the business of older men. Two or three *katuns* before, at the time he was a young priest, A'Ciliz would have thought nothing of those stairs, but today he thanked the absent gods for the landings; he could pause at each one.

He could not know that a thousand years later, the archeologist Alberto Ruz Lhulier would do the same thing.

The younger priests and scribes marched with him for the journey across the plaza, sunning in the cheers and whistles of the crowds. They stopped at the base of the Temple of Inscriptions, parting like a giant river divided by a large boulder, allowing the Chief Astronomer-Priest the honor of climbing the stairs by himself. They formed a kind of guard.

He took the first few steps, beginning to feel the first, faint stutter in his chest, like that of a struggling bird. He paused, making his way slowly, pausing at each landing. The kings, waiting at the top of the stairs, thought his pauses a matter of prayerfulness and respect for the gods.

They were wrong but the air seemed thinner today, A'Ciliz's lungs hungry. Hibiscus watched him closely as A'Ciliz's forehead furrowed in worry, and, as he progressed up the stairs, in pain.

It worsened, beyond its familiar short-lived pattern; this attack seemed different. Normally fading after a brief rest, on this day it maintained itself, robbing him of breath and energy. He calmed himself, taking deep, cleansing breaths, praying to his non-existent gods. And then the pain changed its character, crushing the left side of his chest, as though a giant hand had been placed there. The pain moved, like a jaguar, from his chest to his neck, from his neck to his jaw, from his jaw to his back. From his back to his left arm. The fingers of his left hand tingled as though they had been burned. He looked at them, wondering, worrying.

Finally, thinking that all he had to do was one more flight of stairs—each impossibly farther than the next, each impossibly tall—his world became as black as the Mayan west, like death. He collapsed, pages of the dangerous, malevolent documents spilling down the stairs behind him.

10

EASTERN MARKET CHARTER SCHOOL, WASHINGTON, DC, EARLY MONDAY AFTERNOON

DiShannia Johnson Johns is far more than they expect.

In two heart beats, the room is brighter, warmer, Noah's now-petty fears calmed, dissonant thoughts blown away like autumn leaves. Charisma has entered the room. Not dry words on a page, not the rehearsed magnetism of celebrity, not a poster. She is the real thing.

DiShannia is basketball player tall, latte-hued, fit.

Perhaps the most striking thing about her is her handshake—warm and strong, marked only by the tiny rattle of a pink charm bracelet on her right wrist. Neither the dry cold limp of many girls of her age, nor the nervous encounter with a damp hand barely clasping another's, this is the muscular grip of a mature thirty year old. Her face is lit from inside, generating a smile to match the handshake. Her eyes are set, deeply black, intense. They appear hungry, wanting to know the person whose hand she grasps. She carries herself with beyond-teenage grace. She hugs Cor Van de Vries tightly, her science teacher, and then turns to meet the rest. She is a 110 pounds of Prozac, smiling, introducing herself to Kate, then to Noah.

"Hi," she says, making up for her absence in one simple word. "I'm DiShannia," taking each of their hands in turn, emphasizing 'Dee-*Shann*-ia'. "Please call me Shanny."

Something almost palpable in DiShannia immediately appeals to Noah. She apologizes for the delay, the product of a CNN interview, the traffic. Her time is limited—she has a visit to the White House this afternoon where she'll meet President Sofia Lopez-Black, the country's first woman president, and a presentation to the National Academy of Sciences tomorrow. The Academy has described her work as "transformational."

She is more interested in what their day was like at the school, concerned that she express her gratitude for all their help. More interested that they meet her mother, Sharron Johns.

Noah is hooked.

What is it that brings you to like—even love—someone on first meeting them? A touch? A look? The memory of an old friendship? Finding something of yourself?

The others, except for Nick the COO, leave the room, allowing Kate and Noah, DiShannia and her mother to sit like four points on the compass of the square table. Nick watches from outside the group working his iPhone, keeping one eye and both ears on the table talk.

"How'd you first become interested in the Mayans?" Noah asks.

"I can't really, you know, ever remember *not* being interested in them. I do remember my mom taking me to the Smithsonian several times when I was how old, Mom?"

"Probably three of four, hon," from her proud Mom, much shorter than Shanny, much darker.

"In the Native American Museum, I saw the indigenous people, and learned about them and how they came to this continent, how they lived and how they suffered. I looked at the pictures of the Maya, you know? Imagine living back then, actually *being* there when they developed their civilization, when they built those amazing buildings! I remembered seeing beads and other things they made and traded. I made Mom buy me a book about them once—Mom never believed I could read!" she says, laughing, sending her mother a look. The look held love, like a child is cradled.

"It described the Mayan people, how they built their cities, how they were advanced in astronomy, how they abandoned everything and walked away from it. That did it for me. I wanted to know more. One Saturday, we went to the Natural Science Museum where there's this amazing display of the planets—you know where you press the button and one of the planets lights up and you can read about it?" Her eyes widened; Kate's too—*she was reading at that age?* "Then it came to me that there might be a relationship between the Mayan story and astronomy."

She uses her hands as brushes, her words as paint. The room is her canvas. Her charm bracelet broadcasts tiny clicks as she gestures.

"What do you think caused the collapse?" asks Kate.

"There are lots of theories. Maybe you looked at my poster? It's what I'm talking to the National Academy about tomorrow. There's all the usual theories—y'know, drought, famine, over-farming, wars. But I've been thinking of something different as the explanation and I've talked with experts in Europe and Great Britain. I think, well *they* think it's none of those, or maybe some of those plus another thing, I guess, an *element*. I think it's more mass suicide than World War ..."

Nick clears his throat, checking his iPhone for time. "DiShannia, they'll be coming to pick you up for the White House in a few minutes. We should wrap this up, perhaps have these nice people come back and interview you later this week?" His voice raises into a question. It is no question however; the interview is over.

But not its effect. Shaking hands with Shanny and her mom and Nick at the door, Noah is left with her manner of engaging people, drawing them to her. Her gestures. Her direct, unblinking gaze. Her high watt smile. The way she looks at her mom. In a way he does not understand, something in these outward displays of her personality is comforting.

Native Americans have a form of art that links people, rocks and eagles, lines showing their connectedness. If this were one of those paintings there would have been a wide bright line between DiShannia and Noah, silent but powerful. A lifeline, you might say.

They walk with her to the door of the school, past the security apparatus and out onto the street where a black SUV waits for her—obviously a White House contingent. Seeing it, manned by two black-suited sunglass-wearing federal stereotypes, some of the comfort and familiarity of the interview flees, crowded out by a flood of other—how did Shanny say it?—elements. The dead "Heroes." The federal financial support that Muscles was so clearly unhappy about. The quietness of the school. The episode Noah thought might be telepathy.

He motions to Kate to follow him to the street, *a little side-bar,* the head-gesture says. As they walk he stage-whispers to her, "I think we have a story here. I mean, a *story,*" he repeats. He doesn't need to: she's miles ahead of him, in the familiar way that women are often ahead of men.

"I know," she says. "What about the Mayan theory? What do you make of the COO? The way he controlled the interview? And what do you make of *her?*" she asks.

He is excited too, wants to talk. The dead or missing students. DiShannia's story. DiShannia herself. *Shanny,* he thinks, but Kate is distracted by her ringing phone.

After a minute she says to him, "Noah, I'm sorry about this. I'm living with my parents and my mom texted me when we were in there. My father has Alzheimer's and he's having a bad day. Like really confused, even belligerent, not at all like him. I know you want to talk about this, but I should go home if that's okay. It's not far, just in Georgetown. I'll calm her down, him too if I can. I'm so sorry, it's my first day and all. I won't be lon…"

"No, look, you just gave me an idea," Noah interrupts her. "I should go home too. I'm just a few blocks the other away at Florida and Massachusetts. I can work from there. I want to check some things out about this school, about those missing kids. Could we connect later, maybe in Georgetown for supper?" Hopefulness in his voice.

"I can't promise supper," she says, with *sorry* in her mind but not her words. "But let's aim to meet later this afternoon. I'll text you. I also have a cousin who's an expert in Mayan history. I'll call him; maybe he can help."

Noah is more than a little embarrassed to say why he wants to go home.

It's the pile of laundry in his front hall that's been waiting for him, roughly the size of Belgium. It's been radiating guilt, like some radioactive substance, for several days. He could, the bachelor-rationalizer, do two things at once: investigate the school and have some clean underwear. And, perhaps subconsciously, he might reflect on the great gift of two new people in his life—Kate and DiShannia. The gift of two's.

Only one, sadly, to last anywhere near a normal lifetime.

11

TEMPLE OF INSCRIPTIONS. PALENQUE. YUCATAN. PENINSULA 683 A.D.

It surprised A'Ciliz.

Not that he had collapsed and recovered. He had had similar several episodes before, none as severe. He was not surprised by the quiet, since he was with the kings, not on the hot plaza filled with the thousand sounds of celebration. Not even with the coolness of the room he woke in. He knew that they would carry him to the intended tomb of Pakal, deep inside the pyramid.

It was this: the six kings who filled the small chamber were naked.

Pakal, the leader, bore only his magnificent muscled torso, glistening with the oil and sweat of mental and physical exertion. His buttocks and thighs hardened by years as a warrior and ball-player, his arms made powerful engines honed by swordplay and the ball-court. Two others stood closer to him. Tepeu and Xipil were no less muscled, one taller and lither than Pakal, the other shorter, even more solid. All of them were greased with chicken fat, scarred like the lines of Nazca, several showing recent blood-letting. Two others, Izel and Huracan, were no less impressive—also survivors of the ball court, the product of years of wars. Even Chicahua, the eldest, was naked, though his advanced years permitted him the modesty of a small leather apron guarding his genitals. His stomach flowed over the apron like an obscene, doughy front porch. Hanging like a small, windless flag from his waist, it had been died jade green, the color of greed.

The sight of the men filled his eyes, disturbing A'Ciliz in ways that had not occurred to him in years—what he, the eunuch, had lost—reminding him of the life he had left behind, of a path not taken.

Their nakedness, Pakal had decreed, was necessary to demonstrate their openness to journey on this path to peace: they were allowed no weapons or adornment. He could trust them only in this state. They were allowed to bring a small retinue of guards and priests with them, arrayed like statues lining the steep stairs to the top of the temple. To show his trust, Pakal had named only a handful to advise him, a much smaller number than the rest, placing them well outside the tomb.

It was a mistake of the first order.

The kings had watched A'Ciliz on his painful journey up the stairs, helped him when he collapsed, overseen others as they carried him into the tomb many steps below. They stood around him as he woke, lying in a small antechamber outside the tomb.

"You are well now, priest?" Pakal asked, worried. "The physician-priest has just left, after he massaged your neck. He has told us you will be all right now: your heart has ceased its wandering."

"Yes, Yes, my lord. I am grateful." His gratitude was mixed with embarrassment at being prone while they were standing and at being ill in the first place. More however, he was embarrassed by their nakedness, relieved that he was still clothed. He began to stand, helped to his feet by the gruff Chicahua, surprisingly tender. A'Ciliz was slightly dizzy but much better, his head almost touching the wooden beams above.

The antechamber was dark, illuminated only by wall-torches, their flames licking the stone walls. It walls were a deep, pervasive red, the color of the rising sun. In the next room, the tomb itself, was almost entirely filled with an enormous sarcophagus, its lid carved with images that some would say were those of a rocket ship, and of Pakal himself being lifted to a strange new universe. Some saw him rising to a new universe, split or represented by a giant tree. The image was ringed with symbols and glyphs, the subject of debate for centuries. One thing was clear however: seven gods looked down on their creation from the topmost frame of the tomb lid, viewing their mirrored creation and the great, peace-keeping king, who lay below.

Only a small passage existed between the red walls and the top of the tomb lid itself. It was magnificent.

It filled A'Ciliz with dread.

Despite their obvious external masculinity, they gathered around him like anxious women, pulling small stools closer to them, settling themselves, carefully protecting their genitals from the rough wood. Only Chicahua, *ahoub* of Chichen Itza, stood, his green apron contrasting with the red of the room.

"We feared for you, Priest," said Pakal, his concern for A'Ciliz tied to his role in delivering the message. Without him and the Codex the plan might fail.

"The gods protect me, majesties," A'Ciliz said, looking directly at Pakal, a look as tangible as a touch passing between them. He was now fully standing, gathering his flowing skirt around him, adjusting his breast plate, the gift of a sacrificed alligator—almost the only clothing in the overcrowded, torch-lit room. A'Ciliz's head was clearing, the tightness and the strange irregular hammering in his chest vanished like a bad dream.

"This has happened before, this collapse, but the gods permit me to carry on in my work, to convey these findings to you. Perhaps my recovery is proof of the importance of the work itself," he said. He was also gathering his anger about him— anger at the loss of his genitals, anger at Pakal for placing him in this position.

He looked at each of them, holding their gaze, moving more closely to them. Hibiscus had brought the documents from the outside stairs of the pyramid and laid them, accordion-like, on the table in front of him. He moved with agility, feeling surprisingly strong.

"This is important business, my lords," he said, lifting his head so that the flickering torchlights illuminated his face, marginally warming him in the cool stone chamber.

He spoke quietly to them, like children in a strange classroom. They were spellbound—except for the restless, pacing Chicahua. A'Ciliz *had* them, as though he held their obscene genitals in his long fingers, squeezing them, telling them how the gods' existence guided theirs. How the gods had demonstrated their power by granting eclipses, then, because of their prayers, allowing them to thrive in the re-born sun's warmth. How the gods sent relief from drought. *Some relief*, he thought. *One year is as dry as the next; it's we who build the viaducts and canals!* How much better their trading and prosperity would be if peace descended on the people of the Maya.

His hands raised to the tomb's red ceiling, he explained that the gods—the Mayans counted seven—had created them from corn, then retreated. And now, he argued, they had shown their faces again.

"You must see this new proof of their interest in us," he said, finally, bending his tall frame to them, confiding and urgent. His voice echoed off the small chamber's walls. They were to meet a great secret. They pulled their stools in closer to the table. Chicahua, the oldest and most restless, finally settled with a loud sigh, arranging the small apron to accommodate his modesty. The others leaned closer, Pakal just beside the priest, protective of him, improbable heat and strength rising from him in the cool space. A wall-torch flamed briefly, then died, hissing its good-bye.

The table in front of A'Ciliz held dozens of layers of bark-paper, each leaf bleached, painted white, marked with hundreds of complex symbols and sound-markings, the hallmark of the Mayan. A hush like a silent bird filled the small room, its wings beating in expectation.

"This," the priest said, showing them the first page, "was our early morning sky looking towards Venus nearly fifty years ago when my predecessor first began to record the movements of the planets, of the sun and the moons. It shows Venus against the constellation of stars we call the Seven Gods, our forefathers. It was his life work, as it is mine." The scribes had re-arranged thirty or so of the scattered sheets in order. Turning to the next leaf, he said, "And this shows the same sky, from precisely the same location at the same day almost three *katuns* later.

"What do you see?" he asked, holding the two beside each other, allowing them to examine it. They were puzzled. "This is the great god Venus here in this year as he crosses the constellation," pointing to a small dot on the white page, near the horizon, then moving his long finger to the next sheet, to point at the same dot, "and this is him at precisely the same time, fifty years before." They saw nothing.

"Venus," he said, "has arrived earlier each year. Now do you see it? It is only the breadth of a hair, but there is no doubt, *no doubt*," he repeated, pointing now with more urgency, using the levers of his age and position, "about its movements. And," he said, finding another page to show them, "we have calculated the distance using two points of reference—one here at the temple, one a distance away. These calculations confirm the distance between us and the god. It is certain that he draws nearer."

It was as he predicted. There were doubts at first, like waves on the Eastern Ocean, some strongly voiced. Comments on the methods used. Worries about the implications. Finally, the question Pakal and A'Ciliz had hoped for, "The god Venus must be angry with us, do you think, Priest?" asked Izel, the tallest of the visitors, almost as tall as A'Cliz himself. "He wishes to come closer, like a parent, wishing to scold us, perhaps?"

"I think so, sire," A'Ciliz replied, "but it is not just Venus!"

The questioning stopped, snared by his voice and stature, trapped by the evidence. He watched their heads nodding, coming closer to him, like little planets themselves. He moved more quickly through the rest of the document, with increasing confidence, like a speaker who senses oneness with his audience. He came to the final pages.

"It is difficult to imagine, I realize, but here are drawings of Venus, of the Seven Gods constellation, and even of the other planets themselves. Each shows the same path; each has been carefully crafted by my mentor Nantua and by our current scribe, Hibiscus. For many *katuns*, perhaps longer, each of them is moving closer with every year."

"Is Izel correct?" asked Xipil, the stockiest of the kings. "Are the gods angry with us?"

Pakal's gaze fixed A'Ciliz for a minute. Quiet until then, his deep baritone a contrast to A'Ciliz's high tenor, he said, "We have pondered these drawings for months. I have witnessed for myself the accuracy of the measurements and I have observed the ancient drawings of the skies as well."

A'Ciliz nodded his agreement.

"Moreover," now pulling himself up to his full height, his charisma like a shield in front of him, his baritone deepening, "we have purified ourselves." Pakal pointed to his scars and blood-letting, its pin picks and lines, some still bleeding slightly. "We have sought wisdom in our sacrifices. This purification leads us down the path to truth. Izel is right: there is only one meaning we can draw. The gods draw closer to warn us, to turn us from our ways."

"*What* ways, exactly?" asked Chicahua, restless but silent until now, his hands firmly in his lap.

"Our warring ways," said Pakal calmly, restraining the urge to shout.

A'Ciliz was happy that Pakal had intervened. He himself, the unbeliever, knew that these were not gods but rather solid bodies that hung in space in some unknown fashion. For the most part, he believed that the planets were simple objects approaching earth on some slow predetermined path, not gods who could be cajoled into reversing direction. He had many questions, too. Were there ways in which the process of implosion itself could be stopped? Could there be a code written in the stars themselves?

Pakal continued, persuading. "We have been astronomers for centuries. During this time the god-planets have been drawing closer. And what has happened in all that time? One city believes in one set of gods and fights another city which believes in yet another set of gods. And then there is retribution, one city to another. Look at these charts!" he stood, pointing at several on the long low table. His thick penis, *toon* in Mayan, directed their attention to the charts of planets and stars, a lewd, swollen finger pointing to the future.

While there were nods of agreement among most of the men, Chicahau, the eldest, remained unmoved, skepticism like twin angry jaguars in his eyes. He leaned back, arrogance supporting his back. He smiled. Some would have thought it resembled that of an alligator just before it swallowed its prey.

He stood. "I for one," he said, "do not believe the priest. What are these things? They are only pictures. Any child could have drawn them. Any clever priest could have made up this story. Any clever *king*! And all in the name of what? Of peace? Of laying down our arms so that you can take what is rightly ours?"

There were protests; Izel stood to make his point. It seemed like an hour to A'Ciliz, though in truth it was much less. Two of the kings sided with Pakal and A'Ciliz, arguing that Peace was worth at least the effort—whether the planets had anything to do with it or not. The other two were more neutral at the outset, quiet, pondering, weighing curious facts. Chicahua's anger built, his arguments appearing to sway the two neutral voices.

As the disagreements increased, A'Ciliz became anxious again, his heart pounding like a small caged tiger. Ignoring the growing noose around his heart, he shouted, "*Enough!*" His voice echoed off the stone walls. "You doubt us? You doubt the work of my predecessors, our scribes and me? You doubt the Great Pakal? You doubt the hours we have spent in recording the movement of the planets in such minute detail?"

He pointed to the codex, now spread on the table. His voice was strong. Finally, with some desperation and his own disbelief pushing the words out, "You doubt that the heavens, full of gods, are coming closer? That is insanity, blasphemy, that is… "

Pakal, the closest to A'Ciliz, noticed it first.

A faint loss of color, a subtle twisting of the mouth. And then a grimace, growing over a minute. Pakal's feet were bound by the intensity of the moment, but his heart leapt to A'Ciliz.

The priest's shortness of breath had not settled, was replaced by a pain—no, more than a pain, a pressure—as though many heavy stones had been laid on his chest. *Perhaps there* were *gods,* he thought, punishing him for his disbelief. A peculiar numbness mingled with the pain, spreading down his left arm. The pain scalded like a flame, twisting, radiating to his back, stronger than before.

And then, unexpectedly, there was a welcome absence of pain, a sea of black.

In it, he could not see Pakal rush to his side, holding his head in his arms as he slumped to the floor. Could not see the surprising tears in the king's eyes, spilling down his cheeks. Pakal the Great, who had fought so hard to build this Peace. Pakal, who had come to admire and even love A'Ciliz. Pakal, who saw the fragile argument binding the Mayan peace accord slip away from him. "It is finished," A'Cliz uttered as his breath left him.

12

WASHINGTON. DC. LATE MONDAY AFTERNOON

Noah is a whirling dervish, part sleuth, part housekeeper.

Texting Gerry Watts at WashPO about setting up a time to talk. Emailing Naomi about government's relationship to charter schools in general, the Rose Charter School Network in particular. Making notes on yellow and pink stickies, full of many questions and only a few answers. Researching the Mayan civilization on-line. Realizing how advanced they were. Wondering what caused their decline. Thinking about DiShannia, *"Call me Shanny."* Talking with Naomi, his phone lodged between his ear and shoulder while stuffing his underwear and socks into the drier. Watching his laundry pile shrink while the parade of yellow and pink post-it notes grow. It looks like Easter in his apartment.

The everyday lodged between the profound and frightening.

Kate on the other hand is more nurse than dervish. Arriving home to find her father pacing in the living room, like a modern day Chicahua, demanding that they take him home. "You are home, Dad," she says. He doesn't recognize her. "I'll sit with you." And she does, holding his rough hands—rough for a history professor she always thinks—while she guides him to his favorite chair, one familiar object in his strange new world. Telling him stories of meals they had together, of the two Thanksgivings they always celebrated, one in Canada and one south of the border. He slips into the serenity of a mindless nap. And she calms her frantic mother too, a tightly bundled, black-haired Asian version of herself, only a *katun* older than Kate, that much younger than her father. She's is in charge again. *How much more of this can she take?* Kate wonders.

She also wonders about the brave new World of WashPO, about the young girl she just met and, most of all, about the lithe, intense, dark-haired man she works with. About the way he moves. About the way his black hair falls in front of his forehead like a small curtain, making him brush it away, absent-mindedly. About his intense, black eyes—*eyes that never leave you, eyes you could lose yourself in,* she thinks. About the demons that bother him. And her too, to be fair.

The same man who texts her late that afternoon. *How u doing? Your dad OK? Want to meet at the Georgetown Park? I can b there in 30 mins.*

The Potomac has as many moods as a human.

Years before, bulging with spring, it marched half way to M Street, taking the old park with it. Sometimes the Potomac is loving, its arm flexed protectively against the shore of Georgetown. Today it's quiet, poets would say serene, a fluid avenue. Kate and Noah are high above it in the just-reopened park, high enough to see the new break wall make its serpentine way along the river, low enough to hear the kids' voices playing below it, their parents yelling at them to be careful.

Clouds rush by on their own rapid, elevated journey, casting fast-moving shadows on the river.

Starbucks' creations in hand, they talk about DiShannia, about the school. He tells her what he's found out that afternoon, facts about the Rose School Network, his conversations with Naomi and Gerry, about the Mayans. He doesn't tell her about his laundry, but she smiles when he tells her about his yellow and pink sticky-notes. And then, in an easy transition, they turn to talk about themselves.

Kate has recently moved in with her parents. Her father is a retired history professor in his late sixties; her mother, much younger, was one of his graduate students. Being home is a challenge for an independent woman in her late twenties, but she says it's easily overcome if it helps her parents. Noah would argue with "easily," but is quiet.

"I feel like an orphan," she says, surprising him; he feels the same way.

"They say my dad has early stage Alzheimer's, but he's gone emotionally, the father I used to know anyway. I don't think there's anything early-stage about it. He's okay socially, but if you probe a little deeper, he's not there. And my mom, the woman who was my coach and cheerleader, she's too preoccupied by him to be that for me anymore. It sounds selfish, doesn't it? But that's the truth." A small pause, collecting her thoughts, perhaps the pieces of her life.

"So, a year or so ago, they decided—well my mother decided, my dad can't really make decisions anymore—to live near my dad's relatives here. We really had no family support in Canada. So here I am, too," she says. Regret mixes with sadness. *What has she left behind?* Noah wonders. The truth is there *were* family members in Toronto; they were estranged, unwilling to help, a source of pain for Kate. She becomes brighter; she is a graduate of the let's-make-lemonade-from-lemons school.

"But, you know, I could move here, help out, not so much physically at this stage, it's more emotional support that my mom needs. I'm *so* glad I found work though; I don't know what I'd do if I stayed home with him all the time!" a little non-humorous laugh. Or what she'd do without external yardsticks to measure her worth for that matter; her worth, or the attempt to prove it, is a subject buried deep inside her, like a formative grain of sand.

"What about you?" It's his turn.

"Funny, when you mentioned orphan, that's how I feel. My mom died of cancer a few years ago. She worked at the NIH, the National Institutes of Health, for years. She was a clinical epidemiologist—you know, studying illness prevalence, designing clinical trials. My father is still around I guess."

"You guess?"

"I hear from him two or three times a year. He's a big developer in the city. That's pretty much it: he's all work all the time. He and my mom divorced years ago. A kind-of orphan, like you."

"Do you have any other family?"

"No," Noah replies. "I'm an only child, so were my parents and *their* parents are gone. My dad's new wife is not, um, my favorite. My mother hardly ever talked about her own growing up so I know almost nothing about that side."

Regret and sadness color the sentence, but there is more than a hint of the lemonade maker in him too, traits they recognize in each other. He leans back on the bench, turning to her, an outdoor version of the slouch. The conversation shifts, though not much.

"I really liked her—Shanny I mean," from Kate. "She reminded me of you."

"I liked her too, a lot. What d'you mean, reminded you of me?"

"Oh, just how bright she was, how inquisitive, I don't know, how enthusiastic, maybe her direct look, like those amazing eyes of hers, like yours. She sees right through you. Her eyes never leave yours. Did you notice that? Your eyes're like that too, you know."

He doesn't know.

The talk about DiShannia is easy. What is a little harder, like describing a taste to someone else, is the feeling that something wasn't right at that school.

Noah says it first. "It *was* strange, all that security especially and those odd, quiet kids. I figured well they're all really bright and maybe introverted, y'know, into their computers and iPads and stuff. One thing freaked me out, though." He tells her about the strange episode on the stairs. He calls the teacher "Telepathic Terri."

"Oh my God," she says, "that *is* weird. Maybe he was deaf, though, do you think? Or, maybe he had Asperger's and all she had to do was sit with him to calm him down and he got the question." In the cool light of day, sitting on a bench along the Potomac, he wants to believe her version.

The conversation of their lives continues. Kate's mother is Asian in a family that was still tied to their Chinese roots, even after two generations in another country. And still xenophobic. They could work and live anywhere, speak the country's language, achieve brilliant success, but at heart, in their homes, they only trusted Chinese culture and people. When her mother fell in love with her non-Chinese professor, married him against her parents' wishes, she was disowned. Kate was raised not to know her grandparents.

"Oh, I did meet them once," she says. "When I was maybe twelve, my dad drove me to their home in North Toronto. It was a big place, with a porch out front. It was summer, and there was a kitchen chair outside. I still remember how odd it was to see a kitchen chair on a porch, but there it was, straight backed, hard, by the front door. Painted white. My father drove me there and stayed in the car while I went to the front door and rang the doorbell. My grandparents came out, asked me to sit while they stood, inspecting me. There's no other word for it.

"They shook my hand, asked me my name and a couple of questions, like 'Where are you in school?' and 'What grades do you get?' And then suddenly it was, 'Nice to meet you, thank you for coming,' and I was *discharged*. That's the only word for it. And then, without another word, no smiles on their part, they went back in the house. Even now, you know, I feel that time. I remember the visit as though it happened this morning. It was almost twenty years ago." A *katun*.

Both of them fall silent for a minute, a long time in a conversation. She is still on that front porch. Noah is reluctant to intrude, but his eyes do not leave her, broadcasting sympathy. Kate is right about the way he looks at people, absorbing them.

She says, "So there I was. My father's family was here in the District, the Caucasian side. I guess I was hoping that the Chinese side could open up, that I could learn more about my grandparents and my heritage. All the way home I thought, 'I will *make* you aware of me and my mother!' And I had another thought—that I was neither Chinese nor Caucasian."

"You're *Canadian*. You're both," he says, the first words he can think of to comfort her. She nods. Like him, in a way, he thinks—neither a doctor nor a reporter, somehow both.

They are excused from this overcharged, too-soon attack of empathy, a tiny computerized whistle, Mr. Samsung and AT&T earning a few pennies, announcing a text. She reaches into her purse—the purse that looms large in their future—and rescues her phone from its depths. The message says her mother needs mangoes; her father, now recovered from an afternoon of confusion, wants them.

Their conversation, so intimate, so soon, ends too quickly. Like Kate's visit to her grandparents.

His meeting and the thought of dinner with her cut short, and a long, solitary evening ahead of him, he decides on a walk through Georgetown before going home.

Sometimes feet are smarter than thoughts.

Like the clouds that continue to scroll by on the still-hot late early evening sky, his steps are guided by something larger than himself—in this case, his heart. They take Noah to Wisconsin Ave. where he says good-bye to Kate. She returns to her anxious mother, her disappearing father, her need to make them and her grandparents proud of her.

He continues up the Georgetown Hill, past the stores, past his present, to R Street, his past. Finally, a sweaty twenty minutes later, he finds himself across the street from a door he slammed shut years before, vowing never to return, never to see *them* again. Never, he vowed, to revisit the wound that had almost killed him, the wound that ran from his balls to his brain.

Faulkner said it best, "The past isn't over. It isn't even the past."

He pauses, directly opposite the house where Pete, Deb and he had lived years before. A jogger passes by, oblivious to all but the tiny, tinny sound his ear buds make, and the slap-slapping of his running shoes on the ancient brick-cobbled sidewalk.

At first, Noah refuses to actually look at the house, but he pauses, partly to get his breath (the hill is steeper than the one in his memory), partly because it is time, his heart says, to let this go. He stops to rest on a low stone wall across the street, his hands resting on the worn-flat stones, rubbing them as though they are larger versions of his talisman.

Pete was the third person.

He had entered Noah's life in freshman year, not a little baby, but a grown-up, skinny twenty-plus year old from Detroit, ebony-black, a recent transfer from Wayne State in Detroit. "Jesus," Noah said to him when they met, "does *anybody* still live in Detroit? Hard to imagine." Friends described Pete as solid, with broad shoulders and a narrow waist, like a black *Yield* sign on skinny legs. He was a study in angles, the slope of his forehead, his lips, his pointing jaw.

Pete slid into the seat beside Noah, at the first of the Georgetown Great Lectures, not by accident. The GGL was created so that students could hear and (oh my, yes) *experience* the great scholars of the University. It was true that they were brilliant discoverers of quarks or smaller objects, of economic theories or larger. But speakers? Not so much. This particular speaker was Oskar Drumboski, once an early-career Nobel winner in Physics, but by then a tiny, dehydrated version of his younger self, barely able to propel his body to the lectern. He was several decades past the day when he had met the King of Sweden. Scarcely audible until the technician moved his lapel microphone, avoiding days-old soup stains in the process.

His speech was so Polish-accented that it was impossible to understand. There were no laughs for the first few minutes, perhaps a snicker or chuckle. By the time ten minutes had gone by, Noah could hardly contain the irony of the Great Lecture given by a man who could not lecture. He laughed out loud, then watching his new seat neighbor do the same, trying to contain it, failing miserably. Together, laughing at the level of *God-I-think-I'm-going-to-piss-myself*, garnering stares from the other students, they left the auditorium, bonding their way to friendship.

They had a year to discover that they liked the same things—hockey at first, then biking. Noah said he couldn't believe that black guys biked. Pete disagreed, "We brothers, we be wantin' bikes, we jus' lift'em. They just sittin' around at offices, locked up with some puny chain. We just snip that chain and poof you got yourself a fancy white-ass bike!" His made-up, exquisitely inappropriate African-American street voice pulled Noah further into the friendship. Pete biked to school every day and to work on weekends at one of the local bagel-coffee houses. "Makin' a li'l extra dough, you know man?" with a big smile, "And I get brea-fast."

Sometimes, when their school and work schedules allowed them, they'd go biking for a day, taking the Chain Bridge when it wasn't flooded and when the day wasn't a scorching 110. There, on those long days, the bonding, like the Potomac they often followed, grew deeper. Pete was from a poor family, fatherless. He got into sports early, started to win events, then scholarships, bringing him to Georgetown. There were holes in his stories: large chunks of his high school years never touched on, offering what Noah called a Swiss cheese life. *What the hell,* Noah thought, *Pete just has some things he doesn't want to talk about.* There were times Pete looked as though he might want to reveal something, but his face would cloud over, like a switch had been turned off. Once, his tongue loosened by a few beers, crossing M street after a hockey game, he came close to saying….something. Noah paused, waiting, looking at his friend. At length, Pete said, "Nothing. Fuck. Never mind." His sigh was lost in the M Street traffic.

Noah thought it wasn't nothing.

Inch by inch, story by story, in the way of men, Pete came to know Noah better. Not so much his past—that was of little interest to either of them. But these questions: How could Noah tell Deborah that he wanted medicine, when her goal was a lifetime of working together in physics or chemistry? How it was that she saw medicine as having two not so desirable routes, either working for a primary care assembly-line, or as some high end, arrogant specialist? Neither path appealed to her for her Noah. How could he tell her he had applied to medical school in Georgetown, to other schools? That was the beginning of their trouble.

Pete had a few girl friends in that time, though never anything serious. "What's serious mean?" he'd ask. "Like remembering her birthday, only going out with her? Actually *buying* her something? Like that?" There were parties, mostly beer-fueled, but there was also marijuana and other drugs. Neither Pete nor Noah liked the harder stuff. Deborah on the other hand, didn't drink much, but she had learned to like other things. Harder things.

It was Pete who suggested it, mid-way through their junior year. "Why not get a bigger house, get us all together, you know?" He had heard about a two hundred year old reno, had actually visited the house after class one day.

"It'd be fun," he said, "much easier than you two walking thirty blocks a day, me biking my ass off, nearer work for me. Nearer you guys. And we get kind of separate apartments. C'mon, you gotta see it!"

They did. They liked it, moving in a month later, enjoying double dates with Pete and his lady of the night or day. The hockey games, watching the Caps lose. Friends coming over from school.

Pete was the perfect roommate, possessing only one bad habit—pipe-smoking. To mask the smell, Pete cooked fennel every day of the year, using it like others use chewing gum. He loved fennel; they ate a lot of it that year. They ate a lot of *everything* that year. They each had one night of cooking a week. For reasons he can't explain, Noah remembers that Pete's was Tuesday, always with tacos—Taco Tuesdays. The memory hurts suddenly, like an open wound.

Noah is still perched on the low stone wall for support, his fingers rubbing the stones beneath them. He knows what's coming, sees it, like a survivor remembers the ocean receding just before a tsunami.

He looks up as the jogger passes, the first time he has seen—actually *seen*—the house in years. It is one of thousands in Georgetown: a wide, inviting front porch; a shotgun hallway running all the way to the back of the house, interrupted only by stairs on the right; a family room/living room/dining room combination on the left at the front; a small kitchen at the back, possibly still smelling of fennel. And beside the kitchen, a little vestibule (Noah's mother, of English stock, called it a *foy-ay*), a separate bathroom and a ground floor master bedroom looking into a little garden at the back. His and Deborah's bedroom. A large wisteria has grown up around the porch, twisting the railing and roof supports. There is new paint on the front porch. Someone has taken a stab at gardening—not something that the trio ever undertook.

The house is essentially the same as the day Noah left it, his clothes and his heart stuffed into two suitcases and a laundry bag.

The tsunami is about to swallow him.

13

THE TOMB OF PAKAL THE GREAT. PALENQUE. YUCATAN PENINSULA. 638 A.D.

Pakal was numb, stunned by the death of A'Cliz, apprehensive about the peace accord, momentarily immobilized. A'Cliiz had been a spiritual guide, almost a father, to the king. Naked in his grief and body, Pakal bent over the priest, holding him, feeling the life drain from him like an emptied vessel. He slowly lowered his body to the hard stone pavement of the antechamber.

Bending over Pakal, in his kindest voice, Chicahua asked if the king wished to be alone for a few minutes. Hearing no answer, he placed his arms gently, fatherly, around the muscular shoulders of two of the younger *ahoub*, suggesting that they move away from the antechamber with its overturned table and spilled Codex leaves, joining the other kings, walking into the tomb itself, pausing only at the entrance to the stairs for a moment. Once in the tomb, they stood around the sarcophagus lid, admiring its carvings, the ornate, ancient almost-spaceship.

Chicahua asked them, "What do you make of this? Do you think the priest dying is another omen for us? Do you trust what he said?"

As they talked, he moved them deeper into the tomb, blocking the exit, skilled at moving objects to his purposes. The kings were distracted by the death of the priest, their eyes missing Chicahua's signal to his guards. Finally, standing at the doorway to the tomb, blocking it, Chicahua placed his hands inside his apron in a gesture that twentieth century muff-wearing women might recognize. He grasped two obsidian blades hidden inside its folds, no longer than a man's foot, polished to a malignant fineness. With a speed and ferocity belying his age he struck at the closest two kings, lunging at Izel first. His taller, lankier frame and prominent rib cage became a perfect target. The knife entered his heart, killing him in an instant, crossing the thin quick line between life and death.

Chicahua watched his guards move noiselessly into the tomb, and then quickly stabbed Xepel, the shorter, stockier man, in the trachea, flooding his windpipe with his own blood. His last cries sounded like the voice of a drowning man, which of course he was. His guards quickly dispatched the other two *ahoub*, attacked with such sudden ferocity that their deaths took less than a minute. They sunk, surrounded by their self-pitying sobs and blood, to the floor. Later, Chicahua's men described the deaths as disappointing; they were expecting a fight.

The footsteps of Chicahua's guards and the stabbings and deaths were so noiseless that Pakal remained unaware, simultaneously only a few paces and many miles away. He held the priest's cooling body, paying no attention to the room or the tomb beyond, planning how he would return to the discussion. He might actually use the fact of A'Cliz's death to motivate the others, he thought. *You see? Your doubt has killed the priest!* His motto, *Never waste a crisis*, surfacing.

Chicahua placed his hand on Pakal's shoulder. "Is there anything I can do?" the old man asked, using his kindly voice. "Shall I call for another priest? Seek a physician's help?"

Slowly, as though rising from a deep sleep, Pakal raised his head, turning to the older man. It was precisely the right angle for his trachea to be severed, a windpipe filled with bubbling blood and betrayal. And almost no sound.

Chicahua wiped his hand inside his apron, no more perturbed by what he had done than if it were a ritual chicken-slaughtering. He replaced the knives, donned the vestments left hanging for him outside the mouth of the chamber. He stood taller, prouder. *He* was the greatest king now. Taking his guards, he climbed the stairs to the topmost chamber, then descended outside, making a small, slow procession down the sun-drenched outer stairs. A few noticed the blood stains on his hands, thinking only that he had bled himself, an act of purification, another example of the misalignment of observation and interpretation.

He turned to the groups of priests and others waiting outside, each anticipating an announcement about the accord. He said, smiling, "All is well. The discussion is proceeding as planned. I have decided to withdraw while my fellow *ahoub* make final arrangements. I shall return however. Have no fear."

He did not lie about returning.

It took several minutes for Pakal's and the other kings' guards to become suspicious, to enter the antechamber themselves and discover what we can only describe as bedlam. The color of the blood on the walls was masked by the red walls, but nothing could hide its copper stench, the red stickiness of the puddles on the floor, the torn trachea and chests of the kings, the grotesque angles of their naked necks and arms, one flung entirely over the tomb lid, his body as frightening as anything on the sarcophagus itself. Alarms were raised, calling many to the temple (including Pakal's sons and brother, one of whom would inherit the kingdom) but nothing could dam the flow of enmity and hatred, of hurt and betrayal. Nothing could reclaim the lives lost.

Nothing could reclaim the peace accord.

Late that night, after the bodies had been cleansed by the guards of each particular king, after the fighting had stopped on the stairs of the Temple, one man dared to climb the stairs. Using his persuasive powers to pass through the frightened, suspicious guards, he entered the antechamber. He was Hibiscus, the senior-most scribe of the Temple.

Dried blood covered much of the stone floors. He stepped around the place where the kings lay, their retinue loath to move them; they would be buried in this tomb along with Pakal. Hibiscus focused on the singular goal of finding the Codex, his and Nantua's creation. He knew, as much as he believed in A'Cliz's view of the world, that truth—and the potential for harm—resided in the leaves of the text.

The blood, splashed everywhere, made a peculiar red-brown carpet of carnage. Stools and a low table had been smashed, as though a giant tantrum-driven child had entered the room and played violently with its contents. By some miracle, however, as a mother recognizes her child, Hibiscus found the codex, trapped between a chair and a table.

As stunned as he was by the violence, its sight stirred him, bringing tears to his eyes. It was not entirely ruined. It lay in parts, obviously thrown into a corner of the antechamber—in disgust? In anger? In fear?—but it was a puzzle that could be put together again. Hardly noticing the blood on a few of the pages, he gathered them up, grasping them tightly in both arms, an unwieldy bundle for one man.

As he carried the precious, dangerous pages into the burial chamber, he weighed his options, balancing them as he did the leaves of the Codex. On the one hand, it was too powerful to destroy; on the other, it was too risky to let others see it. It was better to bury it. Finding a space below the eight stone legs that raised the sarcophagus from the floor, he placed the codex, battered and bloody, leaf by leaf, in a separate hidden space, far under the huge, immovable structure. Tomorrow, when they buried Pakal and the others, the tomb would be sealed for eternity, exactly the right amount of time for it to rest, hidden from the world.

His work finished, Hibiscus climbed the stairs to his studio and removed a blank folio sheet from a pile of bark-skin folio pages, painted white. And he— with as much skill and speed as his years of experience would allow—painted the scene as he saw it. Later still, he buried it with the other codex leaves, hidden in a location that he and only he knew. Chaos, recorded and buried for all time.

Finally, the orange dawn arrived, its light bathing the crown of the temple first, like gold.

He called for the other priest-scribes to join him in their march, a poor imitation of the earlier grand procession. They made a somber parade out of the temple, leaving its upper room, in single file, the younger scribes in front, Hibiscus, the eldest at the rear. Each after his brother, they stepped carefully off the east-facing, topmost platform and, one step at a time, descended the steep stairs. All except for Hibiscus. After the last had left, turning to his right at the top stair, not descending with his colleagues, he made his way carefully to the western face of the temple, the face of death to the Maya.

Something unwelcome had arisen in him, speaking questions so frightening as to seal his fate, like nails in a coffin. It precluded any other thought. *What would happen if I speak of this? If others hear me in my sleep? What if Chicahua's forces capture me?*

There was only one answer. On the west side, the Temple steps were absent; the wall of the temple became a straight cliff. At the top, standing on a thin ledge, he folded his hands in front of his chest. He closed his eyes and leaned forward until gravity and the horror of the last few hours caught him, propelling him past the many temple decorations, past the intricate stonework, into oblivion.

His last thought was identical to A'Ciliz's only hours before, *It is finished.*

And so it began, a rapid unfolding of the peace process, like a fragile glass vase dropped, smashed into a million pieces. Like those pieces, the unfolding was able to wound.

At first there was the rage-filled charge on Chichen Itza and its *ahoub*, Chicahua, whose guards had slain the remaining kings. The citizens of Palenque stormed their new enemy in retribution for the killings, a living example of an eye for an eye, murdering and raping. And then Chicahua's sons, enraged by the death of their father, attacked other cities and villages, unleashing another vicious cycle of murder and revenge. Like a virus, the plague of violence and carnage spread to other communities, to other cities, peace lost amidst the blood and the anger. Even acts of kindness were buried by the bodies of men, by the corpse of hope.

Something else fueled the self-harming cycle. Hibiscus was not the only scribe whose work had created the codex; others had toiled on the depictions of Venus, the other planets and the Seven Gods. While A'Ciliz had struggled to keep the recordings separate so as to not let any one person know the complete truth, they had underestimated the scribes' ability to arrive at their own beliefs about the collapse of the planets.

And to spread them.

And with their spreading, to create despair. Like a slow flood, the message of a doomed world inundated the thoughts of the scribes, then their wives and neighbors. The message conveyed the emptiness and purposelessness of a doomed world, infecting the Maya. Coupled with the blood lust and revenge that followed the failed peace accord, it caused them to abandon their cities, to turn from their culture. Within a hundred years, it could be said that the peak of Mayan civilization had passed; within two hundred years, that their civilization had largely disappeared. Later, in our time, it was said that the decline of the Maya occurred for reasons still largely a mystery.

There is no mystery here.

14

GEORGETOWN. WASHINGTON. DC. MONDAY EVENING

S ome details are vague, like an impressionist painting. But these facts are clear, carved in the stone of his memory.

He was home from school early. He noticed the pipe first, sitting on the little IKEA table, just inside the hallway outside his and Deborah's bedroom. Not in the front hall where it should have been, but beside the kitchen, in *their* hallway. And then, his mind at first discarding the noise as though it were irrelevant, he heard the sounds of bed-creaking, the animal noises of sex.

Pushing through the door, pushing through his rising anger and disbelief, he saw it in the room's corner mirror. Pete's thrusting chocolate ass, Deborah's legs wrapped around his waist, a tight, beige vice. The mirror was from IKEA, it occurred to him, his mind trying hard to focus on benign things, away from the betrayal in front of it. And then sounds. First, from Deborah, "*Oh my God*!! Noah's home? I heard the door! Jesus!" They heard more than the door.

They heard Noah storming across the room in three big steps, heard him yelling, "What the fuck do you think you're doing?!" Undeniably a stupid question, from Noah who rarely swore. "Get the fuck out of here!" he yelled at Pete, equally articulate. They could have heard Noah's heart pounding in his chest. In over two decades of life, of teenage angst, of the separation and divorce of his parents, of his isolated youth and adolescent loves, he had never experienced rage.

Or betrayal.

There was Deborah to deal with. For a few seconds, he thought he might have turned his fury on her, but her reaction stopped him cold, or rather, her non-reaction. She stood in the bedroom, her clothes gathered against her breasts and pelvis, a shield against him. The picture of a frozen living Venus stopped him. For just an instant he might have seen tears in her eyes, or the beginning of "I'm so sorry!" on her lips. But if there was one defining characteristic about Deborah—beyond her beautiful eyes and mocha skin, beyond her intellect, beyond the memory of what they had together—it was her way of turning the anger back to its source, like a mirror reflects light. It wasn't *her* in the wrong. *What was Noah doing home?*

It was her fatal flaw.

Years later, other memories flood him as he stands on the street outside the house, sweating, heart-racing as though he had just biked the Georgetown Hill at full-out speed.

Most of the next five days are a smudgy, partially erased memory now becoming clearer as he sees the house. Making love to Deborah, although love may not be the best word, perhaps the memory of love. Smashing the mirror in the bedroom—the mirror where he'd always see Pete's black ass reflected. Using a picture of Deborah and Noah in a heavy old ornate frame to break the glass into a million Scandinavian shards, like the two of them had shattered his life. Remembering where they got the mirror (the IKEA in Maryland), putting it together with the tiny little key thing, where they bought the heavy vintage picture frame. Remembering where they took the picture, biking along the Potomac. How much in love they were, *were* being the operative word.

At the end of the fifth day, Noah had enough of the frequent flyer feeling, the flipping from one side of the knife edge to another, from rage to sympathy and back again. And in the end, in the morning, he paid his share of the rent for the next six weeks (on-line, making the gesture as impersonal as possible); rented a U-Haul to take the mirror and other forgettable items to the transfer center;

threw them with a hugely satisfying grunt and *fuck-you* into the dumpster; packed his things into two suitcases and a laundry bag. He had loved them both and they had wounded him deeply, their actions like the knives of long-dead kings.

Noah considers himself a decent reporter and yet, those feelings—the way they stripped away his skin and left him screaming, alone—leave him wordless.

Noah has experienced all this before, but looking at the house for the first time in years evokes other memories. They surface from the sea of self-pity, struggling towards consciousness, rising fast. Somewhere, he hears a siren off in the distance, blocks away. The jogger is gone; it's the only sound.

The first memory is of Deborah. Her emotional catatonia on the one hand, her anger at Noah on the other. How she must have felt when he, at last, told her he'd applied for medicine and then when he started medical school. His pre-occupation with the first overwhelming year of study, his neglect of their shared life, of her feelings. For a while, she functioned externally, going to school, taking on her teaching assistant assignments, even making a meal when it was her turn to cook. But she was unstable internally, clearly unable to deal with the emotional whirlpool inside her. And, in hindsight, drug addicted.

The second memory is of Pete. Noah had neglected him, too. Pete, whose uncle or somebody had died during the spring, taking him away for a week. When he returned, Noah said something like, "Sorry about your loss," and then didn't pursue it. Noah wasn't even sure who died.

Thoughts and memories accelerate now, faster, larger than a commuter train. Noah has replayed this tape in his mind a million times, his thoughts still trying to alter the ending or the script, but in this, his particular past, there is no editing. They form the third memory, lost until then. He sees Pete pulling on his skinny jeans, trying to stuff his still-hard black cock dick into them, an almost laughably impossible task. He sees himself chasing Pete out of the house, through the family room, out onto the porch, the porch that he sees now. As Pete stumbled down the front stairs, he turned back. Noah saw something in his eyes, possibly an apology, a sadness, moisture caught in the noon sun. It lasted only a second, but its implications are profound.

Maybe, he thought, possibly for the first time, who could blame them? If only he had—what?—been more sympathetic? Told Deb more about his plans?

Been around more? *Cared* more? Pete and Deborah were a couple now, he thinks; they deserve whatever life they've had. He'd heard they dropped out of school, moved away, had a kid. *Good for them*, he thinks, only partly sarcastically.

Irony, invisible like the footsteps of generations, appears on the sidewalk: years later, on a *sidewalk* of all places, he hears his mother's words, the woman who used aphorisms like other people use punctuation. "The universe is unfolding as it should," she'd say. On this street, where memories have come alive, where angry words are heard again, where the pain of loss and betrayal diminish with time and understanding, it is these words which carry the most weight in this story.

The universe.

Noah checks his iPhone. It is seven-thirty, only a half hour from the time he left Kate. He's spent at most two minutes on the sidewalk, staring at the house. A lifetime in 120 seconds. And as he turns to leave, it occurs to him that he is less burdened than he has been in years, less a hostage to his hatred. A psychic shaman might say it's the release of a spirit, but it is clear that something has shifted in Noah's mental machinery, a molecule re-adjusted in the chemistry of rejection and anger. Something has let go.

He has a thought as he leaves, surprisingly lighter. *How could I tell Kate this?*

He walks the rest of the way home, and in fifteen minutes or so he's in his favorite place—a little one-person balcony in his Florida Avenue apartment. It overlooks the street and the corner of Twenty-First Street. If he leans out just a little bit (well, maybe more than just a little bit) he can see Mass Ave. It's on the fourth floor, high enough to feel that he has the western edge of the city almost entirely to himself. At night—alone but not lonely, drinking but not drunk, awake at two a.m. but not sleepy—he can feel a kind of peace, perhaps tonight more than any other in recent memory. At least enough peace to take himself to bed and—reluctantly, he never wants to give up on the day—sleep.

His night table drawer is the treasure chest of the insomniac. The ear plugs, the foil-wrapped *Sominex* pills, the melatonin tablets, and even something from his mother, an old Christmas stocking stuffer, packages of some awful, fruity caffeine-free tea. They reside there with the other debris of bachelor night table drawers. Old Christmas and birthday cards, snapshots, a few matchboxes, several retired pens and the single man's prize—mostly unused but ever-hopeful condoms. He could even find, tucked away in the back of the drawer, an old photo of Deborah and Pete and him in what we might call happier times. He will not find the picture tonight, but if he did, he would keep it.

He skips the treasure chest tonight. It's possible that Faulkner was not entirely right: some of the past has been put where it belongs.

His dreams are of a family life, with Deborah and him, of Deb and him and Shanny, together in the same house. Having dinner together. Bike riding as a family. In the mysterious chemistry of dreams, Deb and Shanny are the same person, alternatively young and old. Near the end of the dream, at the beginning of morning, a phone begins to ring, its iPhone tune-of-the-week the only sound in the room. A Seventies' tune, but insistent.

It's Kate, using his cell phone.

"Noah, *Noah!*

"They found DiShannia dead last night!" Kate, breathless, at work, or *working* at least, the tiny sound on the phone clear but distorted—at first by the long journey from deep sleep to wakefulness, then moments later by his disbelief.

"What? *Jesus*, how?"

And later, much later, *how did she know?*

SECTION II

A DEATH IN THE FAMILY

15

385 MILES ABOVE EARTH. MONDAY

At nearly four hundred miles above the earth, there is only the silent seductive song of space. Swimming in it like a dark, airless ocean, Hubble hears nothing.

Or almost nothing. It might hear the occasional molecule of air or a tiny fragment of space debris as it strikes the telescope's surface, slowing the structure down, a tiny pushback against the forces which hurled the telescope into space in the first place. Those forces are the product of US and German ingenuity, a decade of fund-raising and cajoling, of scientists attempting to explain deep space to politicians unburdened by technical understanding. Or by much intelligence for that matter, a subject for another day.

When it was first launched, the telescope suffered a serious defect: it could not see. It would have had perfect (one might say twenty-twenty) vision had it not been for the lens. It was the world's largest, carefully crafted, but was scratched, beyond fixing. An especially big problem when the technician had to make a house call 380 miles above earth; its repair cost several million dollars.

Today it works perfectly. The telescope, like a lover seeking a lost a lost soulmate, and still quiet as a tomb, has a perfect view of the universe.

What it sees is light in real time, projected from the objects it finds through its now-perfect lens. That light however is not instantaneous. It takes time for it to travel from its source to the lens. Light from the moon say, or the sun, takes only a few seconds or minutes to make the journey. These views—let's call them views from nearby objects—are really pictures of pretty-much current things (well, an eight-minute-old view of the sun; a much smaller delay from your moon). Light from Pluto, sadly now demoted to non-planet status, takes several months to touch Hubble's surface, so the picture that the lens captures is of a Pluto several months before. It is like showing a bride's baby picture at her wedding.

When it looks from its quiet platform very, very far into the distance, as far as it can see, it is looking at ancient images of galaxies, of planets being born, of stars dying, of nova and supernova. The most distant of these are pictures of objects roughly fourteen billion years old. That is the age of the universe—*this* universe, to be clear—at its birth. This view into the long distant past takes it back in time to the origin of the universe itself, to what cosmic specialists call the Big Bang.

In contrast to its outward-looking nature, Hubble is tethered to its earth-home by gravity and electronics. It is this that saddles Hubble with another disadvantage, in some ways worse than the damaged lens. This one isn't so easily fixed: Hubble has only men and women to answer its many questions.

Hubble's human masters and servants occupy surprisingly pedestrian, squat office buildings on the planet below. There, those master-servants fill databases, journals and field notes with findings that fuel the imagination of men and women studying the beginnings of those stars and galaxies—and their movements. It would be impossible to actually measure those distances and their speed in the usual way of calculating the distances of the sun or moon or the other planets. *We don't have yardsticks that long,* said one scientist to a college class.

Clever science has developed its own ideas however, among them the effect of Mr. Doppler, the detection of direction of movement by sound or light. Sound is simple to explain: a train moving nearer makes one sound, when it moves away, another—the product of the changing transmission of sound waves. In the silent vacuum of space however, no sound waves can travel. Here, humans depend on light waves, which, like obedient children, adhere to the same laws. They produce a spectrum of color, ranging from a deep blue, like the night sky, to a bright fiery red, like the sun. Those objects which move *away* from earth shift their light spectrum to the red end, those which move *towards* us shift to the blue. Since the objects in Hubble's view shift to the red there is no doubt that these far distant galaxies are moving away from us. It is one thing on which, unlike other theories of space and time and the physical universe, there is full agreement.

Or almost full agreement.

Perhaps Hubble, left to its own devices, might have imagined an alternative answer: that what we see might not be what *is*. That your manner of recording speed and distance is altered by the universe in some way. That your assumptions are wrong. It is possible that Hubble's human master-servants have made an error of enormous proportions, placing mankind at a serious disadvantage. We can forgive them, though: their imagination is limited by their human-ness.

Perhaps you cannot forgive them this last item, a final example of a lack of imagination. Hubble is interested, you might say obsessed, with the examination of the very edges of the universe, the earliest beginnings. The Big Bang. The farthest away, oldest picture. Hubble's masters suppose that because they see nothing before their dating of the universe's origin, that there was nothing there.

The product of a lack of imagination, perhaps the largest disadvantage, it is a silly supposition: I was there.

I am there.

16

GEORGETOWN, WASHINGTON, DC. EARLY TUESDAY MORNING

DiShannia? What? *How?"* Noah is confused, still occupied by the business of waking up.

"They're not sure exactly. The last time they saw her was when she got into a White House SUV. Only there's some doubt that that's what it was. She didn't come home for dinner. Somehow she wound up in an alley ten blocks from her place, beaten to death. What a waste, Noah, eh?" The Canadian "eh" fills the hollow space created by Noah's verbal absence. In Afghanistan, in Finland, elsewhere on medical training electives, he has learned to separate himself from news like this.

"I can't believe it, Kate," he says, pulling himself out from the bed-covers, swinging his legs over the side. "She is…" He is suddenly, surprisingly, saddened, his voice catching. "She was an incredible person, even that young. Where are you now?" he asks, squeezing the phone between his ear and his shoulder, trying to pull his pants on. She isn't at Bezos 1 yet; she's on her way.

"I'll meet you there. Give me an hour, maybe two. Check with the police, would you? Find out all you can? I have an idea."

And he does. He follows a rapidly deflating erection to the bathroom. Like him, it's diminished by the thought that such a brilliant star could be snuffed out so quickly.

He is even more convinced that there is a *story* here. One that won't of course bring her back, an impossibility in this particular universe. *We can*, he thinks, *help find her killer. Killers, maybe.* There are many uncertain, suspicious things swimming underneath the surface of this story: his hunch about a problem in the school; the backpedalling on federal funding; the timing of her death just before her presentation to the National Academy.

It's just the two of them assigned to her story though. Neither of them has enough crime background; they need help.

For a minute, he thinks of texting Sydney but realizes he needs to go over her head and involve the Executive. Unlike its singular name, the Exec comprises the directors of each of the information services (they called them product lines, like the news was a toaster or a *Lay Z Boy*) plus of course the EIC, Eric. The Exec is a hungry beast, not just for news. It meets every Tuesday for breakfast, at a nearby high-end place called the Tulip Club. If he hurries he can just make it.

Thirty minutes later—a quick shower, a fast pull-on of pants and shirt, a hurried walk to the Tulip Club— he does.

The Tulip Club: white table cloths; maroon, velveteen banquettes around the walls and in rows; little hanging vase-pockets of Murano glass imbedded in the clear, wood and suede-covered walls of the place, each big enough to hold a fresh, just-flown-in tulip, the hallmark of the place. There are several hundred of them decorating the walls and room dividers, colorful little reminders of Queen Juliana. And there, away in the back, cozy behind a glass wall, Noah finds the Exec. The chiefs and their hangers-on are just moving their chairs back, brushing the toast-crumbs off their shirts and blouses, leaving the detritus of breakfast behind. One lonely bagel sits in a large basket in the middle of the table, unwanted.

He nabs Sydney and Erich, non-identical news twins.

"I'm glad I caught you," he says, "I think I have an interesting story; can I get your read on it?"

They look mildly pissed off. Syd pulls a *Jesus, not this again* face. To be fair,

Noah has tried this a few times with stories that he thought were hot and which turned out to be, well, not so much. Erich looks at the watch on his skinny girl-wrist, raising his eyebrows as if to say, *Better make this fast.* Noah has learned to play the game, though: making things sound like they are at least partly their idea eases the journey from idea to story. Ignoring their automatic first responses, he accompanies them to the door, walking backwards and slightly ahead, awkwardly, almost hitting a waiter. The kid is busy defying gravity, carrying a mountain of dirty dishes.

Noah tells them about DiShannia—her research, the science award, her death, the school. He lets them connect the dots.

Using his faux-humility skills, he says, "This is one of those cross-theme stories you've always stressed to us." More than the murder of a fourteen year old girl, it's the Presidential Science Award and the White House reference that hooks them. Erich is a constant room-scanner, looking for somebody better to talk to, using his super-power, eyeball radar. His eyes rarely focus on one individual, an act too perilously close to commitment perhaps. When his gaze does land on someone, it's as though they are an object like a pen, of use at times but not worthy of anything but a casual glance. This attribute is most noticeable as he shakes hands, looking over the shakee's shoulder to see who else is in the room. He does all of this during the backward Noah dance—grasping the hands of a table of well-dressed political types, smiling at the room—but in the process, he says to Noah, "You said DiShannia? She black?"

Sydney, bless her heart, has assumed a form of suspended animation, checking her iPhone for messages, waiting for the boss. Two beats and one room-scanning search later, Noah agrees that she is indeed African-American. Finally Eric says, speaking to the door, "We received some criticism last year for not enough black interest. Not justified in my opinion, but then who am I?"

He shrugs his tiny shoulders, the servant-leader. "If you can get me something more than a simple crime involving a black girl for Chrissake, I'll look at it—more than just black-girl-got-killed interest. No extra resources, though, huh, Noel? You know what our budget is like, right? Work it, just you and whoever Sydney thinks is good. How about twenty-four hours? There's nothing worse than a stale story. If you get something more, let Sydney work it up the chain to me."

His voice on high-whine, he disappears beyond the revolving door. Some freaking chain, Noah thinks: *there's me, there's Sydney, there's you, period.* But he puts on a pleased face and says something profound to Erich's back like, "Good, thanks." The story of DiShannia is more important than his ego.

Then suddenly, Sydney is off her phone, transformed suddenly into Miss Enthusiastic. "Yes, good idea, Chief!" And a nod to Noah as he holds the door for her, "You and the new girl run with it. Maybe a couple of others if you need help. And oh," she says as an afterthought, exiting the door, "you can have a team room."

On the one hand, Noah is happy. He has a green light to pursue the story and the promise of a team room. On the other hand, as the door closes, he thinks, *Noel. He called me Noel. She didn't remember the new girl's name. They're really into human interest stories. Her name's Kate, for God's sake.*

What a joke.

It doesn't take long for the Whirling Dervish v2.0 to take over.

Noah charges into the Bezos 1 Plaza in full story mode, the slouch long behind him; he has a plan to find out about DiShannia's death. He smells something here—not the burnt-urine smell of the streets as he speed-walks to the office from the Tulip Club. Not the fine wine of homelessness—the dirt, grease and cheap zin—of the family sprawling just outside WashPO's front door. It's the smell of a story. This time he's charged not by his ambition, but by the loss of a remarkable teen. Something took her life, something bigger than she was, possibly bigger than WashPO. He's doing it for her mother, Mrs. Johns, and for, to be truthful here, the young woman he just met and whose life was ended too soon.

For reasons he can't explain, he feels compelled.

Team rooms hold much more than their writable white walls and flat screens, movable tables and easy-swivel chairs. They hold the potential for people-to-people collaboration, for idea-sharing, for new thinking. In fairly short order, he's asked green-shirted Hernando to clean one, texted Kate to let her know he's back in the building. Once he's settled, he erases the whiteboard, filled with story ideas from the room's previous occupants—global warming, rising seas, fires, disappearing islands and receding shorelines.

He searches, downloads and photocopies a slew of stories about DiShannia and the Rose School, grabs a roll of scotch tape off of someone's desk (he's thinks it's the twentieth century's greatest invention. That and stickies of course) and places the pages on the whiteboard, re-arranging them, thinking.

Kate arrives half an hour later, delayed by meeting someone she knew, an old co-worker. Noah has converted the all-white walls into a gerrymandered version of Shanny's poster. One big panel is devoted to recent stories about the school and its funding, its successes. Another panel contains a Wikipedia print-out of the Mayan civilization and a map of Central America. A whole wall, the one nearest to the flat screen, is dedicated to DiShannia's murder, her diabetes, her poster, her discoveries. Above them are labels for the major themes: the Rose School Network/Eastern Charter School, the murder, and DiShannia herself.

Kate brings a competence to the room, along with the scent of crisp linen and soap falling off her like small cool waves. She dumps her oversized purse onto the nearest chair. Noah has come to call this her suitcase. He is suddenly aware of how sweaty he is, like after a workout, a product of the hot walk-run from the Tulip Club, the tension of this story. She takes the marker from him, her hand cool on his for a brief second.

"You didn't waste any time!" She walks to the white board, impressed, baffled. Like him. "It looks like one of those CSI crime scenes," she says, looking at their wall-mystery. "I think like you do. There's something about writing a story down that helps me understand it." She begins to re-organize the items, moving them so that they fit the themes better, trying to make sense of the questions that Shanny's death compels them to answer.

"I talked to her mom," she says, adding her own items, standing closer to him. In a few minutes, Noah's wide-ranging and somewhat chaotic elements are arranged in a more chronologic (and logical) order. She writes in a hand much more legible than his; she lacks the benefit of his medical school bad-handwriting training. Finally, they both stand back, looking at the walls:

- *DiShannia: her background, upbringing, precociousness, diabetes. How did DiS's mom support herself?*
- *The Rose School: COO, funding, quiet students, training. Is there telepathy there? Something else?*
- *The Mayan story: related to her death? Is her presentation to the National Academy important? Where did she get her information? Why would someone want to steal it?*
- *DiShannia's last twenty-four hours: Monday AM CNN interview;*

noon, visit to school; afternoon, meeting at the White House; afternoon-basketball practice: then ???

- *Her death: evidence of a struggle?*

He adds a question, *What happened to the other missing Rose School students?* Finally, she says, "We're going to need some help here, Noah."

He pulls a chair around, straddles it backwards. "I've been thinking about people I really want to join us. There's Gerry Watts, that tall, mustached guy, with his eye on you yesterday morning? And Naomi Zaltser? Maybe you don't remember. A kind of tight, compact woman? Hair in a bun?"

She remembers them both.

He's restless, turns the chair around again, and slouches. His feet are stretched out in front of him, his rear slides about a foot forward on the chair. Hands clasped behind his head, he says, "I'll tell you more about each of them."

There is no doubt that they need a crime reporter. While there are many creatures in the WashPO fishpond, Gerry Watts is the pond's brightest. Gerry was the reporter who blew the whistle on Hiram Bombardier, the governor of Maine, a couple of decades ago. Hiram, running for president as a third party guy was caught, literally and figuratively, with his pants down. The Tea Party (now styled the New Patriots) would have forgiven him if the persons at his feet were women, but not if they were boys performing what we might call oral tasks, often crossing state lines in the process. Gerry wrote it up: goodbye to Hiram's political ambitions.

And hello to Gerry's career, a Pulitzer nomination on that one and on several other crime stories. And hello to his being on Noah and Kate's team.

"Naomi Zaltser is also perfect for us," Noah says. If Gerry is a koi in the fishpond, Naomi is the shark. An amazing potential contributor, the odds that she'd join them lies somewhere between slim and none. There is also a mystery about Naomi, not of the sexually alluring or dark-past sort, but rather that no personal history attaches itself to her. Naomi never married to any one's knowledge, never showed any predilection for either sex, or any sex for that matter.

"What about the Mayan question, Noah?" Kate asks "Is there anyone here who writes about archeology, or about ancient cultures?" She has spotted a gap in their team. WashPO has lots of staffers who can research a topic, probably find sources at the Smithsonian or one of the city's universities, but Kate has another idea.

"I told you I have a cousin in Toronto, the only one I know on my mother's side, right? We could Skype him. He's a world expert on Middle American civilization. He'd help us, I'm sure. Can we invite outsiders?"

"Of course," his nod says, as she writes the name Wai-Ching Lam into the right side of the board along with Gerry's and Naomi's.

She's on a roll. "I have another idea. I met a guy in the hallway just now, a young computer whiz, a researcher I knew in Toronto, at GlobeCan. He's really smart. He joined us maybe a year ago, from England. He's awesome. He helped us investigate a couple of terrorist cells, did work on a government scandal. I was surprised to see him here, but he said he's been angling to work at WashPO for years." She adds "*Harry Foley-Bennett*" to the white board.

Noah nods again, brushing the hair back from his eyes, unfolding from his slouch as quickly as he fell into it. The Whirling Dervish is taking over. "Why don't I tackle Naomi and Gerry? You talk to your cousin and the IT guy. See you back here in—what do you think? An hour?"

Half an hour later, when Noah has his two team-members, Kates tackles the IT department, knowing that Harry will need permission from his chief. That department is a mosh pit of those who avoid human involvement, preferring the intangible and less hurtful connections of a cyber-world. The inhabitants of this universe concentrate on their devices, their curved backs almost all she can see. The soft clicks of their devices are the sole sounds in the speechless room; keyboards have replaced tongues and lips for communication. She wonders briefly if their great-great-grandchildren will be born without them, tiny Darwinian examples of an electronic evolution. Until she met Harry, she had always seen them as relatively interchangeable pieces of an Asperger puzzle.

She searches out to the manager.

"Kind of a compliment, don't you think?" the manager, M'iniqua says. M'iniqua's done her hair in corn rolls, bleached the color of a North Carolina orange, conjuring images of Hallowe'en. Kate is too new to know that people send emails around the office in code when M'iniqua's done her hair in a special way. *M'n—ringlets today. Gotta see*, the emails read.

"What is?" Kate asks, a little distracted by the bright orange color.

"Well, you come lookin' for Harry, y'know. And just last week, he heard you was hired, he say he knows you from your last job. He'd *love* to work with you and Mr. Scott, he says. You know him better, but we think he's that good, real fast, helpful, cool with teams. A big story like you need him workin' on? That'd be great!"

Kate finds him hunched in his open-space white-white cubicle, intent on finding the loose, amorphous thread of a story on-line, a sports fraud. He's overweight, a little over five feet high, slightly less across, the product of low physical activity. The accent gives him away: Harrison Edward Foley-Bennett is as English as crumpets and the late Queen.

"Oh my goodness, Kate," his eyes registering surprise at seeing her so soon. Pleased. "Of course I should like to work with you!" he replies. "Smashing. In fact, to be quite honest, I don't find the task I have currently so interesting. I do like soccer rather, but this," he says, pointing to one screen full of NBA stats, and another showing a list of thrown games, money passing through hands that should only hold a basketball, "this work, I am not so fond of." He says, *teddibly*, his upper-bracket speech hard-shifting the consonants. His smile brightens the oval olive of his face, like a back-light. One final analysis of the NBA stats, and he's more than happy to leave his sports-and-money pursuits.

Each one of them—Kate, Noah, Harry, Naomi and Gerry—are able to reassign meetings or work to meet over lunch.

It's the last good luck they have.

The team room, now marked by Hernando with a red sign, *Hold until FRIDAY, October 7,* is theirs to use whenever they want, booked for the rest of the week. When they return, the white board still contains Kate's and Noah's notes. They gather, spend a few minutes (fewer for Naomi, more for Gerry) on small talk. They settle.   At first, Noah feels like the primary care resident presenting a case to specialists, radiating varying levels of arrogance and certainty, sitting in judgment.

"So here's what we know so far," he starts. Only the rustle of Gerry's sandwich unwrapping disturbs the room. It's a gigantic Reuben; sauerkraut spills onto the wax paper.

The resident-feeling fades fast. He's caught up in the story of DiShannia— how they met her, what was in her poster, her background, the suspicious timing of her murder just before the National Academy speech. What Kate and he felt about the school, the possible tying together of individual threads. He is good at this, articulate and compelling, just as he is when he finds himself in front of a camera, reporting. Like him, the story attracts and compels them.

The team forms, an unusual constellation of talent—Gerry the womanizer and schmoozer, Naomi the bunned, dour workaholic, Harry often a short round fountain of good suggestions. Kate is a master group facilitator, an excellent reporter.

In the end, they assign themselves tasks: Gerry takes on the crime scene; Naomi will tackle the Rose Schools. Kate has tried to reach her cousin, but failed; she'll try again. Harry says, "'I'll dig. That's what I do, rather," a large smile lights up his face. "I'll explore DiShannia's knowledge of Mayan history, where it came from. I have some ideas, chaps." They are all chaps to him. "I'll also see what we can do about communication." Kate tells them that she telephoned Mrs. Johns to offer condolences, and to suggest that Noah and she drop by that afternoon. Noah will handle the medical aspects of DiShannia's death—her autopsy, her diabetes.

There is clearly something about this case that is contagious, attracting each of them in turn, moths to a flame.

They do not know—and will not for hours—how damaging the flame can be.

17

THE *QUEEN MARY,* BOUND FROM NEW YORK TO LONDON, 1938

She was a good girl, well taught by nuns, but a good girl would never contemplate doing what Mary Catherine was about to do, in a public place at that.

She thought she was alone on ship deck, somewhere mid-ocean, riding the giant slow waves of the North Atlantic, looking at the perfectly starred night, leaning against the railing, taking in the living smell of the water below her. *How close the stars look*, she thought. She was on the *Queen Mary,* returning from New York, in the heady, frightening days of war threats. One might easily imagine that she was returning to the solitary and scholarly life of a historian, but the adjectives no longer fit. Two recent events had stimulated her beyond the scholarly and solitary.

The first was a missive from her director, the equivalent of a command from Her Majesty. He had unfolded a letter held in place by a small glass paperweight, the light from a nearby desk lamp diffusing it into the colors of the rainbow. It was an invitation.

"Here it is, Mary Catherine. '*We are seeking a representative of the British Museum as a participant in the program we have tentatively called,* Defining the Field of Mathematics: An Anglo-American Conference. *The conference is to be held at the Willard Hotel, April 13-15, 1938 in Washington, DC. In particular, we have scheduled a panel on the history of mathematics, a subject in which we believe your institution has considerable depth. It is a relatively small conference to which less than a hundred English, Canadian and American scholars have been invited, but we are hopeful for a lively and informed discussion. We understand that current geopolitical difficulties might hinder your attendance but are hopeful....*'"

His glasses had reached that perilous point at the end of his nose when they might drop off by themselves. His finger saved them from that fate, shoving them back up the long ramp of his nose. "There. I think you see what they have in mind. You would attend the conference as a participant. Are you up for a presentation? You could speak easily on Mayan mathematics."

She was nervous: it would be her first international speech, her first trip to America. There was the risk of war. She weighed her anxiety however against the heft of her university experience, her seminar presentations. The interview was almost over, signaled by his rising from his chair, its ancient coasters like small castanets on the oak floor. Sensing the hesitation in her, he ended with, "It will be a chance to present yourself on the global stage, Mary Catherine, good for your career. There's one more thing. Could you also transport something back home with you when you return? The Smithsonian appears to have found itself the owner of a Mayan codex and doesn't know what to do with it. You do, my dear—would you be willing to bring it back with you?"

Of course she would.

It was there that the second magic thing had happened, the thing that was about to disrupt her good-girl self-image.

Mary Catherine's role on the panel was to respond to a brilliant young English mathematician who spoke on the *future* of mathematics, and—causing some rustling of papers in the audience—how we might one day create an artificial intelligence. She had been intrigued by the way in which his mind worked, taking, maybe *making* leaps of faith. He appeared as interested in her talk on Mayan mathematics as she was in his.

That interest, scholarly and collegial, carried them to the post-meeting reception in one of the hugely elaborate meeting rooms of the Willard. Plush carpets held virtual gardens of roses and hibiscus, ornate Louis Fourteenth chairs and sofas. Baroque mirrors reflected every one of the hundred-plus guests. A table laden with high quality and expensive "heavy hors d'oeurves" seemed out of place for the times, she thought. They were standing together when she noticed, *truly* noticed, him for the first time. He was surrounded by congratulating participants when he put his arm around her shoulder and whispered to her, "We should d-do this again next year." And then winked at her.

She was instantly, totally lost.

Until then she had little use for men, remembering her father, a brutish cattle raiser and her brothers, never less than crude. The way they rubbed their crotches when they were talking to her about boy-girl things. "*Ya know what they all want, don't ye, Mary-C? They just want to put their things inside ya!*"

Instead, her focus was on things of the mind, things that couldn't hurt. Through her middle school years, spent mostly with nuns and other girls, she won awards and scholarships, finally finding herself at King's College, Cambridge. There, in a single-minded pursuit towards a master's degree (one of few awarded to women before the war), she honed her interests to a love of Mayan civilization, its mathematics, its astronomy.

And now on her return voyage, filled with the excitement of her first trip abroad, she was gripped by the rolling cycle of the ship and the tense, rapid vibration of the ship's engines. Both kinds of waves washed over her, through her feet, through her midsection, resting on one of the rails. There she felt a different, internal kind of wave, as though she were astride a stallion, a feeling *inside* her. She was a scientist. She could compute the length and interaction of these waves, but she only wanted to experience them—and the strong, welcome wetness that accompanied them.

She could see him now, clearly, in her mind. His straight black hair angled over his right eye, his dark deep-set black eyes burning through her. The smell of him. Not the rough masculine smell of smoke and ale, but the faint reminder of soap, perhaps cologne, almost feminine. The feel of him as he placed his arm around her shoulders, the sound of his slightly stammered, whispered voice.

She had discovered a small space on shipboard wedged between two life boats and a heavy piece of equipment for which she could not fathom a purpose.

A private space. The vibrations had all but carried her away when she looked over her shoulder. To her simultaneous horror and delight, she saw him watching her. She had been so *close* to doing something she would only have done—but would never admit to doing—in the privacy of her own room. He was behind her, between two small down-turning spotlights, almost invisible in the darkness. She couldn't know that he was waiting for one of the ship's young crew with whom, in the silent conversations of the homosexual—he had arranged a meeting. No matter, the young man was late, the tryst forgotten or delayed.

Instead, he said, "I apologize, I h-hope I didn't f-frighten you. I was trying to figure out if it were you or not," a gentle lie. And then after short pause, "I am g-glad that it's you," much closer to the truth. It took a moment to recover from her surprise.

For over an hour they asked each other questions, learning more of each other's field, becoming increasingly engaged, the young man forgotten. The stutterer had, to be fair, never really engaged with a woman in this way. His work, and let us say his tendencies, offered him little entrance into a female world.

He was particularly interested in her theories about the Maya and their study of astronomy and mathematics. In turn, she was intrigued by his ability to decode messages, his understanding of the ways in which all thinking could be described in mathematical terms. A thinking machine? Impossible of course, but tantalizing.

She made a decision. Another woman might offer herself. Instead she said, "I have something with me about which I should like your opinion," precision in her language, just as it ruled her scholarship and life. "I have not been told to make it a secret, and given your standing in the academic community, I believe my director would not be averse to your seeing it."

He was intrigued. She continued, seeking a way to hold his interest, a magnet to iron filings. "It's a codex, a sort of book, dating from the first millennium. It has astronomical and mathematical symbols that differ from those I am used to, but I am confident that they are decipherable. Would you like," she asked, her heart pounding, recognizing there was more at stake here than a book, "to look at it?"

Alan Turing would indeed, changing the path of both their lives—one short, one long—that neither could foresee.

18

SOUTHEEAST WASHINGTON. DC.
TUESDAY AFTERNOON

A virtual, invisible line divides leafy Washington from its gritty alter ego.

Some use zip codes or the District's north/south, east/west descriptors to define the boundaries, but the line is more mischievous than that. On one side live tall, stately, intricately designed art deco apartment blocks with classical names and well-bred residents; clean, sleek businesses and office buildings; restaurants and bars. Alfresco cafes full on moderate days, packed with the young and not-so-young. Well healed developers, members of the leafy sect, have moved the line, pulling up tenement weeds and planting new, shiny condominiums and steel towers ten times the size and twenty times the price of the slums they replace. Not heard in the civic applause that follows the re-planting, are the cries of *Where will we live?* from the other side.

If the north and west of the line has been energized by preening wealth, its southern and eastern counterparts are fueled by poverty and its offspring. Here lie the tenements of any city, windows abandoned by water or soap for decades, houses pushed almost to the street, leaving a tiny crack of sidewalk on which to spend too-hot summer days. Cardboard, flags and tinfoil pasted to the windows. Junk crowding the back and side yards—old cars, children's tricycles, derelict refrigerators, old TVs. The pavements cracked and bleeding with weeds, some taller than young boys. And the people, showing the effects of unemployment, of failed relationships and fake marriages, of neighbors playing music too loud, of alcohol and drugs, of the slap across the faces of children.

It is in this gritty portion of the city where DiShannia met her death, bravely, even—if such a thing can be described in this fashion—smartly. The killing field has been marked temporarily by yellow police tape outlining the area like some giant yellow highlighter. It is marked forever by the ghost of a young woman taken long before she or the world was ready for her departure. It is a small triangular patch of green near the Eastern Market, a place called Turtle Park, named for the giant concrete animal that children jump on, whose rounded back they slide down.

This is what the turtle sees, even now, in its mind's eye.

DiShannia, minutes before her death, is forced out of the back door of a black SUV at midnight, falling, scraping her knees. She is tied, thrown onto the pavement as two men in anonymous athletic gear take turns with a baseball bat, hammering the side of her head, smashing her skull. The turtle still sees a kind of malicious delight in the attackers' eyes, apparent as they pass the bat back and forth. The turtle watches the girl as they abandon her, assuming her death. Instead, she rises, staggering across the street, entering an alleyway behind the nearest houses, seeking her mother and her home, if only with a portion of her mind intact. It is an exceptional mind, even injured. Several houses down the alley, the turtle sees her trip over a garbage can, struggle to her feet and her full height, fall again over an abandoned baby stroller. She collapses finally, slumping beside the high rear fence of a house. This taped-off area where she finally lies is roughly the size of a family's dining room. DiShannia has never actually sat in a dining room in her life, and must await some celestial meal if she is to do so.

A small shiver touches the turtle's spine at the finality and the awful, pedestrian nature of the moment, offsetting the brutal heat of the day. If a concrete inanimate object could be moved to tears, the turtle would have shed them. Finally, the turtle cannot not forget this: in her last, confused moments, DiShannia undertakes a final act of defiance and intelligence, ripping a charm bracelet from her wrist, taking the brightest pink segment in her teeth, swallowing it.

Noah and Kate cross the leafy/concrete line that afternoon, walking south and east, beyond the Eastern Market into the tenements. After a bit of searching, they find a corner bar, a faded *Eastenders* sign the only visible indication of welcome, a living tribute to Edwin Hooper. Maneuvering around a garbage can, they enter a side door leading to the apartments. The stairs are open at the first landing to the bar itself.

Something gets to Kate. Not the narrow dark stairs with fifty year-old mats that were once rubber or linoleum. Not the single light bulb hanging over them, dangling what may be the last remaining tungsten bulb on the planet. Not the bar downstairs, with its early Tuesday afternoon clientele. Not the heap of garbage left on the first landing, the detritus of trips to McDonald's and candy-wrappers. Not the one dusty, used condom left the side of one of the stairs, deflated, absent its member, absent love.

None of that. It's the smell of beer and urine, of puke and unwashed bodies, of grease from the kitchen below. And dirt, the odor of poverty.

Each door in the long hallway is marked above by a faded letter. Some have been re-done in black magic marker, a feeble effort to improve the surroundings. At the end of the hallway, waiting for them, is a small island of grief.

Exhausted from an agony of overnight waiting, of talking with the police, of absorbing in increasingly painful waves the death of her daughter, Sharron Johns is a tiny, flattened vessel. She would only allow one set of reporters into her home, after the police had left. "Mr. Scott and the nice lady, I forget her name. Shanny really liked Mr. Scott. I'll see them but no others, please."

DiShannia and her mom occupy—occupied, for Shanny—two rooms at the end of the hallway, marked by a window between them, unwashed for years. How could this girl have moved with such grace between this place one morning and the White House in the afternoon? What gifts of self-presence would that take? Living in two worlds, at once—like Kate, like Noah.

None of the other tenants have noticed, or perhaps have the capacity to notice, Sharron's grief. Several of them are schizophrenic vessels unable to carry sympathy. Kate says nothing at first, using her arms as voice, encircling Sharron's shaking shoulders.

Then she says, like a soft mantra, "DiShannia is, was, such lovely young woman. We are so sorry for your loss, *so* sorry. We truly liked her; she was a wonderful girl. We won't take much of your time but we have some questions for you, and we'd like for you to tell us DiShannia's story. Perhaps another day if this is too hard for you?" Somewhere down the hallway a television is turned up, loud, echoing. Someone shouts, and it's quietened. There are few other sounds, a siren growing louder, then fading away. And then nothing. It is as though the building holds its breath.

Sharron says, "Might as well talk to you now. It keeps her alive a little bit, y'know? Even talking to the police today, showing them pictures. It might seem funny, but it," a long pause while she composes her face, keeping it from crumbling, "helps."

Sharron takes them into one of the rooms; the other door is closed. This is the living room and kitchen, and, when the couch folds out, her bedroom. It's a small rectangular space, filled almost entirely by the narrow brown sleeper sofa, a hot plate, a small fridge, a little table for two. By one chair. They fill the room, although the grief and loss have done that too. Sharron sits on the bed, Noah beside her.

Kate kneels in front of Sharron, taking her hands. They shake, a small palsy of disbelief. Noah thinks, *What can you say?*

"She was such a *good girl*, such a good girl." Sharron repeats. "Never mindin' that insulin pump. Never complain', always lookin' out for me, always ...."

Kate continues to hold Sharron's hands, a small gesture of comfort. The kindness unlocks a cascade of facts. How she has raised DiShannia on her own right from the beginning. How it was hard but she had help—it's unclear if it was DiShannia's father or another man in Sharron's life. He was busy, away, but visited regularly. The stories tumble out fast. Noah and Kate are afraid to stop the cascade.

How DiShannia had blossomed so early that it almost frightened her. When she was two she started to actually point at the words her mother was reading to her. By three she was speaking in full sentences, her reading not far behind. How, one day, a stranger came to her at the daycare center, telling her about the Rose School program, offering entry into a charter school with no tuition.

How she wrestled with a decision that would see DiShannia gone every day. How it broke her heart to see her go off on a little school bus the first day. She was doing simple arithmetic at five, more advanced arithmetic soon after. "I couldn't help her past when she was maybe five," her mom said, laughing but not smiling. How taking her to the Smithsonian became a regular thing. How she was in good spirits almost always, except when she developed her diabetes. Then she was tired and irritable, lost weight, was peeing more. She got good care though, "In that Kaiser System, y'know, and just seemed to take it in her stride. So long as she was learning things, she was fine."

Mostly how good it was to be around her. "She was like electricity, you know that? She come home, everything would brighten up."

And then, suddenly, like somebody had shot her, she was on her feet, taking them across the hall, "I want to show you something…"

In hindsight, the suddenness is intended to shake off the next wave, the terrible peristalsis of grief—the realization that the electricity in her life had been turned off. She says, "You'll be wanting to see her room. The police saw it but I couldn't go with them. I'm ready now."

She leads them across the hall, opens the door, its final *squeak* the only sound in the now-quiet hall. Unlike most mother's and daughter's rooms, DiShannia's is the neater of the two.

They are surrounded by adolescent wallpaper—posters of a fourteen-year-old androgynous kid singer with something like a thousand nose studs, blown up pictures of the universe, photographs of Mayan temples, of the night sky, including pictures of the Pleiades. Kate remembers her father calling it the Seven Sisters. On the opposite wall, a crowded desk and a chair with a sweater slung over the back, and pictures of bunnies—bunnies on the wall, a bunny-themed binder, a small pad of notepaper with bunnies around the edge. The kid-adult.

"It's gone!" Sharron says, suddenly. Where the hardly-ever-worn sweater is slung over the chair and desk, the chair is tipped. There's a blank spot on a crowded desk, a space where her laptop always sat. It's now empty. "Her laptop. It was always there!" "

They stay with her, helping with this new situation, now a robbery. Kate comforts her. Noah contacts the police. While they wait, Noah asks is he can take pictures. When Sharron agrees, he uses his iPhone to take pictures of the room, of the night-sky posters and the empty desk and thinks about the layers: a murder, now a robbery and stolen information. *What's on the laptop?*

They pause, pulled by needing to investigate DiShannia's death on the one hand, and the desire to stay and comfort Sharron on the other. The former wins. "You go," Sharron says. "You been so kind. The police are coming back. You go help find out who killed her, please. I'll be all right. And you can come back and visit me any time, y'know?" She walks them to the top of the stairs, passing the closed and open doors. One man, unshaven and overly thin, sprawls on his daybed in his underwear and a hunter's flannel shirt, despite the heat of the day.

As Noah takes the first of the cracked, linoleum-clad stairs, she says, as much to the empty stairwell as to him, "She never knew, you know."

"Knew what, Sharron?" Noah asks. The grief and upset of the afternoon permits first names.

"That I was her grandma, not her mom," she says to Noah. "I know it happens a lot, but I never got 'round to telling her about my son and his girlfriend and how she came to be. Never thought it was the right time."

"I was her grandmother, not her mom," she repeats. This time definitely to the stairwell, or to her son, not to Noah. Perhaps to the universe.

19

CHARTWELL, ENGLAND, SEPTEMBER 19, 1942

Paulson!" he yelled, though he never considered it yelling—that would be vulgar. Clementine, the lady, would not approve.

"I want to talk to Paulson!" this time his shout was loud enough to penetrate the thick, creaking, sliding double doors of his study. Loud enough to bring his secretary, the bunned, bustling, tightly wrapped Mrs. Hodgetts, a small notebook in her hand.

"Yes, Prime Minister," she said, looking pointedly at the clock, both of whose hands had edged past midnight. She was checking the on-call schedule. "*Shed*-yool," she would have said. "I believe he's in bed, sir. He's already put in two shif…" Then, seeing *that* look on his face, she turned, leaving the room, trailing the distinct impression that she'd call him directly.

It took nearly fifteen minutes—time for Mrs. Hodgetts to call the night secretary in the out-building that housed the Prime Minister's wartime staff, another minute or two for the secretary to put his book down, to check which room Paulson currently inhabited, and go knock on Paulson's door. It took time for Paulson to disentangle himself from the bedsheets and the other person wrapped in them, for him to pull on his trousers and shirt, to comb his ample, reddish-brown hair, and to rush down the back stairs heading to the PM's room.

In that time, the Prime Minister had time to ponder what lay before him.

Ponder was too mild a word. Worry, perhaps. There was the latest report about post bombing damage to the city: several dozens killed, a darkened pub flattened, filled with older men mostly, the younger men on duty elsewhere. A row house in the east end, equally flattened, though many were in shelters, avoiding a final fiery death. Russian U-boats spotted off the coast of Scotland and—more worrisome—near the mouth of the Thames. The fractious alliance of Germany, France, and England against their shared enemy, the Bolshevik emperor. A small shiver ran through him. The account of the Duke of Windsor's latest attempt to walk the tightrope of treason, this time with a female Russian spy. Who would have thought that a member of the royal family would occupy himself so?

The early planning for an invasion of Eastern Europe and the Russian empire. Head counts, loss-counts.

His face darkened at the last report piled on his desk, cigar smoke passing over it like a small cloud. It was the one he needed to speak to Paulson about. Small ashes drifted from the end of his cigar, enough to make a mess. Mrs. Hodgetts would scold him.

As he picked the report up, knocking the ashes to the floor, he moved to his reading chair, leaving the desk and its piled worries behind. There was nothing he could do about any of them this evening. This report however, had implications of action, and he was—despite the image of him as an overweight, ponderous figure—in personality and performance, a man of action. The report was labeled simply *TURING*, a single dry word at the top of the page. Below it, a slanted *For Eyes Only* stamp.

He was waiting for an explanation and the beginning of a plan, alert to the creak in the sliding doors that would announce Paulson.

If the PM was anticipating Paulson's arrival, the very junior agent now attempting to get his enormous, unruly crop of reddish hair back in some semblance of its normal state, could best be described as anxious.

Meetings with the PM would never be described as "laid back" affairs, as his American colleagues would say. Indeed, his balls and cock, so recently in a state of pleasurable engorgement, had shrunk roughly to the size of a half-penny bag of peanuts, causing him some discomfort. He hoped that the blood was rushing northward from this highly valuable geographic zone to his brain, an organ which needed every ounce of help it could get. He knew what the late-night call was about, was rehearsing what he recalled about the report. Mrs. Hodgetts slid the doors open on their squealing, unoiled tracks, announcing him. And he found himself, staring for only the third or fourth time at the Old Man himself.

"Sit," the PM said, not unpleasantly, from deep within the wing-backed chair. It was upholstered in a terrible tartan-red plaid, covered mercifully by a knitted throw rug and the large bulk of the man himself. Several holes were visible in the throw rug, tiny remnants of cigar ash arson.

"Scotch?" the PM asked, pointing to his own crystal glass. "A small compensation for disturbing your beauty sleep."

"Thank you, Prime Minister. I think I shan't, sir," thinking that he needn't muddle his brain any further. Margaret's hands and mouth had done enough muddling.

"It's about Turing, of course," the PM said, confirming Paulson's suspicions, waving the report in front of him, finding yet another ash to brush away, taking a sip of a fifteen year-old single malt, sniffing its tiny fog of peat. The pleasure only lasted a second. "Tell me what you know."

Paulson began. "I know that you understand the importance of Alan Turing to the war effort, Prime Minister." Others had told him it was wise to phrase background material as though the PM had full knowledge of it. "He is the leading code breaker, as you know. His team developed the *Enigma Machine*, cracking Russian spy codes. He is a true genius, I am told."

Inwardly, the PM was satisfied. Outwardly, he expressed irritation however, another trick of working with staff. "I know all this, young man. What is this *new* information?" waving the report at him like a square fan, spreading yet more ashes.

"It appears that Turing has also been moving beyond his usual activities, sir. He has been seen in the company of several individuals whose security levels are unclear. He has expressed a strong interest in astronomical, er, phenomena. He is quite agitated about this, speaks about it regularly and publicly. And it appears that on hearing what he has to say, individuals appear to become disbelieving, then anxious, even despondent."

"Despondent? That's a strong word, Paulson."

"Indeed sir, but there is a report—I doubt it has reached your desk—that one of his closest friends walked into the Irish Sea and drowned late last week.

Some say alcohol was involved but the report indicates the man was a teetotaller. Of course, his suicide could be anything."

"I suppose so," the PM said; he couldn't care less for the occasional suicide. Instead, he said, "I expect that I might have a death wish too, if I believed his nonsense."

"Oh yes, sir. We of course have checked out Turing's theories, sir, and have consulted with experts in the field, none of whom believe his calculations. They think him quite, um, possibly deranged. What is worrisome is that he appears capable of causing instability in others."

The old man took another sip of his scotch, slowly and thoughtfully. The chair seemed to swallow him further. Unmoving physically, the PM progressed quickly to the heart of the matter. "And yet he is, as you say, a genius and widely respected. His views *would* be considered legitimate, could cause widespread concern. Especially damaging when wartime morale is already only marginal, wouldn't you say? We do not need this, do we, Paulson? What does MI5 propose to do?"

"There are two schools of thought, sir. One approach is that we discredit him entirely, undertake some action which would condemn him in the eyes of the public. Some of my colleagues advocate however for a wait and see approach, not undertaking any activity detrimental to such a national hero, but rather watch his actions carefully, particularly his public utterances."

The old man paused, a puff of smoke the only indication of the calculations taking place beneath his balding head. Turing may have been able to work mathematical equations brilliantly but no one mastered implications better than the Prime Minister.

"I agree with both courses of action, Paulson. Take this down," he said, all business now, throwing off the mask of the ponderous man of thought, pitching a pad of paper (no ashes this time) and a pen at the young man with the too-abundant hair. The PM came forward in the chair, his bulk alone reassuring.

"Let us create a small task force to watch this individual and his team, Paulson, to plan for the possibility of discrediting him, perhaps thinking of other more drastic ways to curb his—how shall we phrase this?—overly dramatic interpretations of his findings. I will of course not need to know *how* you would terminate more widespread communications from him." A shift in his thinking occurred; the PM sat back in the deep chair. "What shall we call this task force, Paulson?" He liked this young, tousled MI5 representative. He might have to do something with all that hair, though.

Paulson thought for a long minute, thinking mostly about the effect that Turing's theories had on his listeners. At last, he said, "What about *Hemlock*, Prime Minister?"

The hint of a smile then. "Ah, perfect, Paulson. I like your thinking, focusing on a possible outcome, not the process." he said, taking yet another sip of his scotch, itself a form of hemlock. Far slower-acting definitely, infinitely more pleasurable, but hemlock just the same.

"Perfect," he repeated. "A good name, Paulson. You of course will be the liaison from my office to MI5 and its creation of the task force. You will keep me informed of the broad strokes or your work. I will have only verbal reports, and I shall have them regularly. Let's say on a monthly basis, more frequently if there are developments. Are you up for that, young man?" the smile widened on his face, brightening it for the first time, a rare event, a brief showing of the sun on a cloudy day.

"Of course, sir!" he said, nodding, his hair moving in an agreeable tiny rhythm of waves.

Neither man—the younger, naïve man with the good hair and retreating genitals or the older peat-soaked seeker of knowledge and action—could foresee the remarkable trajectory of *Hemlock*.

20

WASHINGTON. DC. MID-AFTERNOON TUESDAY

Morgues and emergency departments—small settings of chaos strung along the high singing wire between life and death. They are both on Noah's hit list this afternoon.

Kate has gone back to the office, trying to track her elusive cousin down, regretting that she suggested his name. He is a gifted researcher, a good resource for them, but his presence in her life has represented something less than pleasant. A decade older than she, the son of her mother's sister, he was the successful *Chinese* grandson, the one who gained praise from his grandparents, the one who was still *in* the family. Unlike her. She leaves the business of a morgue visit to Noah.

He's in familiar territory, although he stops in the Howard University Hospital Emergency Department to ask a nurse he knows about DiShannia's record from the night before. She divulges an interesting fact, "The chart says the fingers of her one hand were inside her mouth." Her time with him is limited however: it's another extraordinary, under-resourced day in the crowded, noisy department, where the major complaint, she says, is, "Heat prostration. It's awful. They're too poor to afford AC, come in here, almost dead, dehydrated like dried fruit."

In a minute, Noah arrives at the morgue, a reporter's pass getting him through the swinging steel doors, the smell of formaldehyde and industrial disinfectant greeting him before the pathologist does. Dressed in greens, a long once-white apron spattered with tissue and blood, Daniel Carlson is just finishing up the autopsy. The soft *snip, snip* of his scissors, weaving their way through bowel tissue, seems noisy in the quiet room. In the corner, on the steel table, under a too-white sheet, lies DiShannia. Noah does not allow himself to think about the body that she so recently occupied, her head so damaged. He experiences a melancholy so deep it's almost as though *he* has lost a child.

The pathologist turns to Noah, his hands still in the sink, his head craning awkwardly on his long body. "Be with you in a minute!" he says. The voice, surprisingly deep, comes from a tiny-ish head atop a frame that left six and a half feet behind years ago. In a heartbeat he's finished his bowel-cutting, snapped off his gloves, undone the back of his rubber apron.

A warm, formaldehyde- and soap-roughened palm greets Noah's. Noah thinks that he recognizes the pathologist, or his basketball-player height, placing him somewhere in the small village that is medicine in the District. The more links that Noah can develop with him the more the chance of full disclosure.

"You were at Georgetown, right?" Carlson asks. "Are you," a silent 'um' divides the question, "practicing?"

"Not like you'd think," Noah says, "I'm the medical lead for WashPO."

"Oh," flat at first, then brighter, pleased, "good for you."

It comes back to Noah what they called the tall, studious, quiet guy. *Ichabod Crane.*

They pursue a few shared memories—classmates and faculty members in common, past newspaper stories born in Carlson's morgue. Finally, Noah says, "I'm covering DiShannia Johns. Our office called earlier. You have anything on her?"

He nods. "I sure do. I'm just finishing up her autopsy now. Your timing's perfect. Just give me a sec' to finish examining the bowel and stomach." He moves back to the sink, this time with Noah in tow, snaps on his gloves again. The tan anaconda of intestine slides along his hands as he moves from the stomach to the small bowel, to the large colon, holding it with huge forceps. They both examine the flat, pinkish brown mucosa, now washed and clean in the sink. "No," he says, "There's nothing there either, no surprise." He turns quickly, anxious to get his report to the police. As he turns to go to his desk, he doesn't see Noah reach into the sink, pocketing something.

Carlson says over his shoulder, "I'll just leave that there while I talk to you. That was the last though. Let's do the easy stuff first and get it out of the way. The heart, bowel," nodding to the sink. He likes to nod. "The lungs, spleen, they're all okay, you know, not surprising for a teenager. No evidence of rape."

Forgetting Noah's medical background for the minute, he launches into a plain-English version of his findings, "There's just a couple things to comment on. There's a moderate contusion—a bruise—on the liver, where I think she fell. What's interesting is her brain. She must have suffered terrible damage to it, but wasn't totally paralyzed. She got herself down a back alley to where she was found. She does have a fractured skull, indented: I'm betting it was a baseball bat, maybe a steel pipe.

"And there's something else, something really interesting."

Noah joins him at his computer. "Take a look at this," emphasizing *this* as he folds himself into the frighteningly tiny $59.95 IKEA desk chair. He shows Noah a few pictures of a skinny, pale pink organ, the color of an oyster shell, like a tiny peeled potato. A few microscopic photographs of what he recognizes as pancreatic tissue.

Carlson explains, "The gross photos – you probably think they're all kind of gross, right?"—a little pathology humor—"….are of the pancreas. Looks normal but it weighed half what it should. Totally fucked, I mean, damaged, even more than you'd think in a diabetic patient. And so I took a couple of microtome slices, got them processed by electronic microscope. Take a look." Pictures appear on Ichabod's monitor.

"Islets of Lagerhans, right?" Noah asks.

Carlson nods. "Exactly right—the insulin-producing cells of the body. In the real diabetic patient, they'd be shrunken, useless. But they're not. They're perfectly normal. But her pancreas hasn't grown. I've never seen that before."

"No doubt," he says, nodding again. "She might have been killed by a baseball bat, but she was already being slowly damaged by something else, something shrinking her pancreas. No way she was diabetic though."

For a something the size of a dime, the small pink object that caught Noah's eye (and that Ichabod's missed) weighs heavily in Noah's pocket. Noah recognized it as a piece of DiShannia's charm bracelet and he's done something entirely outside the rulebook—he's stolen it from a hospital morgue, technically part of the crime scene. It was an instantaneous decision, prompted by a nurse's remark an hour before and these questions: *Why would she do that?* It's more than a simple charm. It's a tiny version of a thumb drive, a tiny disk that pops into laptops and other handhelds, capable of holding *tons* of data, at least until the next generation of device storable data units arrives. Noah thinks, *She must have swallowed it at the end, when she was—what?—going in and out of consciousness? In terrible pain?*

The tiny object had called out to him, as clearly as though she had written a note in the ground where she lay dying.

The morgue and Dr. Carlson long behind him, stimulated by the verdict of a small-but-normal pancreas and the diagnosis of her diabetes, Noah reaches out to one of his old university professors, Jay Levine, a world-famous diabetes specialist. His office assistant slots him in for mid-afternoon, a scheduled, if laughable, coffee break time. Laughable because it rarely happens.

Levine's waiting room is a model of Costco-couch neatness and pale hues, a huge contrast to the professor's office where Noah is ushered. There, chaos reigns. On every horizontal surface lie journal articles, whole journal issues, open text books, CME (that's continuing medical education) brochures, medical newspapers, drug company monographs. Even the professor's $750 soft-roll, ergonomically perfect chair sports a ten pound stack of journal articles topped by a text book and the remains of a tuna sandwich. The walls are only slightly less crowded, a place where framed degrees, awards, certificates and pictures live. The walls tell a story just by themselves. There are pictures of him with dignitaries, even the last president.

If by some miracle visitors miss the resume and the walls, there is a little brochure laying on a coffee table highlighting his most recent accomplishments, providing the details of his latest award in Stockholm. Not the Nobel, but close enough.

And then, as though someone has opened a door and a hurricane has blown in, Dr. Levine arrives, filling the room. Morris Jay Levine, professor and Nikon-Mitsubishi chair of the department of medicine; professor of epidemiology and biostatistics, professor of public health, Georgetown University; Fellow of the

American College of Physicians and a handful of other colleges world-wide; Director of the Pzifer-Poseidon Center for Research in Diabetic Metabolism. One of the nation's largest figures in research.

And one of the smallest.

If he manages to edge a little over five feet on a warm day, it's a miracle. He is the consummate academic entrepreneur, his research achievements piled as high as a research tower. Noah is a foot taller, but thinks his life is much smaller than this man's.

His entry has created a wake, and in it follow two residents, a fellow and a visiting Japanese professor. Without missing a beat he introduces Dr. Sachs and Dr. Mohammet (the residents; Noah hopes they get along), Dr. Bernstein (the fellow, a larger but junior version of Professor Levine), and Dr. Kinoshita, from the University of Osaka.

"This is Mr. Scott—I'm sorry, Doctor Scott—from the *Washington Post*. You were a graduate from here, right, Dr. Scott?" Noah nods, surprised; Levine has done his homework. "Dr. Scott is here to interview me about a patient. Would you mind if we attend to patient care business first, though, doctor? I'm sure you won't mind."

It doesn't matter if Noah minds or not, Levine is off—a virtual, pint-sized gusher, the essential medical Napoleon. Directions about the inpatient volume on Ward 9A, specific orders for several patients, a quick rifle through his papers to find articles for Dr. Sachs and the Japanese professor, directions about what patients to present at Diabetes Rounds. Finally, a kindly but firm out-the-door-you-go hustle for the Japanese visitor, even speaking a little Japanese. All in under five minutes.

He sits on the edge of his desk while Noah stands; there is nowhere to sit. He checks his cell phone and says, "This is a busy day. Can we do this in ten minutes?"

Noah presents DiShannia's case to him. He stresses that she was diagnosed several years previously, had been in good control until recently when she had spells of fatigue and lethargy, episodes of hypoglycemia or low blood sugar. How the pathologist found no evidence of diabetes at all, though the pancreas was tiny. Carlson promised to email the results of lab tests to Dr. Levine.

"Let's see if they're in," Levine says, hummingbirding his way across the desk, shuffling several papers off his keyboard. In a few clicks, his brow furrows. Looking at the lab results, he mutters to himself, something like, "Nothing here, nothing...." Then finally, "Look at this. There are traces of alpha-1-misoprostyl here. It's one of the Mitsubishi-Nikkon early phase two trials that we're conducting. Its intention is to regrow the islet of Langerhans cells by..." Noah loses him here; Levine has just leapt beyond Noah's medical knowledge base.

He does know enough to question. "If it was re-growing islet cells then why was she hypoglycemic, wouldn't she be in better control, not worse?"

"It's the isomer—the mirror image—of the drug, Dr. Scott. Almost but not quite identical to the original. It tricks the pancreas into thinking it has lots of insulin on board, so much so that the pancreas doesn't even grow. The drug has the reverse effect. No wonder she died! She was pretty much poisoned. Her Islet cells would look perfectly normal in the pathology lab, but her insulin production would be totally blocked. Normal cells but no hormone. You said she was found murdered, right? Why do that if she's already been compromised?"

So many questions. *Who killed DiShannia? Why kill her if she was already being poisoned? What role does the Rose School play?*

21

WASHPO. WASHINGTON. DC. LATE TUESDAY AFTERNOON

Noah is late from the morgue and the visit with Dr. Levine. He arrives just as the day-crowd is leaving—some of his fellow reporters, other staff, even the green-shirted Hernando.

"You working too late, Noah!" he says, holding the door for him, his smile as wide as the doorway. Nothing is too late when Noah has a story, but he returns Hernando's grin. He rushes to the IT floor, finds Harry, hands him the nail drive he's freed from its travels in DiShannia's stomach. He doesn't tell Harry how he got it, just who it came from.

He hurries back to the team room, afraid he might be late for the six p.m. deadline for first-in-the-morning news submission. He's developed the story in his head on the impossibly crowded hot taxi-commute from Howard University to Bezos 1. He flips open his red laptop, and his fingers—the tongues of the twenty-first century—begin to fly over the story. His hair falls in front of his eyes, a small black curtain.

He tells the story of DiShannia, her murder, the connection to the White House, her life's work, adding a quote from Dr. Carlson, "Two things killed her: the blow to her head was the immediate cause, but something was wrong with that pancreas, not diabetes, something induced." Submitting it through the WashPO internal website is a relatively simple matter, getting it into the queue for Syd to review it. He texts her, telling her it's on its way, reminding her that Erich has approved it. He sits back, looking at the digital wall clock click to six, time for the all-powerful News Cycle to begin. And sighs.

The team has agreed to meet at six-thirty at a bar across the street. His brain is on *overwhelm* today, as much as Howard University's Emergency Department; he needs to collect his thoughts, currently scattered like the pieces of a jigsaw. The lingering after-effects of DiShannia's death have stirred more in him than he's prepared to handle in a noisy bar and pub.

Many evenings he uses the roof of the building as an end-of-day refuge, overlooking the traffic on Massachusetts and New York Avenues and a tiny triangle of green that may be the world's smallest national park. Too hot to use during the day, by late afternoon it's cooler, the breeze or wind allowing committee members, staff reporters and other workers to cool off. Today's group, just winding up, is the senior editorial board of the enterprise. It's a big deal; it's occupied Erich, Syd, and their bosses all day.

Noah meets them as they're coming off the elevator, still wearing their name tags. Some he knows: the District's current congressional representative, a leading black activist, an oil magnate and a military-looking guy that Noah recognizes but can't place, his name tag lost or misplaced. Others are interchangeable with patrons of any country club across the nation. He nods at them, then heads for the roof patio, now all but empty except for the green-shirts. They're almost-invisible helpers, clearing the wine glasses and little hors d'oeurves plates, rearranging the chairs. Hispanic for the most part. Finally, he's alone, moving into his favorite position where the building and roof come to a point. Sometimes he imagines he's Brad Pitt, standing at the prow of the Titanic.

He is not however invisible to the green shirts. One of them is engaged in text messaging.

It is quiet, quiet for DC at least—only a few sirens, a little less honking. Noah uses his elbows to lean on the low Plexiglas wall that separates him from a twelve story free-fall into eternity. Putting the pieces together, looking for the connections, he's mired in something he can't understand—he is grieving for DiShannia.

Suddenly, occupied by the noisy fact-checking voices in his head, he catches a glimpse of green reflected in the shiny Plexiglas railing to his right, a little flash of lime. It moves towards him, too quickly for activity on a patio. He takes no more than half a step back, turning to see what it is.

The tiny half-step saves his life.

He is hit by someone, powered like a running back, intent on throwing him over the side. He crashes into the Plexiglas, his shoulder landing with a massive, painful *thump* against the railing. It threatens to crack the barrier, shakes it as though it were cheap plastic. He manages a quick look over the edge before he hits the patio floor, staring straight into the abyss of the tiny green triangle, staring stupidly at his death. He is stunned for a second, possibly briefly unconscious, but yells loudly, pushing himself up off the railing. He turns to see a brief blaze of lime head down the stairs. He begins to chase his assailant—two steps, three, four—angry, scared, wide-eyed.

And throws up on his shoes.

It is minutes too late to chase the guy. There is a little bathroom just inside the kitchen. Alone, he locks the door, cleans his shoes and listens to his internal voices: *What the hell was that? Was this guy alone? Should I call the police?* Muddled, without answers, he can think of only one thing—to get with his team. Throwing the now-soiled paper towels in the waste basket he notices a sole, discarded name tag. It reads, *Maj General Gerald Wilcox (retired)*. One of the board members, the one he couldn't name from a few minutes ago.

Every sense on high alert, he takes the elevator, makes his way across the street—it's crowded, *crowded* is good—to Poets and Busboys, where his team is waiting for him. A message pops up on his iPhone, a message without a sender, a scary thing just by itself.

"Leave DiShannia and her story alone," it says.

And then, even more frighteningly, it disappears like smoke, gone in five seconds. He's not even sure he saw it. Watching him from across the street, in a darkened alley beside the Bezos building, Hernando pockets his cell phone.

22

BAKER STREET. LONDON. ENGLAND. 1953

It was a grueling business, visiting Dr. Cunnington-Smith, feeling the numbness in his feet, thinking they were molasses-glued to the sidewalk as he left the office. He was sure this doctor was not the average, ethical Baker Street physician—the strange, back room lacking even the comfort of a chair, the deep, painful injection in the hip, the lack of eye contact.

He had just received the fifth or sixth of his monthly injections.

In their immediate wake, his mind functioned even more slowly than his feet, his gut registering a kind of emptiness, a coldness. His own red scarf, a color he loved, seemed faded, somewhere between a maroon and a dull, lifeless gray. That's how he felt right after these injections—lifeless. And he told Dr. Cunnington-Whatever that they continued to make him feel that way between treatments.

The truth was different; their effect wore off quickly. He had learned to counter them with a recipe of vitamins, cocoa leaves and cannabis, the miracle leaf. He smiled; he was clever, cleverer than this physician.

Several other things propelled him: his mind had always been able to muscle its way beyond an immediate situation to see a larger picture; he could communicate his findings or rather suspicions, about Mary Catherine's codex and its implications to a wide audience; and he loved. Oh, how he loved. If his loving was somewhat less than it had been—not quite the aggressive tumescence of younger men—he at least could love with his heart, and other parts of his body.

He willed himself to walk faster, to stand upright. Two people in particular occupied his mind.

Mary Catherine was the first.

He remembered meeting her on *The Queen Mary* years before, Irish and intelligence in her eyes. Not that it was anything like the shipboard romances of movies and women's books.

She had showed the codex to him first in her stateroom. It was not what she wanted to show him of course—her heart, for example—but it was enough. There were few people in her life: only her father, now rotting in a nursing home which she rarely visited and whose malodorous hallways she dreaded; a mother's grave; brothers she never saw. In contrast, the mysteries in the codex were numerous.

The stateroom seemed to sway that first evening. The seas were heavy, but her emotions caused the feeling, not the swell of the ocean. Two single beds occupied either side of the door, both covered with a seascape of some sort. "I have the room to myself as it turns out," she said, hope heavy in the statement. She reached to turn on the light over the bed, leaning slightly, thinking that she might fall, wishing he would catch her.

His mind however was on the object laying on the unused bed, a box roughly the size of an elongated, narrow telephone book. He watched as she undid the leather binding, flipping open the lid's clasp. It revealed multiple bark pages, covered in a white limestone paste and a mystery of writing and symbols. Figures. Paintings. Images of the night sky with tiny dots indicating—*what?*— Stars? Planets? Measurements. Colored pictures—mostly red, red-brown, orange-red, still vibrant. Black lines and tiny squares against a white background. It offered a great, complex mystery, beckoning him, just as she herself was.

If he had been mildly interested before, the codex and its symbols, drawings and figures left him intrigued.

"This is only the fourth complete Mayan codex known to us," she said, pulling on a pair of white gloves, taking it carefully from the box, placing it on the bed covers between them, supporting the leaves like one might hold a newborn. "There were many books like this in existence when Spain invaded the Yucatan in the sixteenth century, but most were destroyed by the Catholic Church and the conquistadors. Such a tragedy, really," she spoke with some heat. With each subsequent page, turned over lovingly by her cotton-gloved hands, he grew more fascinated by the figures, the stylized glyphs, the writing. Each spoke to him in a language he did not know, in symbols he did not understand. Yet.

"I sh-should like to spend more time with it if I c-could," he said, his stutter demonstrating the depth of his excitement. *And with you, too,* they both thought, but neither said.

The war years fought against their working together, but they were able to exchange letters, written extensions of that first ship-board conversation. There were sketches of the text's pages, of the drawings, attempts at interpretation. There were occasional phone calls, although their conversations were less than private at Bletchley, irritating him.

Trips to London took him to see Mary Catherine in the British Museum, visits precious to her. Rare during the latter years of the war, they became more regular after when he moved to the University of Manchester. There, as chair of the Department of Pure Mathematics, he had only a cramped, shared office to work from—a converted closet, he thought. He had come too far to be closeted.

She had an idea. They called it "his office," a large, unused storage room at the end of a basement hallway in the museum, crammed with artifacts. Pieces of small Egyptian sculpture. Statues from Thailand. The top of a British Columbian totem pole. Small pottery shards arranged like a pulled-apart jigsaw puzzle. A multi-armed Indian goddess that they named Sadie. Roman and Greek artifacts. A trio of bronze Buddhas, one of them badly damaged. A discarded couch from a former director's office. She cleared a large table for him to work on, carefully labeling the pottery shards. The desk was perfect, she thought, a large space for a large mind.

And it was there that he had helped her work over several months, spending as much as a day a week inside the museum, studying Mayan astronomical predictions and the puzzle of the codex. Working for weeks on several pages,

Alan and Mary Catherine had broken through the maze of icons, deciphering them one by one, then finally, like a dam breaking, paragraphs and pages. They had uncovered the events leading to the last days of the Mayan civilization.

The codex chronicled the slow inward motion of the planets, the long slide towards collapse. It told the story of a complex peace process, of warnings issued to kings by astronomer-priests. It revealed a final leaf, sloppily done as though sketched in haste, picturing several kings lying prone, dead, bloody. The blood appeared to be everywhere—the red-brown on the walls, the floor, on an overturned table laying near one of the kings.

What the codex had not revealed to them—because it could not—was the period after the collapse, the wars, the tearing apart of the fabric of Mayan civilization, the despair.

Late one day, when most of the staff had gone home, she found him in his "office," bent over their codex. It was spread out, filling almost the whole table. His thin shoulders seemed even more compressed as he bent over the object, as though he could squeeze knowledge from the document. His jacket was off, hung carefully on the back of the chair. His tie was undone, the collar of his white shirt open. "Look. H-here," he said, sensing her presence.

"Mary Catherine, I think I have the w-words—Venus, seven, gods, collision." He pointed to symbols on the pages before him, lines, dots, graphics, icons. "What do you think? Does it say that the M-Mayan people actually had visions of the planets crashing in on earth? Or did they c-calculate them?"

"Calculated, I think. They were adept mathematicians after all. Look here, and here," she pointed to several of the earlier pages, astronomical projections.

"What you told me yesterday helped enormously. I c-compared their other forms of writing, the alphanumeric, the numbers and letters, here and here," he said, pointing, as animated as she was. He had found yet *another* form of writing: tiny dots and squares requiring a magnifying glass. She could almost hear him think. She leaned over his shoulder, wanting desperately to touch him, bending to him. Her breast brushed his shoulder.

He barely noticed, his mind light-years away, racing, comparing the position of Venus over decades, using Mayan calculations. His efforts occupied sheets of foolscap, spread out, a virtual codex in itself. He brushed the hair back from his eyes, that thin black curtain. His suspicions, widely disseminated to his friends, were now confirmed. He would have to broadcast them even more widely, possibly an open letter to one of the nation's tabloids.

It was then that he noticed her, her body curved to him, her breast almost caressing his shoulder. He turned to her to explain more of his findings but stopped, thinking, *There's something different about her,* perhaps a new perfume, a soap possibly. Perhaps the blouse, open enough to see the swell of her breasts as she breathed deeply, like the ocean that brought them together. He saw, perhaps for the first time, the white brassiere strap wedged in the narrow plane between the blouse and her skin.

She undid the top button of her blouse, and then—deliberately, slowly—a second button and a third. A current existed between them, one which he was simply—intentionally, genetically, it was of no importance—unaware of. Until that moment.

"Alan," she said, her voice different, lower, "I am not your mother."

And she did what she had done a thousand times in her dreams, had longed to do from their first encounter. She brought her lips closer to his and kissed him deeply, her tongue exploring the hidden, foreign terrain. An intruder, it met with some resistance at first, but soon encountered his own tongue making forays into her mouth, exploring, tasting, sucking. Her fingers found his tie, loosening it further, opening his shirt, and then with enormous boldness and shaking hands, unbuttoning his fly. They moved quickly, hurriedly, locking the door, discarding the remainder of their clothing, using the couch for something other than the numbering of pottery shards.

If it was less than perfect—less him entering her and more her enveloping him, riding him like the dark stallion of her dreams—it was enough.

In a few minutes (and a lifetime for her) they were spent, lying beside each other, experiencing a dozen emotions, some conflicting. Delight, relief, regret, embarrassment. In the end, pleasure.

At length, Alan managed to break the silence. "You know, Mary Cath, this was wonderful, but I can't be the m-man you want me to be. I c-can't...."

She placed her finger on his lips, not wanting him to spoil the moment with his speech, his constant staccato speech. "What you gave me tonight is enough to last a lifetime, Alan. I'll never need anything else from you. I shall always *want* more from you, of course, in any form you can conjure, but needing you? That is something for teenagers." She offered a small laugh, "We're definitely not teenagers."

Later still, in their own beds, they would both remember the phrase, "last a lifetime." It was a phrase that held both promise and threat. Neither knew that it would last longer than a single lifetime.

That had been several weeks ago. Each subsequent week, though he spent time with her, neither attempted to re-create the event. Neither mentioned it. They both thought of it however, she more than he. She had more reason to think of it. On this particular day, when he left with only a brief, "Good-bye. See you next week!" she thought, *There's time, I'll tell him when I see him next week.*

An event not, unfortunately, ever realized.

A second person occupied Turing's mind as he left the doctor's office, looking for a green grocer. Even more than Mary Catherine, it was this person, a man, who had stimulated his rushed departure from the museum.

There is more than one kind of love, some more dangerous than others.

23

POETS AND BUSBOYS, WASHINGTON, DC, TUESDAY EVENING

Noah can never remember if it's called Busboys and Poets or Poets and Busboys.

Whatever its name, it's a two story box holding a huge central winding staircase. The stairs link the diners and noise on the bottom and the quieter kitchen, bar and bathrooms on the top. The dark fieldstone floor absorbs conversation like Washington people absorb each other, that is to say, not very much. The walls are painted with faux-impressionist street scenes. The space contains more Salvation Army refurbished chairs and tables than any crowded second-hand furniture shop on the planet. Like a remembrance of Easter, someone has injected dozens of aqua, green, pink and yellow neon loveseats and tulip chairs into the mix. The furniture and the funky painted do-over would have looked out of place two decades ago, but for some reason is back in vogue, they say.

There are no poets and only a few busboys here—an irony lost on most of the after-work drinkers. Loveseats pulled together to make little huddles of conversation, sometimes two people, sometimes, in Noah's case, more.

Still breathless, Noah tells his team about the attack, calmed a bit by their presence and by an unconscious rubbing of his talisman. He wonders if he should have called the police right away, debating out loud what it means, questioning. Gerry reaches across the table, pats Noah's knee.

"Noah, hey, we're just glad you're here, buddy. You're safe with us. I called a detective friend of mine to join us tonight. He'll be here soon. You can tell him. He'll give it more attention than just a random call."

And with that, exhausting the story, embracing their company, Noah's heart rate descends to normal. Kate, not showing the fear that his story builds in her, joins in the Noah-patting, her touch—on his back, feeling the hard, tense muscle of his shoulder—lasts a second longer than the others. He doesn't see Gerry texting someone, urgently.

The team is a half hour ahead in their drinking—tea for Naomi and Harry, a scotch for Gerry, a beer for Kate, small lubricants to make the conversation flow. Naomi is more animated than usual, even though filtered through her diffident, cool exterior.

Surprising no one, Gerry starts. "I gotta admit," he says, "this is interesting as hell, this story of yours, the Mayan connection, the young girl, the big national award." Somewhere upstairs, a waiter drops several plates, the racket making its way down the stairs, bouncing off the impressionist walls and flagstone floor. Someone applauds.

"First off, the cops found her laptop this afternoon. I'm trying to get one of my police buddies to email Harry with what's on it." Noah knows the police won't release any details, not for days or weeks. They have an ace up their sleeves though—the little nail drive that Harry has. Harry nods, anxious to talk, waiting for Gerry and the others.

"I talked with the investigating cops, two guys in homicide I know." Gerry continues. "Arjay Singh was on that evening, the guy joining us tonight." He checks his watch.

"It's clearly not a *simple* crime though. Here's what I got. Let me trace it from when she left the school. We know she went to the White House right after lunch. She spent like two hours there, getting photos taken, meeting other award winners and the president herself. They drive her back to the school. She goes to class till three-thirty, then has basketball practice. They pack up their stuff and walk out the side door around six—the one by Twenty-Fourth and N there?—to pile into the school van to take them home. But DiShannia doesn't get on the mini-bus. Instead, she sees the same SUV that took her to the White House and gets in it, waves good bye to them and gives 'em a big smile, like, '*See? Check out the cute driver!*' But the White House says there was no pick-up later in the day; high school award winners don't warrant further attention.

"That's the last they see her. Then there's a four-hour gap. The next thing we know, Sharron, Mrs. Johns, she's calling the police around ten maybe saying her kid's missing, didn't come home from school. Well, nobody's gonna pay attention to a call about a kid who's like three hours late!

"Then around ten, they get an urgent call from some neighbor. He's found her body in the alleyway behind his house, head smashed in. You know that part of the story."

Naomi interrupts, verbally this time, "What about the SUV?"

"Okay, there's a ball-buster for you," Gerry says, nodding to Naomi, a small raise of his shoulders, a sort of apology. "Arjay went right to the top, contacted the head of Secret Service, goes to the White House and interviews him. They went through the records carefully—there's a *lot* of traffic going in and out of the White House, every day. Who knew? All their SUVs are accounted for."

"That's all I got. Arjay'll be here in a minute. We should wait for him."

Naomi is happy to be next; she has something to tell them. She is after all the most workaholic reporter in the group, maybe anywhere. And she's been busy.

She also knows her charter school history. "They grew out of a need in Canada, the US, Australia; we all had them. Public schools were underfunded and pretty much hell-holes, physically and more importantly, educationally. There was chaos—poor teachers, terrible social environment, virtually no learning. And the high end, very expensive private schools were definitely not for everyone." Naomi was no member of the high end, expensive set.

"So they needed a different business model, a third way. Charter schools secured grants from agencies like the Gates Foundation, or private smaller donations. They call it "Third Way" funding, definitely not government, not entirely private sector, more a combination of the two aimed at helping the public good."

There are two questions at once, a strange stereo. Harry asks, "What about the Rose Charter Schools?" From Noah, "Do they ever get federal funding?"

Naomi takes Noah's question first. "None of the charter schools are *supposed* to use federal support and the Rose Schools are the most successful example of the Third Way model. There's more though." She shoves several loose strands of hair back into her bun, escapees from last month's dye-job. "I talked with a senior director at their head office in Bethesda. They have scouting programs that reach far into the inner city, into upper middle class schools, everywhere. What do they scout for? Talent, she said, talent of any sort, especially in mathematics and sciences. But there's no doubt that this school has some kind of government involvement, given what you've said about the interview yesterday. We'll have more tomorrow for sure."

It's Harry's turn. He's been drinking in the conversation as much as sipping his tea, his pudgy hands wrapped around a mug the size of a small vase. Tipping his iPad up so that they can all see what he's found in the half hour or so he's had DiShannia's nail drive, he begins to scroll through her pictures. Her classmates, a boy she apparently liked (there were lots of shots, one a selfie), dozens of the current male teenage singers, a piece on someone named Turing, a four-decade old article on Jonestown, her mom. Many images of Mayan temples, some of them in bright colors—aqua, red, blue, yellow—as they might have been in the past. Many as they are today, in ruins. One temple in particular has a number of pictures. There is text attached to the temple.

"This is the Temple of Inscriptions in Palenque," his upper-class British flows like a scholarly lecture. "And right below it, there are pages on something called the Palenque Codex, and an array of equations that uses foreign symbols, some of them highly complex."

There's more to come. "There are sub-files after sub-files here, chaps." Harry's face is furrowed like a small potato patch. "They're sealed behind firewalls, each file locked by separate passwords."

Noah adds the autopsy report to the list of clues and findings.

"It was what you'd expect, you know. Almost normal autopsy, only the large head injury, the cause of death. The pathologist says that the indentation in her skull matches a heavy, rounded object, probably a heavy pipe or baseball bat." He doesn't tell them how seeing her body on the cold steel morgue table has affected him. He uses tight, clinical language. "There *is* a problem with her diabetes. Her pancreas appeared normal, but very small, the size of a young child's. The microscopic slides appeared entirely normal also, no damage to the cells that produce insulin. The pathologist is puzzled but it's clear that there is no way she was a diabetic. There's more."

He tells them of his visit to Jay Levine, the specialist's opinion that the insulin DiShannia received was altered in a way to make her blood sugar fluctuate, to give her the symptoms of diabetes. In short, to poison her.

There is a moment's silence while this sinks in. "What?" Gerry says, "They treated her for years, didn't they?"

From Kate, looking at her notes, "From the time she was twelve." She looked at Noah, brushing the hair back from his eyes. "Why would they do that?"

Noah says, "Fluctuations in blood sugar level can affect mental function, causing confusion, light-headedness, irritability, possibly even more serious in a teenager. Repeated drops in blood sugar can also cause her to be less intelligent. Somebody was trying to make her less smart."

The sound of other conversations is loud in their ears, but louder still are the questions in their minds. Noah thinks about the near-miss on the roof. Kate thinks about DiShannia's theories and her death. They're both increasingly convinced this is more than just another story.

Harry fills the quiet void. "It's true, chaps. We do have rather a lot to discuss. But I have something that will make our conversation easier. It is," he says with a little flourish, turning his iPad around for them to see, "an app."

"To do what?" from Gerry. They all think it.

Precisely, as though they're all a little mentally impaired, Harry delivers an apps-for-dummies lecture: "You know that an app is an application, correct?" Four heads nod in unison, little toy dogs behind the back seat of an old car. "I have designed it to be our private, secure communication method, with a space for pictures and text, notes and comments, all sharable. One way to think of it is as a virtual team room. Shall I load your phones and iPads with it now, do you think?" he asks. They agree, handing him their phones and laptops, one by one. Even Naomi the unenthusiastic is enthusiastic.

Finally Kate, the last one to speak, offers an apology.

"My job was to contact my cousin, the Mayan scholar, in Toronto?" The little end-of-sentence question again. "I finally reached him, during what he calls his 'office hours.' He was friendly, but very hesitant to talk; he sounded harried. He will *not*, under any circumstances, speak to us by phone or Skype. I offered him a secure videoconference line, but no way. Sorry." She doesn't tell them about other parts of their conversation—personal parts.

Their problem with finding out more about the Maya is interrupted by Gerry. He spots Arjay Singh, a big black guy, across the room. Arjay, the rumpled senior detective of the DC crime task force. Arjay, the son of an Indian rug salesman and an African-American mother. Arjay, far more at home in Southeast DC than Southeast Asia. Arjay, one of the best on the force, although his two ex-wives and rarely-seen daughters would remember him more as the picture on the mantle than anyone invested in their lives.

Noah met him once but the details of the case are vague. Details about Arjay are never vague however; no one who's ever met him has forgotten the experience.

He makes his way to the group, dodging the chairs and the tray-bearing waiters, his toeing out as obvious as the pain in his knees, a grimace accompanying almost every step. His beer gut precedes him by a foot or more, his belt angling downward at forty-five degrees, holding back the giant bulk of his belly. He impales himself on a straight-back chair, obliterating it from sight.

Arjay's oversized DCPD jacket must have taken extra yards of material and his white shirt long ago forgot how to close at the neck. It makes small O-rings, one of them showing an inch or more of hairy black stomach. A sad little DCPD blue tie hangs from his open collar, looking lost against the vast prairie of the shirt.

"Fucked if I could find a parking space. *Jesus*," he says, offending Christians and obscenity-sensitive ears in one breath.

In one motion he grabs a fist full of peanuts, shakes hands, manages something between chews that come close to *"Pleased-to-meetcha"* and orders a double shot of Dewars with a beer chaser.

He has something to tell them. Impossibly, he leans his massive stomach farther over the little bargain basement coffee table. It's crowded with their drinks (though now devoid of peanuts). Arjay has done his work. His voice carries more New Jersey than New Delhi in it. He turns to Gerry to talk, but each one of them moves closer, drawn by an invisible gravity, as you all are.

"This is some case you got here, folks. There's something fucking strange about it, which is why I'm seeing you guys. You gotta understand this is all off the record, no reporting from a reliable source, right? Nothing. You can investigate all you want, but no pointing to me, okay? I'd be in a fucking pisspot of hurt." He receives, in reply, little verbal nod-agreements. Even Naomi agrees, her disdain for the vulgar dismissed for the moment. Noah is anxious to tell Arjay about his incident on the roof, but waits.

"There's two things strange here, maybe more. First thing is this. I started retracing DiShannia's steps from late afternoon or whenever she's killed, after she's been at the White House. I interview a few of her classmates." Gerry's already told them some of this. "They're all set to get on the school bus and they notice the same red-haired guy standing beside the SUV that took her to the White House. He's calling to DiShannia, says something like, 'We'll give you a ride home, DiShannia. Special White House treatment.' It's the last they see her.

"So I gotta investigate, don't I? I mean this is serious. I visit the White House Security agent in charge last night. They *didn't* send a car for her. They have no red haired agents. There was *no* White House SUV signed out late yesterday." They've heard all of this before. Somehow it sounds more real from Arjay. More tangible. More painful, knowing what happened to her next.

That isn't all. He shifts his weight on the impossibly tiny chair and makes the Dewars disappear, orders another in the secret language of frequent bar-flyers. He tells them what he knows of the last few hours of her life. How they found blood and scalp fragments in a small triangular park called Turtle Park, in Southeast. There were signs of a struggle in the park itself, gouges in the grass, drag marks in the street beside the park. A trail of blood for nearly two blocks, down an alleyway, traces of her attempt to find her way back home.

"And there's more. This one's even stranger. So I'm figuring out the last known events in her life, and I think, *Fuck, I better see the crime scene for myself.* It's in the alleyway where she died. I got three of my best guys—well, two guys and a gal—working the scene but I want to eyeball it personally. So I get there this afternoon. It's all taped up. It's a typical alley in Southeast, right? It's got used baby buggies, lots of other old shit, garbage everywhere, like that. But the crime part, the part where she died? It's fucking perfect, clean as a whistle. There's no tracks or foot prints around the body or where the body was, no drag marks like she was killed and then pulled there. There's no footprints, well, almost no. It rained a little bit last night, right? So footprints would've shown. There's some shit left where she fell against a garden gate, hair, scalp. No prints. The entire scene's been raked clean of everything. Oh, and we found the baseball bat back at the park, right? No fucking fingerprints there either. Nada.

"So, I'm trying to piece all this together you know?" Another Dewars appears magically, the waiter nodding to Arjay like they do this all the time. "And I do what I normally do. I put on my little booties and I walk around the scene, tryin' to think like the perp would. I stand way off to one side, where I think he might have stood after it was all cleaned up, him seeing it the way I was seeing it, right? And there's a little hill kind of, just opposite the gate where they found her, maybe ten feet away. It's no more'n a little rise. It's just like the bump where they found her, a twin to it, kinda. And I stand there, and I look down, and there it is—a perfect foot print, in the mud, in a little depression just beside the hill. So we do a mold, and send it off to the crime lab.

"That's why I'm late, that and the fucking parking. So, first there's the White House thing. And now there's this shoe print. Fortunately, I have taken a picture of the print," He taps his forehead, the gesture saying *See? Not so dumb, huh?* "And I send it to this guy I know. Used to work at the crime lab, but he had a problem they say with boundaries, whatever the fuck that means. All I know is he's sharp, does a little work on the side. And here, just like ten minutes ago, I get this answer from him."

Another swig. Half the scotch vanishes. Chug, chug.

Wiping his mouth, liberating his cell phone from a hip pocket, he finishes. "I'll read you what he texted me. '*Really unusual foot print. Product made in Germany, not sold to the public. The product has been purchased in the last two years by two main organizations.* Here they are," he reads in a German that would make Angela Merkel laugh, a rare event in the old lady's life. "*Das Amt des Deutsch natürliche Tierwelt Rangers,* that's the German Park Rangers. Or," he pauses, makes the rest of his second Dewar's disappear, "The Swiss Guard."

"Bloody hell," Harry says, as much as to himself as anyone.

"You mean the force that guards the Pope?" Kate asks.

24

BAKER STREET. LONDON. ENGLAND. 1952

He walked slowly, leaving the faux-doctor's office, quickly gathering speed, gaining strength, like a stone rolling downhill. The molasses in his mind thinned, less viscous this morning, his depression lifting with each step. The memory of his and Mary Catherine's brief time together raised its strange head. And *that* raised the question of another kind of love, of Lorenzo, the object of much of Alan's ample stores of romantic affection.

Lorenzo, his lover for tonight and hopefully some time to come, Lorenzo of the incredibly black curly hair. Lorenzo of the muscular back and ribbed stomach, Lorenzo of other rather incredible parts. More than anything, this second thought lightened his step as he crossed Baker Street, stopped to buy pasta, tomatoes, basil and wine. He would cook for Lorenzo tonight, a small compensation for impotence, the temporary gift of the doctor's treatment.

If he couldn't fuck him, at least he could feed him.

+++

Alan had a third love, something so unusual he rarely discussed it with others—his devotion to the story of Snow White. *How many adult men*, he wondered, *keep such a secret in their heart?* He never cared about the answer. His bedroom, in a small walk-up flat in Chelsea, was a veritable shrine to the memory of a fairy princess who never existed. She was, in some eccentric fashion, like himself, isolated, surrounded by smaller beings. Pictures and sketches of her lined the walls of what anyone might suspect was a woman's bedroom. A dozen or more books of Snow White paraded along one shelf like tiny colorful row houses. Just below it, another shelf was filled with Snow White dolls of all shapes and sizes, from two inches high to over a foot, and from thirty years old to a small set of the seven dwarfs he purchased recently.

The evening with Lorenzo went very well. In the hurry of the afternoon he had forgotten dessert, but Lorenzo, bless him, had brought his favorite thing—bright red, shiny apples, a half dozen. They were meant for dessert, but instead they had found themselves in bed, enjoying a different kind of after-supper treat. The dishes sat, sticky with tomato sauce and spaghetti; the wine bottle open although almost gone; the two candles on his small kitchen table burned to oblivion.

An early morning business call kept Lorenzo from sleeping over. A devoted, loyal lover, he told Alan he would make it up to him on the weekend, demonstrating his promise with a hug, a kiss and an impressive pelvic thrust. Closing the door on Lorenzo, Turing became suddenly ravenous, happier than he had been in days. He turned to the kitchen, found the apples and ate two, wiping his hands on the little apron that protected his skirt. He saved a third for bed.

Where, the next morning, he was found dead by his housekeeper.

Leaving Alan's place, Lorenzo entered an iconic red telephone booth, morphing from lover to MI5 agent. "Let me speak to P," he said when he had finally rung through. He waited a further highly annoying minute before he heard the Eton-educated voice at the other end ask how "it" had gone.

"Perfectly. It went entirely as planned," Lorenzo responded to P's question, deploying his imitation of an Eton-bred accent. P never got that he was being played. Intent, eager, a corporate thinker, gifted with generous ginger-colored hair, Paulson was ultimately a stupid man. "He never suspected a thing. I am quite sure he is happily consuming one of the apples as we speak. More perhaps—he loves apples."

"I still think it's an insane idea. Quite bizarre, indeed. Still, I am glad that it went as planned."

Lorenzo knew his trade as well as any skilled carpenter or artist. He said, impatience entering his voice, "You're quite wrong about the insanity of it all. You'll see. You know he has highly unusual tastes that'll become apparent when the coppers have a go at his house. Why, he was even wearing a Snow White outfit last night. This will be seen as flamboyant, just like him, a suicide in this case. It is precisely how Snow White died, by eating a poisoned apple. He has ample reason to be hopeless—his depression, his jail sentence, his medications. It will be a discrediting, final sensation. Just as you ordered, P, a concluding chapter to Operation Hemlock. And just in time; I found a copy of his open letter to the tabloids on his desk. It's destroyed, you'll be pleased to hear."

The call ended with this reassurance and something from P that could have been, "*Good show, have an evening off then, mate,*" but the mushy peas of P's accent wreaked havoc on the serious vowels and consonants.

Lorenzo was not done making calls. Moreover, his transformations were not finished. Instead, he dialed a number leading to someone housed in the Vatican embassy. He spoke seven words, not in his *faux*-Eton, but rather in his native Italian.

"*È finita. Sarà morto mattina,*" the dual agent said, "It's over. He'll be dead by morning."

The call's recipient, a monsignor with the pedestrian title of Observer, had a highly unusual job. He called Lorenzo, "Padre."

"You've done well." The Observer's accent was hard to place, its origins Southern Italian, Calabrian, possibly. "You've saved the flock from the weight of enormous worry and angst, Padre. Disconnecting him from the human race and discrediting his voice at the same time? An enormous gift to civilization and to the Church of course. You're to be congratulated."

A slight pause, "But we are not done. We have an even larger task for you, Padre."

There was something in his voice that caused Lorenzo to shift uncomfortably, a change of tone, like the advent of a minor key in a lighthearted piece. He readied himself, straightening his back, unconsciously adjusting his tie with his unoccupied hand.

"There is evidence that you've been working for two masters, collecting two paychecks. Please don't insult my intelligence by denials, Padre. For this particular period in our history, the two have similar goals. We simply want to, how to say, *capitalize* on the dual relationships. I wish to meet him, your *Signore P.* It's as though you have both a wife and a mistress, and one wishes to meet the other. It is not uncommon is it? We need to expand P's horizons beyond this particular incident, to tell him a bit more about the world, in fact about the universe. He'll be receptive. It is your job to *make* him receptive. Shall we say tomorrow, at noon? Near his office? In the Church where we have so often met?

"I'll do my best," he said. "I'll do my be..."

The Observer interrupted him. "Oh," he said as he hung up, "I know you will."

25

WASHINGTON. DC. LATE TUESDAY EVENING

Arjay is insistent. Noah and the others must have protection tonight. Noah particularly, after he describes the incident on the roof to the big detective.

Over their objections, Arjay arranges a police escort home—Kate to her parents, Harry, Gerry and Naomi to their condos and houses in leafy Washington. Naomi refuses, claiming that she's able to look after herself thanks, but the rest agree. Noah will get a police car located outside his apartment, the others will receive drive-by attention and Arjay's private cell number. He's already got two detectives working on the attempted murder.

"Don't take this lightly, folks." Arjay says, "This was a serious attempt on Noah's life, not just some accident. And I think this shit is all tied together with a big freaking bow. You guys be careful."

As they leave, none of them are aware—are you ever aware?—of the small homeless tribe sitting just outside the outdoor patio at Poets and Busboys. Noah would have recognized his ankle-grasping friend from yesterday.

Later, in his apartment, Noah finds it impossible to sleep. He's put the laundry away, has tackled the dishes in the sink, researched a dozen topics on the internet. He finds almost nothing about the Swiss Guard for example, frustrating him. He is driven to find answers.

It's tempting to see it as the same force that has fueled him all his adult life: a strong desire, a cousin to compulsion, to *do something.* His favorite T-shirts have a giant Nike checkmark on the front and the motto, *"Just do it,"* on the back. He wears one tonight over his boxers as he keeps busy, trying to solve the puzzle of DiShannia, trying to push back the anxiety nibbling at him like the nightly visits from the rats of insomnia.

It's the same force which drove him to become a physician, in his twenties, thinking that he would be able to help people, diagnose their illnesses, make them better. Such simplistic thinking. He admires those who can take up this role with grace and skill, but he's found two things which have driven him elsewhere. The first is the nature of many patients, many *people,* at least in safe, developed nations, to cause their own illnesses: the obese diabetic who continues to eat badly despite warnings; the smoking asthmatic; the self-defeating depressed patient.

The second is an even greater force, discovered on rotations in international settings, some of them spent with *Doctors without Borders,* then with its cousin, *Reporters without Borders.* In Syria, where Shia fought Sunni, where children still died, where blood still ran in the streets. In this and other settings, he found the well-intended but tiny services that he and his colleagues performed in makeshift emergency tents barely adequate. *Band-Aids,* he thought.

Instead, a more powerful tool became apparent to him—bearing witness.

Alone in his tent at night, he'd blog about the patients he'd seen, thinking that the pen was mightier than the scalpel, his scalpel at least. The blogs argued for peace and developed a readership in the world of social media—never millions, but dozens, hundreds world-wide, several thousand at one point.

One of them was a senior reporter for the Washington Post who reached out to Noah, offering three gifts, like the Magi: congratulations on his writing; the suggestion that reporting, especially *doctor*-reporting, might be a career option; and, finally, an offer to introduce him to Jeff Bezos, the famous, now deceased, owner of the Post. The rest, they say, is history. The email exchange changed his life.

It drove him to switch careers, or, rather merge them.

Tonight, alone in his apartment, Noah is unaware of another force at work, a force as small as a gene, as large as the universe.

Like the homeless people outside Poets and Busboys, like the homeless man behind the police car, out of sight, Noah is unaware of it.

26

WESTMINSTER CATHEDRAL. LONDON. ENGLAND. 1952

The giant phallic tower of Westminster Cathedral loomed in front of him. This was the *Cathedral,* not to be confused with nearby Westminster Abbey. The ancient Abbey was a huge, vaulted, gothic, dark gray structure; the Cathedral was unmistakably a late nineteenth century bright stone-and-brick creation. As instructed, he used a side door, surrounded by cherubim and seraphim frozen in quiet stone song.

And entered a marble forest.

Small chapels made their homes along the walls, like dark caves, separated by pillars, as big as giant trees, disorienting. Blood red columns from Nordic countries, reminders of the Precious Blood. Great brick piers clothed in Greek *cipollino* used in ancient Rome. Forest green columns, also Greek, mined from quarries that supplied Santa Sophia. Other pillars faced in red from Ireland, and in *campan vert* brought from the French Pyrenees, near Lourdes. Even the floor was marble, a light blue-grey *faux* forest from Tuscany.

It wasn't just the Byzantine forest that fed Paulson's discomfort. It was the urgent early morning call from the agent he called Lorenzo, a man of many talents. Lorenzo was genuinely persuasive in his call: this was an urgent problem, an issue of some delicacy. A grave matter, the double meaning of the word lost on Paulson.

Paulson found the Chapel of the Holy Souls deep inside the cathedral, a small alcove, home to a statue of Mary and a raised altar framed in marble and mosaics. Two small rows of pews faced the altar while a polished brass rail surrounded it, ringed by a long kneeling bench, thankfully padded. A small donation box sat in front, the tiny slot an invitation to generosity or guilt. Lorenzo had already arrived, kneeling, his elegant body hovering over the altar rail, tightly wrapped in a tailored black suit. A perfect example of piety to the outside world.

Somewhere, a choir began to rehearse the *Te Deum*.

Paulson knelt beside Lorenzo. Paulson viewed the man's transformation with sizable interest and not a little suspicion. Lorenzo was no longer a lothario in tight leather pants but a young priest, his black curls more controlled, his dark eyes downcast, his Roman face more kind than seductive.

Looking ahead as though transfixed by the altar, the pseudo-priest whispered, "In a minute, P, you will meet a Monsignor Albinoni. It's not his real name of course, so you needn't strain to memorize it. He has thirty minutes in which to tell you some things that are beyond my level. During that time, I'll make myself scarce in one of the confessional booths. I do have rather a lot to confess don't I, my friend? Then I'll return, at your disposal."

As quickly as a candle snuffs out, Lorenzo was gone, the soft click of a confessional door signaling his presence elsewhere. On cue, the kneeler moved, rocked by the frame of a large man, dressed in a monsignor's full black cassock, a giant cross hanging on his chest, a rosary in his left hand. His back was arched by the task of carrying his massive stomach in front of him, a pregnancy of overindulgence. Paulson could picture the man late at night, reading salacious novels, a single malt adult beverage perched on the platform of his stomach. He could also *smell* the man. Apart from the incense of the candles on the altar, it came to him in waves: the unwashed cassock's dried sweat, stale after-shave, tobacco.

Extending his right hand limply, briefly, Monsignor Albinoni, or the Monsignor of no name, or no monsignor at all, began, "Please to listen carefully. Incline your head towards me so that I may speak quietly, as though we are having an earnest discussion. Perhaps you are dealing with a sudden loss." Vowels insinuated themselves between words. *Italian, Sicilian possibly*, Paulson thought.

The priest started, "You know of course that the Vatican has an embassy in London. I am, shall we say, both from that embassy and not from it. It will also not surprise you that the Holy See engages in the art of information gathering on a regular basis, just like any country. Knowledge of course can be very powerful. Look at the way in which your master-mind, your *genius*—What was his name? Ah, I recall, Alan Turing—solved the riddle of the Enigma, and, it is said, saved the war for you." The game of trying to remember Turing's name was lost on Paulson.

"I understand he is now sadly departed our world, a death perhaps not entirely by his own hand, and not entirely outside the knowledge of MI5." The choir rehearsal stopped, re-started, the only sound in the Cathedral.

"You might ask what role the Church could possibly play in world events, apart from our homilies and our presence? We have no army, apart from our small troop who protects us. We hold no sway over the money markets, we possess no or few weapons. Ours is the territory of the soul. Yours is the terrain of the visible and the worldly. How indeed," he continued, straightening his back, impossibly raising his stomach, a small feat of anti-gravity, "could we possibly play any meaningful part in what I have to tell you? It is the reason I have called you here today. It seems that a text from the Mayan period has survived."

The small chapel held its breath, Paulson also. Only the choir continued, echoing in the dark marble forest.

"It tells the tale of an astronomical discovery by the Mayan people centuries ago. It appears that your Mr. Turing had also learned of this text, studying it at the British Museum. He received this information from his friend at the museum, a Mary Catherine O'Rourke."

He had Paulson's full attention.

"So, my friend," groaning slightly, the kneeling position not entirely to his liking, "what I have to tell you this afternoon is not information from today or yesterday, or perhaps especially last *night*," a pointed nod to the confessional where Lorenzo had lodged himself. "But rather from centuries ago."

He appeared to shift the conversation. "Do you know the name Diego de Landa?" Paulson shook his head.

"Ah, no matter; few do, except perhaps for scholars of the ancient Mayan people. De Landa was the Spanish Bishop of the Yucatan in the middle of the sixteenth century. Spanish Catholicism was an exceptionally, let us say *strict*, brand of Catholicism. De Landa saw his role as eliminating the barbarism of the natives and in that effort he was conscientious, perhaps too much so. He destroyed the writings of the Mayans. And he denigrated their religion as uninformed, crude, even evil." Vowels continued to insert themselves like little dividers.

"He was very industrious, examining the texts with great precision. He found a prophecy that decreed the end of time for all mankind, a fiery cataclysm of the solar system. I will spare you the details. It is enough to say that its message does not conform to the beliefs of the Mother Church."

Paulson's occasional nodding stopped. This was familiar territory, the guts of what he had begun to call the Turing Story. There was also the taste of acid in his mouth and a shrinking feeling in his groin; he wasn't about to like what this priest had to tell him.

"He considered them the scribblings of an ignorant people with little knowledge. The truth is, the Maya were brilliant astronomers, their writings as advanced as any from the ancient world. Their books," for the first time he moved beyond his blasé diplomat-spy persona, "their *books* were magnificent, beautifully crafted and detailed.

"De Landa destroyed them all in a massive book burning in 1560, receiving criticism even from the Church. In reality, the burnings involved only the destruction of those codices that were considered barbaric, showing the sacrificial rituals, and, most important," his voice became more heavily accented, "those books he thought were astronomically disturbing." "It appeared not to be enough, however. He heard persistent rumors that another text existed, containing a proof of the prophecy, why, they say, the Maya abandoned their civilized world five hundred years before.

"It is no accident that it was precisely at that time the Holy Church became interested in astronomy." He paused—for emphasis, to catch his breath, to let the words settle into Paulson's consciousness.

"Let me continue with the next phase of the story. In 1932, a Swiss German archeologist, Ruiz Lhulier, discovered a tomb in Palenque and inside it, a treasure of writing, the very prophecy of the collapse of the planets, the codex about which de Landa had heard. In time, the codex found its way from Palenque to America and then to the British Museum, where its Mayan specialist was Mary Catherine O'Rourke, the woman who was a close friend..." He hesitated, speaking now almost entirely into Paulson's ear, the tobacco and stale sweat overpowering even his cologne, "...a *very* close friend of Professor Turing."

"Surely, this nonsense about the planets is bollocks!" Paulson's squeezed the altar rail tightly, the veins on the back of his hands prominent in the soft light of the chapel's candles. His bluster fooled neither of them.

"Oh no, Mr. Paulson, not at all. For decades the Church has maintained an observatory at Castel St'Angelo." He raised his eyebrows, turning to Paulson as though conveying a great secret. "What business, you might ask, has the Vatican got in building an observatory?"

Nothing surprised Paulson about what the Holy See did or didn't do.

"The official story is this: faced with the criticism that the Church was anti-science, Pope Gregory XIII undertook several reforms, like the modern calendar for example. He also ordered the building of an observatory, first at the Vatican, then at the Papal Summer Residence, and even to this day, the Holy See undertakes several important, one might say 'stellar,' research programs." His attempt at semantic humour fell flat. "And now we have a larger observatory in Arizona, in the United States.

"This is no superficial interest in the sciences, my friend, and it is no coincidence that at the time of de Landa, the Holy Church decided on its next steps, *secret* next steps, I must say. I will trust you with them, since in turn, I have some interesting details in hands to hold your silence. Some of the Jesuit community has been entrusted with the care and science of the Observatory. They are called the *Astronomi*. They have devoted their priestly careers to the study of the movements of the sun, the moons, and the nearer planets. And we have extended ourselves to American and other European colleagues. You might ask, 'What have they found?'"

The obese monsignor shrugged, a gesture holding nothing, or everything. Paulson had believed the rumor of the collapse was held by only a few colleagues in the circle of knowledge defined by *Hemlock*. The older priest stood, the pressure of kneeling finally too much for his back. Paulson stood with him, turning, facing the marble forest.

"I have two rhetorical questions for you," he said, straightening his back, groaning slightly, wordless regret from an epicurean. "One. Why would the Holy See spend its resources on *several* observatories? Two. Why would the newest be located thousands of miles from Castel St'Angelo so that astronomers can observe the moons, the planets, the sun *with the naked eye* from two locations, as though they wish to measure its distance from us?"

Paulson's eyebrows, as endowed as his head, raised slightly at the twin facts. *Focus,* he thought. He needed only to protect his own and MI5's role in the matter, and to raise this more earthly question with the priest, "And what of the girl, the woman rather, this Mary Catherine? If she knows of this, she knows about Turing's death. Surely she knows about his, um, beliefs? Won't she be able to spread these tales?" He couldn't allow himself to label it anything more than a tale.

"You're perceptive, Mr. Paulson," signaling for Lorenzo to join them. "We, rather, our young priest friend here, went there this morning to make our interests in her known, only to learn from her roommate that she had come home yesterday in some turmoil, quickly packed her bags. Quite distraught, her friend said. It appears that she has decided to leave Great Britain, we think for the United States. While we are not without resources in America, your connections are much deeper. We need your help to find her.

"We have no idea where she's gone. We believe she knows much about the codex, has studied it." He placed his arm on P's shoulder, a gesture of confidence. "It may be more serious than just a woman vanishing, Paulson. Her roommate says that she was…" He paused, the celibate priest exploring unusual terrain,

"…. pregnant."

The word hung in the air, like the sound of a bell. Only the choir's final responses of the *Te Deum* entered the silence, *"Miserere nobis, Domine, miserere nobis."*

Have Mercy on us, O Lord. Have mercy on us.

The choir fell silent, the last notes echoing in the marble forest.

27

THE TEAMING ROOM. WASHPO. WASHINGTON. DC. WEDNESDAY MORNING

Even the dust motes seem hot.

It's only nine o'clock, yet Noah is sweaty, has had enough of the too-bright sun's slanted rays. He unfolds himself from the noiseless, sliding chair and lowers the blinds, their mechanical purring the only sound in the quiet room. Even the sirens are quiet for the moment. He's managed a couple of hours of solid sleep, more than standard for him. The police guard outside his apartment building was a welcome babysitter; the guy even drove him to work.

There are five in the room, each of them deep inside their own electronic mini-world. Gerry and Kate on their iPhones, the rest on laptops or iPads, outwardly silent antisocials. The team room is just as they left it: their thoughts, Noah's notes, others' reports, printouts taped to the walls, DiShannia's death, her diabetes, the Mayan story, the crime scheme, each occupying its own territory. Small countries of doubt, provinces of questions.

Looking up from her phone, Kate says, "Good. I finally got my cousin to agree to a Skype interview. There are *complications* he says." She doesn't mention the complications that his presence in her life have caused.

Suddenly, they shed their isolated devotion to the electronic devices, becoming members of a group. Harry couldn't look more English if he tried: his striped Eton tie and a maroon sweater-vest strain around his belly. He is surprisingly cool, apparently used to the heat. He's been monitoring police calls, has done some background work on Rose School financing. He reassures them about the app's security. "Un-freaking-hackable," he says, trying to adopt American jargon, failing miserably.

Noah's sadness is leavened by the team's efforts to solve her murder. He moves to the white board to lead the conversation when Erich surprises them, a rarity outside his office at any time.

"Don't get up," he says, needlessly.

He moves at close to the Erich-version of warp speed, pulling up a rolling chair, inserting himself into the group. He pats the seat beside him, indicating for Noah to sit.

"I do hope you're all right," he says, another surprise, the worded caring. "The police called me early this morning. They told me the whole story. Must have been awful for you, Noah. Very frightening. And for all of you. Bizarre." He says it like it's a place.

For a minute, Noah sees another level inside Erich: there is a genuine person inside, or at least the appearance of one. And he has news. The police have arrested Hernando, or at least the guy they have called Hernando. Erich is appalled, he says, that employees of this organization have such malignant intent.

He surprises them even more: he wants to hear more of what they're working on. Harry is new to Erich and he introduces himself, his exquisitely perfect Brit-English adding some class to the room. "I'm Harrison Foley-Bennett sir, originally from the UK." Kate is similarly new, explains where she last worked. Gerry and Noah are familiar to him. He appears most interested in Naomi, however—Naomi and her political, White House connections. Power, or the search for power, is in Erich's blood.

Naomi starts with little preamble, clearing her throat, shuffling papers in front of her, transferring the material on her laptop to the flat-screen with the flick of an unmanicured finger. "I think I might have something. Figuring out where the Rose Charter's schools funding came from seemed the best place to start, so we searched their public annual reports. Harry was enormously helpful. Look here," she says, using her cursor. "First we identified all the corporate donors, like Kaiser-Gibraltar HealthCare Inc., groups like that. Every one of them checked out; their donations were listed in *their* public records. But there was one corporate donor called 'Poseidon' that I couldn't find anywhere." She appears excited, though *excited* in Naomi to be fair is indicated by a tiny widening of her eyes, a slight raising of her voice.

"I remembered hearing the name at a Senate hearing on clandestine funding years ago. It helps to have been in this business a long time." A tight smile accompanies the comment. A siren careens through the glass windows momentarily, loud and shrill. "I tracked down one of my contacts, a retired senate staffer. He said that Poseidon was two or three administrations ago, a large terrorist-finding network of agents who worked beside Homeland Security. That was the problem: their work was 'parallel play,' both involved in the same business, but not really cooperating. He believed Poseidon was shut down, and its leadership, one or more two-star generals, were demoted."

She pauses then, bending over her iPad and her paperwork, scrolling to find more documents, the growing gray line in her hair indicating her dedication to fact-finding. Staffers say you can tell how long she's been working on something by the width of those gray margins.

"And now it gets interesting," she says, as though the first part wasn't.

"We didn't stop at the public pages; Harry knew some, let's say, back routes. And we found the name Poseidon, still active, with huge donations to the Rose School Network in the previous year. This is all," more finger pointing and scrolling through the back route documents, "years after Poseidon was officially shut down." A look falls between Erich and Naomi, as loud as the siren.

Erich's cell phone dings, a reminder or a message interrupting him. He stands, grasping the back of his chair as he leans in to the group. "You're certainly on to something here, folks. I don't know yet where it will lead but I'm grateful to Noah," not Noel this time, "and to the rest of you. One of our reporters has been threatened. I want you to give this a full court press. I want this to be on TV, newsfeeds, even in print. I want you to travel if you need to. Remember the stories are out *there*. Use the exceptional travel budget line to do it. I want you to drop everything else for this; it's possibly as big as Watergate decades ago. It'd be good for WashPO!" he exclaims, exiting. He means it would be good for Erich.

The little show of support energizes them. They are interrupted by an impossibly loud rock and roll song of the Seventies, annoying Naomi, making

Gerry laugh. One of his kids loads his phone's ring tones for him. Today's phone ring is *Stairway to Heaven*, one of Noah's favorites.

"It's Arjay," he says after a minute of listening. "I'll put you on speaker phone. Everybody you met last night? They're here. Go ahead."

It seems impossible that the big man's voice can squeeze into the speaker's tiny microphone. "Hey. Good morning everyone. Noah, you got through last night okay?" Noah replies, "Yes, thanks," to the phone. "Okay, here's what I was telling Gerry. It's about the boot print, the one that nobody could track down? The one that could have had two sources? My little buddy figured it out. The German park rangers have four tiny cleats in their little booties so they don't like slip on the Matterhorn or wherever." Arjay's geographic knowledge isn't as good as his crime information. "And our bootie prints don't have any cleats. So, what the fuck, pardon my French, is the Pope's guard—or at least their shoes—doing in DC?" he asks. His voice is infinitely smaller than the size of the question. Noah erases *German park rangers* on the white board. The heading now reads *Boot Print–Papal Guard?*

Arjay has a few last words for them. "Sorry, gotta run. We're busy as *shit* here. Homeland Security has tied us up with a weapons of mass destruction leak in the US. *Fuck*." He's gone.

Harry's face has been, one might say, interesting. He has been quiet, even throughout the little profanity-laced exchange with Arjay. He almost-shouts, "The bloody password, chaps. I think I've got it!"

Harry has figured out Shanny's password on her nail drive. He's been working on it all morning, using what he calls "a rolling, scrolling algorithm." Kate looks at Noah as if to say *Whatever the heck that means*. His shoulders lift slightly, the universal gesture of *Beats me*.

Harry explains, "I showed you just what was immediately accessible yesterday like her pictures, but there is a *lot* here, I must say." Like an excited ten year old, he wants to tell them how he did it. "It was totally shambolic at the first. Those posters on her wall? They're of some boy band called *Aliens in Dallas* though how one identifies aliens in Dallas may be the question of the year. Her favorite was Dalton, the lad with all those nose studs." He shakes himself slightly, trying to rid himself of the image of Dalton. No one can blame him. "So that gave it to me." No one could see it. "*Dalton*1007. October seventh is her birthday. Was, I mean."

His manner implies ease and simplicity but the group knows otherwise. Noah knows something else: they're prying into her personal life, not a comfortable feeling. "And we have a treasure trove of information here, lads."

His eyes never leaving the screen, his fingers fly over the keyboard, "Files on the Maya, files on the British Museum, files on of all things CERN, files on…..Give me a few minutes would you?" Like some modern hunter-gatherer, Harry is sifting through hundreds of photos, documents, appointments, notes.

Kate suggests that they leave Harry to study the museum of DiShannia's files. They have a half hour before the Skype call with her cousin.

Minutes later, in line at the local Starbucks's with Noah just behind her, Kate says, "I'm feeling like it's going to be awkward with him at first. There's our family dynamics for one thing, but he's not easy to talk to. He's pretty much got a one-track mind."

It's more than simple family dynamics.

28

THE TEXAS BOOK REPOSITORY. HOUSTON. TEXAS. NOVEMBER 22, 1963

T**he truth was, he hated books.**

Every Saturday, from the time he was little, say five, his mother would take him to the library. From their fifth floor one bedroom, down the front stairs with its cracked and peeling linoleum, spilling onto Flatt Avenue, turning right on Aberdeen, a whole seven or eight blocks. Then it was another three long blocks before you found the fake English cottage with a big sign that said *Welcome, Hamilton City Library*.

He hated the way the older boys on the basketball court would yell "Harvey Lee's a faggot!" and worse at him as he was dragged by the hand, dressed like he was headed to some funeral. His mother insisted, "Dress up, boy! You're going to a place of learning. You want to be exemplary, you got to learn to read." As though it were a university or something—laughable, the idea. Years later when they asked him where he wanted to go for his training, he said, "Anywhere but England for Christ's sake."

He hated the musty smell, the cardboardy, tobacco-damp aroma of old books, the straight-as-arrow rows of tiny brownstones, the shelves disappearing into a five-year old's distance. He hated the long aisles. Once, when he was eight, when his mother and his little sister were in the children's room, reading *The Princess and the Pea*, he explored the adult section. At the back of one of the rows he saw a man dressed in a too-big brown suit, holding a book just below his waist. The book was open, its altar holding a plump, pale snake, sticking out from the man's zipper. The man looked at him and mouthed, "It's okay, you can touch it if you want." It scared him—not that the man might hurt him, but that a part of him was curious enough to *want* to touch it.

He ran crying, forever the suck, back to his mother.

Even the army psychiatrist, the pain-in-the-ass, probing guy they assigned him when he failed to fucking *meet expectations*, even *he* didn't know that story.

Irony filled the room. He, the book-hater, was stuck in a book repository, working yet again in some menial job, being told what to do. Even worse, he was caught on the floor where they put books that nobody wanted. His supervisor, a black guy for fuck's sake, said, "We put'em on the top floor where they the hardest to get to. Know what I mean, son?"

And there they were. Boxes and boxes of school books, each one carefully labelled—*Middle School American History, Twelfth Grade Algebra, Cursive Writing for Fifth Graders.* One book label per box, some neatly piled, some boxes thrown off to the side as if to say *Nobody wants this lot*. A few books just by themselves piled by the windows—total rejects, a bit like him, he thought. Row after row of books just like the aisles in the fucking Locke Street Library. And the smell! Like the bottom of a dirty damp cardboard box. *Jesus.*

Fortunately, he could get some air in the place, had to in fact, if he was to get his job done. He moved to the window he was told to use, the second one from the left. It slid open smooth as anything, greased ahead of time. Looking across the way at a grassy knoll, he saw him, the guy who had recruited him, months before. Then the man was dressed as a priest, one of the European kind that had the long black dress right to the floor. Today he was just a normal tourist, his skinny white legs in khaki pants and one of those plaid—*Madras, that was it*—shirts. What would a priest want with a man like him? What did he want with somebody who hadn't really done much to be *exemplary* all his life?

Opening the window relieved some of the smell of the room. He could hear the crowd, excited, dressed up for the event. He could see the ladies in their best skirts and the men looking like it was a Sunday. From this height, some of the ladies looked like little puffy flowers on thin-legged stalks. They were gathering along the streets around Sam Houston Plaza, a dozen or so deep, some parts a little patchier, buzzing like the circus was coming to town. Maybe it was a circus. Here was another irony for you, ladies and gents, a fucking big one this time, *Dress up for a party, stay for a funeral.* He smiled.

He checked his watch, knowing he had lots of time. Whatever else they said about him, he was organized; German trains could run with his precision. He had been to Germany; it was where he had met the priest. In a whisper just loud enough to hear, the man had said, "I have a job for you, a very sensitive and pivotal one. You will be able to say to your grandchildren that you led an extraordinary life and accomplished great things. The job has danger and risk, but it is very important."

He went on, encouraged by his companion's nodding. "There is a powerful man who holds a highly dangerous secret. It is not that he would divulge the secret himself when he is in a public place or making a speech. But he has a very serious problem: he sleeps with women all the time." He spoke as this act by itself were distasteful.

"*Many* women, I must say. Sometimes there are two and even three in a day, even at one time. And when he is with them, he uses drugs to keep his stamina up." There was no doubt what he meant by "stamina."

"Drugs to calm him, drugs to keep him awake. And it is during this time, especially after he has made, er, love to these women, that his tongue becomes loose. It is one thing to tell small secrets, like gossip about this person or that. It is another thing to tell secrets of national plans to those who are not his wife. But this secret, *this secret*," he repeated, his voice carrying the hiss of a snake, "….is not a state secret, this is a *world* secret. It is much too devastating to broadcast. We have to intervene." *Intervene* became sinister in the priest's mouth. "We have tried other ways to dissuade him, but the man is a stallion and he feels he is above us. We need to stop him. Would you consider taking on this task? You would be, I believe it is safe to say, exemplary at it."

In a way it was like the bald man showing his penis to his eight-year-old self. This time he decided to touch it.

And now there he was, minutes away from the task, his plans at work, the incredible ticking weight of an assassination marching in his mind, the pieces like soldiers on a parade field.

He took his gun from the carrying case, assembling the pieces rapidly with the precision of multiple practices and well-worn neural pathways. Laying it so that the barrel was just an inch from the window sill, sighting on the spot where he was told the lieutenant governor and their two ladies would pass. Straining a little bit. He could hear them now, cheers from the crowd as the motorcade was approaching, ahead of schedule by a minute or two. The barrel wasn't right though, the gun was too low. He had to raise it. He tried to inch it higher, but this strained his back and shoulders, made his aim unsteady. No, he needed *something*, the position and timing had to be perfect. He grabbed a flat book laying at his feet, sliding it under the rifle barrel, a perfect, one-and-a-half-inch raise. The flat green surface of the book was just right, the angle was just right, the motorcade, ahead of schedule or not, was just right. And so was his aim.

He watched it, fascinated, as though someone else had done it.

The head of the hypersexual Adonis-president exploding, his mushroom-colored brains, some of them anyway, flying away, spoiling the first lady's blue dress. *There'll be hell to pay about that*, he thought, smiling. The lieutenant governor turning around to look at the back of the car only to find his shoulder a painful bloody mess. The first lady trying to escape the car, turning to climb over the back of the convertible, a pitiful site really. Needless, you might say— she could have died in an instant if he had wanted her to. The secret service agents trying to meet her on the trunk of the car as it sped away. He didn't need the "okay" sign from the priest on the grassy knoll that he had done an excellent job, even, he felt, an exemplary one.

He always supposed—at least until he died, not a long time at all as events unfolded—that one day he would be told what the secret was. Surely if they could trust him with the act, they could trust him with the mystery. As he threw the gun to the floor, ripping off his gloves, leaving no fingerprints or trace of himself, he knocked the book to the floor. It was *Mystery of the Mexican Pyramids,* by Peter Tomkins, Harper and Row, Publishers—a book read so infrequently that it had found its way to the sixth floor of the Texas Book Repository in Houston of all places, and then not even boxed.

29

WASHINGTON. DC. WASHPO OFFICE. WEDNESDAY MORNING

I t takes a minute or two to get the Skype connection right, to do the introductions, to make Dr. Lam look like something other than a pixelated cartoon. At first, before he joins the call, the team—Naomi and Gerry, Kate and Noah, Harry—see his office, another example of the academic habitat. Marginally neater than Morris Jay Levine's, it's long and narrow, like a train car. One wall is lined by books, papers, journals piled on the other. Decades before, someone had tried to brighten the office by painting it yellow, a color that had morphed in time to something both more and less than the original, altered by urban pollutants, by time and by the almost-prehistorical use of tobacco.

While they wait, Kate is deep in her own thoughts. Wai-Ching's presence here is part of a larger story. Years before, the estrangement caused by Kate's parents' marriage was deep, but not total. Her mom's older sister maintained contact, visiting periodically, bringing stories of their parents, and—most of all—bragging about her son's accomplishments. How her cousin had leap-frogged over others at school, how he won prizes. How he was admitted to university, how he had become a full professor, both at early ages. Especially, how his grandparents had doted on him. It reinforced Kate's decision to bring similar honor to her family, perhaps healing the family's estrangement, hoping that her grandparents would learn of her achievements, would reach out to her, could love her mother again. Only partly unconsciously, Kate worked tirelessly to be the best—at school, in athletics, in her early writing career—all, sadly, for nothing. The estrangement was as solid as a kitchen chair placed on a porch.

Her feelings about her cousin are, it's safe to say, mixed; despite its futility, the inner treadmill caused by her grandparents' estrangement continues to operate.

There is a little intake of breath from Kate as Wai-Ching enters the room, late, greeting them. Kate thinks, *It's been years since I've seen him. He's aged.* No longer the optimistic, energetic overachiever she recalls, his face is drawn, his eyes tired. They begin the introductions. Noah starts, "Tell us about your interests in the Maya, Dr. Lam. May I call you Wai-Ching?" He nods.

The door to a conversation cracks open.

"I have been very interested in ecology since I was young, Dr. Scott," he says, not looking directly at the camera, a product of natural shyness. His is a formal speech pattern: it holds no trace of an accent but has the cadence and flow of a Mandarin-speaker.

There is a small clearing of his throat, "For my doctoral thesis a decade ago, I studied the Mon River delta in Africa. Its people have suffered greatly from climate change. That work led me to the development of a theory which intertwines river flow and economic impact. This theory was published in the *European Journal of Ecology* and received international acclaim." His look towards Kate says, *See what I've done with my professional life?* Noah feel a little less than warm and fuzzy about Dr. Wai-Ching.

"My success also caught the eye of private donors, and I was subsequently named, also very early in my career, to the Li Ka Ching Chair of Eco Studies." Naomi, not impressed by most things, says, "You must have felt very honored, Dr. Lam."

"Thank you. I was. But it seemed I was not truly in charge of my research. The chair of my department, with encouragement from the donors, desired that I prove the theory in *past* civilizations. It was not enough that I had done my studies on current civilizations like the Mon. Not enough," the *enough* almost spat out.

"And so, I elected to study the Maya since it was thought their civilization ended because of a drought. By that time, I was able to build a small but impressive research team. I have asked that one of my graduate students join me." He looks down, checking his iPhone. "I do apologize. He is late. How much do you know about the Mayan people?"

Naomi answers, "We've seen pictures of Mayan temples and pyramids, but we have no real *knowledge.*" She says it as though it were gold. In many ways, it is.

Wai Ching continues, "I understand." Warming to the Skype experience, he fills in details of the Mayan Empire and its demise. After a few minutes, like a good teacher, he turns to his audience, asking the question, "You might ask, *What caused the collapse?"*

They might indeed.

He answers it himself. "For years, scientists thought that severe drought caused the population to leave the Mayan cities, but the Maya were very smart people; they could easily have figured ways to cope. And I have analyzed lake beds, looking for evidence of rainfall. I will share my screen."

It takes him a minute, then, suddenly, he occupies only half the picture, the other half fills with graphs of rain and drought projected on an ancient Mexico. He shows them a map of the Yucatan with the drought-stricken areas about 800 A.D. perversely marked in green; the deeper the green, the deeper the drought. He uses his cursor to point out several cities that were totally abandoned by 900 A.D. None of them had any green at all; there was no drought there. The screen reverts to showing his face, the tired eyes more visible. "It is clear, is it not? Drought was not the problem. Nor was over-farming or a pandemic or any of the other theories widely argued." He hesitates then, as though he were standing on the edge of something, a giant cliff. After a long moment, he says, "I trust this line is secure."

Harry assures him, "You can see the *https*, doctor," indicating the website on which their conversation smolders. "It's as secure as a bed bug."

Reassured at least partly, he re-starts, "And that is where my graduate student's research is important. Our grants have allowed him to lead a team in explorations near the old city of Palenque, where the temples are so well preserved today. Here we discovered proof of cities abandoned, fields not tended, children left to starve, myths about a cataclysm."

The room is silent for seconds, only the ever present sirens of the city interrupting the quiet. Overcoming her own feelings about him, Kate asks, "Wai-Ching, I know you are reluctant to talk about this but can you share your concerns about publicizing your work?"

"I have tried to publish this work, but have been turned down by almost all journals. A year or so ago? I was having *no* problem getting anything published. Now, nothing…"

"This must be difficult for you, Dr. Lam," Naomi says. "Can you tell us more? We'll treat it confidentially; perhaps it will help explain why this is happening to you."

He seems to agree, a hint of Asperger's continuing to make eye contact difficult, but the group has warmed to him. Only Harry appears focused on attempting to understand the treasure trove that DiShannia has loaded into the tiny nail drive. His brow furrows; he has hit another wall.

"There are other things I would like to share with you but they are shared with my grad student, Mr. McClintock." Wai-Ching checks his iPhone again. "I do apologize for his tardiness. I will go check on him. While I do, I will put up the pictures from our last expedition to Palenque. Many are self-explanatory." As he does so, his assistant appears behind him, whispering in his ear. She appears upset.

"Please, look at these," Wai Ching says. "I'll be back in a minute or two. Something has hap-" his assistant pulls at him with some urgency, and suddenly his half of the screen shows only his empty office, the yellow even more intrusive as the sun brightens it. The white teaming room is silent, its occupants looking at each other, half of the large flat-screen at the front void of anything but the aggressive yellow office walls. Their eyes are fixed on the other half of the screen showing the map of the Yucatan a thousand years ago. Strangely, they hear shouts and cries in the background, wailing, like a fire engine, Kate thinks.

Suddenly, Wai-Ching is back, clearly upset, "I am so sorry, I will need to leave this call. You see, R.J. is my assistant's fiancé. I asked her to check on him. He's *dead*. I wondered what had kept him so long. It is R.J., he has…" he leans close to the computer's microphone, almost whispering, "He has taken his own life." The screen goes blank.

For a moment, so are they.

They are stunned, looking at each other, the native connections between them almost tangible. Naomi breaks the silence, "It must be connected. Dr. Lam can't publish in this area, then his grad student takes his own life." She shakes her head. Noah is also stunned, quiet at first but he sees an arc spanning the last forty-eight hours—from meeting DiShannia, possibly to the Rose School deaths, now to this. Gerry, the crime reporter, intent on his own laptop, he says, "I'll see what I can find out."

Harry, the least attentive to Dr. Lam, has been trying to get their attention. "I think I have it, chaps. Well, rather a part of it. I didn't want to interrupt, but

Shanny's nail drive has *tons* of information here." They are eager for a diversion from the sadness of the last call.

"I've been able to break into two of her sub-files. One is marked 'Maya— British Museum' where she's stored pictures of the Mayan pyramids that we've seen previously—nothing new here—but she's had extensive correspondence with someone named Miriam al-Ansari, a researcher doing post-doctoral work at the British Museum. There are reams of notes, emails and reports, pages deep. The second file is marked 'CERN-cosmology.' It's detailed and complex, quite marvellous!" he exclaims. His copious brown hair is messed, his tie askew. "Un-be-*leiv*-able."

As though a dam has burst, they are all talking now. Gerry interrupts. "Here," he says, "I've got some information about R.J. McClintock, graduate student at the University of Toronto. Sound right? Okay, I have a breaking news alert from one of the local stations, and I found a few pictures from his girlfriend's Facebook page. Only took me a minute." He shoots a little look at Harry, *See Kid I'm not the only one with IT skills*. It's a friendly, teasing look just the same.

"It's here, on the news. They say he's the first jumper from the so-called suicide bridge in years. His body was found just before lunch—it's, oh, it's pretty awful, a drone shot from above. I won't show it to you." He shakes his head.

Kate breaks in, "That's not what it's called, really. It's actually the Bloor Street Viaduct. It was a magnet for suicides for years, but I thought they'd fixed that. I'd have thought it'd be impossible to jump from it now."

"Whatever," Gerry says, "It's pretty clear he went over all right. Let me show you this from Facebook," and in a couple of clicks, it's on the flat screen, replacing the absent Dr. Lam. He's found a picture of a group, labelled *Our engagement party—Dr. Lam's backyard.* It's a group picture, Wai-Ching standing shyly at one end of the photo, with a smiling couple in front holding hands. R.J. and his fiancée are just off center. While most observers of pictures like this would describe the bride or bride-to-be as beautiful, this one could also describe the groom in those terms. A crop of tight brown curls cover his head perfectly, a masculine jaw that years ago defined the Marlboro Man, deep-set, intelligent eyes, a welcoming open smile, and, through his tight-fitting T-shirt, muscles sculpted in a gym.

He is just half the bride-to-be's height, less than three feet tall. And he's in a wheel chair.

To the entire group one thing was clear: someone, or more likely a pair of someones, had catapulted him over the side of the bridge. They see what Noah saw minutes ago, the linear connections between these deaths.

There is much yet to uncover. Harry is frustrated by failing to break into a third file, labeled "Red Shift" on the naildrive.

Finally, Noah takes charge of the team, "I don't say this very often but I think Erich is right. You heard him, this is a major story: we shouldn't be here. We've got Gerry on the police connections, there's still lots more there; Naomi has to work her White House and government connections further. Harry has more to get out of Shanny's computer and naildrive. He can make sure that we keep in touch with the app. We've got to get *out there.*"

Harry interrupts, "Brilliant, chaps. Exactly right. You need to get you to meet those people Shanny used as her advisors. There is a lot I can decipher here, but you really need to go there, I think. Perhaps you and Kate can visit them?" It emerges as *p'raps.*

There are head nods everywhere, glad not to sit and wait for the next death. Harry continues, "She was in touch with people months before she was killed; there's a long string of emails between them. There's this Dr. Al-Ansari and another, a Dr. Ivaan Something at CERN. I don't know what's in the emails yet and I do not trust my IT friends to help me break into the messages. At home, tonight, later, I'll do it. And there is more," more scrolling of his e-screen. "Here's a picture of this Dr. Al-Ansari, in the Meso-American Section in the staff pictures of the British Museum. Here," he says, as he flips her Facebook picture onto the big screen. *Facebook* is rather a misnomer; she's totally veiled."

He is matter-of-fact. Does Harry know how risky this was, this sending them out into the world, naked but for their reporters' credentials?

They know this much. The British Museum is the most resourced center for archeological research on the planet. In some ways it is so similar to, in some ways so different from, CERN, the European Center for Nuclear Research, one focusing on the past, one on the future.

Harry is energized. "London is easy-peasey from Dulles, then we can get you to Geneva to CERN." Harry's fingers dance over the white keyboard, a contrast. "There's a six-thirty flight tonight to London, United 7998. One day should do it there. Then I can book you to Geneva the day after, at nine-thirty in the morning on Lufthansa"—more scrolling now—"Flight 671." Kate is slightly reluctant, thinking of leaving her father alone with her mom in the evening, but she nods agreement; she and Noah can leave tonight.

"There's more, Kate and Noah," Harry says, a smile crossing his intent face. "I just checked with Dr. Al-Ansari about her availability. She returned my email right away: she is expecting you about eleven tomorrow. Go home. Pack. Get your passports. You have lots of time."

Time.

It is quiet after Noah and Kate leave, the little team of three taking next steps. Naomi has her Poseidon contacts to pursue. Gerry has to meet the head of White House Security again and has his other police connections to follow up. Harry cheerfully works away at breaking the next sub-password and the next. An hour passes, more. They're gathering up their notes and electronics to leave when Sydney surprises them, entering the room. She appears anxious, pressed, her forehead and cheeks flushed, geographic shapes brightening them both. She ignores the chair that Gerry pulls out for her.

"There's been a change," she says, urgency pressuring her speech, "about the story that you're working on, the one we okayed yesterday. I want you to drop it."

Gerry erupts, his hospitality gone. "Drop what? Drop this story, Syd? For Chrissake, this thing has legs, we learned even more this morning. Erich's been here already. He's given his blessing."

She stops him with a stare. Many men have been the brunt of the Stare; some have said their balls shrink. She repeats, "I said drop it."

"Sydney," Naomi says, using her full name, "You haven't been on top of this like we have. There's more here than meets the eye…"

"Jesus! Are you *deaf*, both of you? You'll fucking *stop* reporting on this, this instant!" Sydney is almost shouting now, clearly at the far end of control. Someone walks by, sticks her head in the door, making sure everything is okay. Sydney, suddenly charming, dismisses her, then turns to the three of them. In an almost-hiss, she says, "Find something *else* to work on. There have been some changes." As she turns, her pony tail flicks, dismissively.

Even Naomi's eyes widen.

SECTION III

OZ NEVER DID GIVE NOTHING TO THE TIN MAN

OZ NEVER DID GIVE NOTHING TO THE TIN MAN
THAT HE DIDN'T. DIDN'T ALREADY HAVE. © *AMERICA. 1972*

30

CASA PERDIDA (THE WESTERN WHITE HOUSE). SAN CLEMENTE. CALIFORNIA. 1978

He despised flowers, or rather, hated what they did to him—his eyes, nose, even his throat complained loudly about the airborne attack of multiple unbidden allergens, tiny little assailants. Paulson had learned about his allergies in hospital rooms and funeral homes where enormous bouquets surrounded ailing or dead MI5 chiefs and colleagues.

He blew his nose on the remnant of his last Kleenex, now roughly the size of a postage stamp, and parked his horrible rental in the front drive way, leaving its crumpled maps and the worry of driving on the right behind him. He was on the curved entrance to the well-guarded, so-called Western White House. His eyes accustomed themselves to its white-washed, red-tiled, modest Spanish grandeur—and all those flowers.

"Wait here," a nameless black-suit said to him, one of the Secret Service agents who appeared out of nowhere. Paulson was about to visit the disgraced American leader in his office behind the main house, *Casa Perdida*. It was the retreat of the thirty-eighth president of the United States, now retired in some infamy, the result of a train wreck of problems—a paranoid, vindictive mindset, a robbery and a pair of dedicated, too-inquisitive reporters leading to a story. The office was its own separate building, laying quietly in the lower back garden of the *Casa*. More flowers basked in sun-drenched splendor sprinkled across the too-green back lawn—dozens and dozens of them. *Bloody roses,* Paulson thought.

The lawn cascaded to the sea in casual elegance like a giant evening dress, divided by a brick path and covered by a carpet of light morning fog. The pathway allowed visitors a full, up-close view of the ocean as it deposited them at the bottom.

Two decades had passed for Paulson, a *katun* in Mayan.

Years had slid by, greased by days and hours, telescoping themselves. There had been the death of the PM in 1965, Paulson's mentor. There were transitions to other, senior roles in MI5 and MI6, then other desks, even a stint in the US with the British Embassy, involving a visit to the Nixon White House. It was his only connection to the man who resided in *Case Perdida*. One constant strung itself across those years: the ultra-secret brief he kept on the whereabouts of Mary Catherine O'Rourke and the remaining friends of the deceased Alan Turing.

He had learned that Mary Catherine (he felt he'd earned the right to call her by her first name) had delivered a child, raising him or her somewhere in the US, most likely in the Northeast. That Mary Catherine had generated much of the original work on the codex, providing Turing with the clues that ultimately led to its translation, just as he had conquered WWII German codes. That Turing's friends at the University of Manchester and from his war years had remained highly loyal to his memory, some participating in university-based symposia on the topic of planetary movements, some even giving clues to reporters. More troublesome, many of his circle had begun to implicate "unnamed government forces" in Turing's death, some with gut-tightening accuracy.

Turing's friends and his one-time lover were potentially more dangerous than Turing himself, like bombs, armed and ticking. Paulson's Vatican sources either had no knowledge of Mary Catherine's location or weren't divulging it, despite an exchange of secrets that would be the pride of any free trade agreement. None of them—the Vatican, its network of Astronomers, MI5, the US government—had been able to find her.

It was good that there had been a drumbeat of competing news in the twenty years: the assassination of a president, the Vietnam War, the transition of the almost-impeached resident from one White House to the other, the fracturing Soviet Empire. It helped that other demonstrably false prophecies predicted an end to the world. It helped that scientists had clear, irrefutable evidence from spectral observations of an expanding universe, that the light from the planets and stars indicated that they were moving *away* from earth.

The monsignor, another constant over the years, had confided in Paulson most recently on a visit to the alliterative Gregory the Great Church, "You and we, we have had a good run at keeping this quiet, but we are losing control. Turing's friends appear even more active as they grow older, and we still lack knowledge of Mary Catherine, where she is, what she knows. Do you think we could persuade the Americans to come on board?" He paused, running out of breath; the only physical change in him over the years was his increasing girth. His kneeling days were long behind him. "The former president is interested in, and still capable of, making events happen, if you know what I mean."

Paulson's disbelief in the truth of the Palenque Codex had grown over the years, buttressed by the string of failed world-endings, by scientists' findings, by his Western expansionist-optimist thinking. His unit had been instrumental in promulgating the more believable universe-is-expanding language, using tabloids and press conferences to spread the word. As much as anyone, he believed the message. On the other hand, the monsignor and the spreading rumors were compelling. More urgently, there was that budget memo laying on Paulson's desk, warning of defunding Operation Hemlock.

He thought it unlikely that he'd be granted an interview with the former president or that the man could actually do anything. Still, Paulson had been the intermediary between the British government and the then-vice resident years before, and agreed to reach out to him. Surprisingly, the reaching out worked; Nixon agreed to meet him in his California office.

Casa Perdida sat dangerously close to the ocean's edge as though it could be carried away with one giant wave.

"Come! Down here!" The deep voice resonated, carrying clearly from the base of the hill, over the wordless roar of the ocean—the rich baritone of a former Commander in Chief. He waved at Paulson, motioning him down the path, thankfully away from the flowers.

Casa Perdida was decorated as though John Wayne could appear at any moment, tying up his horse. Perhaps Ronald Reagan in *Rio Bravo*. Paulson entered a large cavern, nearly two stories high, its wood-beam ceiling crisscrossed by rough timbers, making a perfect upside-down X's and O's game. Huge windows ran from floor to ceiling, allowing the rooms' inhabitant to keep watch on the ocean. A giant, antlered chandelier hung over a nest of three buckskin-upholstered couches, forming an overstuffed square "U." Smaller lamps and tables, antler-gifts of now-dead deer, elk, perhaps moose. A loft above the giant open space, possibly an extra bedroom. A steep set of stairs leading to it, made of half-logs, shellacked within an inch of their lives—*treacherous,* Paulson thought. A huge desk, a steroid-induced version of the one the resident had known in the White House, occupying the space under the loft balcony, facing the sea. The two stories of glass were divided vertically by a massive, open fireplace, its mantel a masculine redwood slab the size of a linebacker's thigh and its opening framed in stone, large enough to house several dwarfs. At the moment, it only held unlit white birch logs.

White birch bark, Paulson thought. *What the codex is made from.*

"My small office and meeting room," Number Thirty Eight said, blending needlessness and understatement smoothly. "I'm writing my memoir, as you can see." The desk, with enough mahogany exposed to build a modest home, was laden with papers, notepads, memos. The deep baritone again, "Can I ring for anything for you? Coffee? I could use some myself." Without waiting for a reply, he picked up the phone and ordered, "Refreshments please—coffee, some of that banana bread from yesterday?" Then noting his visitor's Eton tie, the tweed sport coat, "….and tea, we could also use some tea."

This little exercise, followed by a quick tour of the lofted living room and the pictures of better days allowed Paulson to blow his nose and clear his head. His recovery was thankfully unimpeded by any giant bouquets in the room.

The coffee and tea arrived, the hospitality evaporating like the morning fog.

"I understand you have a proposition for me," the deep voice said, settling himself on a side couch, leaving Paulson to choose one of the other masterpieces of overstuffing. Nixon leaned back in the seat. He was dressed casually—an open shirt, khaki pants, loafers—the perfect retiree wardrobe. He held a flimsy sheet of paper which Paulson recognized as his own letter. "You realize of course that I have little power anymore."

It was all pretense: in the labyrinth of government, he retained influence over many of its levers, like a Minotaur. The pretense was displayed with such outward innocence that it made both of them smile simultaneously, a small bridge in Anglo-American relations.

"Mr. President," Paulson began, wondering, *Why are former presidents still called "president?"* "I've come seeking your advice. Very briefly, you will recall that we have had problems in what we might call a predicted astronomical catastrophe." Paulson was referring to his visit to see the then-vice president in the mid 1950's, shortly after the death of Turing and the departure of Mary Catherine O'Rourke. "It is not of course that we have come to believe that such a catastrophe might occur but rather that some *believe* it might occur. Several individuals in particular are in danger of spreading this, er, rumor, two of them here in America, in fact." Paulson opened his hands, a small gesture, demonstrating *spreading.*

"We're not alone in this of course. The Catholic Church has been studying the phenomenon for years, in secret. The real risk, it seems to us in MI5 and MI6, is that the message has become global in scope, and that if it were widely believed would wreak havoc in the markets. In particular, we think it important that we find Professor Turing's friend, this O'Rourke woman about whom we spoke many years ago. She might be playing a role."

The resident replied, his gaze not on Paulson but at the loft, "Yes, I remember the story. As you said, you and I visited on this subject years ago. Of what use can I possibly be to you now?"

"Mr. President, two things have brought me here. First, the situation is not fully embraced by my current, er, employers. The PM wishes to disband our little unit, the one called 'Hemlock.' At the very least she wishes to see it merged into MI5 proper, to have it report more openly to Parliament." He cleared his throat of the annoying post-allergic drip.

"Second, I have had contact with representatives of the Catholic Church who have expressed an interest in collaborating with American authorities. I have come to ask whether the American government, or perhaps an *aspect* of that government, might be persuaded to help us find this O'Rourke woman, to help curtail some of Turing's friends' communications. I myself am happy to help but am unable to continue this fight—I fear it is a losing battle—with my superiors. Your own government's handling of Area Fifty-Two some years ago strikes me as a perfect model, and..." a final deep breath; he was trying to scale the increasingly unsmiling human wall opposite him. "I recalled your sympathy to this issue many years ago."

For a beat, the ocean was the only sound in the room.

"Stop," said Thirty-Eight, his face radiating negativity, surprising Paulson.

Paulson had taken their recently shared smile as an indication of an agreeable solution to Paulson's dilemma. He was wrong. Using his famous profanity for punctuation, Nixon said, "Let me be perfectly fucking clear. I am not able to help you. I am no longer the goddamn president. I have zero control over any aspect of government. I have neither sympathy for 'Hemlock,' nor your shitty situation. Furthermore, I have no wish to form an alliance with the Goddamn Catholic Church." Then softening slightly, he continued, "I do not mean to be unsympathetic to you personally, but please understand me: I cannot help you." As he finished the last four words he leaned back, as though he were giving a speech.

Only minutes later, following an apology and a quick final sip of his tea, Paulson was gone.

The entire visit, the allergic attack, the tour, the refreshments and the failed effort at collaboration had taken less than thirty minutes. Paulson left, a diminishing trail of sneezes marking his progress up the path to the main house. A car door slammed, possibly more loudly than politeness would allow in the genteel neighborhood—a heavy, metal-on-metal slap. In that time, the president had reached over to his desk and clicked off a small, high-end tape recorder buried in one of the small apartments in the condominium that was his desk.

"You guys still up there?" he yelled. Of course they were up there; where else could they go? "You can come down now!"

31

THE DULLES TOLL ROAD. VIRGINIA.
WEDNESDAY AFTERNOON

The several year old 2021 *Prius* is safe, fuel efficient, the product of hybrid technology. The backseat holds Noah and Kate, their fears and demons. It also holds their backpacks and electronics—their laptops, video equipment—and Kate's purse-slash-bag. "It's as big as a refrigerator," he says, laughing, "What do you *keep* in here?"

Between them lie the remains of two Starbucks lattes, a half-eaten spinach and goat cheese sandwich and the shell of an orange. A refugee from Syria—one of several million in the new world—is behind the wheel. Noah has an iPad on his lap, fingering through the day's news, focusing on Toronto and the headline about Wai Ching's young colleague. He watches Kate. She's put on black pants and a white top, comfortable, she says, for an all-nighter in a plane. He watches the way she holds her coffee, her face and eyes attracting his attention. Her smile. The way she fills out her blouse. The nape of her neck. She is not without occasional glances turned towards him either, admiring the way his skinny jeans tighten themselves around his legs. His big arms, his profile. The way he brushes the hair back from his eyes.

They are making good time from downtown. There's not much traffic on the road; the recent Sunni-Shia wars have jacked gas prices to nearly ten dollars a gallon, beyond the reach of many travelers. The only slowdowns occur where the heat has buckled the roads, the 495/Dulles toll road merger for example. There, crews have narrowed the roads to one lane, slowing traffic. They pass the Beltway, the end of the known universe for most DC residents. Midway along the toll road, they notice cars slowing, stopping, the cabby muttering, worried.

"What is it?" Kate asks.

It's Noah who answers, the cabby's mind occupied by weaving his way through the slowing cars and even some people wandering onto the road. Some hold signs.

"Must be one of the homeless camps, Kate. There was a newsfeed on this one last night."

The camp is on a hillside to their right, spilling over onto the westbound lanes. There are hundreds of people. The police or at least what pass for police, possibly private militia, have managed to secure the shoulder, but barely. More people are crowded against the barricade as they creep by. Ragged clothes, bearded men, underfed, unhappy children, no fat visible on any of them. Women screaming at the cars, some yelling obscenities, some pleading, some saying nothing as though poverty had robbed them of speech. The cabby is frightened, perhaps reliving scenes from his refugee years before. One kid, his belly impossibly large and swollen, shakes his fist at them, pounding on the car's hood.

One woman pulls her baby from her breast as they approach, leaning in towards the car, offering the child to Kate and Noah—partly a gift, partly a plea. "*Take my baby!!*" she screams at them. Her breast is flat; it's held no milk for days or weeks. Kate's mind thinks the baby is a rubber doll, but she's wrong: it's an infant, dead for days.

Kate flinches. Her right hand moves to the window control, instinctively, her sympathy driving the movement. Like Noah, she is driven to *do something.* A black policeman scoops the woman up, mercifully, not unkindly, taking her away from the traffic. Noah has seen the scenes on videotape but is immersed in the experience, lost at the stages of anger or denial that this could happen at all in his country. And then suddenly, the crowd parts. They squeeze past.

They do not see, at the margin of the pack, one homeless man whom they would recognize in a heartbeat. From the Dupont Circle metro, outside Poets and Busboys, and now here, a familiar tattoo on his arm.

Noah's phone rings. It's Harry, at home. Noah's iPhone screen fills with his oval, olive face and that of his two year old. "Anna," he says, "say hello to the nice people." She sits on his lap, trying to take his glasses off. He puts her down, gently.

"Naomi, Gerry and I have left work for the time being. There is a *lot* going on, rather, since you left."

"That was only four hours ago, Harry."

"I know but, please listen. I am very definitely worried. The others have asked that I call you. They're lying low, working the story, not at the office. It began almost as soon as you left. Sydney rather marched in just before noon as were packing up, announcing that we were *not* to work on this anymore, absolutely not. That threw a spanner in the works, I tell you!

"Right afterwards, two men announced themselves at Security as federal agents and proceeded to escort Erich out of the office. Erich kept repeating 'What did I do?' quite loudly for him. And then, just at the door, you know where the floors overlook the atrium? At that very point for us all to hear, he shouted, 'There's no fucking freedom of the press, is there? Not since Congress weighed in!!' Please forgive my profanity, Kate. My God, I have to tell you we are very, very concerned. Maybe it's that Congressional reporting mandate!"

Harry is referring to Congress' recent public-reporting bill directing every licensed information service to report all major stories to a joint Congressional-White House agency. It followed the burgeoning crisis of so-called fake news. It was done in full compliance with the Fourth Amendment, not limiting freedom of the press, just, shall we say, *channelling* it.

Harry's head comes closer to the screen, filling it, his intense brown eyes holding theirs. Anna is no longer visible. "I believe the story that we are working on—DiShannia's murder, the Rose School, the poster, the Presidential Award, everything—is what has triggered this. Bloody hell. Unless of course Erich has been embezzling or something, our story is the only major new story line we filed this week. All the rest are regular, ongoing things like shootings, like fires and flooding. Am I correct?" He is correct.

"So Sydney is…" Noah starts. Harry completes the sentence, "…the acting editor in chief."

Kate is fearful. "But she's shut the story down, right Harry? We shouldn't be going."

"Gerry and Naomi gave me strict orders, Kate. They want me to pass on what we think, well *they* think, is best. I will lie low here, at home. I will say I have child care problems but will be extracting more information from the nail drive. No one knows about our app. I built it at home, remember? I will continue to communicate with you through it, no email exchanges, no phone calls, since they're all traceable. Gerry and Naomi, also. You can honestly say you didn't know about the freeze at work, since you've already left for Europe. I suggest you follow up on the leads we found today."

Noah says, "You've got a point, Harry, but why would anyone be interested in a story about a dead civilization, for heaven's sake?"

The question hangs in the air.

"One final thing, Noah and Kate, maybe two. Since I've been home, when Anna and the little one leave me alone, I've done more sleuthing for you, and I have an appointment day after tomorrow for you with Dr. Ivaan Horkonen at CERN, someone DiShannia's corresponded with extensively. His assistant confirms that he is working on Friday, lecturing at a public forum or something, but that he would see you. Here are their coordinates…"

Anna, the little lady, now climbs back up on Harry's copious tummy. She waves *Bye-bye*.

Noah is busy entering the information about the appointment. "And the second thing?" he asks.

"Oh yes. Please, lads, be careful."

32

CASA PERDIDA [THE WESTERN WHITE HOUSE], SAN CLEMENTE, CALIFORNIA, 1978

Thatatat was well-timed, wasn't it? That little show?" the president said as they began negotiating the half-log steps, cousins to the giant redwood mantel. The loft and its treacherous stairs disgorged them, one at a time.

They managed the steps carefully, worried that the highly shellacked half-logs would fail them, tricking them into an embarrassing fall, or worse, a fractured hip. That was wise; they were not young for the most part. Their footwear offered small insights into their personalities. The rubber-soled practical shoes of the compact, muscular Vincent Battigelli, automotive CEO, over thirty years since he had left the plant floor. The highly polished, upmarket shoes of the former deputy secretary of the treasury, Conrad Bitterman. The regal figure of Morgan Pierpont III, used to slippery boat surfaces, his dark blue, trimmed-in-white deck shoes held the stairs perfectly. The slightly raised black pumps of the only woman in the group, Dr. Christine Bishop, past rpesident of the National Academy of Sciences, former professor of physics at Northwestern. And finally, a pause for the fifth person, announced by the soft staccato of basic, rubber soled shoes owned by the youngest of the group. He managed the stairs in a staccato burst, announcing his presence like a teenager rushing out the door.

The overstuffed sofas absorbed the noise.

Arnold Edelstein was the fifth person. Energetic and slightly rotund, he had been the president's deputy press secretary in his White House days. The period had been shortened by Nixon's determination that Arnie could be very useful to him in other aspects, especially in his post-White House work, managed from Casa Perdita. Arnie was often asked whether he missed the White House and the power of the presidency. He would praise the current weak and vaguely incompetent administration, but secretly—this was a man who could keep secrets —he felt little difference.

Arnie never reclined in soft, suffocating furniture. He grabbed a straight-backed dining room chair instead, straddling it backwards, placing it just outside the overstuffed "U" of the couches. It was where he could listen to the conversation, alternatively resting his chin on the high back of the chair, sitting upright and standing, stretching his back. They were the outward signs of a brilliant if impatient inner mind, thinking of a thousand things at once. Someone had called him a modern Napoleon—Napoleon, who had once kept six secretaries busy simultaneously.

"I apologize for the interruption," the deep baritone began, "but I thought the timing of his visit was perfect, don't you? A little example of how our British friends are playing the same game. I was tempted to put him off, but I thought—what the fuck?—let's see if he has anything to offer. Nothing, fuck-all, that's what."

Their nods were modified by uncertainty about the nature of their visit. Weeks before, there had been a polite inquiry on *Casa Perdida* stationery about their availability on a certain date, a generous invitation to spend a day with "like-minded colleagues to explore issues of the day." It was followed by a telephoned request from Arnie to keep the invitation confidential. Finally, a flight to California and a limousine pick-up at their hotels early this morning. And that was all.

"Let me summarize what we have here, friends," the president's baritone continued, captured by another hidden tape recorder. "You know most of the story already." Their meeting had begun several hours before Paulson's arrival. Over croissants, orange juice and possibly the best coffee any of them had ever tasted, they had begun to explore the history of the Palenque Codex and its prophecy, the financial and social chaos if its contents were released.

"So this man, Turing," the baritone continued, "a Brit, the Enigma code-breaker during the war, believed that he had discovered a goddamn terrible secret, one derived from a Mayan codex—some cockamamie ideas about the end of the world caused by the solar system imploding. Something scientists say is bull shit."

"If I may, it is truly *not* believable," offered Dr. Bishop, the scientist in the room, her hair held prisoner in a tight silver bun. It shook briefly, emphasizing her refusal to believe the idea, possibly her reaction to the profanity. "We analyze light patterns which emanate from the stars. The light waves all appear in the red zone of the spectrum, indicating objects moving away from earth, in fact away from each other. The evidence is uncontestable." Her bun twitched again, then stopped.

The president continued. "Well, it might be obvious to rational people like scientists but this Turing guy, he was so smart, so believable—they credit him with inventing the computer, remember—so much a treasured fucking genius, that a few have spread the nonsense, like some kind of manure, from Britain to here. His former colleagues, some of his students, some woman named O'Rourke. We tried to find out about her years ago, got nowhere. And this group that Paulson leads or led? This Hemlock thing? It had Turing killed, made him appear deranged. Even that didn't stop the story. It actually fueled it."

"So what if the story gets out there, Richard? You said it yourself, it's crazy. No one would believe it." Pierpont spoke for the first time. Richard and he had known each other since college, allowing him to forego presidential protocol. Only the former first lady or his brothers used his first name and never in public. Never of course, his three daughters. Pierpont resisted the urge to put his dockers on the expansive wooden coffee table.

The president, not noticing the lapse in manners, said, "You're right of course, but Turing has persuaded others, some of who have even shown proof, *naked-eye proof,* of the planets moving their orbits closer to ours, closer to the sun. So then what? If the word gets out? If others believe him, if the press gets hold of this?" his famous eyebrows raised, "Fucking *chaos* that's what! No one wants to buy a car if the world is going to end. No one wants to invest in the stock market. No one...Jesus. Anarchy, that's what happens."

Battigelli added his two cents. "You're right, Richard," he said. He was remembering what it was like to be poor, what angry mobs of frightened people could do. He continued, his mind conjuring scenarios. "It's one thing if a run-of-the-mill scientist talked about it, but a world figure?"

"What makes you think it hasn't happened already?" asked the president, now quieter. Even Arnie, the one-time press secretary who knew it all, leaned forward, his caffeinated mind slowing, a rarity for him. It was possible he might *not* know it all.

The president leaned forward also, the couch's soft grasp diminished. His voice softer, careful, like a cat's tread. "Let's suppose that at the beginning of each presidency there is a series of briefings. Suppose that at least one of these is a very high-level top secret disclosure with the head of the National Intelligence, the CIA and the FBI. Suppose that the president is told about this—what should we say?—potential catastrophe. Suppose he is sworn to secrecy but is not able to keep his fucking mouth shut. Supposing the people he tells this secret to are not government employees or close White House staff or elected representatives. Suppose they're women he sleeps with, who would sell secrets like that without batting an eye, perhaps without even understanding them. What would happen to that president?"

"That can't be true, Mr. President," Dr. Bishop said. "No leader would ever be that stupid or careless."

For several seconds, each member of the group shared one thought. There was only one president who had been that careless.

Finally, quieter still, Nixon spoke. "For years, we thought it was the Russians who did it to him, a product of the cold war. And then we imagined more complex theories: it was the Mafia, then the Cubans, a combination of the two, plus the Russians of course, they're always in the mix." He laughed, a sound without humor. "It could have been a jealous husband, for all we knew. God knows there were enough of them. He must have fucked every woman that came within twenty feet of him!"

He knew he had them. He leaned back, enjoying the moment, the instant of surprise and fear, the use of anger. He could feel their testicles in his hands, even Bishop's. "But, it was none of them, not the Russians, not the Cubans, not the Mafia."

For several hundred heartbeats, the ocean remained the only sound in the room.

33

LONDON. ENGLAND. THURSDAY MORNING

Noah and Kate have two hours to kill before their meeting. They find a small restaurant on Montague Place, a treed chunk of London, a stone's throw from the British Museum.

They've become acquainted with Dr. Miriam Al-Ansari, the product of Googling and reading the email chain between her and DiShannia, resident in Harry's app. Trained in her native Saudi Arabia, Miriam moved to London to finish her PhD, her brother chaperoning her journey. In the same way that the past lives with you, she works in the same office that Mary Catherine O'Rourke occupied decades before.

Neither of them are aware that Mary Catherine is as much a presence in their lives as Kate's grandparents are in hers, or as Deborah's and Pete's are in Noah's. A ghost-presence.

The restaurant is called *La Bodega*. Too hot to sit out all summer in Washington, this place is a relief, nursery-rhyme perfect, not-too-hot-not-too-cold (though cold, to be fair, is hard to find on the planet any longer). It may not be safer, but several thousand miles from Washington, it feels that way. They find an impossibly small table outside, roughly the size of a medium pizza, the patio ringed off by a little metal chain. Kate sits with her back to the street. When he wants to, Noah can stare into the street, the traffic moving from right to left, a reminder that this is England. He can also look directly at Kate.

Harry pings them. Moving their coffees, they finger the app on the table between them. A series of questions, a kind of tiny cartoon cascade, pops up. And a set of pictures.

He texts, *Did u make it OK? Have u seen Dr. Al-Ansari yet? Pls ask her about this set of photos I extracted from DiShannia's nail drive.* The pictures look unlike anything they've ever seen before—black on white dots and dashes. *I have no idea what these are. Maybe they contain clues.*

There's also more from Naomi on the app. Harry forwards an email from her, dated yesterday. It says, *Continuing my digging in the Rose School files, chasing down some leads. The Wilcox investigation is interesting. Take a look at who's on our board. See attachment. There's more, Poseidon, for example. There's a connection between it and that Li Ka Ching Foundation that Wai-Ching mentioned. It looks like the Rose School is more than just a chain of charter schools. It's also developed a network. And it's not the only network in this space. There's another one, something called the Astronomers. I'm pursyinh....*

The message ends with an uncharacteristic typo mid-sentence, like a conversation cut short. The attachment lists the current board of directors for WashPO. One of them is Margaret Hyde-Pierce, wife of General Norman Hyde-Pierce III. What's interesting is her maiden name, which Naomi has scrawled in the margin of the page, nee *Margaret Wilcox.*

Harry's text ends with *More from Naomi and Gerry later today, I hope. Stay safe!*

They order a late breakfast. The eggs, bacon and the toast are just like home but the addition of mushrooms and baked beans reminds them this is England. They struggle to find a place for everything on the tiny table. Noah, the table architect-builder, starts to make a tower of the salt and pepper to make room, making them both laugh. They've begun to unwind.

With one impediment. Across the street from them, behind Kate, is a homeless man. He's as much a part of any modern cityscape as telephone poles and heat-buckled pavement. They occupy most major cities, often invisible, even in England with its larger social consciousness and net.

One of them holds Noah's attention. He seems edgier than most, sitting beside twin garbage containers and a grocery cart, alert. He is only the width of the street away from them, looking at them with intelligent, focused eyes. Kate says finally, "What are you looking at? Something interesting across the street?" She thinks it's another woman.

"This guy. He's been there almost since we sat down. He's pretty intent on watching us, or watching you, maybe." He smiles, hoping not to spoil the easy relaxation.

And then, in less than sixty seconds, all hell breaks loose, or perhaps a tiny slice of it.

Montague Place is a one-way parade of slow moving cars, inching their way behind Kate. Out of the corner of his eye, Noah sees a black SUV moving slowly, the passenger door open. *Why drive with a passenger door ajar?* As he becomes aware of it, the homeless man sees it too. He jerks his head, jumps to his feet, charges across the street, using a shopping cart as a kind of battering ram. He runs between cars, making horns honk, forcing pedestrians onto the hot street. He bursts into the upmarket breakfast scene, knocking some empty tables over, disturbing several of the other couples, making a mockery of the little faux fence that marks the patio/street boundary. He crashes full-on into Kate, hitting her left arm as she turns to grab her bag. His knees make a two-pointer on the rough patio stones.

"Hey!" Noah yells, for the most part unhelpfully, getting to his feet to help Kate and push the surprisingly strong man away, shoving him to the ground. The intruder is pinned between the waiters and one of the other eaters, mouthing something, desperate. The doctor in Noah checks Kate's arm first as it sprouts an impressive-but-not-worrisome bruise. He sees the man wanting to tell him something, pulling on Noah's pant-leg. He tells the waiter to bring ice for Kate's arm. He kneels beside the man, checking his heart and pulse, bending to hear what he's saying.

"Careful, you gotta be careful!" Homeless keeps repeating, stunned by the sudden push to the ground, hitting his head. Through the grime of his hair, Noah sees a nasty cut the size of a thumb, bleeding profusely. He grabs a napkin from the table, applies pressure. Suddenly, he's dragged away by two burly men, their black suits two sizes too small for them. Noah struggles to keep the man lying prone, but they reassure him that they've, "Got this, Mate. We'll look after him."

They take the man, lifting him roughly, bending his arms tightly behind him, dragging him to the street and into the SUV Noah saw minutes earlier. Noah tells one of the black suits to keep pressure applied to the cut, to get him help.

Later, Noah swears he hears the man say as he's dragged away, "No! No! Be Careful! No!" with each tug on his arms. Later still, he knows what he hears is, "Noah! Noah! Be careful, Noah!" The warning isn't directed at the suits.

That certainty is lost in the confusion: the wait staff rushing to their assistance; the chattering crowd of tourists walking by; the bustling but unhelpful attention of the Thai restaurant staff next door. Noah sees the two men throw the stranger into the back of the car, plastic-tying his hands and feet. They turn to have one final look-back at the mess the man's made, like some minor tornado.

Much later Noah remembers something else. Kate's oversized bag hangs on the back of her chair, holding her notes and things-in-purses that are mysteries to men. Homeless has jammed a crumpled piece of paper into it.

34

CASA PERDIDA. SAN CLEMENTE. CALIFORNIA. 1978

The ocean, it's fair to say, couldn't have cared less.

For a while—a heartbeat in the universe, a fully tangible moment in the room—the pulse of the expanding ocean was all that filled it, hitting the rocks below the *casa*, then receding, hitting them, then receding. This is the rising, patient ocean, the product of thinning ice caps, human waste and extravagance, and something else, something—astronomical.

For several moments, no one spoke. The president broke the silence, "We have every reason to believe it was the Astronomers." Over the whispered *"Who?"* and the puzzled looks that flew around the room like trapped birds, he continued. "The Warren Commission, the FBI, the CIA, even the private investigations, none of them really approached the Goddamn truth. It is true that Oswald killed the man, and that Ruby killed him. It is true that Oswald had a Russian connection and, in ways we don't fully understand, the Mafia was involved. What isn't known is this: there was a hand behind all of it. We thought for some time it was an Italian connection, and we were close: it was the Vatican, more precisely some fucking group called the *Astronomi*, the Astronomers.

"They are, as best we can tell, a several hundred year old organization, highly secret, based at the Vatican Observatory. They're far-flung, and we're only now understanding the huge fucking scope of their work."

They were, as the saying goes, all ears.

"The Vatican has reason to believe that the solar system is collapsing in on itself, that is, the distances between the planets and the sun are diminishing. And at some point, who knows, maybe a millennium from now, Earth will be annihilated. The Holy See conveyed this to major world leaders years ago, every one of whom vowed to keep it a secret, me included. And of course it would have *remained* a fucking secret until Kennedy began fucking and worse, *talking* to, every female on the planet."

"So why aren't we pursuing this?" Bishop asked, an idea that inspired nods of agreement around the room.

"Here's the problem," replied the president. "If the Vatican hadn't killed him, we would have had to do it ourselves. Ironic, right? The first godamn Catholic president, the Vatican gets to assassinate him. Most important, the predictions are correct. The timing may be uncertain, but the predictions appear factual." It was the second unwanted gift, still, to some extent, unbelieved. In the stages of grieving—denial, anger, depression, acceptance—they were stuck at denial.

"That's impossible!" from most in the room. From the lone female, "There must be *some* truth behind it, Richard." Reluctance in her voice, as well, the scientist.

"What's true or not true isn't really why I brought you here today," he said, his deep voice surging, overcoming that of the swelling ocean. "We can use this secret, this prophecy, *whatever it is*, to our advantage. It's unlikely that a collapse is imminent. It may not be true at all. But the beauty is, it *doesn't matter.*"

It was Arnie's turn. "The president's right. We've been looking for a way to," there was a small pause, a word-search, "*augment* our abilities to penetrate the CIA, the FBI, to create a secondary, um, enterprise, in order to move markets and people in a direction we consider desirable. This knowledge is a perfect vehicle to create our own messaging, perhaps even to develop strategies to prevent this collapse, or to flee from it. Those are all huge weapons for us. And we should be in control of them. Just think how we can use this knowledge to manipulate people and events!"

He was nothing if not persuasive. The older men began to respond. Conrad Bitterman was the most vocal, sitting at the edge of his seat, his experience at

Treasury guiding him. The stock market ran in his veins like red and white cells: he could see the huge, rolling, negative psychological response if the message were believed. The others joined him, successful, bright people easily grasping the brass ring of the secret. *The Solar Collapse*, one of them called it.

Of them all, Vincent was the most creative, skilled at using the tools of business development—marketing, product development, sales, messaging. He sat forward, fighting the seduction of the overstuffed couch, his muscular body reflected in his posture, "It seems to me that we *do* have an opportunity here, though we'll need to be careful—letting a bit of the story out to create some uncertainty in the market, allowing for selloffs, or building on related theories, like this global warming thing. If the sun's getting closer, the oceans will rise won't they?" He owned land in Florida's Naples.

Bishop was more guarded, the only mother in the room; mothers are naturally cautious. "There's *certainly* no conclusive evidence that I know of, but at a minimum, the theory deserves exploration." Her bun shook briefly, then was still.

"It needs a plan," Pierpont added.

If the cue was as silent as a look passed between the president and him, Arnie felt it like a drum roll. It was as though someone had shone a small spot light on him; he was on, finally.

There were many things about Arnie that stirred admiration in the observer but when he shone, there was no one more likable or more persuasive. He had an eclectic intelligence, a child of his ADD. It gathered facts like a vacuum cleaner, taking them from any source, academic or pedestrian. And then there was the way in which he could take a highly complex problem and distill it to its core, a chef's reduction. In the days before an impending impeachment, Arnie had saved the administration on more than one occasion. He was used to collapses.

He was also physically engaging. He used his small, just-slightly-overweight body to demonstrate processes and plans, his hands and physical energy engaging his audience. His wife said it was his hands that she fell in love with. "Let's start with what you think we might be able to do," Arnie suggested. "There's no right or wrong here. Let's just start a list in your heads of problems and potential solutions. You guys think for a minute or two. I'll be right back."

He jack-rabbited up the stairs to the loft and returned with a large flip chart, causing at least one of the guests to smile. She knew Arnie loved flip charts. He loved smelling the ink of magic markers, hearing the sound of the paper being ripped off, the feel of them as they were plastered around a room. Most of all he liked the way he could use them to create ideas, or, better, let others take his *own* ideas, making them think they were their own.

"I'll use this to get your thoughts down." And it began, an afternoon of sending questions like fishing lines into the group. *How could we use the markets? How to determine if the "solar collapse"* —they agreed that was a good phrase— *was actual or not? Could they begin to develop a way to escape the solar system if they needed to?*

Capturing the ideas like little fish, Arnie ensured they found their way to his flip chart.

Finally, the afternoon and the audience exhausted themselves. The men's ties were off, Christine's shoes lay under the coffee table, a couple dozen pages of flip chart notes had spread themselves around the room as though some tornado had visited. Arnie summed up.

He took his left hand from his pocket, the hand his wife fell in love with, and began, his thumb upright like a hitch-hiker's, "One: you all agree we need to build a workforce here, one able to ferret out those with the knowledge of the collapse. We should be able to at least control the message, or failing that, to discredit the messengers, like Turing's girlfriend or whoever." He was referring to Mary Catherine. No one doubted that he was talking about a spy network.

"Two," the chubby thumb and index finger collided, "We need financial support. I loved your ideas here. It sounds like," nodding to Bitterman and the others, "Wall Street resources could be leveraged easily. Do you agree?" Before they could respond, the thumb and middle finger had found each other. *Resources*, he thought, *such an all-encompassing word.*

"Three: we need smart people. Why? It's obvious that something is going on in the solar system, something that most astronomers say is nonsense, but a few suggest otherwise. We need to know the truth, develop a solution, investing in space travel for example. That's why we need smart people. How do we get them? That brings me to four."

His ring finger and thumb made a perfect circle. "Screening and training programs. I think this was Christine's idea. We need a way to find and educate the most intelligent among our kids and young adults. We need new ideas, better ways of space travel, better astronomical data. It might sound like science fiction but think what we could do!" The voice of optimism and youth. "We've already been to a moon. By the next century, we could have conquered space travel, getting us away from the solar system if we need to. *If* we need to."

"Tell us how," the president asked, "you see accomplishing this." Spoken as though he didn't know.

Arnie took a deep breath, plunging a summary, "What I hear us proposing is a network across the country. And I hear us describing a way of infiltrating the school system, perhaps creating our own, like a special type of charter school, separate from the public school system. The schools could be funded privately by Wall Street and other investors, even government, able to screen for the super-smart math and science kid. And the teachers, we can think of them, well, some of them anyway, as more than teachers, maybe like guidance counselors, like investigators, like….."

"Like spies," someone said.

"Such a harsh word, spies." Arnie shook his head, admonishing a child for a small mistake. "I think more like knowledge experts, knowledge brokers maybe. Mentors, guides, docents. There's so much more in this vocabulary than spies." His face made a small comical downturn.

They laughed. He had them then. He loved that feeling—that and the flip charts of course. It was almost more than lovemaking, certainly more than the best meal in the world, beyond any achievement in his just-over forty years—winning people over to a plan, making them think it was their own.

"Agreed. Wall Street is a natural ally here," Bitterman said.

They were all agreed. Arnie finally searched for the right word, his forehead furrowing. "What should we call this, um, network?" He could care less what it was called. It was his and the president's idea, spun like a giant spider's web over several late night conversations. *Never go unprepared into a discussion like this, always have the big plan in mind,* POTUS had taught him. *Let them make decisions over the unimportant things.*

But the plan, starting like a small trickle, was now a swollen river. Bitterman stood and stretched, arching his back, taking in the ocean and the beds of roses, a sea of color.

Arnie smiled at the president. It was like magic. At lunch, they would never have imagined the creation of a national network of this size and capacity. But, a few hours later, given the right players, plus of course the little show that POTUS had arranged, they were off, talking between themselves, seeing the possibilities. It was as complex as the Manhattan project years before. They agreed to continue to meet on a regular basis.

Finally, as the black suits announced that their limos had arrived, the president asked, "Arnie didn't get an answer when he asked what to call this fucker. What do you think?" *Give them control over the little things.*

The CEO offered, "How about the Manhattan II Project?"

Someone else said, "Or maybe the *Case Perdida* Initiative. CPI, we could call it."

"I have a better idea," Bishop said, her face flushed. "We're speaking of a recruiting and training program here, aren't we? Essentially a new school system." She looked outside the window, where the pink-orange-reds of the Peace roses, the Mr. Lincolns, and the Darling Debutantes were all in full bloom. "How about the Rose Charter Schools, or the Rose Network?"

Arnie said, serious, "Perfect name, Christine. Perfect. Roses require fertilizer. Fertilizer, like bull shit. Roses show signs of promise. They're ubiquitous. They need care, the right soil to grow in." Christine nodded, now almost permanently immune to profanity.

"And have thorns," Pierpont reminded them. "Don't forget; they have thorns."

After they had gone, the president and Arnie were left to do the straightening up; no cleaning staff would see what they had created. Rolling up the flipcharts, bundling them into the fireplace and then lighting them along with the white birch bark logs.

"You're not keeping any of this?" asked the president. "Want to take the notes? Something this fucking big needs a written plan."

Smiling, Arnie reached into his briefcase, the tan, leather-bound gift from his wife on his fortieth, a large *AE* monogram in gold in the leather. "Here it is, boss," he said, tossing him a twenty-page document, watermarked *Highly confidential/POTUS eyes only*. "Just like you like it—background, resources invested, short and long-term outcomes, assumptions, costs."

The president, never really surprised by Arnie, raised his bushy eyebrows a millimeter or two, furthering an almost-affectionate bond. He had no sons, but this young man came close. Neither of them could guess the size and scope or the impact of the Rose School and its network, thorns and all.

35

LONDON. THE BRITISH MUSEUM. THURSDAY LATE MORNING

The huge white-vaulted dome looms over their heads, a giant inverted bowl.

Like the Eastern Market Rose School, it has at least one anomaly, the dirt- and age-darkened exoskeleton of a centuries-old building and an inner, bright-domed, modern court yard. It rises several stories above the neck-craning visitor, whispering, *Here is all the world's knowledge, under one roof, accessible to you all.* And if the message isn't conveyed by the dome, the Enlightenment Gallery—a two story, wood-lined football field filled with statues of discoverers, authors, poets, historians, philosophers, and their works—could arouse the intellectual curiosity of a brick.

The seduction of knowledge.

Dr. Al-Ansari's email said that she'd meet them in the Gallery Café, at the rear of the main lobby. *You'll spot me readily. I'm dressed traditionally,* it read.

"Traditionally" hardly does it justice. Apart from her eyes and hands, she is entirely covered. Her henna'd hands demonstrate long fingers, untended nails, evidence of anxiety-inflicted cuticle damage. Her *niqab or* veil, her *hijab,* her head scarf, her full length *abaya.* All black, the color of night, of the west, of death in the Mayan tradition.

Her eyes rivet them first. They are hungry, hiding. It's not just that they are virtually the only thing visitors see; they roam like two caged animals.

She is prompt, meeting them in the café at exactly eleven a.m. They feel their post-economy class state, their stale clothes, the less-than-crisp appearance broadcasting that they've spent the night in them.

"I am Dr. Al-Ansari. I am pleased to be able to help you," she says, her voice a thin flat line projecting from the microphone of her *niqab.* Her voice betrays no emotion, only her darting eyes permit some insight into who or what was inside the small black, shapeless statue. She leads them into the Gallery, the two story monument to the Age of Enlightenment. She stops at the bust of Voltaire, also a searcher for illumination. Culturally sensitive, Noah doesn't offer to shake her hand.

"Your colleague, Mr. Harry, was very clear about how important this was for the story you are working on." Her English is perfect, but it plays to Arabic music, the sibilant *s* drawn out, the sound of *er* broadened, widened. Noah and Kate both nod, looking for a table and chairs. Miriam's eyes fail to convey anything but fear. For his part, Noah feels the asexual, isolating burden of her dress. Kate, still reeling a bit from the attack at breakfast, feels nothing.

The Enlightenment Gallery sits quietly at the rear of the building, as though existing in another century. It is a miracle of discovery—of ancient Greek and Roman civilization, of the Middle Ages and their Renaissance, of statues of great minds, discoverers, navigators, inventors. For a minute, Noah thinks of the Great Minds Lectures of Georgetown and his once-best friend Pete, but he pushes the image underground, stored for another day. The age-stained oak display cabinets are abandoned half way up to make room for cream-colored walls and open spaces, perhaps making room for new knowledge. *What if,* Noah wonders, *the dark gives way to more dark?*

She doesn't say it, but the place of their meeting speaks to Miriam's needs. It's not the tiny office that her status dictates or the overcrowded Reading Room. This is somewhere in between.

"You know that DiShannia is dead, Dr. Al-Ansari?" Kate says, half statement, half question.

"Yes, Mr. Harry told me." She looks only at Noah; men occupy a higher rung of authority than someone like Kate.

"I was very sad to learn of her passing. She and I had never met, you know. We only Skyped and emailed each other, but I must say I was impressed with her enthusiasm and wide knowledge. She was very mature for her age." Noah feels her prejudice; she was about to say, *mature for an American girl.*

The gallery has recently added a few tables to create the feeling of a tea house, a move not without its critics. They find a small table in one corner. It's bigger than a medium pizza though; it'll do. Dr. Al-Ansari sits with her back to the wall, and holds what we might call a coffee table book on her lap like a precious six month old. She continues to scan the room with her eyeball radar. Noise and activity surround them—a small child spills his orange juice to his mother's disgust, people balance their drinks and scones, their backpacks, their travel brochures and maps on the tiny tables. To discuss something privately but in the open, it's perfect.

"Miriam, tell us how you and DiShannia…" Kate begins.

Miriam is miles ahead of her, interrupting Kate. She is in a hurry, unburdened by doubt. Though Kate has asked the question, Miriam continues to respond to Noah. "She reached out to me first, for a school project, she said. She got my name through someone at your Smithsonian. My doctoral dissertation was on the Mayan codices, you see." They did.

"It soon became apparent to me that she wanted to know much more than a simple high school project would require. She wanted to learn about Mayan writing and language, and about the Palenque Codex, my specialty."

"How did you become interested in Mayan culture?" Noah asked, the question he had asked of DiShannia, days before.

"Do you mean, why would a person of my culture and background become attracted to it?" Miriam replies, raising her face a little, a sliver of arrogance or self-pride showing itself. "You must understand that the Arab people were astronomers and mathematicians long before your *Western* civilization. In fact, there is evidence that the two cultures collaborated; their interests in astronomy occurred at about the same time."

"There have been many Arab astronomers who studied the movement of the moons or the sun. In what we now call Uzbekistan for example, there were highly developed astronomy schools and observatories, some of which appear to have used Mayan mathematical principles, although how this came about, we don't know. I too was immersed in this knowledge, and then became interested in comparing them to ancient American theories and science." She is not unkind; she is simply making a point. Their heads nod.

"I have brought this recent publication to illustrate what I will tell you. It is a wonderful compilation of images of the Mayan civilization. It shows their pyramids and temples, their way of life, the brilliant sarcophagus lid of Pakal the Great, and even very small carvings." She flips to the last third of the book, "And brilliant pictures of the codices. It was published before the final work on the Palenque Codex. I cannot show that codex to you of course since it is kept in our lower levels, in a humidity-controlled facility." She nods towards the floor, as though they might not know where the basement is.

Warming to her tiny audience, she shows them more, like a gardener displaying her favorite flowers, possibly roses. She flips through several pages. "Those who created the codices were highly valued by society. They were the scribes and painters, people who had a special talent for drawing and stone carving."

She is enjoying herself; this is *her* specialty, using a text book to illustrate its intricacies. The eyeball radar continues, searching, though more slowly.

"Each codex is an amazing piece of work, the product of months or effort. They are made from the inner bark of fig trees, or white birch, folded like old-fashioned screens, covered with layers of starch in a thin, white paste. Some of their writing used pictographs, figures were outlined with black ink made from coal, drawn with cactus thorns or bird bones and their details created with animal hair paintbrushes, using symbolic colors. There were other forms of writing, too, more like ours, using symbols to represent sounds; we call it alphanumeric. And a third kind, in which dots and squares and lines represent— well, we do not know what they represent. Here's an example," she opens the book to a strange object. To Noah, it looks like a warped QR code.

"Now, to the Palenque Codex itself," she says, leaning into the table, using her eyeball radar again. It's safe; the little orange juice vandal has vacated the table beside them. "The conquistadors burned most of the codices, except for a few. One of them was buried under the tomb of Pakal the Great in Palenque, and found its way here where it sat, untouched, for many years."

A young woman appears from behind Francis Bacon, the nearest statue, to take their order. Her mahogany hair is clearly the product of some Vidal Sassoon bottle. Tats almost completely cover her bare arms, as undecipherable as Mayan script. They order three teas; this morning's British coffee was, to say the least, a disappointment.

Noah says, "Talk to us about the other codices, Dr. Ansari." They've heard about them just yesterday from Wai-Ching, but this is a little test. She passes with flying colors.

"There were, until just recently thought to be three major ones. The oldest Mayan text we call the Dresden Codex, perhaps the most beautiful, the most complete of the three, and a marvel of information about medicine, about time and farming. It was badly damaged in World War II but as you can see," she finds a yellow stickie in the book, flips the page open, "it's been recreated rather well." Noah, an appreciator of stickies, smiles.

Mahogany-hair brings their tea.

"The second codex also has a very interesting history," she says, sipping her tea loudly, raising her niqab. "It was found in a garbage basket by a French scholar in 1859; we call it the Paris Codex." She continues to flip through the pages, finding another yellow page marker. "It refers to questions of ritual. Then," she says, "there is the Madrid Codex, which found its home in Spain. The text describes farming rituals.

"And that brings us to the fourth codex, the one that your DiShannia was interested in. The one I have worked on for almost two years. This one…" A tour group has entered the room. The radar eyeball intensifies for a beat, then, reassured, settles. She leans even closer to the table, placing her hands on the book, as though to protect something. From her lap, she produces a large manila envelope. "This one was uncovered by the team of Alberto Ruz Lhulier in 1935, a most amazing discovery I must say. It was discovered in the Yucatan, in Mexico," she reopens the book to show them a fold-out map, moving the tea cups slightly.

The room has begun to fill. The tour group is noisy, their guide using a small voice amplifier to communicate with her flock of elderly couples, from Israel or the US, each sporting a blue and white name tag that broadcasts, *Shalom, my name is…..* Just behind them are several families with small, sticky-fingered kids and one with a teenager who might, at any moment, die of boredom. There is a striking Swedish or Danish pair, tall, elegantly Nordic. Miriam's eyes widen, coming to rest on an odd, out-of-place group of Rastafarians, their dreadlocks either set free for the world to admire or piled high under yellow, red and green knit caps. Even more than the teenager, they seem uninterested in the dead people, the Alexander Popes and Francis Bacons. They are interested in the live ones.

Miriam continues in a softer voice. Looking around her, especially at the Rasties as they edge their way closer to their table. She adjusts her veil. Noah and

Kate lean in. She unwraps the figure-of-eight red string that holds the envelope shut, wary.

Now huddled together, she says, "These are pictures from the final codex and some other items I have collected. We were going to include them in the book, but our publishers suddenly changed their minds, saying we were still unsure of its provenance. It was at this point, when we were debating including these and other pictures, that DiShannia contacted me. She apparently watched the internet regularly for anything Mayan."

The pictures she places in front of them are striking. Even more graphic than the others, they remind Noah of an out-of-this-world adult cartoon book. There are pictures of the codex's pages—the sun, moons, planets. A mix of text, of pictures of kings and servants, of pageants and processions, and of sacrifice. It is a breathtaking creation, equally as well preserved and beautiful as the Dresden Codex. It is hard to imagine why it wouldn't be published with the others. Along with it, she shows them pages that DiShannia has scanned and sent to her— copies of the teenager's attempts at translation of Mayan into English, using the three kinds of writing.

Miriam says, "She said she thought of the writing in the codex as a kind of Rosetta Stone. What is strange is that, on her own, she duplicated translations I inherited from a predecessor many years before, a woman whose work has helped inform mine. She was a Miss O'Rourke. Here," Miriam says, pointing. "You can see where Shanny has begun to translate words, where she's written questions over pictures of Pakal's sarcophagus cover, and on pictures of the Codex itself."

"She is writing about things that the Maya and Arabs understood, Venus for example. Here," another point with a tiny tea spoon, "she writes about it crossing a constellation she translates as 'seven gods.' Here, she describes 'collapse.'

The Rastafarians have gotten to within a couple of meters of them, catching Miriam's eye.

"And so," she says, straightening her back, speaking more loudly, closing the book, surprising them. "I would like you to take this small gift, this book, to DiShannia's mother. Would you do that for me? And," she says, taking a pen from her sleeve, "I should like to write a small dedication to DiShannia, inside the front cover. She was truly a remarkable person."

She writes in the book, then presses it into Kate's hands, a gift or a curse. Softly she says, "Read this when you have left the museum."

It is true that DiShannia was a remarkable person, but it is no dedication.

36

THE WASHINGTON ZOO. WASHINGTON. DC. 2003-2010

Thy were twins, she was sure.

The one on the left was a boy, in blue shorts and a powder blue muscle top, a tiny miniature of the ones teenagers wear, maybe not so appropriate (*It's too chilly for that outfit*, she thought). The same size, in pink of course. The same smile, the same rounded, placid oval of her face, the same hair as her brother, blonde on the way to something darker. Twins, maybe. Each of them was tucked into the concrete giant **ZOO** sign at the entrance, the boy sitting inside the left squared-off 'O', the girl on the right. Their dad and mom taking copious pictures, parent-paparazzi.

This wasn't her first visit to the zoo, or more precisely the National Zoological Park, Washington's zoo, the equivalent of every other national capital's attempt at capturing and displaying the wildlife of the world for its inhabitants. Perhaps acceptable a hundred years ago, but increasingly less so. It *was* a nice park, though.

Her visits had started years before when she was able to watch a younger woman push a baby in a stroller. The visits were pre-arranged, sometimes through a third person, sometimes by a cryptic phone call, "I'll put the laundry out at ten-thirty Saturday morning. Yes, the usual place." It became a familiar, hesitant pattern. The younger woman and the baby would walk slowly by the older lady a few times, allowing the baby to be seen but never touched or spoken to. Later, when the boy was a toddler, the younger woman would walk by, holding the boy by his hand, watching the animals, pointing them out to him in the classic parental gesture of zoos. This allowed the older woman to stand beside them, sometimes talking quietly to the boy. Finally, when he was five, the boy was allowed to sit beside the older woman, like a casual encounter.

It was anything but.

A close observer might have noticed that both women were hyper-alert. Each would watch the other visitors in the park as though searching for someone, protecting the other, certainly as though they were guarding the boy.

More meaningful visits started when he was six or seven, able to carry a conversation. An only child, he was precocious in a world in which adults were almost his sole companions. This was his mother's friend, someone he could call Auntie. Later, as he grew, he was allowed to meet her on his own. Once, near Christmas, they took in something called "Zoolights" on a surprisingly warm December evening when the cages, pathways, and trees were illuminated. It was one of their favorite visits. Later, an almost-teen, she took him across the street to a restaurant. They sat at the back, facing outwards towards the street and the square **ZOO** sign.

When he was little, he thought that she lived at there. Realizing that was a silly idea ("Where? In the cages?" his friends mocked him) he asked her, only to be told that she was a volunteer and had gotten to know him and his mother over several years.

Auntie had a habit of surprising him, commenting on how well he had done in school, a prize in mathematics for example. He wondered how she knew some of those things, but, in the egocentric world of the child, assumed that his achievements were common knowledge. Occasionally, she'd comment on his looks. "You're growing into a handsome young man," she'd say nonchalantly, molding his self-esteem.

The nonchalance hid a huge sea of emotion, running with deep currents, debris from a lifetime of running and hiding, memories of abuse and unrequited longing. Or unrequited for the most part. When she commented on his looks, she thought only of one man, the man she called Mathison.

He was known by his other names to the outside world of course, but they had decided on using their middle names in correspondence and when they were, all too infrequently, together. He had said, "Middle names are appropriate, d-dear. They're hidden, rather inside us, rather central." And so she became Margaret; he was Mathison. His looks, skipping a generation, had landed, squarely if not perfectly, on the boy. It was mostly in the dark eyes, although his straight, flat hair resembled the older man too. Rebellious strands persistently blocked his vision, until he learned the magic of gel. When he was fifteen, on their last visit, he looked at her from Mathison's deep set sockets, with Mathison's almost-black eyes, the ironic twinkle locked inside them by the magic of genes.

It was chilly that last day, the chill both inside and outside.

She had decided to spoil herself.

For years she had stayed at cheap, out-of-the way hotels, always using an alternative name when she registered, the Day's Inn several blocks away for example. But this weekend she splurged on the Marriott Woodley Park, in an upgrade of all things, in what the brochure had called a queen-suite. None of her early fears about being followed, or that the boy and his mother would be traced to her, had materialized. And so, today, when he was a teenager and she well past seventy, they decided to meet at the Panda House and have a coffee at the zoo's Starbuck's. Coffee was a mark of his impending adulthood, with a woman at that. He hadn't told his friends, knowing they'd make fun. He hadn't said a word to his mother; this visit was his secret. He had even saved enough money to make it his treat.

The freezing temperatures had cut their visit short. Bo-Bo the panda, now a year since he had come from China, was as lazy as ever, chewing on a bamboo and eucalyptus salad, reclining on his rock couch as though he were watching a boring television program. Shortly, they decided to leave the zoo, finding their way to two grande-sized lattes. He told her several school stories—about a funny teacher, an escapade of one of his friends, a girl he liked, what he wanted to do at college and beyond (he was conflicted). He could tell her anything. He loved his mother, but she was busy, overly occupied by her agendas and expectations, and by her anxiety. His father was absent for the most part. But this woman was deeply interested; even in his decade and a half view of the world, he knew she loved him.

On that day, she was not alone in her interest.

The Starbuck's store manager had been told there would be a "random inspection" that day, someone arriving for a periodic inspection. A man wearing the darkly pinched face of the refugee arrived at noon, examined the books, helped out behind the counter, checked the supplies, reviewed the employee attendee records. Took extra care with the two cups that the older woman and the teenager left behind, using napkins to put them in his back pack, like priceless artifacts. He was a stranger to them; they were not strange to him.

He was also a photographer. He paused to take several pictures of them in the front window, using a surprisingly tiny camera, stepping outside to get a better picture of the boy, lit by the mid-day sun. It was a shame that neither of them got to see the pictures, the only record of their last visit.

Their goodbyes—after the short lattes and longer conversation—acquired a special poignancy for her. As she turned to walk back to her hotel, she wondered if she would see him again. Several weeks before, she had discovered a lump, secreted in a place where neither she nor anyone else except her family doctor had visited. It had grown in the way of its species, a sort of small Trojan horse, quietly spreading, unheralded by pain as it spread into her lymph channels, into her nodes and lungs, announcing itself by tiny specks of blood in her tissues when she coughed in the morning. She knew enough medicine that she wasn't surprised when the doctor gave her the diagnosis, showing her the x-ray pictures himself. She supposed that viewing them was like being exposed to a kind of pornography, that she'd be embarrassed and ashamed.

She was neither. If anything, she felt liberated.

It mattered little now if she were discovered. The secret that she bore inside her—secrets, plural—would die with her. She had led a life exactly as Mathison would have wanted. She wanted only to see the boy thrive, the young man who had occupied so much of her waking imagination and her nightly dreams. She was proud of his mother of course, but especially of him. She extracted nuggets of satisfaction from the thought that he might carry more than just Mathison's external characteristics. She hoped he might have inherited some of his internal ones as well—his patience, his humanity, his humor. His ability to love. His puzzle-solving brilliance.

Although she had survived much in her life, the cancer proved a particularly resilient enemy, beyond her skills, well past the meager weapons carried by the physicians and oncologists of the day. No zoo could hold this monster. In only a few, pain-shortened months, she succumbed.

Although she thought of the boy frequently, she had no idea that he might in fact have that last brilliant quality, or that, like Mathison's before him, it might save the world.

Though not in a way that anyone could have imagined.

37

TOTTENHAM COURT UNDERGROUND, LONDON, ENGLAND, WEDNESDAY AFTERNOON

MEET ME 3PM IN THE TOTTENHAM COURT ROAD UNDERGROUND, PLATFORM 2, the book's inscription says, in a perfect, neat hand, one that broadcasts nothing of Miriam's anxiety.

Kate and Noah fill the three hours. They immerse themselves in a small room in the museum, a sad reduction of Mayan life and culture into four square meters, learning nothing new, only deepening the mystery of the collapse. They risk a call to Harry but can't reach him. Finally, they find their way to the Underground station, its circle and line symbol as memorable as any icon on the globe. This particular station has a long and distinguished history, its platform walls marked by mosaic tile patterns that the Maya would recognize, and that were based on sketches made decades earlier, some of the drawings signed, "MCO'R."

The station is a small node in London's subway system, one of the world's great organisms. Daily, a million people pass through it like some giant alimentary system, bustling up and down the rapidly-moving escalators, pushing their way onto and off of crowded subway cars. Taking risks. Human parts of a living, underground world.

Not unlike Kate and Noah.

They take the skinny escalator to the second level down, finding Platform Two. A few minutes late when she arrives, Miriam's eyeball radar is even more at play, with cause: there are disapproving stares from some people on the platform, visual reminders of rampant anti-Islamist sentiment. She ignores them, as she has most of her recent Western life; they are not what worry her. From under her *abaya,* she takes the manila envelope she showed them earlier and hands it to them, explaining again, needlessly, that they contain important pictures of the Palenque Codex and its messages. Kate places the enveloped carefully into her bag, beside the book on Mayan culture.

"DiShannia had part of this, but not *all* of it. You must take it, now," she says, urgency in her voice.

Kate is puzzled, "But why, Miriam? This is your work!"

Her look stops them cold. "It is, but I am forbidden officially to go on with it. Today, after I met you, the director told me that all funding on the Palenque Codex project ends this week." She is clearly distraught, small wells of her tears just visible, in fact almost all that is visible. But defiant, too. "He offered no reason, no more than the publisher who wouldn't publish. But I have made copies of what's in the envelope and I *will* publish the material!"

Miriam, relieved of the package, gathers her *abaya* around her, a symbol of her strength. *I will go on,* the gesture says. She makes an unusual request. "Will you take my picture? It's important." She moves to a spot on the platform, standing beside an elaborate mural done in the Mayan style, using small, inlaid pieces of colored and black and white tile. It's a strange marriage of Byzantium and the Yucatan, of the Arab and Mayan worlds. Of the modern and the ancient. Of the past and the future.

"Please. I will stand here." She is quite insistent, raises her hand as though to demonstrate one piece of the mural. Noah takes the picture with his iPhone, then a second one, a tourist thing.

Four Rastafarians appear at the far end of the platform. They are the same men from the Museum, hours before, their colorful caps visible above the heads of other passengers. They move quickly towards them, as Kate grabs Noah's arm, stage-whispering, "Those men from the museum? They're here! I think we should take Miriam and leave."

As she turns, she notices two others at the far end of the platform, and something even more frightening. The two are carrying knives, and the crowd has dispersed, like animals seeking shelter before a storm. One young mother has headed immediately for the exit, shepherding her young son and a baby stroller up the escalator, moving quickly. The others huddle against the walls where Kate has wisely left her bag. Noah, Kate and Miriam face the Rastafarians, seemingly alone on a tiny unsafe island.

They come closer, obviously challenging them. "No Muslims here, no Muslims here!" they chant. Strangely, they sound more Arab than Jamaican.

Noah, finding bravery—and anger—not far beneath his skin, confronts the leader, "She's with us, buddy. Leave us alone!" He's rewarded by a powerful knee to the groin and a large hand grabbing his neck, pushing him to the ground. Two of them kick him with boots the size of anvils, then hold him down, pinning his arms. He is furious, struggling against their hatred.

Kate also tries to protect Miriam but is held back by one of the men, probably double her size and triple her strength. She watches in horror as two of the remaining youths hassle Miriam, issuing a string of anti-Muslim slurs. From one of them, she hears, "You got a veil on your cunnie too, bitch?"

"Ignore them!" Kate yells, as though that were possible.

But the horror has just begun.

The two remaining men pick up their tiny black-clad parcel, an easy chore despite her screaming. As a train approaches, they throw her—past the yellow *Mind the Gap* line, past the last few cracked floor tiles, past the fragile boundary between life and death—into the wide black mouth of the subway track, and into the gory maw of this universe.

In the last seconds, as she flies through the air, free of their hands, her *niqab* flies up, revealing her face for the first time. Her mouth, framed by a surprisingly red lipstick, shapes a giant "O," a scream drowned by the roar of the train.

And then, in seconds, the Rasties, or possibly the pseudo-Rasties, are gone. When someone rushes to use the pay phone, seconds later, he discovers that the cord has been cut, severed by a tall Nordic couple.

In less than two minutes, they are all gone. Kate and a bruised Noah are left with only the memory of a scream and the incredible sound of the too-fast-to-stop train, a memory replayed in their minds and nightmares over the weeks to come, unbidden and unwanted. As they grab her bag and rush to leave, they're left with the horror of what they've seen and of course the questions: *Who killed her? Why? What does this have to do with her work? With her being told to stop it?*

Not all knowledge, or the answers to their questions, is contained under the dome of the British Museum.

38

CERN, GENEVA–MEYERIN, SWITZERLAND, THURSDAY–FRIDAY

At first, they think only to flee the subway pursued by more immediate questions. *How many others were involved? Would the police detain Kate and Noah? Would it help if they had stayed?* The terror-filled minutes settle into something more controllable when they exit the Tottenham Court station, past the bobbies running down the stairs, past the crowds streaming from the station, past the screaming sirens, past the *Station Now Closed* sign.

Instead, running across the street, they think only to call Harry like teenagers stranded far from home. Hiding inside a pub entrance—The Flying Horse—they use the app. In minutes, they connect with Harry, still at home, and in a further minute of electronic wizardry, with Gerry. Even in the tiny app-picture, relief is evident on Kate and Noah's faces. Gerry and Harry are both appalled at Miriam's death and fall into a heated discussion about what it means for the investigation. Two little faces on Noah's phone argue with each other about its significance. "It could be connected," Gerry says, "not just a random act aimed at Muslims."

Harry is not so sure. "The Brits don't have much love for Islam, you know," he says with surprising heat. Kate and Noah are certain Gerry's right; they were there after all. In the rush of the moment, they forget to ask Gerry where he was for hours.

Guys, *guys!*" Noah interrupts. "This is no hate crime. They were in the museum earlier today, sniffing around Miriam and us, looking for her. She had something that they wanted!" And now Noah and Kate have it.

But there is another argument: should Kate and Noah stay and turn their information over to the British Police? It generates more words bouncing back and forth from satellites to earth, from fear to certainty. Harry is firm. "Bloody hell, whatever you do, Kate and Noah, don't go to the police! What you have? The envelope? The pictures? Maybe other materials? Those're integral to the story, to DiShannia's death. You show up at the coppers' door, those'll be the first thing they'll want. And they'll keep you, interview you. Plus, you know, what can you really *do* at this stage?"

The argument, simultaneously as heavy as death and light as words, wins Kate over.

They hail a cab to Heathrow, running late. They jump the queue in the security line, barely managing to catch their flight to Geneva. They make it, drained but safe. Kate, exhausted by the long flight yesterday and the horror of today manages to sleep at takeoff, but wakens with a shudder and moan, crying out. Noah reaches to comfort her. Over the years, he's been able to build up mental muscle, a sort of immunity to the trauma of the afternoon: tragedy and loss have hardened him.

Or so he thinks.

There is an irony in CERN, the European Center for Nuclear Research. It lies in the image of a circle, the Large Hadron Collider, a seventeen mile-across tunnel laying hundreds of meters underground, like a giant ring. *You can start wherever you like,* the irony whispers, *but you'll always return to the same place.*

For Kate and especially for Noah, that place is DiShannia.

The LHC finds its home beneath ground that others would recognize as French and Swiss. It lies closest to Geneva, Switzerland, but its headquarters are actually a few kilometres away, in the village of Meyrin. Constructing the LHC was a feat of mental, physical and impossible-to-visualize science. It operates like some fantastical hammer, the world's largest and most complex scientific instrument, smashing particles together at almost the speed of light, studying the fundamental building blocks of nature. The process provides insights into the laws of the universe, into the Big Bang, into the structure and function of subatomic particles. Into the universe as a whole, its beginning and ending. Simple matters compared to DiShannia's death and its tentacles.

One of its principals, Ivaan Horkonen, is a Russian-Finnish genius, one of the twelve principles of CERN. Some call them the Apostles, though who is the Christ figure in that imagery is uncertain.

The little desk-sign says *Pat Maisonneuve*. Not Patricia. Not Patrice, a natural, given her Francophone looks, her dark hair and elegant figure. Just plain Pat. She is not, however, plain.

She stands away from her desk filing papers in a surprisingly dated, almond-colored file cabinet when they enter the room. She shuts the drawer, a thumping metallic *click* the only sound in the room.

Harry has organized the meeting with her boss, Dr. Horkonen.

"You must be Monsieur Scott and Mademoiselle Forest, am I correct?" she asks, her voice husky. She moves her auburn hair away from her forehead, like lace curtains in a breeze. It's an elaborately feminine gesture. "You were to meet Professor Horkonen, but he," she smiles, engaging them, "is giving a public lecture this morning." She says, "publeek lec-ture" with such Gallic grace and charm that Noah smiles.

"He says," picking up her phone to read the message, her long fingers caressing the case, "that you are free to join him there. He will be about one hour, perhaps more. He *loves* the public lectures." Her mouth loves the word "love."

Another smile, this one a little bigger, framed by red-red lipstick, Revlon's *Honeymoon Cerise Number 109*. "It is your choice."

She takes more files, turns to put them away, an extravagant, deliberate gesture, allowing her guests to view her upper body and—as she stands—her miniskirt and beautiful legs. Finished her task, she sits in one sultry motion, lowering her bottom onto the chair. In another setting, this would be a sexual act. There is a small aberration in the picture however: her too-feminine gestures are practiced, almost choreographed.

At one time, Pat was Patrick.

Despite all that is in Noah's head, he would like to stay to interview her, but there's an urgency in the need to see Dr. Horkonen. Pat peels a little map from a pad and shows it to them, using her red fingernail to trace where they need to go.

"You are here," she tells them, all business now, "in the main administrative building. You will please to take the monorail entrance on the second floor; it will get you to the new Sky Tower. There, take the elevator to the top floor, to the Cosmos Auditorium. Dr. Horknonen will be lecturing there. It started perhaps five minutes ago." *Meen-oots.*

The monorail, built just last year, looks strangely dated, outpaced by the advances that occur daily in the tunnels hundreds of meters below it. It connects the main buildings with a new feature, the Sky Tower, mimicking Seattle's Space Needle. In an attempt to woo more support from the European Union and its fractious parliament, a wealthy donor built the tower as an attraction, a symbol of high hopes and easy-to-understand science. The regular public lectures have the same goal, explaining the complex theories and experiments that are CERN's daily bread. The funding drive has worked; donors have contributed. The names of only some of them are public knowledge.

It takes a few minutes of waiting while the elevator swallows its mandatory load of ten tourists per ride, rising silently to the top floors, passing through a glass enclosure that allows them a view of Meyrin, the countryside and Geneva. They emerge into a gift shop full of tiny space needles and coffee cups decorated with atoms, and find the Cosmos Auditorium. It's the circular, temporary home of just over fifty people, roughly divided into two age groups—teenagers painfully assigned to a field trip, and white haired tourists. Three teens, in glasses and writing in notebooks, occupy the front row, separate from the others.

The designers of the auditorium were clear in their intentions: the red carpet and light mahogany paneling instill a solid confidence in the presentations; dark red cushioned seats intend to comfort; and the curved, arching ceiling invokes heaven. In case there's any doubt about the last feature, stars are mimicked by hundreds of tiny small halogen lights.

Dr. Horkonen has just started, using slides, another not-so-modern technology, illustrating the origins of the universe. He's addressing the question, "How do we know the universe is expanding?" If nothing else, the topic, and the plush seat cushions, reassures them. They're in the right place. It's a relief after worries about collapsing solar systems for the last four days.

Has it only been four days?

Dr. Horkonen occupies the small stage at the front, elevated by a foot or two, enjoying his position. He is a bear of a man, well over six feet tall, his gray hair trimmed in a military-style brush cut, his large hands virtual paws. He dwarfs a small table on the dais in front of him; it holds a pitcher of water and a small glass.

BAM!

He slams his hand palm-down on the table in front of him, almost sending the pitcher and glass into a shattered death on the floor. Kate jumps, the trauma of the last twenty-four hours still with her. Noah steadies her.

"What was that?" he asks the teenagers in the front row. It's a rhetorical question.

"That was my little imitation of the Big Bang. And it was *nothing* compared to what really happened. For one thing my slapping the table was very long, and for another, it had no matter in it." However pale an imitation, it garners attention.

"Almost two centuries ago, a Belgian priest named Lemaitre described what we now call Big Bang, thinking that universe began from a single atom. He was right, but you must not to think of Big Bang as an explosion in usual way." He fixes on the teenage group, stares at them for a second, watches them magically come to life. "No, universe did not expand *into* space, as space did not exist before then; it *created* space. Also time. There was, how to say, a *moment.* Since then space itself has been stretching, carrying matter and time along with it. We also know that universe cooled as it expanded, forming matter, all very quickly. For example a second after Big Bang," he slaps the table again, "universe was filled with the particles we study here at CERN—neutrons, protons, electrons, anti-electrons, photons and neutrinos." He shows them several slides representing the early expansion of the universe, the creation of the particles.

Another slide asks, "Is the universe continuing to expand?"

Horkonen, the bear, turns to his audience, "The answer is 'yes.' How do we know this? Theory is supported by observations made from watching light from planets and stars, light which shifts to red side of spectrum, meaning that stars are moving *away* from us. This is Doppler Effect; it exists in the world of light as much as it does in sound." His Russian-Finnish mind continues to eliminate the English "the," a nuisance word at the best of times.

"You might ask, quite rightly, 'What might happen in future?'" In a way, it is *the* question. "You might think universe is full of matter and matter means gravity and that should halt the expansion, shouldn't it?" The teenagers nod.

He smiles, "Well, you're wrong!"

"Do not feel badly, please. Many scientists have been wrong too! Indeed, stars are moving *away* from our solar system, even speeding up. Maybe there is force stronger than gravity that causes stars to move away? This is so: we have named that force dark energy. To balance that, we call other property of space dark matter. Why do we call it dark? It gives off no light, so it's not in form of stars and planets that we see. And so, we have created a theory with two entities —dark matter which holds the universe back and dark energy, which makes it expand."

There is more, a cornucopia of nebulae, of new galaxies, old, collapsing stars. Of planets not in the solar system. Of light so ancient, he says, that it represents the very earliest creations, billions of years old, just after *the* Big Bang.

A minor miracle has happened: none of the teens are on their cell phones. There are nods in the audience, the slow comprehension of an invisible subject, followed by questions. Most begin with *How*? *What*? No one asks *Why*? Only I know the answer.

The three front-row students, their interest overcoming their outward reticence, have most of the questions.

Finally, the auditorium clears; across the red-carpeted distance, the speaker spots his visitors.

"Dr. Horkonen," Kate begins the introductions.

The bear is chillier up close. He radiates disinterest, like a refrigerator whose door has been left open. A cropped salt-and-pepper beard has wrapped itself around his face like an aggressive moss, a moustache plummeting from his lip sideways, two matching linear marks indicating disdain for those with lower IQs, namely everyone on the planet, including two American reporters. His handshake covers their hands—Kate's tiny one especially—with cold palms, squeezing out a microgram of welcome.

"We understand that you've been corresponding with a young woman in the States, DiShannia Johns," Noah says. A small smile lights Horkonen's face momentarily, killed by the next sentence. "Sadly, she was murdered this week, and much of her work has been taken, right after she received the Presidential Award in Science. We think her murder has something to do with her project...."

Horkonen absorbs the news, his face darkens, sad at first, briefly angry, then settling, uncommitted, to its neutral posture. He is after all, a Finn; he will not give himself away on a first visit. Noah's time with Aija has reassured him that this is a national personality trait. Noah says, "We've come to find out what you might know about her. It might help us solve her murder."

Kate tries a different tack, softly, lace against his steel. "We know from her emails and phone contacts that you were in touch. We're hoping you could help us understand why she might have been murdered." If his manner was meant to be intimidating, it wasn't working on Kate. "She was bludgeoned to death, I'm sorry to say."

His eyes widen slightly, absorbing, "bludgeoned."

"You will forgive me," he says. "My first thought, was, you *Americans*, you have such a high murder rate that I am not at all surprised. She was just another black person, am I right?" Stressing *another black person*, saying what the rest of the world thinks about America. He reaches behind him to take a drink from the glass on the little table. His hand shakes slightly.

Finishing the water, he says, "I apologize for anti-American sentiment. There *is* much more going on here?" It's not a question.

"I feel so sorry for Shanny. She was quite remarkable. I regret I never got to meet her in person, but we talked frequently on the Skype. I have all her emails you know. She was so full of the life and excitement. We had talked about," a momentary sadness pauses his speech, "a scholarship for her to study with me. She had fine mind in general, but also very highly developed *mathematical* mind. I do not often see such. She saw connections in complex equations that very few could imagine, let alone describe. Even *I* could not see some of connections she made."

His face is still unmoving, but his speech is more sympathetic. He asks, "How much do you know of what we worked on together?" The refrigerator door closes; it's warmer in the room.

Kate says, "We only have the poster and a portion of her electronic files to go on."

"*Well,*" he says, "What do you think we can accomplish here today? What is it would help you most, do you think? You've traveled a distance and I can give you," looking at his watch, "next hour. We can meet in main office." Impeccable English, despite that little problem with "the."

On the monorail ride back to his office, he points out the buildings of CERN. They glide over CERN's giant, inverted U-shaped laboratories, the wooden-slatted half-dome administrative building, a new amphitheater and exhibit hall. Over the parched grass, burn marks from the last mid-European grass fires. Spontaneous, frightening.

A march through security protocols that puts WashPO's puny electronic moats to shame. Ivaan unlocks his office with a palm and eye scan. He glances at his watch, showing them a small couch, a holdover from Ikea, and two matching chairs sporting an impossible design, surprisingly comfortable. "She reached to me two years ago through a mutual colleague at George Washington University. Her science teacher made this connection, but it was apparent that her areas of research and interest were beyond my friend's expertise. It was at first by email came introduction, and then in a Skype interview and in subsequent emails."

There is a tap on the door. Pat enters, whispering something in Horkonen's ear. "You will excuse me a minute, please, I have experiment to oversee."

His absence allows them to check their iPhones and the app. There is good news from Harry on one front: he's been able to use the Mayan language guide to break the password, giving him access to more files. He's working on several at the moment, hoping to have something more for them soon. Under his breath, Noah comments, "It must be five a.m." And there's an update from Gerry. They can't determine if any of the deaths of Rose School students over the past five years have been anything but what they appear to be—on the record, they are random accidents or killings. But, *I'm working on it,* his text says. A little happy-face emoticon appears with a moustache, typical Gerry. There's no word on Naomi.

Horkonen returns, his face flushed. "There is small problem with our experiment. We delay until after lunch. This is no matter. It allows us more time to discuss Shanny. Come." He says, now gesturing for them to join him around his desk, filled with the scholarly detritus of most academics. They snug up to him, dwarfed by his oversize presence. Beefy fingers fly over the keyboard. The giant computer has three flat screens, one for each of them.

"Here, I will show you our correspondence." He scrolls through emails on one of the screens, "Here DiShannia shows interest in Mayan predictions of a collapse of Venus and solar system, all nonsense of course. I was never able to move her away from her theories but it got her interested in cosmology and beginnings of universe. And that is what mattered. Well...." His voice becomes less crisp.

$$\Gamma = \frac{\varepsilon}{\mu}$$

He points to the second screen. "Here are recent conversations. You perhaps do not recognize them as such. They are discussions about a complex formula, well beyond her, about rate of expansion of the universe. I did not expect her to understand it, or you. I only show it to say how advanced she was."

Noah looks closely at the screen. It is a complex series of letters, numbers and Greek symbols, filling almost the whole screen. "Explain it to me, Ivaan," he says, becoming too familiar and too pressing in one sentence. "Just explain the symbols, I mean." Horkonen, hiding his skepticism behind the impossible Finnish mask, fights to hide his condescension; there is no way Noah will understand this.

"It is basically about rate of expansion of the universe—r—based on our analysis of red shift I described earlier in public lecture. The forces which drive it forward we call dark energy, symbolized by Greek letter epsilon, ε. Second, there are forces holding expansion back, made up of weight of all planets and objects in the universe and more, what we call dark matter. We call this mu or μ. Of course, if r is positive then universe is expanding. If it is negative, then contracting. There are many other elements in this equation of the expansion/contraction equation but this is its core. Do you see?"

He's right, the screen is packed with other symbols and numbers, but the three essential elements stand out as though they are in boldface to Noah. To Kate and Horkonen's eyes, Noah simply stops, transfixed. His eyes focus only on the screen. There is a full minute of study in which Noah leans closer to the screen, asks Ivaan to explain several additional symbols.

For Noah, it is a strange event. The room drops away, its floor and furniture vanishing for him. Even Kate and Ivaan disappear and others—in the room, in the building, in his life—cease to exist. If he were a composer, he would have heard individual notes, then melodies, then a symphony. Instead, he sees literally a universe of numbers and equations, of balances and checks. Of possibilities. No less surprised than Horkonen, Noah understands at least the basic meaning of what he sees.

At length, still immersed in the equations, Noah questions their host. "What if r is wrong, Ivaan? You've worked backwards. The real equation has three unknowns, doesn't it? You act as though you know what r is, based on your assumptions about red shift, but you don't really. And based on those calculations, you've built arguments for the weight of dark matter, the inward-driving force, and dark energy, the outward-pushing force? Is that possible? What if your spectral analysis, your analysis of red shift, how you've calculated the expansion of the universe, is wrong? That would change all of this, wouldn't it?"

The expression on Horknonen's face, unmoving until now, shifts slightly. His eyes widen, in part surprised, in part taking in a wider view of the world— one in which others are as bright as he. Slowly, the ground under him providing a small tectonic shift in his world view, he responds, "Is what DiShania believed also. And yet, Doppler shift and our observations say that universe continues to expand. So you are assuming there is something wrong with this calculation, is it not?" Noah points to calculations of red shift, complex numbers and equations. He is lost in their jungle for a minute, possibly longer. At length, as though wakening from a sleep, Noah manages a single word.

"Yes."

"May I ask question, Dr. Scott?" Horkonen is puzzled, massaging his beard. "Where did you get your training? You are one of only handful of people who can understand this equation. Myself, I have studied this field for years to fully evolve what you have grasped in just over," he checks his watch, precision his only refuge, "ten minutes."

"I have no idea, Ivaan," Noah responds frankly. It is another mystery. It lives in two places—in the stars of course, but also in the genes.

39

CASTEL ST'ANGELO, TUSCANY, ITALY,
MARCH 21, 2000

R udy was perplexed. Usually it was His Holiness in the rear seat of the limousine, the Holy Father, John Paul II. The Pope was on a tour of the Middle East however; Israel was today.

Instead, the elderly man with the high-security briefcase and the copious almost-white hair was receiving royal treatment. Well, papal treatment. He was seated in the rear of the Holy Father's own limousine, armed with several bottles of water and a drop down desk guarded by four outriding motorcycles positioned as if His Holiness were the passenger—two ahead, two behind. The road was the same serpentine Tuscan highway slicing through the hills like butter.

This passenger was the product of an early morning briefing by Monsignor Diamonte, the assistant deputy camerlingo, who thrust a picture of the man into Rudy's hands. Holding it the timid light of the garage, Rudy could just make out the white hair, the bland, self-satisfied smile and the rosy/pink complexion. It screamed *Englishman* at Rudy.

Clearing his throat, mustering his inner tour guide, Rudy began, "*Signore*, most people, even many Italians, think that the Castel is only the summer home of the popes, a kind of spa and summer retreat." Extra vowels peppered the sentences like heavy confetti. Paulson just hoped the roses weren't in bloom. "We are going to the residence, the Apostolic Palace. Many are surprised it is not Italian. I mean, it is a property of the Holy See, not part of Italy itself." His passenger nodded, whether from fatigue or interest was debatable.

Minutes ago, he had unlocked the battered leather briefcase, using today's code (Neville Chamberlain's birthday preceded by the word COWARD—someone's warped sense of humor at work). And now, partly to distract himself, partly to send a message to the annoying driver-cum-guide, he had begun to move papers from his brief case to the seat beside him, spreading them like large playing cards, jokers perhaps. They were in an old yellowed file: memos about Lorenzo, hand-written notes about the death of Alan Turing, typed records of the Church and its astronomers. Evidence of efforts, all failed, to find Mary Catherine O'Brien. Newer elements about the surprising rise of so-called Rose Schools in the United States. And, the oldest of all, a special fifty-year-old memo, a handwritten, "Farewell, Paulson, keep up the good work!" from his ally and colleague, Winston Churchill.

Earlier in the week, after all of this had lain quiet for years, there was a call from the current prime minister, a man half the age and a quarter of the intelligence of Churchill. It was a call which dragged him out of retirement and into the back of a papal limousine.

The PM said, "Something's going on over there, Paulson. I don't like the sniff of it. Care to go over and have a peek, old man? You're the only one who knows how all the pieces fit. It's all about this tired notion of the planets collapsing onto the earth or something. You've had the file for so long, you're the only man for the job. You will go as my official representative, won't you?" He hung up, not waiting for an answer.

There *was* no answer except, "Yes, sir!" when the PM or the palace called. So here he was, slicing his way through the Italian countryside, driven by a short, pudgy, middle-aged Italian who apparently had no turn-off button.

And he was increasingly uncomfortable.

"How much longer, driver?" Paulson asked, increasingly aware of the need to urinate. He had been rushed from the plane, hustled into the back seat of the limousine, had to pee for over an hour. "Fifteen minutes, *Signore*," came the tour guide's answer.

About fourteen unbearable minutes too long, Paulson thought. "Driver, just pull over and I'll use the side of the road. It's still early; no one will notice." Stopping was no little production; the motorcycles had to pull over too.

Rudy rotated his ungainly paunch to the left as he swung open his door and then the passenger's behind him. Paulson's impatience was as full as his bladder however; he had already exited the right side of the car, was standing on the roadside untangling his blasted zipper. The little choreography left both rear doors open at precisely the same time, inviting a gust of too-hot wind to scatter Paulson's papers onto the road—several dozen of them, each marked *Eyes Only*.

Rudy rushed his overweight body to bend and retrieve the papers. Thankfully the early morning held little traffic. His efforts to place the papers in some semblance of order required him to at least look at the page numbers. As he was counting, bent over, using the rear seat lights, he looked up to see his passenger peering into the car from the opposite side, his eyes scolding.

"What did you see, driver? Did you look at the pages?" Paulson asked with some urgency.

"I, I didn't actually *read* them, sir," Rudy stammered, "but I did see the headings, and the watermark. I was trying to re-arrange them. I am so sorry." A cascade of apologies followed—about the door opening, about not asking whether the visitor needed the bathroom earlier.

"No matter. Here," Paulson said, annoyance bubbling just below the surface. *So like Englishmen*, thought Rudolfo; *an explosion would have been better.* "Give them to me." And he proceeded to re-arrange them himself, moving across the seat, slamming the door behind him.

The rest of the trip was spent in silence, Rudy questioning what he had seen, the white-haired gentleman counting the pages marked *The Turing Affair/UPDATE/HIGHLY SECRET.* None were missing, thankfully. He scanned the headings: *Recent Findings Confirm Turing Hypothesis, Venus-Earth-Moon Axis Shifts,* and the most damaging of them, *Sun-Earth Distance Shortening.* They were not the only mysteries though.

None of the papers gave him a clue about what this meeting was about—the sniff of this place.

40

CERN. GENEVA-MEYRIN. SWITZERLAND. FRIDAY

I never went beyond college calculus," says Noah, puzzled, his eyes darkening.

"Nothing in the university, in medical school? In journalism? Then, how…?" Horkonen doesn't finish the question. Kate finds another face of Noah, her brow darkening, wondering.

"I have no idea," Noah says. "It just seems, well, intuitive," nodding to the computer screen with the scrolling equations, the rows of numbers and brackets, the *epsilons, mus* and *rhos*. "Once you explained the legend, I was fine. If you're surprised that I know this, then that makes two of us."

Three if you count Kate.

"You know," Ivaan says, his furry question marks lowering, "it was this way with Shanny too. She wanted to know equations, what they meant, to know theory. DiShannia had even less training than you I expect, although she was advanced in high school…." The sentence dies, killed by Ivaan's growing awareness of the degree of loss they have suffered, and—a new sensation for him—his own confusion. The real world has offered him very little in the way of tangible puzzles, only the theoretical.

There is suddenly a fourth presence in the room—a paradox.

On the one hand there are millions of observations about the expanding universe, possibly more. Every day, in every observatory. On the other hand, there is an equation which appears contrived, designed to meet others' observations. *Cooked,* you might say. Noah and Shanny have raised this issue: the way in which we know that the universe is expanding is based entirely on a set of analyses from starlight, the red shift of this morning's lecture. There were millions of such observations from every observatory in the world. Was it possible that they were wrong? That they had created equations like the one that Noah deciphered with the *assumptions* of expansion, using figures to match those assumptions? Was it possible that models using dark matter and dark energy were made up just to balance the books?

Horkonen is not prepared to accept this new theory yet. He argues, as much to himself as anyone in the room, that red shift has been well established, but something has shifted in *him*. He's aware that he's in the presence of another genius—untrained and naïve—but a genius, just like DiShannia.

It makes all the difference.

"Would you like," he says, "a tour? I would like you to see experiment. I should like your opinion about our advanced work on Higgs boson." These are only names to Kate and Noah. "Perhaps lunch? Pat can bring sandwiches." He appears uncertain for the first time. They agree to stay, will see the experiment if the timing works. It is true that there is much for them to learn here, but there is much more in the world outside CERN, a world in which DiShannia's death and life occurred.

The tour is a marvel: walking in a gently curving circle, passing preoccupied lab techs in white coats; seeing miles of curving pipes above their heads, some color-coded, others bare aluminum or plastic, some man-sized, some smaller, like water pipes; viewing windowless rooms, full of computer screens; meeting security guards at every exit. They finally emerge into a large open space, surprisingly bright and devoid of almost all extraneous equipment, occupied by an array of large flat screens and a half dozen technicians.

Horkonen says, as if to reassure himself, "We are *increasingly* sure of the ability of mathematics and physical theory to *predict* something and then to see it realized. Just as we will prove the existence of dark energy, of *epsilon.*" He is less than certain however. Their talk is like CERN itself. Circular. Self-fulfilling.

The security guards are distinguished by dark blue European Union badges and suits. Two in particular seem to follow them, their manner implying military training. They're differentiated only by dark curly hair on one, a trim Marine-style haircut on the other. There are no smiles. *The place must be full of Finns,* Noah thinks. Finally Ivaan—he's Ivaan to both of them now—returns them to the control room to witness the experiment of the day.

Ivaan introduces it, channelling his inner professor, never far below the surface. "We have been successful for nearly two decades in creating Higgs bosons, thinking this is an important way to understand basic physical properties of universe. You will recall that we found so-called 'God Particle,' or Higgs boson, by studying protons. We increase speed in vacuum tubes you saw today and accelerate particles using electro-magnetic fields generated along path. We take particles to nearly speed of light, then smash them into each other. And out of the millions of such collisions created we 'catch' small handful of bosons. They are very unstable and disappear rapidly. Today we have slowed the process down so much that we can watch their very short lifespan, here, on computer screens."

"Very short" is about to take on a new meaning for them.

The experiment passes quickly, too fast for Noah and Kate to register more than a giant grinding noise, like the sound of a huge MRI machine, and to watch the technicians. In turn, their eyes are fastened on their computers, looking closely at the representations of the tunnels, of the ramping up to light-speed, the effect on the ramming protons. They have it at last—a picture of the Higgs boson as it exists for a millisecond and then disappears, vanishing into nothingness.

After the experiment, they believe they're finished, but Ivaan presses them.

"Ah, Pat has bought sandwiches." They've made plans for a late afternoon app-mediated conference with their WashPO team but decide that they're hungry after all. Pat lays out the food, piling plates, putting some salad into a little bowl, all with the practiced grace of the newly-feminine. She gives them her sixty-watt smile, red lipstick making its mark on their memories.

Midway through Kate's first bite, Ivaan explains his team's frustration at not being able to determine precisely what happens to the Higgs boson; they cannot account for its disappearance. The particle goes nowhere, does not dissolve or dissipate, does not break up into smaller particles. One second it's there, the next second, or much less than a second, it's gone. It is, he says, after a long and satisfying career of thinking about this, and a stab at an uncooperative piece of lettuce, a mystery. Noah is seized by an idea he had when he was watching the experiment. He takes the pile of stacked plates and asks a question that takes a while to digest, longer than his food.

"Ivaan, what if the particle isn't gone?" he asks, imagining the plates as different worlds. "What if it moves to a different plane? Possibly to a parallel universe?" The plates have become universes. It isn't as though Ivaan and his team haven't considered this, but coming from a novice, one whose field is entirely different, one with mathematical intuitiveness, it makes the suggestion seem real to him, possibly for the first time. He says nothing.

As they clear the plates, Kate checks her iPhone. They have a new message from Harry. He's been able to break into more of DiShannia's files. One of them contains references to CERN and particle physics.

"Perfect timing, boss," Noah texts him. "We're at CERN now."

In three clicks, Harry's face appears on Ivaan's wall-mounted flat screen. Introducing him to Ivaan, Harry begins, stumbling over himself. He has read information about Dr. Horkonen, is impressed. "Well, linking to CERN like this, and to you, sir. It is quite an honor, sir." Two "sirs" in one breath are not typical for Harry.

"I've met you only through DiShannia, from her writings." He fails to mention his own searches. "I must say she was thrilled that you would take her on as her mentor." He becomes all crisp British business, "I have not worked through all the equations, but here is what she says in her 'private notes.' A month before she died, she writes, 'What if red shift does not mean what we think it means? What if dark matter is actually so large that it alters red shift itself? What if what we interpret as red shift, as expansion, but what if the universe is actually contracting? Check Mayan calculations, compare with current observations.' She underlined *universe*."

There is more, but not for Horkonen's eyes and ears.

Suddenly, Harry has to leave. Looking at Noah and Kate on his own screen, he says, "Let's chat later, chaps, shall we? Lots going on here." In the private language of WashPO, there is too much to reveal with another observer in the room.

Noah and Kate are struck by something, almost at the same instant. Until this moment, they have been thinking that the contraction only related to the solar system, and that if there were a collapse it would be survivable, at least for humanity. It would involve a superhuman effort to move human civilization to another planet, but a tangible feat. But, surviving the collapse of the universe? That would be impossible. For a moment, they feel what the Mayans and possibly others must have felt. Empty. Helpless.

Ivaan is nothing if not persistent.

"You *must* stay so that we can discuss this idea, what DiShannia has to offer from her final calculations, how you could help us with your insights," Ivaan says. He is not used to being refused—by his team, by Pat, by any one. Kate wonders briefly if there's a Mrs. Horknonen, someone mild, subservient, she thinks. She's wrong.

As he puts the plates back, it strikes Noah that the feeling of the invitation has moved from a friendly offer to a demand. Unable to refuse, they agree to come back tomorrow. Their main concern is DiShannia's death, not this—what would we call it?—this red herring, this anomaly. Neither of them recognize how much the red herring is key to her death.

"It's settled then, tomorrow, let's say eight." He will ensure that their stay at *L'Auberge St Antoine* this evening is picked up by CERN, will also have a car take them to their hotel this afternoon.

Kate is insistent, "You are very kind, but I would like to get back to town on our own. We have had so much on our minds in the last few days, some horrible events, including DiShannia's death. We need time to clear our heads. Please understand."

She's just as firm as he is. They are struck with the loss of DiShannia, struck by the horror of Miriam's and others' death, struck by a set of puzzle pieces—the Maya, the question of mathematical genius, a suspicious school system, several deaths, and now a collapsing universe. They had come with many questions; they're leaving with more.

And a promise that they would return tomorrow. A promise they would not keep.

41

CASTEL ST'ANGELO, TUSCANY, ITALY. MARCH 23RD, 2000

Pulling into the little piazza at the Apostolic Palace occupied Rudy's full attention. Considering that His Holiness was absent, abroad in Israel, it was far busier than he expected.

Paulson had also pictured a placid scene, a place of reflection and prayer. He was wrong: there was as much commotion as at Monaco's casinos. Dozens of cars lined the circular drive—Lamborghinis and Lexuses, Bentleys and Buicks, Maybachs and Mercedes. Cars of the wealthy and the clergy, the categories overlapping in surprising ways. Servants carried bags, luncheon trays. A helo circled noisily overhead, overseeing the tension below. The bustle achieved at least one unintended purpose: it succeeded in diverting both men from questions that consumed Rudy's past quarter hour. *What is in those papers? Who is this person?*

Rudy could only guess; there were hints in those papers of something astronomical. He knew that the Apostolic Palace had an observatory, among the world's oldest such research institutions. He didn't know that it was linked to a sister observatory in the University of Arizona, in a place with the unlikely name of Tucson, halfway around the world.

There was more mystery. Signs flanked the main door, "WELCOME OUR MUSLIM BROTHERS," in Italian, Arabic and English, the graceful Arabic scrawl in the green of Arab renewal and the black of oil. And in red of course, the color of blood, a color Mayans would be familiar with.

Taking his small overnighter from the trunk and holding fast to his briefcase, Paulson was met at the door by a willowy young priest, Father Adolph. *I am from Germany,* his name tag read. Paulson followed the priest, or rather his aftershave, down a long marbled hallway, its ceiling covered in sky blue, its walls holding photos of summer scenes at the Castel: prior popes as they met world leaders, senior members of the Catholic hierarchy, a picture of Pius IX with Himmler, Pope John playing crocanole.

Paulson was led to the intersection of two main hallways, four Gospel saints guarding each of the corners, then turned left, passing between Mark and John. To his right, he caught a glimpse of a man in a wheelchair, an ancient, bent priest, followed by several others garbed in white. Were they priests in white robes or Arabs in their thobes? Both were possible here. Perhaps *anything* was possible here.

This was the 140th Conference of the Catholic-Muslim Alliance, a phenomenon few in the world knew existed and which was, in truth, ten times as old as its announced age. On its surface, it was a celebration of brotherhood under one God, of collaborative pacts and achievements. In contrast, something hidden just below the surface had, as the young PM said, a sniff to it. *I'll give him that,* Paulson thought. *He has a good nose.*

Finally unpacked and freshened, Paulson found the solarium, a forest of white wicker chairs and tables, of Persian rugs and Boston ferns and yet another family of marble saints. Father Adolph, his aftershave faithfully accompanying him, introduced Paulson to dozens of other conference-goers—priests and imams, monsignors and mullahs, two cardinals. All of this, from the Boston ferns to the cardinals to the movements of Patrick Paulson—was reflected in a mirror resting on the floor at one end of the solarium as though it watched the proceedings. Garage door-sized, its surface was ancient, cracked like a thousand other mirrors in the Vatican, in Europe.

The next two days held meetings of the hundred or so conference attendees. The meeting drew on the large toolkit of his experience: language skills—Arabic from his days helping to solidify the British role in the new United Arab Emirates, Italian from his years as British attaché to the Italian embassy in London, even Latin from his public school days; observational skills, honed by his time in MI5 and MI6; and exquisite if not innate diplomatic skills. He could see why the PM had wanted him here.

And, despite his preoccupation with who might have read highly secret papers, Paulson began to accumulate the pieces of a giant puzzle. It helped that no one knew he spoke Italian or Arabic fluently: he could listen to conversations without appearing to do so. It helped that he could read lips across a room (with a bit of squinting, to be sure) with the finesse of an elderly James Bond. *Almost eighty and still in the game,* he thought, *sharp enough to put the puzzle pieces together.*

And what pieces they were. He heard whispers about the *Astronomi*, an old order, an offshoot of the Jesuits but separate, responsible only to the Pope, their headquarters here in the Apostolic Palace. He learned that the Swiss Guard were considered the military arm of the *Astronomi*, that they had an outreach, espionage role, like MI6. He learned that the Taliban had an ancient connection to the Church, possibly over a thousand years. He learned that Catholic-Islamic connections ran deep, not just to the vast majority of well-intended Muslim communities but to the tiny terrorist-driven fragments usurping Islam. In the acoustically revealing rounded dome guarded by the Gospel saints, he had heard, "We are of course, supportive of our brothers in the Taliban, and its cousins," as clearly as if he had been in the conversation itself. The sentence, as lethal as an atomic bomb, was uttered by a cardinal.

Despite his dislike for the modern, too good-looking PM, he was glad he had made the trip.

The man in the wheel chair had watched it all, some of it through the window of the heavy mirror that rested against the wall of the *solario*, some through the eyes (his worked badly) of his closest colleagues, in particular his almost-constant attendant, the young priest with the distinctive aftershave. Father Adolph confirmed the elder man's suspicions: Paulson was more than a retired, out-of-touch senior but rather a gifted agent, far more inquisitive than his eight decades would suggest. One who, it was clear, knew too much about the greatest secrets of the Church, its Nazi sympathizing, its neglect of aberrant sexual behavior, its huge multinational holdings. This secret was worse.

Father Adolph continued, "This Paulson has been keeping an eye on the Turing Affair and its, ah, related activites for over fifty years. He has had access to new information on the, shall we say, astronomical issues, but he knows nothing of the woman O'Rourke, nothing that could be of help to us. His knowledge is dangerous to the Church. We have no need to keep them alive—neither him nor the driver who also knows too much. They are a cancer."

The elderly man, his speech rendered almost absent by Parkinson's, nodded, agreeing.

It only took three days for the telegrams to arrive from the Holy See. Enough for a Saviour to rise, but not, it appeared, long enough to see Paulson resurrected. There was one phone call to Paulson's widow from the prime minister. There were letters to her mentioning Paulson's years of great service to Her Majesty's government, his enormous diplomatic and bridge-building skills, his commitment to service, even to the point of coming out of retirement. The words expressed deep regret at his death—his and his driver's—in a tragic car accident. They mentioned the attempts to save them, their bodies extricated from their mangled car, found at the bottom of a steep hill.

They could not mention that this was the last chapter in a story called "Hemlock." Or the severed brake cable that caused the accident. Or the nod of an elderly, wheel chair-bound man in ordering their death, supposedly on a mission of peace in the Holy Land.

Or what Father Adolph called him. *Santo Padre.*

Holy Father.

42

MEYRIN-GENEVA. FRIDAY AFTERNOON

He is about to hail a cab over her objections. "Noah, let's take the bus back to the hotel, and then maybe take a walk along the river." She holds up a piece of paper with another little map from Patricia/Patrick, in her elegant, flowery script.

He tries to tease her, "*What?* You didn't walk enough?" using his best Long Island-Brooklyn accent. "Several miles of walking in a circle today, that's not *enough*?" His attempt falls flat. She is at the end of a long tether, adamant.

"I want to clear my head. I don't know if it's him, or the security guards, but there's something not right. That's all I can say."

It takes about an hour, partly on the jostling bus from Meyerin to Geneva, partly walking along the Rhone—half-country, half city. It is hot, but there has been rain and *dunnerwedder,* thunderstorms leaving the smell of ozone fresh in the air. It's cooled to a manageable high eighties, rare for Geneva in the last decade. But there's something more. While he was absorbing equations, she was able to watch the security guards at CERN.

"Those guards were looking at *us,* Noah. Studying us. And that was no 'invitation' to come back tomorrow, Noah. He was very insistent that we return tomorrow. I have a funny feeling about this." The car that follows their bus, disgorging two security guards on the street near their hotel, escapes them.

As they get off the bus, Noah and Kate avoid the family of homeless now occupying the Plexiglas bus enclosure, one of many such families across the city, a virtual underworld of crisis-survivors, the result of religious wars, economic meltdown, rising ocean tides and worse. They engulf many nations; Switzerland, despite its strict separateness, is one of them. This particular family looks Syrian to Kate, the mother begging, the father and children sleeping, listless. Kate shivers in the afternoon heat, remembering the homeless camp outside Dulles, the dead baby, deaths over the last forty eight hours.

In less than an hour they arrive at *L'Auberge St Antoine*, a hotel in the modern world, anchored in five centuries or more of history. It rises four stories from the *Rue Ste Marie de Vincennes* in baroque glory, trailing painted vines and flowers on its tan stucco surface. Bucolic scenes frolic between the windows of the third floor—happy farmers, milk-maidens, plump blonde children. Four dormer windows peer like nosy school neighbors over the street; small balconies sprout ornate wrought-iron railings, remnants of the eighteenth century. The number *1793* is painted over the door; it's not the street number.

Inside, it has the single peculiarity of many old European hotels: no elevator has ever found its way into the design. An elderly bald gentleman is noisily tugging a suitcase roughly the size of a refrigerator up the stairs, one profane bump at a time. At almost each step he complains, "What the hell did you pack in this thing?" She, the blonde, younger suitcase-filler, is two steps ahead of him, a purse in one hand, and a shopping bag marked *Printemps-Geneve* in another. If the bag weighs more than five ounces, Noah would be surprised. He smiles for the first time in hours.

Noah and Kate have rented two rooms. Hers, on the top floor, can keep an eye on the street. They take it, as she says, "to huddle." For just an instant he thinks she says *"cuddle"* and he smiles again, a small bulwark against the heat and fear. It's a very small room, cramped, filled almost entirely by two overstuffed seats, a small table, one straight-backed chair and a narrow bed—tourist blogs would call it "cozy." A small window-seat fills the bottom half of a little dormer window. She claims it, wanting to look out the window, dragging a straight-backed chair over to face it. There's no hint of cuddling in the way she's organized the seating.

She turns to look out the window, adjusting the seat cushion, "You know what? Let's *write* out what we know, like we did at WashPO? We have all these details on the app and on your iPad, but maybe we'll we see things differently if we sketch them. And I'm worried about the app. Harry *says* it's okay, but they can be hacked, can't they? They can trace us! There's just *so* much…."

As she says it, her face melts, tears filling the wells of her eyes, spilling over. The mask she's worn for him crumbles. The tears flow readily as she says, "Watching Dr. Al-Ansari die like that? Not knowing what's happening at work? DiShannia's horrible death? And then there's watching my dad, too…" She doesn't say, *And the useless years of trying to get my grandparents to accept us.* The move to Washington has finally killed that dream.

Noah's also not unmoved, either by her or by these horrible, sudden events. He sits beside her on the window seat, holding her, eventually taking his thumb to clear away her tears, an ancient gesture. He says nothing; his heart does all the talking. At length, she apologizes, smiling, "I'm sorry. That wasn't very professional, was it? I just had to let it out."

While she blows her nose, she says, the lemonade-maker, "We should start, eh? Can you get me my bag?"

The "eh" makes him smile again.

Noah, in some ways as tired and frightened as she is, thinks only to humor her. He grabs her bag, thinking about the chubby tourist lugging the suitcase up the stairs, and looks for paper. There's none in the room. He retrieves a handful of little white napkins with German beer ads on one side (*Bitmeister,* they say; an aproned, massively bosomed waitress holds several tankards of beer) and nothing on the other. He pulls a little ornate wooden table over for them to write on, its baroque carved scrolls the product of long-gone furniture makers. He takes a dozen of the napkins, writing something on each of them, spreading them like some malevolent card game on the table. *Mayan Codex, DiShannia's death, DiShannia—who killed her? Why did she die? The universe; expanding? Contracting? Red shift. Rose School. Miriam/British Museum—Who killed* her? There are several others.

Twelve little napkins. A dozen big questions.

"We're going to need more paper," she says, reaching into her bag. He almost says something about lunches and underwear—she is a *long* time in there after all—but decides this may not be the time; his genius is not confined to mathematics. She looks up, puzzled, holding a little three-by-five card.

"Noah, look at this. This isn't mine! Look, it was way in the bottom of the bag."

He's distracted, looking out the window. A small gang of college students has gathered on the street outside, acting as though they spent the afternoon in an Octoberfest tent, singing, holding giant beer mugs. It's not the crowd that catches his eye however: it's the curly hair of one of the guards from CERN standing quietly to one side, watching. Noah blinks, leaning closer to the window.

"Sorry, I was looking at something on the street. What's that?" he asks.

She looks puzzled: her mind races through the days since they met DiShannia. Then, "Remember that homeless man yesterday in London? I think *he* must have dropped something into my bag when he grabbed me."

Noah rewinds the mental filmstrip: the man ramming his grocery cart into Kate's chair, scraping her arm with the sharp edge of the cart, grabbing her shoulder and—the memory returning in a rush—shoving something into her bag.

"Is there anything on it?"

"Oh yes. It looks like it came from DiShannia's room. Remember the way she liked that bunny rabbit stamp? This is hers all right." Kate reads a name written in DiShannia's oversized handwriting, the puffy graffiti of the teenager.

Isaac Zapinsky, Lugenstrasse 17, Heidelburg, Germany.

The name Isaac Zapinsky is not unfamiliar to a health/science news lead. Zapinsky was a famous astrophysicist and Nobel Prize winner in the early part of the century. He was also a talented (*and very good looking*, Noah's mother once said) presence on public television, explaining hard-to-grasp facts about space science. Late in his life, Noah recalls, Zapinsky's credibility plummeted, he was drummed out of CERN and finally, most memorably, set himself on fire. He lived—until now at least—in obscurity.

There's not much on the card, no phone, no email, just an address. "How did this," she asks, waving the card like it was a tiny fan, "get from Shanny's room in Washington, to the homeless man, to here?" It is just what they need: another mystery to add to their pile.

Noah checks the street again and spots the same man, caught in the reflection of a Starbuck's window, framed by the reflected ghosts of coffee aficionados. A modestly tall, angular guy, unsmiling—perhaps no one ever smiled at CERN—with curly black hair. There's no doubt: this was the security guard they had seen earlier in the afternoon. Kate finds another person in the doorway of a small pharmacy down the street, his marine-shaved head a tip-off, drinking beer in the little sidewalk café adjacent to the hotel, trying to look like he belongs to the Octoberfesters. He doesn't. They're both CERN security, each poised to follow Kate and Noah.

It's her idea. There's no doubt that security guards from CERN have followed them back to the hotel, blocking their exit. Not used to surveillance work that goes beyond their normal job descriptions, the CERN employees make poor, even comical, spies.

Oktoberfest in any German-speaking city means that most bars become magnets. Not so much during the early weekdays—these are the Swiss after all—but on Thursday nights and the weekends, definitely. Young people especially congregate called by the silent, siren song of social networking. Then, lured by the same phenomenon, move on to the next, talking and laughing about nothing and everything. Many of them dress in costume—long skirts, hats, *lederhosen*, a few masks. The masks are a license to do things their wearers would not normally do.

She has an idea: they could make new friends at the bar, get them to help them somehow (this part of the plan is vague) and slip by the watchers outside the hotel. She is as good as her word. In fifteen minutes they pack up their little napkin-clues, take their bags, check out (much to the consternation of the front desk clerk) and join a small group sitting at the inside bar. It's lined with wooden shelves filled with beer steins; the music, noise and laughter echo off the walls. They are invited to sit with a young couple, a process eased by North American smiles and an offer to buy drinks. Kate spots them first. "They're just married, I bet," she says, their identification made easy by their hungry looks and hand-holding. Kate is right.

"I have a serious problem. Can you help?"

She is Angela with a hard "g." He is Heinrich, the word ending in a crunchy mush, like chewing ice chips. Their English is good; it rides the roller coaster of the Swiss German.

Looking almost solely at Angela, she says, "My husband works at CERN as a consultant. He is so cruel!" It's not hard for her to generate tears, remnants of those recently shed for Miriam and DiShannia. She rolls up her sleeves. "See? Here?" She points to the bruise and scrape on her left arm left by the grocery cart, and the now-visible marks of the fake Rastafarian's massive hand prints. They're on their way to an impressive purple, like an eggplant.

"I need to get away from him. I do have a good friend in Noah, and he's promised to take me away to"—a pause, her mind searching for the address on the card—"Heidelberg tonight, but my husband has planted men outside, maybe private detectives or CERN security staff. Can you help us get away?"

She doesn't have to say anything more; it's enough to stimulate a plan, especially for Angela with the hard "g." Heinrich is dubious.

"I have an idea," Angela says. "*Haff.*"

She takes her cell phone from one of the folds of her peasant skirt and finds a German crowd-source site. "In half an hour, we will have fifty people here. We will make a swarm? And you can leave in the middle of it. You can also have my skirt and this cap, and Heinrich will give you his hat and his vest. It will be loose on you Noah, but okay, I think. And then we will drive you to the *Banhof.*"

This is clearly news to Heinrich, but the early matrimonial bed does marvelous things to a man's ability to reason. Soon the vest and hat come off him and onto Noah. The exchange of skirts requires a bathroom break and the order of another beer for Heinrich. In the meanwhile, Angela's texting does not achieve fifty friends. She manages more; the bartender has to send two busboys downstairs to haul up more cases of beer. Enough so that many of the young people spill onto the sidewalk, some dragging their bar stools, obscuring the door to the hotel.

It happens suddenly.

The four of them are on the street, drinks in hand, making overloud Octoberfest sounds, keeping their heads down and caps on tight, acting drunk, just like most of the crowd. They maneuver past the three CERN agents, oblivious and untrained in the arts of espionage. They jam themselves, like circus clowns, into Heinrich's little Mini. Noah thinks it's a slightly larger version of a sewing machine; it's half as comfortable. They manage to fold their bags and themselves into a back seat that's never held anything more than a week's worth of groceries. In the same instant, they are cramped and relieved, grateful and frightened.

At the *Banhof,* a few minutes of ducking crowds and back streets later, the two women embrace. Fake story or not, there are real tears in both their eyes as they say good-bye. *How do women bond so quickly?* Noah wonders. On the other hand, Heinrich can't wait to get out of there—the call of the conjugal bed and the fear of a jealous husband propels him. He offers one stiff water-pump handshake to Noah and a firm, "*Gutt Luck.*"

They believe they're safe, finally on their own.

It is not quite true. Across from the *Banhof,* a homeless man watches intently, someone Noah and Kate would recognize. The cellphone looks out of place in his hand.

They have decided to take the first train out no matter where it goes, then connect to Heidelberg, hopefully throwing Ivaan and his little team of spies-for-a-day off.

They make a show of announcing in loud, atrocious French that they want two tickets ("*doo bee-yay*") to Paris, and then in a quieter voice say, "No, Heidelberg." They pay twenty Euros to the agent to buy his silence about their true destination, hoping it's a good investment. They have just enough time to get a small loaf of bread, some cheese and two bottles of terribly overpriced water before they board. It doesn't dawn on them until the train leaves how hungry they are.

And tired. To cloak themselves, they purchase their way into a small coach rather than buy general open car tickets. There they're alone for most of the time, talkative at first, then quiet and reflective. They are both exhausted, human vessels drained by the events, deaths and confusion of the last few days. Finally, Kate takes a deep breath, the inhaled part of a deep sigh, and falls asleep on his shoulder, where it, they both think, fits very nicely.

Trains. The metronome of the rails, clicking beneath their feet and in their ears. The industrial back-doors of buildings, of tenements and factories. The graffiti—the visual piss-marking of tribes—decorating sidewalks, fences, buildings. The abandoned vehicles left to oxidize and die. The strange designs of overhead wires. The burnt grass and dry woods, visible even at night.

The peace inside the coach.

In it, they hear the soft staccato of the wheels building to a soft, almost-invisible white noise. They smell the memory of cigars long gone, of old farts, of baby talcum, of old ladies' cat-perfume, imbedded in the upholstery. They feel the tired seats, their ersatz velveteen worn flat by pregnant ladies, young people off to see their mothers or girl and boy friends. By old men gone to visit a faraway sister. By children not used to sitting, using the seats like velvet trampolines.

By a young couple, falling into love.

Just across from the *Banhof Centrum* in Heidelberg they find a narrow three story hotel, graffiti marking the first floor, old wall-paintings marking the second and third stories—scenes from a world in which lives proceed, music is played, children grow, dance, have children, and die naturally. Not the world they find themselves in.

Heidelberg's *Gasthuas Schraeder* offers has a blinking *Unbesetez sign*. *VACANT* flashes onto the street, stops, flashes again.

"*Ein Zimmer?*" the lady asks, not looking up. Her gray hair makes a perfect half circle of curls around a face that Kate thinks looks like that of an old apple doll, displaying the many wrinkles of a dried Granny Smith. There is no smile; boredom or age or both radiate from her like a cold front. *One* room?

"*Nein, Zwei,*" Noah answers, two rooms, chivalrous. He feels Kate's arm around his waist, *low,* squeezing. Something has shifted in her mental machinery, just as it did for Noah only days before on a street in Georgetown. The deaths, the pursuit—and this man—have throttled the importance of issues like pleasing absent and uncaring grandparents, leaving them flattened in the dust. They are behind her, not part of her future. Noah hears her say, "*Nein, bitte,* Ein *Zimmer.*"

Something profound happens in that moment; it is possible that time stands till. The lady looks up. Her face, still wrinkled, becomes younger, brightened by—what?—her own memories? Another hotel room? She smiles and warms the space between the three of them. She takes an old key from the tiny prehistoric drawers behind her, pressing one into Kate's palm, like a gift, closing her own arthritic fingers over Kate's. It is the gift of youth.

And turns to Noah, surprising him with a full-on, honest-to-God wink. *Good for you,* it says. He could hug her.

To be fair, it has been building for days—a small ebb and flow at first, a higher tide flooding the days between the Eastern Market Rose School and *Gasthaus Schraeder.* Time is the most elastic element for you, isn't it? Four days? It could have been four months or years, so much has happened. And there is the other, too. A brush of Kate's breast against his arm in the subway, the smell of her hair on the train. The inviting curve between the small of her back and her bottom.

And for her too: the long lean look of him, the intensity in his eyes, the way in which his shape narrows from the width of his shoulders to his thin waist. The black hair he brushes back from his eyes.

What a difference three words can make, even apparently in a foreign language.

"Ein *zimmer, bitte.*"

One room, please.

SECTION IV

THE HAT TRICK

43

PIER 39. SAN FRANCISCO. CALIFORNIA. EIGHT WEEKS PRIOR

He smells the ocean, leaning against the railing, holding his paper coffee cup, listening to the honking of seals, the flatulent, nasal choir of a hundred or more sea lions. He pulls the coffee cup's warmth closer to him; coffee is the only thing in the American landscape that he savors. The cup's recycled surface offers a modest amount of heat, a small cylinder of warmth to combat San Francisco's almost-frozen fog, containing thousands of minute, painful ice cubes.

The girl in the coffee shop is blithely polite to him, a stupid blond thing he thinks, her ears covered with studs. She offers a vacuous, "Have a nice day." *So like American superficiality*, he thinks, so unlike Mumbai and the Islamic life of his first family.

The anger warmed Aabis. It was the product of many things, like logs on a funeral pyre—a long string of grievances that had made him who he was. His status as a Muslim in a partitioned Hindu country. The rape and strangulation of his sister Neela, named for his grandmother, her *hijab* used to strangle her. The beating death of his father Parvez by a gang led by Atul, months later, while attempting to seek revenge for Neela's death. Atul watching, as was Aabis, age nine, standing in cow shit. His mother's suicide, caused by her husband's death and a bread knife struck far into her belly. His stay in a Catholic orphanage, treated as a number until he left, adopted by a couple playing out a colonial scenario.

It was then that Aabis discovered some good things: schooling, in which he excelled; his light skin, rendering him acceptable in his new, adopted country; and an exceptional ability to adapt, to be a chameleon.

And this: an ability to exact revenge. In Sanskrit, *Atul* means incomparable, matchless. In Aabis' mind it meant arrogant, evil, murderous. For weeks after his parents' death he watched Atul, learning his daily routine, finding out where he lived, plotting. Finally, just before he left Mumbai, he rolled a large rock into the middle of the steep dirt laneway leading to Atul's house, causing Atul's motorbike to flip over in the dark early morning, breaking his neck. Aabis also learned about the benefit of a back-up plan: to be certain of his death, he had also tied a wire at neck height at the end of Atul's laneway.

In the honking morning mist of an American pier, Aabis smiles with the memory of Atul's death and the presence of a new plan on a much larger scale, something to crush the story of solar collapse, like his family's life had been crushed years before. He pictures an abyss, not unlike his name.

Even in the bitter cold morning fog, she is hard to miss.

She advances through the frozen fog, treading the hard planks of Pier Thirty-Nine like some women command a fashion runway. She appears unbothered by the early morning tourists, dressed in a long black skirt made of material that clings to her like sweat on a hot day. It is as though she is naked. Her cleavage is on display, a tiny sweater covering shoulders which he is sure are bare underneath. Against every ounce of a profoundly Islamist view of the world, he finds himself aroused, the work of the devil, the same devil that prods his dreams. He feels none of this when women, like his wife, are wrapped in unrevealing black swaddling, none of their shoulders or cleavage—*Oh Dear Prophet, their cleavage*—visible.

He shifts his briefcase to cover his groin with his left hand. *Insha'Allah*, she will *not* notice her effect on him. God willing. He shapes his face into one of welcome.

"Anna! I'm glad you could make it!" He extends his right hand, another affront to the Prophet.

She has never met him before, though she has heard of him of course. He is an Astronomer, perhaps *the* Astronomer, although, like the fog around her, the details are unclear. It's a relief, finding him; she's searched for nearly half an hour. She takes his puffy right hand into both of hers, tucking her iPad under her arm. His hand is surprisingly soft, clammy.

"I'm glad too. I have a lot to share with you and this seemed like the best route. We're a little like spies, aren't we?" she asks, slightly giddy with the clandestine thought.

"A little, I suppose, yes," his seriousness balancing her giddiness. "We do have to be careful, though. This will have to be it, I'm afraid, until the, er, *event*. The *only* route we'll be able to use. Pity, rather."

The *event* is eight weeks away; it is the subject of their meeting.

They return to the same coffee shop he's just visited, despite the presence of the obnoxious metal-ridden barista. It's like thousands of other Starbuck lookalikes across the country, olive green-yellow walls, more green or yellow depending on the light in the room. Today, before the fog lifts, green wins. Quiet groups fill the room. Two young businessmen, not talking, both of them on iPhones. One family of tow-headed, rambunctious boys and tired-looking parents. The smell of roasting fair trade coffee. The sound of an espresso machine, grinding foam out of thin air at occasional intervals. Some of the morning fog enters the room with them, creating a strange dance between it and the green-yellow walls. A small wooden table calls to them, perfectly tucked away in a corner by a bowed window, divided into squares like a relic of Dickens.

The timing is ideal, a narrow window between the early morning coffee rush and the ten a.m. break. Tourists are hiding, avoiding the tiny frozen darts of the summer fog. Anna and Aabis' table is as far away from the vacuous attendant as possible. Miss Ear Studs takes their order: a tall grande macchiato for her, more coffee for him. When she delivers them, she places a jar full of artificial sweetener packages and organic sugar cane lollipops in the middle of the table. She smiles benignly, stupidly, Aabis thinks.

The instant they're alone, Anna leans forward, taking her iPad from its purple-flowered case, opening it, becoming more professional with each deliberate movement.

"We're all set," she says, summarizing, raising her eyes to meet his. They show him no diffidence; her giddiness is gone. With a few delicate hand movements, her screen shows him pictures of the Federation Convention Center in Melbourne. The lollipops and sweeteners find a space between them, moved slightly to one side.

She continues, "The scaffolding is in place. Most of the work has been done. We're all set to go, weeks ahead of time at that. Let me walk you through this and tell me if we're missing something." His reputation as a master planner has preceded him.

He nods. The temperature in the room drops. The front door opens, closes, letting more fog in, though it is more than fog chilling the room.

She continues, leaning closer to him, lowering her voice, "We started nearly two months ago, before they announced officially that the CG conference was to be moved to Melbourne."

CG, he thinks. *Clinton Gates. Initials and acronyms. So American.*

"We wondered how we could get the gas into the conference center. And then we looked at the building." Her scrolling finger finds just the right picture. The center is all angles and glass, like a giant jewel, sitting above the Yarra River, above train tracks.

"All you see are glass panels, right? They're our route of access. We got one of our people to act as a window washer, to loosen several of the panels. The next week, one of the panels fell, injuring a tourist. Not a serious injury, but enough that city council voted for a massive repair. You'll smile at this: it wasn't even one of *our* panels that fell." She flips to several more pictures of trucks unloading the metal framework, men climbing on the scaffolding.

"The rest was easy. We put two men on the crew. One of them was an AC guy who knew his way around ducts and air vents. The other was one of our senior agents. He had a little difficulty at first maneuvering the scaffolding, but he got our, um, package in place. In two places, actually. I am told you like to build redundancy into all our projects."

"Indeed," he nods, taking a sip of the still-hot coffee. Its oiliness burns his tongue.

"Well. Each of the canisters is now attached to the intake vents, in areas that no one will ever visit. They're both fixed with tiny, remote devices," another flip of pictures on the iPad, "that will release the gas on your order. We think it should be at the press conference, right? We're working on building interest and hype, issuing a press release days before, naming our speakers…"

She takes a breath and a sip of her grande macchiato, untouched until now. "With proper timing we should be able to release the gas at the top level, driving participants down the escalator and the stairs to the main lobby. And, with the second canister we should be able to deliver gas at each of the main exit doors. There's no way out for them. They'll be trapped." Neither of them mention the name of the gas.

Sarin.

For a minute or two, they are both engaged in thinking through next steps. He asks several questions but in the end is satisfied with her plans, compliments her on the built-in redundancy, a hallmark of his work as an Astronomer.

He's satisfied. "I must say," he says, "the plan is coming together very well. I'm grateful for the update today; I feel as though I know enough." He is not the only one who knows enough.

Ear studs and nose rings convey so much, don't they? One would hardly imagine that the person wearing them might be highly trained, intelligent and— on this occasion, across a room—listening. One of the ear studs is a speaker linked to a tiny microphone in the little glass jar. Only the occasional steam from the espresso machine hampers her listening.

The erotic hand gesture again. Anna thumbs through the plans, summarizing what they've decided. "That should do it, don't you think? In a few weeks, they will all be at the press conference. None of them will survive. And if they do, any trace of their story will be drowned by the terrorist hype."

He holds his hand up, *enough,* it says. He sips his coffee, its temperature finally just right.

Wanting to impress, Anna probes. "What about *Operation Headrick*? This is a part of it, right?" She is nonchalant, folds the iPad into its little flowered case, drags the sugar bowl back to its original position.

He is stunned. He snaps his briefcase shut, a small negative sound in the room. He had only recently named the project himself, and she didn't even get the name right. *How did she know?* This is entirely beyond her paygrade and security level.

"That should not trouble you," he says, his voice suddenly as cold as the mist outside. "We have all our plans in hand."

Unfortunately, the last is lost in the movement of the sugar bowl on the table, in the snapping shut of his briefcase. It would not, in any event, have given any clue to the alternate plans—sarin was only the beginning.

If you could peak into his briefcase and look at the plans in his laptop, you'd be able to see that plan laid out—pictures, text, maps. A scanned newspaper clipping describing a break-in at a nuclear waste storage facility in the Urals. A malicious Google Map, highlighting a journey beginning in Moscow by train, touching on Hamburg, moving through the Baltic and North Seas, progressing through the Atlantic Ocean, rounding the Cape, crossing the Indian Ocean, reaching Melbourne. Architectural plans of a large convention center in great detail, containing floor plans, air conditioning ducts and its underbelly—a giant train complex. Conference agendas. Blueprints for something that resembles a large briefcase, perhaps a unique, double one, lead-lined and suspicious.

And a file name for his meticulous master plan.

44

LOEW'S MAGNIFICENT MILE. LAS VEGAS. AUGUST 14TH. 2006

He loved Fox News.

Not necessarily the reporters and anchors, although the two women he saw most frequently on air were definitely easy to watch. The blonde often leaned forward over the anchor desk, pushing her cleavage toward the audience, a view he would have liked to have enjoyed more in life. He liked the newscasters' ceaseless conversation; it matched his own internal voice, the drumbeat of the authoritarian right wing. The funding that found its way into armed conflict, supported wars in lands where the outcomes were vague and complicated. Where oil wealth lay just underground. Where American soldiers could easily die, their passing marked by the perfect oxymoron of mourning and celebration.

The voices weren't those of the soldiers however, they were those of the one percent, the wealthy and powerful, the few who truly ran the country. Led by him, of course. Not the puppet president, the one who occupied the White House but lacked the guts and intelligence to run America. The other man with the family name might have been playing the role of president, but the greater title—the Commander in Chief—fell by default to the vice president.

He loved Fox News so much that his agents and guards were told to tune all TVs to the local channel in whatever hotel suites housed him. His hotel visits were frequent and often hidden from the public view. The names of the inviters spoke volumes—White Patriots of America, Right Now—organizations which did not appear in the final public documents issued weekly by the White House.

His code name was *Heart*, a small irony wasted on most of his security agents and handlers. And on him, to be fair. He had none.

"What's he doing tonight?" asked one of the black suited agents, turning to his partner. They sported identical blue-tinged sunglasses, spoke in a clipped internal language, only their bulk marking any difference between them. They were sitting in an anonymous Dodge van, outside a plush five-star hotel, inside a city as empty as the man they were guarding.

"He's got two visitors at five," the shorter, beefier of the two said, using a chubby, manicured finger to scroll through the man's schedule, "then a break until seven when we to escort him to the convention center for a speech at the Republican Governor's Assembly." "Escort" was an understatement: it took ten motorcycled policemen, two long armored limousines, four SUVs with rifles poking out of their barely-open windows, and a black ambulance.

The two five o'clock visitors were already waiting in an adjacent room. The VP's office always booked several suites, some for the agents, one for less-than-public meetings. This was one of the latter, an exuberance of Las Vegas baroque, a yellow, gold and gilt rebellion against the sleek, minimalist design of the last decade. Kings of France would have felt right at home.

A casual observer might be forgiven if he thought the young visitors unrelated. Karla and Kym Mandeville were identical twins, a fact obscured by their birth. Karla had an uncorrectable scoliosis, her neck almost absent, twisting her head into her chest. While Kym reached nearly five foot-six, Karla was much shorter, her view of the world often confined to her shoes and the floor. The impediment hardly mattered: they excelled in high school and college, became active Republican volunteers, campaign organizers and fund-raisers.

Early in the days of the administration, the vice president read about the twins' fund-raising and planning prowess, two muscular wunderkinds on a beach of weaklings. What he hadn't known about was their extra-financial skill set, their problem-solving gifts, their ability to think outside the box.

Heart had come to count on them. In time they became prime agents in the nationwide Rose School efforts, now his since the enterprise had lost its founding architect twenty years before. Interesting, he often thought, how powerful some vice presidents were. Some became presidents. Some *were* presidents.

"Tell me what you've got," he said, closing the door and starting the conversation simultaneously, ignoring the stuttering thump-thump-thump of an arrhythmia in his chest. He never wasted time—never on niceties, never on neurotic self-worry.

In the almost-square formed by the ornate love-seat and two matching wing-back chairs, he took the love seat, one young woman on either side of him. There were two mirrors, one behind him and one in front, the latter one sitting high above a mantel, tilted enough so that he could see his tweed jacket and striped tie, his round face, his bald head. They reflected dozens of times between the two.

The "What you've got?" unleashed a torrent of details and updates. There were several major threads.

Kym started. "It's been a hugely successful last six months, Mr. Vice President," she said, a little of West Virginia left in her voice. "We've added five new schools in the Northeast, more in the west and south, sixteen in six months. That brings our total up to 141 schools, ten percent above last year's goal-setting. And funding is up too. We used the 'Search for Genius' campaign last year if you recall. S4G brought in," she checked her figures on a yellow lined pad, "over eleven million dollars. Teacher recruitment is also up and our student enrolment has jumped fifty percent over last year. We've reached what we think is a critical mass."

"Mostly, the curriculum has focused on advanced but traditional maths and sciences. Several of our kids have even been accepted into advanced NASA programs." Karla added, pride in her voice.

There were details about the Rose Charter enterprise of which he too was proud: how the teachers were ignorant of their true purpose; how they tested students to determine math and physics aptitude. And test them genetically, naturally. Their work had answered dozens of questions. Could they select students equipped to answer questions of space travel? Could they detect those who might be dangerous to the cause, too garrulous for example? Could a network of agents infiltrate marginal groups and discredit them? The answers were like the room itself: the overwrought baroque mirroring the multiple networks of intrigue and money-flow of the Rose School Network.

And then there was the other, larger picture.

Needing to keep countries unsettled so that the military-industrial beast (his beast, after all) could be fed. Destabilizing the world order, upsetting world markets, so that his supporters could profit. Creating new funding sources out of old, some governmental, some private. Ensuring that his own company, Muskoka Enterprises, survived. Engaging colleagues—General Wilcox for example—riding high on his investments, riding higher on his increasing control of the nation's media. Remembering the hidden secrets of Poseidon, deeply buried, like the sea.

"Very good," he said, the hint of a smile indicating his pleasure at their progress. He had chosen them to be co-chief operating officers, twin staff leads of the Rose Network, much bigger than the Rose Schools. "Anything else?"

There was a pause in the room, as though time stopped.

Kym had been chosen to start the conversation; she was the braver of the two.

"We've concentrated on the thought that we might at some point need to abandon the planet, selecting some of the human race, sending them into space to colonize other worlds. We've focused our efforts there because we believe there's direct visual evidence that the solar system is slowly closing in. But," she said, the slightest hesitation in her usual march of sentences, "what if...."

"... the entire universe were collapsing." Karla finished the sentence, exhaling. They had thought about this conversation with *Heart* for a long time.

For a minute, the vice president's heart galloped. A hundred beats a minute, 110, 120. 140. Like a wild horse.

Time stopped, stretched, restarted. Like his heart.

He stared at his reflections for a minute, pushing his vision past them, trying to imagine the unimaginable, attempting to regain control. To reign his heart in.

"Should we start thinking about a backup plan?" from Karla. "A plan B?" from Kym.

"What in God's name would a Plan B look like? A plan B in case the universe is collapsing? What? In a billion years?" he asked. There was anger in his voice, the worst kind, fueled by fear. He wasn't expecting an answer. He was incredulous that his planning would be questioned. Here was a man who lived by thinking well beyond Plans B, and C. He had considered the *possibility*, of course, but certainly not a probability. He felt, above all, a challenge to his authority. That and his fear of course.

"There is a theory of parallel universes, sir," both women said, a mildly disorienting stereo in the room. They had rehearsed this. The room seemed to breathe, an inspiration in any sense of the word.

"Science fiction bullshit," he said, as though the two things were synonymous. His words were fueled by the unusual feeling of not fully understanding something, like the global warming nonsense that was becoming more bothersome. Cold spread from his gut to his heart.

"We've been thinking," one of them said. The other continued, "...less about the collapse, or possible collapse of the universe, but rather that someone, *someone* will discover parallel universes. You do know, Mr. Vice President, that scientists at CERN and elsewhere have studied their existence."

"What possible use could that be to us?" he asked, not expecting an answer.

"We have two thoughts," said Kym. She rarely thought of herself as a single individual.

"First, the idea of parallel universes is more than just theoretical. Scientists say that subatomic particles can move between them. It's not too much of a reach to say that, in time, there could be a transporter of some sort, moving us from one plane to another, just as we move from one time zone to another. And if there *are* parallel universes and someone invents a means to travel between them, we might monetize the process, much as we do space travel today. It would be an investment with huge payoffs in the future."

Her tone said, *Now who's thinking outside the box?*

"And second," from her twin, "we have the perfect educational *factory* to find and grow those scientists. We've focused on the more traditional sciences, sir—space travel, engineering physics, mathematics. We rarely focus on particle physics, on subatomic studies."

Her sister's head made a tiny negative head-shake; her twin was diving too deeply into the details. Karla was more intense now, leaning ahead in her seat, her back's curvature more noticeable, half a question mark. She reached for her iPad. She had just reviewed the results of the latest screening tests which highlighted students considered risky and "removed." She had begun to reflect on those losses. "What if we found and trained them to answer these questions, sir? Questions about particle physics."

He was quiet then, the irregular metronome of his heart marking the forward progress of time. His eyes took in the drapes, the mirrors, the ornate, over-carved furniture. The mirrors caught his tie, reflected into infinity.

Multiple universes, he thought.

Finally after twenty or thirty beats, he said, "I don't say this very often, but you've convinced me." He smiled, a rare event. "Doesn't happen very often. What you propose has merit, but it needs a plan. Could we train our teachers to spot this talent? How we would choose and train our students? Could we use CERN or create another laboratory?

"I want," he said, looking at his watch; they were nearly out of time. "I want a full report by next week. Can you manage that?"

They said "Yes, sir," in unison (sometimes the stereo was annoying) and stood to leave. The report was already done, like their predecessor's decades before; they had worked on it for weeks. The Rose School curriculum, the selection process, the outcomes, the product, all about to turn inward, not the external business of space travel, but the internal business of subatomic physics. Of parallel universes.

The hour was up. He adjusted his jacket, straightened the crease in his trousers, tightened the knot on his tie, the tie that was reflected a million times in the mirrors, the one he would wear at the Republican Governors' Association that evening. He had one last question for them as they left the room, "Have we ever learned anything about that woman of Turing's?" As though there could be "that woman" in Turing's life.

"We were reluctant to mention it," said Karla, twisting her body to see the vice president. "It's not confirmed yet but we think finally we have a lead, after fifty years at that."

Kym continued, "DNA findings from one of our Rose School students and from a Starbuck's of all places, but it's still preliminary. We'll keep you posted."

Soundless, with only a nod, he was gone. He knew they'd let him know.

They left the room, the door shutting behind them, an expensive, soft *thunk* marking its closing. The baroque furniture remained quiet, inanimate. Only the mirrors were alive, reflecting each other a dozen times, a hundred, an infinity.

45

HEIDELBERG. GERMANY. SATURDAY MORNING

Why do you call it "sleeping together"?

So little of it is actual sleep, at least at the first. Cat-napping or catching a breath, resting or recovering, yes. But sleeping? Not so much. There is so *much* to see and do in the new country of love.

Despite their exhaustive exploration of this new terrain, Noah and Kate aren't tired when they make their early-morning way from the *Gasthaus* to the address on the back of DiShannia's bunny rabbit-marked card. Motorcycles, *lots* of motorcycles have awakened them earlier; it's Friday the thirteenth, a day for bikers worldwide to travel, often in packs. One of those packs gathers just outside their hotel window.

Kate and Noah are famished, stopping to buy coffee and croissants at a café. Noah's croissant is gone in three bites, leaving his face flecked with tiny pastry bits and a large smile. They find reasons to touch each other for no reason. They have a small hotel map in their hands, typical tourists one might think, but they're watchful, their eyes searching. Crossing the old bridge over the Neckar they emerge just below the castle. Hundreds of padlocks hang like small trophies from the bridge's iron railings, souvenirs of love. They have their own memories, less visible but no less real. They make their way up stone stairs smoothed by hundreds of years, by thousands of visitors. They're looking for the house of Isaac Zapinsky, laying across the Neckar from the *Gasthaus*, behind the ancient, decaying *Schloss*, the castle. Built several hundred years before, it still watches over Heidelberg and its river like a parent.

Remnants of summer, yellow leaves the size of large wallets, carpet the steps. Dampened by last night's rain, they make walking treacherous. Noah and Kate hold on to the stone wall at the sides of the steps as they climb from the river level to the top. A light fog surrounds them, scented by the earthy, decaying leaves. They emerge from the stairs a little out of breath into a different world, all the visual markers of the castle softened by the *Nebel Herbst,* the fog. The Neckar is one of those rivers that makes the mist sleep on the hillside and not in the valley. It mutes sounds as well as sights.

Perhaps it's a combination of post-coital and real fog that makes them feel secure, the first time for that feeling in hours. With no evidence, they believe that the bubble of fog and mist, the carpet of decaying leaves, protects them; it's another deception.

"We're pretty early to go knocking on doors, unannounced," she says. "Want to find a place to sit?"

She's right. It's still early, before eight. The adrenalin of fear and those pesky motorbikes have acted like early morning alarm clocks.

In a few minutes, they manage to find one of the remaining ramparts, a small alcove allowing them to sit, observing a living map of the city below them. It's an impressionist's view. They settle, unaware of the discomfort of the rock and stone alcove, looking down at the carpet of blood-orange roofs and leafy trees below them. Behind them are the tooth-like remains of the castle fortress.

Catching their breath, they look at an old fashioned Google-map (no more cell phones; they printed this at a cyber-cafe). Turning it several ways before they get it right, they find where they need to go. Behind the *Schloss*, this part of the town is marked *Neue* Heidelberg, the *neue* referring to a section built almost five hundred years ago. Everything is relative; it's new compared to the thousand-year-old *Alt* Heidelberg, laid out before them across the river.

They have also Googled Dr. Zapinsky in the cybercafé. Wikipedia describes an expansive career shrunk to a pedestrian two pages: a Nobel prize winner; a brilliant but renegade astrophysicist; an early television celebrity, known as *Dr. Zap*, a movie-star handsome explainer of scientific facts. The Wiki-writer said he had set himself on fire years before, the product of a "paranoid and unorthodox view about the universe." Whatever that view was, it was condemned by the scientific community, especially by CERN physicists.

Number eighty-four *LindenStrasse* lies a few blocks away, slightly up the hill from the castle, the *Schloss*, in a row of connected homes, sitting quietly side by side in the fog. Many homes on the street display small brass squares imbedded in their walkways. In front of the house, the plaques mark the lives and deaths of a Jewish family who lived there, now long gone. Their plaques live underfoot, placed there by guilt, their names erased by the footprints of time, like the career of Dr. Zap.

The house has a distinctly non-German look: an untended garden fills the front yard, full of tall weeds, the remains of a pizza box and other litter. Some of the debris sits on the front porch. Perhaps, they think, no one lives there. Perhaps this is not the home of Dr. Zapinsky.

Hidden from them across the street, a pair of homeless men lurk, as surprising as an untended garden in the orderliness of Germany. At least surprising in *Alt,* the old Germany. In the New, refugees from wars and floods overflow the giant well of guilt-born generosity of the German people, filling many side streets and suburbs with tents and their own debris. The two men occupy a tiny cardboard village across the street in an alleyway, hidden by several large recycling bins and remnants of the dissipating morning fog. Noah and Kate are not hidden from them.

The wait seems like minutes. Kate becomes anxious, fighting memories of another porch and its unforgiving kitchen chair, years before. Finally a muffled voice says, "I'm coming!" and they hear the door's several part unbolting. The doorway frames a durable young woman of moderate height. Her square Slavic face displays no smiles, the professor's housekeeper, perhaps nurse, they think. Seriously blond, her hair tied almost cruelly at either side, she says nothing, waiting for them to speak.

She listens to their story, no invitation in her voice or gestures. As they tell her about themselves—who they are, their role at WashPO, their pursuing a murder in the US, how they learned Dr. Zapinsky's name—the day brightens somewhat, the fog burning away. She weighs each of their reasons separately, her brow furrowing, then lightening, temporary clouds casting shadows on her face. And then like the day, her face brightens.

In only slightly accented English, more Brit than Slav, she says, "Well, you *have* come a long distance. It is not a bad day for him. Some days he is so confused he can see no one. But today he seems brighter. Do not be alarmed if he has outbursts. This passes quickly. He is having his breakfast now. Come in." Short, staccato bursts of information, like gunshots.

They step across the threshold into the vestibule (the *foy-ay,* Noah's English-raised mother would have said), the *squeak* of the ancient door the only sound. In one moment they are back in time, one hundred years. More.

Decades have passed between the original design of the room and today.

The vestibule is as dark as the day is bright, impossibly cluttered with Victoriana or its German equivalent, a virtual, crowded furniture store. On one wall is a muscular, gorilla-sized gilt mirror, its cracked surface wrapped by a huge baroque frame several inches thick, even wider where little cherubs frolic in gilt abandon. The mirror reflects the odd trio: the blond attendant; the skinny man with black hair and dark, dark eyes; the petite Eurasian woman, more Euro than Asian. The attendant's name is Ingrid. There are fractures in the mirror; the trio look like a jigsaw puzzle.

Wallpaper is everywhere. Brown tree trunks, yellow flowers and green leaves chase each other over a deep red background. Stiff, heavily carved wooden chairs sit expectantly on both sides of the mirror. Dark oak frames the doors and a small window beside the front door, now bolted shut. Across from the mirror, stairs lead up and to the left. There are pictures everywhere mercifully covering the wallpaper, almost as ornately framed as the mirror. Most are of a young, handsome man, with thick, unruly hair, accompanied by figures in science, and, in one picture, by the King of Sweden.

It is an excess of color, of the baroque.

For an instant, Noah experiences a sense of *deja-vu* so intense that he almost staggers, losing his balance. His hand comes to rest on an elaborate hall stand, embellished by hand-carved deer heads serving as surprised coat hooks. He grabs one, his mind considering the impossibility of knowing this place. The feeling is so strong that panic fills him. He tastes acid, the sweat running down his back. It lasts only a few seconds, conquered by focusing on Kate, and by rubbing the little talisman through his shirt. *How could I know this place?* he thinks. *I've never been to Germany.*

They move from the vestibule into the parlor. It's more of the same. The couches and chairs are framed in dark wood, enormously padded, laden with pillows two or three deep. Thick drapes at the front of the room block out any trace of the brightening fall day. They are a dense maroon-brown. The Persian rugs sop up sound like giant floral sponges. Ingrid leads them to matching grandmother and grandfather chairs. She leaves them for a moment, making the first real noise in the overwrought space as she slides two giant oak doors back, dividing the living and dining rooms. They complain, squeaking on their tracks like a stiff stage curtain, revealing the world famous astrophysicist, internationally-acclaimed professor of physics, the Nobel award winner and former public television star. He wears a bright blue bathrobe, a stained T-shirt and soft, floppy pink slippers.

And nothing else.

He's just finished his breakfast. A telltale debris of eggs, bacon, cold meats and cheeses remain on the short housecoat, the pale blue highlighting the egg and coffee stains, a sort of culinary paisley. He moves sideways like a crab, exposing his right side to them, his slippers making light flop-flop noises, instantly absorbed. It takes him several slow minutes to maneuver from the dining room table through the large doorway to stand beside what seems to be his chair, the impression of his bottom firmly denting the soft, over-padded seat. A product of age and weight, the irony of gravity seizing him. He has the profile of Falstaff. When he turns to greet them, his left side—his scarred left arm and leg, his cruelly disfigured cheek and scar-closed eye—becomes visible, the remnants of his attempt at self-immolation. For a minute, he says nothing. He stands, staring at them as though they are from a different planet.

Perhaps they are.

They introduce themselves, explaining, stumbling over themselves a bit, intimidated by the memory of who he was. Their story emerges, one well known to us. As they tell it, its improbability appears in the light of day (even in the darkened space) as an elephant in the room. The professor however is moved to sit and engage with them. He knows this elephant; he is partly responsible for it. Ingrid helps him move the stout trunks of his legs, a match for the trees on the wallpaper, the calves swollen and red, engorged by blood and fluid, the infected cellulitis of the elderly and obese. They try not to notice something else—his aging, pendulous genitals, also the victim of gravity. They are quickly, mercifully covered by Ingrid with a sudden tug on his house coat.

From somewhere deep in the chair, a half whispered, half spoken German-English. "You have come to see me, see me, see me?" he repeats.

Noah asks, "Dr. Zapinsky, do you remember DiShannia Johns?"

He turns coy, looking upwards at the ceiling while he speaks, a child who hasn't eaten his peas but rather knocked them on the floor, pretending not to see them. "I *may* know her," he says.

"Can you tell us about her?" Kate asks.

"It is possible that she wrote to me not so long ago, asking me—it is hard to remember you see—perhaps certain questions." There is a small battle in his face; a smile wins, though just barely. "I cannot tell you everything in the letter, except," he says, smiling more, "she was afraid to use the internet and the email. Or perhaps she knew that I do not use them anymore. They won't let me."

Noah lets that go—who *they* were—matters for later on the reporter's checklist. Instead he says, "We think she reached out to you because you are an expert in dark matter and in red shift, and because she herself had some unorthodox views about these things. She wrote your name on a piece of paper, one of the last things she did."

The word "unorthodox" unleashes him. "You think my views unorthodox? My views unorthodox? My views unorthodox?" He repeats the question with growing anger.

Kate intervenes, "I'm sorry professor, we only mean to say that it's possible that you both had the same views."

And then they watch it happen.

It's like a pinball machine in motion, something from the last century. He moves from topic to topic with apparent randomness, careening from conversation point to conversation point, ports of call on a stormy sea. Emotional ports, as well. He is animated now, waving his arms, the fat underneath them like doughy wings. "It was too much for them, too much for them, too much for them," he says finally, exasperated, launching into another pattern of threes.

He swings again, becoming calmer, shifting his persona to the professor, not the angry discredited scholar. Years before, in a medical school psychiatry class, Noah saw videos of women who suffered from Personality Identity Disorder, what doctors used to call Multiple Personality. He recalls one woman who presented as a gentile, middle-aged housewife: she put her head down, closed her eyes, and opened them, becoming a foul-mouthed, rebellious teenager, all in the space of thirty seconds. Parallel personalities.

He is fully the professor now. "This, this unorthodoxy you call it, is not new, you know." He says, "*iss.*"

"Many years ago, since we could not really see objects with the naked eye, telescopes were built to measure the light from distant objects. We discovered that the spectra of light from many of these objects shifted to longer wavelengths, the red end of the spectrum, as these objects move away. This is the Doppler Effect, no?" They know. "At the same time, Einstein described an expanding universe, and even the *great Hubble,*" his voice makes giant air quotes, "said the red shift of distant galaxies increases as their distance increases. The only explanation that can tie these two observation together? The universe is expanding, is expanding, is expanding. Do you see?"

Before a reply forms inside them, Isaac shifts again, now the angry, rejected scholar. He almost-shouts, making a tiny cascade of egg and cheese run down the white stubble of his beard. "They were idiots!" He struggles to get out of his chair, falls back, panting. Sweat forms on his brow. He makes another effort to stand, this time succeeding.

"There was a problem," he mutters, sinking back into his chair with a sigh. He is sad now.

"They were not all wrong of course, not all stupid." He becomes quieter, confidential, leaning in to them. Ingrid closes his bathrobe again. "What if what we observe in the red shift is not accurate? What might make it so?" It sounds like *zo* from his lips.

His face says, *aha!* "Here is the answer. We know that the universe is made up of dark matter, that is, densities we don't see, which hold it together, like gravity. And we know how strong is gravity; it even affects time and space!" They nod, watching his face acquire its own red shift.

"But we only *guess* about dark energy. What if our knowledge is wrong? What if the dark matter is so strong that it *pulls* the blue shift into red territory? That it makes us *think* objects are moving away from us when they are actually getting closer? We observe the red shift in light, but dark matter and gravity are so strong they alter our ability to see accurately. In fact, it is possible that instead of these objects pulling away from each other, they are actually coming closer!"

He pauses for a minute; the little lecture tires him. He has been sitting, using his doughy arms and fat fingers as surrogate planets and suns, moving them together as he describes the effect of gravity and dark matter.

He startles them again, becoming the younger, articulate scientist, no longer immobile. Only minutes ago gravity was his enemy, much as it is the universe's; he could barely manage to stand by himself. Suddenly, he uses his arms as pistons, as strong as a thirty year old's, leveraging himself from his chair, using his thick tree-legs to stump across the Persian rug, soundless except for small grunts accompanying each footstep, and the tiny *flop-flop* of his slippers. He is all energy, moving to the bookcase that frames the large central window, shoving a small chair aside to retrieve a book. He flips open the pages. Ingrid watches the shape-shifting with increasing concern, joining him at the window, helping him find what he wants. Worry is a small shadow on her brow.

Noah reflects her worry. "What you said about red shift, professor. It isn't just referring to the solar system, is it? You're referring to the entire universe—all the planets, all the stars, am I right?"

For an instant, there is no sound, as though the universe holds its breath, waiting for an answer about its fate.

"You are precisely correct, Dr. Scott," Zapinsky says as though Noah is a graduate student. Zapinsky is the competent professor again; there is no trace of repetition, no pretense, no anger, no craziness. "The farther away the objects are the greater the red shift, the greater the alteration. In other words, the more they are speeding towards collapse." There is another pause, several minds absorbing this new knowledge. No one dares to ask a question that begins with "When?"

"Let me show you something else, something very important also, very interesting, my friends," Zapinsky says, the "my friends" drifting away as he tries to find the right page, flipping rapidly, but steadily. He is calmer now that he's found the book, more dignified. He stands taller, defiant, the scars on his left cheek almost bright red. The proof is in his hands.

"There is not enough light!" he mutters under his breath, frustrated that the darkened room won't let them see the page properly. He opens the drape, using the elaborate brass tie-back at the side of the window. He hefts the book in both arms, turning to the window to shine more light on the page. He pauses, seeing something outside the window, startling him. He straightens his back, as though defying his critics or perhaps what he sees in the window. He holds the book open to the window and says, very distinctly and finally, as though addressing another audience, "You see they were not only in error about the expansion of the universe. They were also wrong about the nature of the universe itself! They were wrong......"

The left shoulder of his bathrobe puffs backwards into the room.

A small hole appears in his house coat, a circle of red forming around it, leaking into the fabric, shifting its own tiny light spectrum from red to blue. An invisible hand pushes on the shoulder violently, spinning him towards the room, like a bully shoving him to the ground. The last word, *"wrong!"* is a blood-wet whisper as he falls to the ground. For several heartbeats, other than gunshots and the *tinkle-tinkle* of broken glass falling into the room, it is the only sound in the room.

They are frozen for those heartbeats, the heartbeats that mark the line between life and death. Between this world and the next.

It is a very thin line.

46

HEIDELBERG. GERMANY. SATURDAY

Ingrid is the first to respond, the closest to the slain professor.

She grabs the book as it falls from his hands, tosses it angrily on the floor, as though blaming it for his death. She kneels beside him, holding his head, the blood from his mouth running like the Neckar on to her skirt. No longer the cool nurse-companion, she sobs, "*Liebschen.*" Darling is the only German Kate recognizes. It is chaos. His head on her lap, the blood running down her dress, the book open to a picture. There are no more gun shots, but the glass shards from the window fall, caught in the dense drapery material, making tiny, clinking sounds as they fall, out of place in the carnage. The sounds should match what they see. Instead, except for Ingrid's sobbing and the tinkle of glass, it is absolutely quiet.

Ingrid reaches for the book, tearing out the page he wanted to show them, shoving it in Noah's hands. It is blood stained, three fingers of her left hand marking it forever. "You must get out of here, now!" she stage-whispers, urgently.

"Now! They have killed him! You may be next! Out! Through the bathroom at the end of the hall!" She points with a jerk of her head.

"What about you?" Noah asks. The remaining clinician in him checks the professor's pulse, despite the reporter's knowledge that he is dead. The second or third shot has entered his upper left chest. He was dead before he hit the floor. Noah says, urgency in his voice, "It's not just us; you're in danger here too!"

"I cannot leave him!" she says, tears clouding her vision, Kate's and Noah's too. "He is my husband. I cannot. He would not have left me." Noah hears a gurgling in Zapinsky's throat, a death rattle, a sudden exhaling of his last, now useless breath. Of his soul.

It is also useless to argue. Kate tugs at Noah's sleeve, urging him down the hallway and out.

Later, it occurs to Noah that Zapinsky got to say "they were wrong," just twice.

As they race down the hallway to the rear of the house, away from the carnage, the déjà vu feeling returns. This time it comes unaccompanied by its partner, panic and instead, helps him. He knows there is a bathroom underneath the main stairway, its door smaller than others in the house, as though bathrooms were an embarrassment. He knows a panel beside the toilet swings open, leading to a small, dark stairwell, like one in an ancient Mayan temple. He takes Kate by the hand, leading her down the narrow stairway into the coal-black basement. He knows he has been here before.

They hold on to the side of the stairwell like Braille readers. It's their lifeline, ensuring they don't fall. Suddenly, the door at the bottom of the stairs opens. Just visible in the basement light, a man beckons them. An odor hits them—the musk of dust and centuries.

"Quickly," the man says, Arabic in his voice, olive skin labelling his Middle Eastern origins. "Hurry. I must go to Ingrid. But you, you will be safe if you head that way," he points to another door leading to the basement of the adjacent house. More staccato thoughts. "Go through to my place. We connect, you see. Go up the first set of stairs to the outside alleyway. No one will see you there. Turn left. You will be safe. You can run all the way to the *Schloss*. But I must go to Ingrid. Is she hurt?" He doesn't stay to hear the answer. His need to run to her pulls him like gravity.

They are in a small, windowless basement room, its ceiling low. The years cascade off the stone and brick walls in layers. The room holds secrets. It contains a large overstuffed couch, just like its cousins on the main floor. A rumpled blanket and pillow are left on it, their rough terrain marked by the activity of the previous night. Noah recognizes the rumpling; his and Kate's bed looked just the same this morning. A coffee table holds two wine glasses, remnants of cabernet or merlot in both.

The escape route is clear. They enter the neighbor's basement, climb his stairs and exit into a back alley. They run at first, a crunching tachycardia of footsteps along the gravel path at the back of his house, their hearts racing faster than their running. Twenty minutes later they in their safe haven inside the castle ramparts. Breathless, they can watch for the attackers, whoever they are, from a vantage point that's worked for six centuries for that very purpose.

Kate, still winded from the running or the fear or both, manages, "What should we do, Noah? Are they after us? Who killed him?" Too many questions, none of them organized, among them Noah's, *How do I know that place*? There are very few answers.

"I was thinking," he says, also out of breath, "we'd be safer in a public place to figure this out, maybe go to the police."

"I'm not sure that they'd have any answers, you know? What could we tell them? We don't know anything. And protect us? I doubt it. Going to a public place, though? That makes sense."

They find the ancient *Schloss* stairs again, managing them more quickly now that the hot sun has burnt away the fog, dried the leaves. It's also burned away their sense of security, as substantial as the morning fog. They return to the internet café they visited early that morning. Now it's full of students, the homeless and the internet-poor, the air full of marijuana. It has one internet kiosk free. They claim it, ordering teas to calm their nerves. The café has smoke-stained blue walls, small tables where two or three can sit, room for drinks and laptops. Benches line the outside of the room, upholstered in sort of a red-brown, a couple of them occupied by homeless sleepers. A young, attractive dark haired woman walks in just after them, taking a seat by the window. She has a long, black skirt, hugging her hips. A sweater just barely covers her shoulders. Noah and Kate can watch the door, hide behind the private screens that ring the kiosks, like tiny castle walls.

And ask themselves, *What next*?

It's Kate who raises the fear level, "We shouldn't use the app, Noah. I think it's how they traced us here."

"You're right," he says. "But Harry did make a private drop box for us. He said it couldn't be traced. Remember?"

She does. Clever Harry had imbedded the link in plain view, on WashPO's home page. In an easy few clicks they get to the news of the day, including the big story, *The Evacuation of Sydney, Australia.* It's shown in videoclips, nightmarish scenes of cars driving through dense smoke, flames lining the roads, giant sparks raining down on the cars and their occupants, swelling the numbers of global refugees. There is also news on the terrorist front. A report on *60 Minutes* has exposed a serious hole in security in the US facility that stores sarin gas. Dozens of canisters are missing from a locked, Level Four facility outside Columbia, Missouri. Officials deny the theft, deny the facility, deny the existence of sarin on US soil. Activists claim that nearby fracking has caused the break. There are also reports that Russia is hiding news of a Chechen raid on one of its nuclear facilities. As if the terror of a sarin attack isn't enough. There's nothing about Heidelberg; it's too soon to hear anything about the professor's death.

Finally, Kate finds one nugget of useful information. She says, "The conference that Shanny was invited to? In Australia? I think this is it. It says the theme is 'convergence,' ways in which various avenues of scientific thought have come together: mathematics, particle physics and astronomy," she says, reading from a long list.

They have their fill of what the outside world knows. They click on the tiny dot over the *i* in "International," enter a Harry-designated password and are at another level of security. Noah answers a question, "What is your mother's maiden name?" by typing "Mathison." They're taken to another world.

There are updates from Gerry: he's found nothing new about Poseidon, General Wilcox, the Rose Charter Schools. Nothing about Naomi. There is only a coded communication from Harry whose basic message is, "Call home!"

Instead, they return to the public pages, where Ivaan's name rises from the screen as though embossed. Despite the fact that they have fled from CERN, despite his possible accomplices who seemed so—what's the word?—*interested* in their well-being, they might be able to get him alone, explain Zapinsky's theory of reverse red shift, even enlist his help in solving DiShannia's murder. There is no doubt he was moved by her death.

But they have a problem: Noah has twenty Euros in his pocket; there are possibly thirty in Kate's. There is no way for them to get money to travel, to access their accounts, without alerting the world to their location.

"We have to reach Harry, Noah, but how? The app's unsafe."

"I agree," he says, "but you know what? Whoever they are, they were clearly after the professor; they could have stormed the house. They could have killed us! They didn't. We could have been killed in the Underground. By that homeless guy in London. I bet they've had a dozen chances like that. Something's protecting us." Finally, the outburst played out, "I think we're okay to use the app."

They plug in the sim card and reach Harry, still at home. It's early morning in Virginia. He's still in his pajamas and there's a child—a different one this time—asleep on his chest. "It is so *good* to hear from you, rather. My goodness," he says, his voice is distorted by Kate's little phone, but his Britishness projects perfectly. "My goodness. I have been *so* worried about you both. We are," he leans close, his features filling the screen, "in bloody chaos at WashPO."

He almost-whispers, "Sydney has shut down two of our sections as though she's forgotten what news agencies are for. And then there's the FBI. The blighters are going through Naomi's and Gerry's files, trying to figure out what stories they were developing. Naomi is still missing. The upper-level management is useless. Useless." He almost hisses, a rare show of anger for him. "But you," he says finally, "are okay. I am so relieved!"

Sympathy arcs across the thousands of miles separating them as they describe Zapinsky's death, the rest of their story. The miracle of Skype. He questions the wisdom of going to Melbourne at first, but as they argue it's the only place where they might find answers, he agrees with them. His child, a baby not more than six weeks old, becomes fussy.

"That was horrible, *horrible* for you. Worse for the professor of course," he says. "I read about Dr. Zapinsky, maybe a little crazy but brilliant, and to have him die like that! My goodness," he repeats. The baby begins to cry, overwhelming the Skype microphone. Harry looks sheepishly at the camera, a *What can you do?* look on his face. "I'm going to find her mummy," he says, "I can get you out of there. Just hold on."

His face reappears in less than a few minutes, childless this time. "Thank God for mothers; they always know what to do." Noah and Kate are glad of *anyone* who can help.

"I have your flights. I found a late afternoon hop from Frankfurt to Dubai, then Dubai to Melbourne. You will have to hustle yourselves from one plane to the next, but you just have carry-ons, right?" They nod in unison, little dogs at the back of a car. "So. You will be fine. And of course, there's your train from Heidelberg to Frankfurt, which leaves," he checks his handheld, "at three-thirty. What time are you there now?" It's just a little after noon. "Perfect. I will send your flight details to you, but you have a tendency, don't you, children..." scolding, teasing, then serious, "...to take your phone apart, don't you?"

"How'd you pay for it?" Noah asks, meaning the trip, maybe everything.

"Ah, lad!" he says, smiling, "You don't want to know." A little smile crosses his face. "In chaos, things are, um, easier."

He signs off, suddenly very serious, worry lining the tiny movie screen of his face. "I mean this," he cautions them. "You must be very careful, look around you at all times, check for anyone following you. Try to move in public places. I think whatever this is, it is very serious. So are the people involved. And stay on touch! I shall worry otherwise."

"Good luck, chaps!" his sign off. Luck, necessary but not sufficient in this case.

The twin homeless men across the street from number eighty-four are stunned for a second, but their training and resilience re-emerge quickly. Within seconds, they immobilize the gunman, shoot his motorbike out from under him, call in extra help, stop another assassin from entering the house and doing more damage. Minutes later, a rented, anonymous van stops in front of the house, deposits the gunman and his motorcycle and guns into the back of the van and leaves. Apart from the shattered window and the carnage inside the house, it is as though nothing has happened.

Minutes later still, one of the homeless across the street takes a cell phone from his tattered jacket, an unusual thing to wear on a hot day. Stuffing falls from the sleeve like soft confetti. The sleeve holds a cell phone, an expensive security device attached to its case. He enters a number.

"Talk to me."

"They are clever, I gotta give them that. The gunman was in one of those freaking motorcycle gangs that have been going by all day. Fucker just peeled off from the group, veered across and down the street, was here before we could do anything about it. Followed by another guy, dressed like a freaking Hell's Angel for Chrissake. First guy got Zapinsky but we nailed his buddy before he could do any more damage. Didn't get the professor's what you call it, his attendant."

"Wife," said the voice on the phone. It's a voice that Noah would recognize.

"Whatever. Not her, she's fine, one of our guys in the next door-safe house? He's with her now."

"And the Americans?"

"Fine, just fine. They're running, but we have a couple guys on them. They'll be good. Kate looked shaken up but Noah's good." After a second, he says, "*Fucker.*" It's clear that he means the shooter.

"Don't be too hard on yourself. The Astronomers are goddamn everywhere, you know? They're like a cancer. This is all coming to a head, though. Soon."

The homeless man returns the phone to the sleeve of his jacket, pushing the stuffing in with it. Fussing with it to get it back into the zipped pocket, he pulls his sleeve up, revealing his forearm. The tattoo *The Fiery Collapse* is just visible, but only for a second.

47

FEDERATION SQUARE, MELBOURNE, AUSTRALIA, SUNDAY MORNING

The brochure is folded several times over, tucked into Noah's shirt pocket. *The Third World Congress on Science and Technology—Satellite Meeting on the State of the Universe*. It's the same one that Shanny was to present at. It's an invitational symposium held before the Clinton-Gates conference. Ivaan Horkonen is moderating. Noah checks his phone, the watch of the twenty-first century. It's just after eight-thirty.

Once the cabby learns Noah and Kate's destination, his conversation is peppered with references to the conference center. And profanity.

"It's a ruddy fucking waste of money, y'know, mate. Took'em years to build it, way over-budget." He says "mite" for mate.

"Probably the contractors and builders were paying off the government guys, having their hands in their pockets. Jesus Fucking Christ, probably the same in your country, right? Shitty fucking workmanship too. Last month, four glass panels fell onto the walkway below, almost killed a sheila. Fuck. And the biggest joke? The *Ear*-Con! Half of the ducts weren't fucking connected to anything, nothing. And now they got a helly landing pad on the top, for them high-priced arseholes to waltz in an' out. Fucking movie stars, politicians, and the like."

The driver uses "fuck" like writers use punctuation.

"Ear-Con?" Kate asks.

"The thing that cools you." Thankfully he points to the air conditioning vent in the cab just above his head.

"Oh, *air* conditioning," Noah says, glad of the comic relief.

The driver continues, conjuring a reporter's wet dream about construction nightmares and corruption. They stop listening though, focusing on getting into the place, finding Dr. Horkonen, maybe finding the Astronomer.

The last thing the cabby says as Noah pays is, '"Look at all them windows!"

He's right: if nothing else, Federation Square, housing the Melbourne Conference and Convention Center, is almost all glass. It's a giant angular jewel in the heart of Melbourne's Central Business District, every square inch a virtual window on the world.

Windows let light in. If Noah and Kate have their way, it will also let light— some knowledge at least—out. Some knowledge about the contraction of the universe, not its expansion. Some knowledge about reverse red shift. Some knowledge about the deaths of Dr. Zapinsky, of Miriam and DiShannia, possibly others. Who knows how many? Some knowledge about a group at work, pulling invisible strings in government and elsewhere.

Not, however, events to be immediately realized.

They enter the giant rhomboid, all angles and projected planes, as complex as the spider web of lies and deceit that propels them. The sharp angles of the windows are repeated over and over again on the rug beneath them. Acres of rug. Millions of questions.

Press passes are like keys to kingdoms, little magic wands that open turnstiles, allow entry into places and receptions, to ask questions you'd never ask in a normal world. They pass their credentials to the young Asian-Aussie woman underneath the *Press* sign. The satellite session they're interested in is marked *CLOSED*. She scans the bar code on their name badges and her face brightens. She says, masking her surprise, "Oh, Miss Chien-Forrest and *Doctor* Scott, they're expecting you! You should have no problem getting in. it's up the escalator to level three, Room 311."

The Fed Square escalator points its way skyward like a giant finger, angling across the vaulted three-story central atrium. It's a never-ending silver belt, skipping the second floor mezzanine level, ignoring it like a first wife. It's open, busy with several hundred meeting participants, small spiders in an academic and technology-driven net. The spiders visit posters, stop to greet and shake hands, have coffee at impromptu stand up tables. The elevator stops its glide skywards, reaches its apex.

The contrast to the floor below is striking: no one's there. No handshaking, no stand-up tables, no coffee. A few unobserved posters, sad trees in an academic forest. Alone at the top of the long escalator, a tall young Australian man meets them, a gym rat. Perhaps all Australian men are.

"We've been expecting you." The gym rat's words are friendly, but there's something in the welcome that drops the temperature.

"Expecting" is such a pregnant word.

The guard takes them to a room at the end of a long carpeted hallway, the design in bright, happy colors. They're far from either.

He tells them, "Please sit along the side. And," not as an afterthought, "leave your cell phone and your other devices with me." He points to a table at the door where dozens of communication devices have been deposited, business cards taped to each, a marketer's delight. Surprisingly, Kate and Noah hand over their mobile devices without complaint, not a normal action for reporters. An efficient young woman hands them a detailed outline of the day's proceedings with a curt, "Please return this to me when you leave." A printed agenda, leaving cell phones, instructions to return the agenda—all highly unusual.

The room is the size of a small tennis court, bounded by a perfect frame of white cloth-covered tables. Twenty or thirty men and women are seated at the table, their names and affiliations marked in Arial **BOLD** in front of them on white name tents. Across the room from Noah and Kate is a giant flat screen. Several participants have moved their chairs back so they can view it, like fans at a sports bar. On the wall opposite the flat screen, a second tier of staff chairs is filled with more young men and women, twins (or siblings at least) of the young man at the top of the elevator. The room is quiet, listening to what the agenda says is one of the first formal presentations of the morning.

The room has a peculiar smell, Noah thinks, not unpleasant, soothing, faintly maritime.

For reasons they can't explain, Noah and Kate are calm, a cloud of quiet and serenity surrounding them, stronger than when they sat at the *Schloss*. The agenda's highlights—Ivaan Horkonen moderating; modern and ancient theories and beliefs about the universe (Mayan included); attempts at finding extra-terrestrial life—seem reassuring.

The morning proceeds, the conversations flowing like an unobstructed river, smoothly, engagingly, open. The conference reflects DiShannia's work and they feel certain they'll find clues to her death. The ten-thirty break is much more than the fifteen minutes slotted. It allows Noah to meet Ivaan Horkonen in one corner of the room. Ivaan grabs two chairs, pulling them out, patting one of them, inviting Ivaan to sit as though they're old friends. Kate finds out what she can about Zapinsky's theories, about red and blue shift, about parallel universes from others in the room, while Noah does the same with Ivaan. More pieces in a giant puzzle.

Ivaan apologies, "Dr. Scott, I am sorry how I tried to secure your staying with us in Geneva. I was, you might say, overly enthusiastic. The facts are that Zapinsky's theories are entirely erroneous, an interesting story, but nothing more. I would like you to join me later to explore this further. There are experiments we can run, even thought-experiments. And as to parallel universes? That too deserves thought. It is all very interesting but, answers that I can give you right now? I have none."

Noah also has no answers but something has shifted in his thinking: he slots Ivaan into a safe category.

During the final open discussion, a participant has asked for five minutes to propose a theory. He sits directly in front of Kate, allowing her only a view of his back and head. He's young, earnest, his hair unruled by any comb, overly thin. The room is dimmed for his presentation and as he starts, someone else enters the room, sitting to one side with others so that he can view the screen. The presenter pulls the wire-thin microphone closer to him. His speech is the sing-song of the German-Swiss speaking English, the music of science. The speaker is also nervous, and a small stutter adds some anticipation to his bland talk, at least bland from the title that Noah reads, *Collapse or Expansion? The Role of Dark Matter. Dr. Andreas Langenaeker, University of Bern, SW.*

"You will see on the next slide what I m-mean what I say about the dark matter and dark energy, and," he takes a deep breath, "whether they are real or whether we created them to fit our own equations." The word "created" is particularly hard for him, his head bending to shove the word into existence. The next slide is a quote from A. E. Housman, a decades-old reminder of the pitfalls of scientific inquiry.

> This method—the conclusion first, reasons afterwards, has always been in favour with the human race. You write down at the outset the answer to the sum. Then you [fabricate an argument] by which you can pretend to have arrived at the conclusion.
> **The House of Delusions,** A. E. Housman, Professor of Latin, University of London, 1892

"Thus there is an e-elephant in the room."

It's obvious that not everyone gets the analogy. "Let me explain. An elephant is of course a large animal, impossible not to notice, but which, for some reason, we ignore."

The reference to the elephant stirs something in Noah, a memory as frail as a dream, a recollection of an older woman he called "Auntie." A woman who was very kind to him, who met him occasionally in, of all places, the Washington zoo. What he remembers most is how she loved the elephants. "They remember, Noah," she had said, more than once.

He was remembering too. Why now?

Andreas is finishing. "I p-propose," he says, "that we have developed a theory of dark matter and dark energy…" and then a breath, an inspiration in more ways than one. He sits taller in his seat, straightens his back, surer of himself. He says,"…to fit our own foregone conclusions about the expansion of space. I believe, that we do not actually *know* that there is more dark energy than dark matter. We actually do not *know* that the universe is expand…."

Someone interrupts the sentence, "Perhaps this is a good place to stop for questions."

Noah cannot place the voice. It is familiar but its owner is hidden behind others, in shadow, turned towards the flat screen. He is British, like many of the participants. The agenda has Horkonen as the moderator, but the newcomer appears to command their attention. The open discussion ends.

The elephant in the room continues to be ignored. Relieved, Ivaan steers the session into other areas like a skilful navigator. He writes down the order of those who have tipped their name tents up, seeking to ask questions. Questions about early discoveries, even the work of Galileo, and Arab astronomers and mathematicians. In the quiet calm cloud that surrounds him, Noah is struck by an almost plaintive voice.

"How certain can we be," someone asks of Dr. France LaPrise. The agenda says she is the current Global SETI project chair, "….that there is no other life in space?" SETI is the Search for Extra-terrestrial Intelligence.

"Professor," she says *professeur*, the *Marseillaise* in her voice as she presses the little *Talk* button, grasps the thin microphone gently between her thumb and forefinger. "We have quadrupled our efforts in the last decade thanks to funding from the Central European Bank and the largesse of private donors. We have relays of networks across the globe and now in satellites. We have even established a listening and watching station on the moons, and the 2015 unmanned space vehicle, *Gallant,* now millions of kilometers into the void, almost to Neptune, has picked up nothing. No radio waves, no pings, Nothing."

The last sentence is untrue. In CERN, Noah heard discussions about "pings," about their source.

LaPrise's straight gray hair reflects the spot lights above her as she leans forward, like Andreas Langenecker several minutes before. "I think it is safe to say this: if there is any other intelligent life in the universe, it wishes not to communicate with us. I am of the firm belief however that there *is* no sentient life apart from ours in the universe."

"But what of the pings whose source we cannot determine, Dr. LaPrise? Some have said they come from a p-parallel universe. What of them?" Langenaecker asks, grabbing his microphone aggressively with both hands. Two things become apparent. First, the morning has been a carefully scripted, sleepy play, dedicated to putting to rest theories and fears about the collapse of the universe. Langenaecker has not been on script.

And second, Ivaan has lost control of the meeting.

It's like watching something in slow motion. It begins as a small disturbance in what has been a model of the tight scholarly dance. Two people whisper loudly on one side of the room; one man grabs the microphone, determined. "I have plans, Dr. Horkonen. I am sure most of us do."

"Yes, flights," several others say.

Handfuls of people begin to leave their seats, moving towards their suitcases standing at attention like squat soldiers, lined up beside the main exit. The young staffers move to block the door.

"I am sure you do, but…" Ivaan says, leaning into his microphone, rapping it so that a loud, *thump-THUMP* echoes in the room. "Please stay. I have important news for you, a special announcement about funding from a special visitor." The word "funding" ends the mutiny as quickly as it starts. The people who have gone to get their bags return to their seats like sheep, led by the call of money.

Later, Noah recalls elements of the next five minutes like some slow motion video. Ivaan asking for the lights to be turned up. The participants settling back in their chairs, even those who were most anxious to leave. The Aussie gents moving more definitely in front of the exit doors. A young staffer moving between Noah and Kate, removing a small cylinder from her purse. Ivaan inviting the newcomer to join him at the head of the table. Noah becoming increasingly certain that this person is a major figure in this mystery. The newcomer takes the seat Ivaan offers him.

He is a young-looking, overweight man, possessing a British accent, pudgy hands, a trace of olive skin. A man with considerable IT skills, and with, it is apparent, other identities. A man with a warm smile and a cold heart.

A man we know as Harry. The world has other names for him.

He displays surprisingly enormous balls, Harry does, like watermelons, though figuratively of course. He searches the audience for a minute, finding Noah, smiling.

"Good Day. My name is Franklin Church. I represent ACRA, the Alliance of Cosmologic Research Agencies, an agency that may be new to you. It is a multinational third sector organization devoted to studying the questions you have raised today, devoted to funding *your* research. I am sure many of you are surprised that a representative of a funder would enter your conference in such a manner. Believe me, my friends, I have no intention of disrupting your day or your plans. But I have news—spectacular news indeed—about funding opportunities and a request about *directed* research efforts in a particular field. Let me tell you more."

He does. The funding, he says, is the product of years of effort on the part of the Alliance. ACRA's sources of funding—Noah knows exactly what those sources are—will allow them to enlarge their research enterprises. The full announcement has been delayed until Tuesday morning, when all its details will be made clear. He wants them to stay, even those who had planned to attend only the satellite symposium and skip the large meeting. He wants them at the press conference at the end. He stresses *every one* of them.

For a group that only minutes before was anxious to leave, its members now check their pocket calendars, become anxious to get to their cell phones at the front door, to change their plans. Many had not planned to stay for the whole conference. Now *all* of them would. For what purpose?

Only Noah hears the smugness in Harry's voice. Only Noah guesses the source of the funding—not some neutral governmental or quasi-governmental agency, not some ethical private foundation, but some mal-intended group anxious to stamp out any trace of theories which indicate the universe is collapsing. Like DiShannia's research. It's as plain as if it were projected on the flat screen in front of them. Only Noah thinks, using terms rare for him but common in the Aussie cabby's vocabulary, *'What the fuck is going on?!'*

But he and Kate have a problem.

Both of them feel they should shout, "Don't listen to this man!" But they feel weighted down, their feet encased in cement, their heads simultaneously spinning and calm. The young staffer who has moved between them slowly releases the contents of the little cylinder she carries like a fat pen in her hand. It carries the odor of the ocean, such a nice smell filling the area between them. It's the same scent they noticed when they first entered the room, but much stronger. And for a minute or two they engage in what Ivaan might call a thought experiment. *Could they escape, maybe make their way into the utility corridor to find a vent leading to an air conditioning unit? Could they climb up and out through the ducts, those ear-con ducts?* But the thoughts become tangled and the answers to the questions clearly "no."

Soon, the two of them become aware of being helped by Aussie assistants, one on either side, leading them through a service door and down a corridor. They're taken, half carried, to a waiting car, neither able to do much more than obey their captor's commands. As though they were drunk or ill.

For several hours, it's the last thing they know.

48

THE DANDENONG HILLS. VICTORIA. AUSTRALIA. SUNDAY AFTERNOON

Noah recalls this about the ride from Melbourne. The primeval mustiness of a rug wrapped around him, his nose pushed into the cheap pile, dirt clogging his nostrils. The car swaying wildly around corners. Bumps when they hit a pothole, jarring him from fogginess into painful wakefulness and back to oblivion. A gravel road, rocky pings of stone against the car's underbelly. The heat of course—the heat of the car, the heat of the black, melting tarmac radiating upwards, the heat of anxiety. The heat of an advancing sun. Kate has no such memory; the aerosolized tranquilizer has rendered her unconscious.

Terror jars him as much as the ride, as the tranquilizer wears off: a here is he? Where are they headed? Who are their captors? What will they do with them?

The scented tranquilizer retreats, like the anesthetic of a dentist. The pain advances for him, not yet for her.

The small *clang* of metal on metal, echoing in a cavernous space. Hard concrete at their feet, pleasantly cool. Then the odor of a thousand open wine bottles— zinfandel and merlot, shiraz and cabernet, pinot gris and muscatel. Chardonnay. Old, stale, stronger now that the rugs is removed, especially the zinfandel. The sounds and smells are empty, dead, like their hope. Someone brushes Noah's face, a surprising, kind gesture. He has one last thought, *This is a winery*, before his world, like Kate's, descends into a small black hole of consciousness.

Waking, they are in an abandoned warehouse, wine kegs strewn around, some stacked, most small or moderate sized. Sadistic handlers have strapped Noah's hands and legs, even his neck, to a giant keg. His right cheek is crushed into its side. He is spread-eagled, naked but for a pair of two-day old undershorts, like some grotesque, pale toad pinned to a dissecting board. He wakes to pain—in his wrists and ankles, stapled too tightly, in his flank where he has taken punches, in his head. He must have fought them he thinks, not without a trace of inner adolescent pride. And then there is the worse pain, the unanswered questions from the hours before and the terror, the marriage of physical and mental anguish.

From his narrow world view, Noah sees Kate, is relieved but angry. Like him, she's stripped to her underwear, but is stapled with her back to a giant wine barrel. Her head lolls to one side, but he sees the rise and fall of her chest, knows she is breathing, is alive.

He also sees two of his captors, spot-lit in the dark metal cavern by one of dozens of lights hanging high above. One of them, shaved-bald, aggressive, wearing the cologne of sweat, leans in to him, nose-to-nose, brave in the face of an immobilized victim. The other guy is dimly lit, not menacing, smiling, enjoying the view. Noah senses a third behind him, out of sight.

"Here's what we know, *buddy*." Any trace of friendship has leaked from the word. It is spoiled for Noah forever, like the smell of zinfandel.

The man is a snake, not saying much but insinuating everything, inches from Noah's face. "We know where you've been. To the Eastern Market School, to DiShannia's home. To England, to visit Dr. Ansari. Too bad about her, huh? To visit the CERN team in Geneva; we know all about that. Then you thought you got rid of us and met Zapinsky. That went well, don't you think? Now you've met with Horkonen again. How did *that* go? Now it's your turn. Here's where you tell us what *you* know. Here's your chance to spill your fucking guts to us. I guess you can tell we're serious here." *Serious* sounds like a terminal event.

Noah's inner adolescent raises his head, "I'm not telling you anything. Who the hell do you think you are?" a part of him wonders whether rhetorical questions might be permitted. They are not apparently. The two begin to work on Noah—a dull, heavy, sudden and excruciating blow to his left side, just over his kidney, expertly placed, a high kick to his thigh. And from both of them, barely repressed enjoyment. The third person, behind him, remains out of sight, quiet.

Grunting, voting for discretion over valor, Noah manages, "I've got nothing for you."

Nothing is not what they want. Noah manages, through the pain, "We only have hints at things, like civilizations that died because they believed that the end of the word was near. There are theories about the Big Bang and the expanding or maybe contracting universe. I can even write a mile-long equation on that wall over there about dark matter and dark energy and rates of expansion and contraction. And I can give you a *treatise*—if you even know what that is!" This wins Noah another kick in his thigh, doubly painful. Gasping, now, his adolescent retreating, "Yes, a treatise on red shift and blue shift. And I know about the Rose School for example, how kids seem to be disappearing, how the funding flows. I've got ideas about global warming, its relationship to all of this."

He is out of facts for the moment. And out of breath.

"What about your last visit, Noah?" This last voice is meters away, perhaps on a floor below. Although his pain is worse, Noah can see more. He realizes he's on a catwalk, a half floor or more above a cement pad, filled with hundreds of wine casks, soldiers in a war of words and theories.

The voice comes from Harry.

Noah hears Harry's hard-soled shoes on the metal catwalk stairs, making his way to the top, directly behind him. A chair scrapes the concrete floor, echoing, menacing, comes to rest beside Noah, less than a meter away.

"What did the CERN visit give you, Noah?" His voice is much quieter now. He doesn't have to project it. It is more sibilant, sinister.

Noah is consumed by questions about Harry, but is maddened by what he sees as betrayal. He knows betrayal intimately. His rage threatens to overtake him like a tsunami. Using enormous will, he pushes the feelings deep, deep inside him, along with the questions. If he lives, there will be plenty of time.

Time is another question.

"Mostly nothing," Noah manages. The rest is staccato fact-telling, the story broken by the pain in his ribs and kidneys, his breathlessness. "Horkonen and the others talked. They showed me what they say is proof of Higgs bosons. We talked about parallel universes," he pauses, winces. "The Higgs boson might travel between them. They talked about receiving pings but they don't know their origin." There is a deep breath, painful. The rest comes in a rush, "You can't be thinking there's a Higgs boson machine, like a time machine!!" He laughs, a breathless, humorless sound, then continues, "Parallel universe traveling isn't like stepping into some magic telephone booth." He's out of breath. Out of facts, the reporter's currency.

Even more strongly, Noah feels *this* doesn't add up—the chase, Kate's capture, the game-playing with Harry as the referee. His anger swells, overwhelming everything else, even the pain. He takes a breath and yells, the tsunami breaking, "Why would you kill Dr. Al-Ansari? Or DiShannia? Professor Zapinsky? Why?"

Harry's rises from his chair, scraping it on the floor, like a cat's cry piecing the space. He defines calmness, precision. "Oh, you'll learn about that soon, Noah." Noah turns slightly, enough to see Harry's smug face, watches as Harry grasps his cheeks in his pudgy hand, an obscene imitation of a mother's gesture.

Noah can count on the fingers of one hand those people he hates. A bully in high school. His father's new wife. Betrayers like Pete, his once-best friend. Like Mohammet, in Afghanistan. And now Harry.

He doesn't know that Harry has other names. We also know him as Aabis. As the Astronomer. As Franklin Church. As another dozen names, one of which may be Evil.

Noah's heart rate rises, fueled by Harry's calm, by his fear for Kate.

"How you have disappointed me, Noah, you and little Kate, the tiny bright spots on my team." *His* team? "We have led you, no, *I* have led you to every possible source of information to solve our little riddle and you have not provided us with the answers we *want*, " a tiny rise in his voice.

"Let me be precise here: you've given me nothing. *Nothing!*" he shouts, all pretense at acting the British gentleman gone. "Nothing about red shift, nothing about CERN, nothing really revealing about the Higgs boson! Nothing through the app. Why do you think I created the *app* in the first place?" It is no question.

Noah draws Harry's anger into himself, "I asked you questions, Harry. Why would you kill DiShannia? Why kill Miriam?"

"Ah," he says, Harry-the-wise. "They had some answers, but not the whole picture. And their timing was all wrong, Noah. Timing is *everything*. And there is something rather exquisitely precise about the timing of all of this. We cannot tell our story too soon, can we? And if we tell it too late, well, we might miss, let us say, opportunities." He leans close to Noah. The coffee smell of his breath is almost overpowering.

"And then there's the Fiery Collapse, the final crush, isn't there Noah? We must avoid that at all costs. Perhaps not you so much, but *we* must. And that's the question isn't it? Is there a Higgs boson mechanism that could lead to a parallel universe? And you, my skinny friend, you have given me nothing that would help answer that question. You, of all people, should have been able to figure this out!"

There is something else in his voice. It holds layers of anger and disappointment like geological layers, but also something more ancient. For all of his bluster, Harry-Aabis is still only a poor, orphaned boy, out of place in a Hindu country, out of place in a Christian home, unaccepted by his peers. A child who learned to be a chameleon to survive. And later, a priest, rising in the ranks of the Astronomers, still feeling inferior to Noah, the unknowing genius. Noah was to be Harry's ticket to a future.

Noah has had his fill of pain and loss. He yells, "You're a sick, sadistic fuck!" For someone unaccustomed to swearing, Noah uses the only tools he has—words.

Harry-Aabis replies, suddenly as calm as a pond, "To be fair, if I were truly as you say, *sadistic*, I'd stay and watch you and Kate die. I never do that. I leave that for my, um, three staff members here."

Harry has glanced at his watch several times during the little exchange, almost nervously. An appointment? A flight out of Melbourne to catch? Harry turns on his heel, grabs the slim metal bar of the catwalk railing and descends the stairs, his hard shoes making the only noise in the room.

Not until much later does Noah learn his real name, or his story. Or the reason for the anxious time-checking.

49

DANEDONG HILLS. VICTORIA. AUSTRALIA.
SUNDAY EVENING

Minutes pass. Hushed conversations flow between Noah's two captors and the third person, still out of Noah's line of sight. Two of them move closer to Kate, dressed alike in tight black T's, standing over her, menacing. Leaning in to her like some distorted version of teenaged boys talking up a girl.

In a second, the third person is inches away from his ear. Noah sees a fraction of his face, as black as his T-shirt. He leans into Noah, grabbing his neck and arms with hard, rough hands. They pinch the soft space between Noah's neck and shoulder, sending unbelievable pain down his left arm. And then, from his pocket, like some magician, he produces a box cutter. Noah is momentarily terrified. He stifles a yell, steels himself. *My face,* he thinks, *he's going to cut my face.*

The man takes the box cutter and slowly, precisely, cuts the strap that fixes Noah's left arm to the barrel.

"Keep it there!" he says. "Don't let them know your hand is free." It's a stage whispered mystery: *Why free one hand? Why whisper?* Noah's body slumps for a second, but his arm stays steady. He also smells something on the man's breath, something strangely familiar.

Noah watches the two other men with Kate. In her off-white bra and panties, she's pinned like an elegant, pale frog in a high school science class. If he stretches, expanding his shoulder joint, extending the joints of his fingers, Noah might just touch hers. It would be easier now that his left arm is freed, but he obeys the man's instructions.

Noah watches the slow steady rise and fall of Kate's chest. Her second finger is moving, the one that touches his lips sometimes when she wants less talk from him and perhaps something more. It's a small replica of God's finger as it touched Michelangelo's Adam, in this case breathing life into Noah. She is sedated, her head fallen to one side, a marionette whose strings have been cut.

The taller guy, leaning over Kate says to both of them, "You heard the boss." There is Aussie-threat in his voice. He is Carleton. "We're going to walk you through every step of the last week. Everyone you've met. Everything you've learned.

"You're bloody fucking going to tell us what we came to find out. And this bloke, his name is Tyler, mate." He nods to his shorter partner, now beginning to rub Kate's shoulder, grabbing his crotch at the same time. He's going to, um, help us here. He's also going to record everything and send it to your Harry. We call him something else." Tyler moves way from Kate, removes his phone from his pants pocket, starts to shoot a video of Noah as the conversation begins. Like a crazy film director.

Noah thinks he can string them along, perhaps with useless details about his trip to the morgue, about other events over the last five days, but he is wrong. Fifteen minutes of recorded conversation, of thoughts about his freed left arm and the man behind him, he runs out of steam.

Carleton says, "You're skipping over the part about parallel universes, mate. We're thinking there's more there...."

"I don't know," Noah says, a world of truth and a universe of lie in those three words.

"Maybe this will help you remember," Tyler says. He moves back to stand in front of Kate, his left hand now pointing a gun toward Noah, his right hand moving from his defiantly-massaged crotch to a place between her thighs. His fingers move the cotton of her panties slowly back, edging closer to the moist-sacred space that Noah has visited only once, and now maybe never again.

"Fuck you!" Noah yells, helpless to do much else. The battery of profanity.

What he saw in Tyler's eye a moment ago wasn't bloodthirst, it was lust. But the man behind him has other ideas. He puts a choke-hold on Noah's neck, pressing his hard body into Noah's.

"We don't have to do that, Tyler," he says, his voice as hard as the barrel-wood rougheninng Noah's body. *This* guy *is their leader*, not pony-tailed, face-scarred Carleton or his friend, the crotch-rubber. His voice is as close to Noah's ear as a lover's.

And loud, "Get your hand out of there. Now. I got a better way, man. Let me handle this."

He does. His strong right arm tightens around Noah's neck, the cement of his bicep wraps around his windpipe, pythoning his trachea. His left hand holds the cold hard erection of a gun, now shoved into the back of Noah's shorts. Noah's anatomy lessons flood back to him: if the gun goes off it will sever his aorta, shatter his spine in seconds. The panic returns, his heart rate doubles, the sweat pouring down his back like a cold offering. He cannot reach his talisman. The man continues leaning into Noah, compressing him even further. His full face finally comes into view, the sandpaper-stubble of his beard scraping Noah's cheek. Noah can smell something, garlic maybe. In a strange way, long before he figures out what the smell is, it calms him. Those who say that smell carries the strongest memories are right.

But the man doesn't calm him. "You're going to *fucking* tell us everything you know, buddy! This is your last chance, I mean it. You'll watch us kill Kate next!" Very menacing, scarier than if he had yelled it. The others stand, drop their weapons to their sides, reassured that he's taken charge. They move away from Kate and, in whispered voice, Noah hears, "Relax, Noah. *Relax.* I've got your back."

A giant flood gate opens, carrying with it the debris of twenty years, of a triangle of hate and betrayal. It isn't garlic that he smells. It's fennel. And pipe tobacco.

Noah sees him then. Almost twenty years later, twenty pounds of muscle heavier. And twenty years of toughness baked into him, along with the fennel and garlic. And perhaps something else. Why had he said, "I've got your back"?

The only guy Noah ever knew who ate garlic and fennel was Pete. Pete, who wore his manhood like a codpiece, whose only-ever homebody, feminine thing was carefully peeling and slicing fennel, baking it and spreading it on toast, virtually every day of his life. Something to help the bad breath of pipe smoking.

Slowly, Pete turns to the other two men, taking the gun from Noah's back and pointing at the others.

"Change of plans, boys. Drop them," he says, indicating their guns with his own. "Put your hands slowly in the air. Slowly."

They are surprised, angry, releasing subterranean sounds like surprised cattle. But they comply. Pete has them throw their guns his way, lay face down on the ground. He has Carleton incapacitate Tyler with plastic ties and then quickly ties Carleton up himself. He hands the gun to Noah—the reason his left arm was freed—and then quickly cuts Noah free. Together, they cut Kate's ties, and help her lie down, still partly unconscious but rousing. There's a bruise on her forehead but it's reassuringly small. Her arm bruise and the Rasties' handprints are still there, but they're old, harmless. Noah checks her, the doctor still inside him.

The entire time, Noah fights the impossibility that this is Pete, watching him. His muscles straining the fabric of his T-shirt and his jeans, the sweat pouring off him like rain water on a black roof. Pete, occupier of his nightmares, the wrecker of the love affair of his life. He knows Pete, the bastard.

But Pete, his saviour?

50

DANDENONG HILLS. VICTORIA. AUSTRALIA. SUNDAY NIGHT

I've got your back.

Noah knows Pete the bastard. Who was this Pete?

Whoever he is, he's good to his word. He is on his phone, giving directions to someone, then frees them, helping Noah take Kate from the winery to the car. She is drowsy but able to stand by herself with their help. They lay her down in the back of an old Honda Civic. Noah checks her again, thinks she's okay. Ironically, the doctor is in worse shape than his patient, his flank aching, his thigh bruised, his ribs hurting with every breath, but he is mobile. And awake. All she wants to do is sleep.

"I'm okay," she manages, well enough to communicate. "Just let me lie here." Her questions will wait until later.

Pete finds a blanket, helps pull it over her. "Good," he says, "Keep your head down, okay?"

"No problem with that," she says, smiling at Noah. And is sound asleep in seconds.

The Civic is a perfect getaway car, a non-descript gray model from the last decade. Pete gets them to shed their sim cards along the way. "'Pitch'em," Pete says. "We can't have anybody chasing us." He rips out the little plug-in GPS from the Honda, throwing it on the ground, behind the parched yews that line the winery's parking lot.

Noah finds a moderately comfortable position in the car's front passenger seat, its position on the left and the events of the last few hours disorienting. Pete tells him that they only used long acting barbiturates on Kate. "She'll be fine, drowsy for a while, but fine." The air weighs heavily between them—the worlds and years that separate them, the events of the last few days. The discussion waiting, like a visitor, for the two of them. It's fair to say that Noah is very attentive to what comes next.

And so it starts: forty kilometers of driving, nearly twenty years of catching up. Speeding down the sinuous roads of foreign wine fields, in a foreign country, in a foreign car.

"I'm not who you think I am," Pete says.

"No shit!" Noah says, using his new-found profanity as others use their fists. "Start talking."

"I'm not even Pete. We made up that name when I was assigned to you. I'm DeJohn Walker, like dee-*John.*"

"Like the mustard?"

"Like the mustard."

"What do you mean, *assigned* to me?"

"Actually assigned to both of you, both you and Deb'rah." His speech had reverted to African American, the pattern Noah recognizes as Pete's. Perhaps he has to become Pete if he is to tell his story.

"They watched you, man, the Rose School people *watched* you from the time you were little I guess, watched you because of your math scores and your particular, I don' know, your whatever, your genius. And then when they learned you was going to Georgetown, and so was Deb'rah, well, the deal was made, you know."

He becomes quieter, trying to organize the story, the first press of it out of the way.

"They watched me, too, you know in Detroit where I grew up, pretty much from the time I was ten maybe. I was pretty good in little league hockey. I don't know how my mom could afford it, but I was in this real competitive league. That's where I got picked." *Picked* is a bitter word for him, like salt on his lips. Pete takes another look around, eyeball radar looking for other cars. Driving on the left requires a little extra attention.

"Turns out they picked me for my loyalty. *Loyalty* for Chrissake. That was *my* genius," he says with more salt.

"The coaches would give you these scenarios to talk about in class, and then play it out on the ice. Like, 'If you had a chance to score, or pass so that someone else could score, what would you do? Who's more important, the team or you?' And when we'd play, I guess, I passed so that someone else would score pretty much all the time. That was *my* talent that got me picked. Loyalty," said with a half-laugh.

"So that got me into the Rose School. There was no way we could afford it, my mom and me. All expenses paid on a hockey scholarship for fuck's sake, meanwhile they was grooming me for this job, this *career*." More salt.

'What job?" Noah asks.

He appears not to answer Noah, although, as you've learned, appearances can be deceiving. He says, "Do you remember the first time we met?"

Noah nods, surprised at how clearly the memory returns, like a movie replayed. "Yes, we both got laughing in class at that lecturer, the guy nobody could understand."

"No," he said, "Before that. I was the guy telling you not to go into the science nerds' meet'n'greet.' That was me. It was me trying to keep you and Deborah apart, even back then. Pretty much a waste of time, I guess. You were my first assignments. I was kind of green, you know. But you had this thing, this chemistry, with her right from the first. There was no way I could keep you apart. No way. I even tried putting some moves on her myself early on."

"You got your moves in on her later, though didn't you?" Noah says, another expletive sitting at the tip of his tongue. Trying but not succeeding to keep the anger out of his voice. And the pain. Anger and pain, like two strands of the same DNA, are close to the surface. Pete looks over at Noah, his eyes locked outside the passenger window, seeing the final scene with Pete and Deborah in the glass. There is pain in both pairs of eyes.

Finally, from Pete. "That was the hardest thing to do, to make it like she was cheating on you. But I had to. She went off her birth control pills, thinking you were heading off to do medicine, and you'd take up somebody else for sure. Her mind was totally on you, man. So I started to spend extra time with her, be sympathetic. You made it easy, you off in class all the time. She was hurt, didn't think you wanted her. She started to cry on my shoulder for a bit. That made it easier. Then she told me one night that you and she hadn't, you know, done it for a while, and well, you saw what happened."

And then Noah sees something else, something missed in the darkness of the car, or the darkness of his thoughts. Another car speeding toward them, its high beams shining directly at them, makes it possible. It's a small tear, tracing its way down the little valley between Pete's nose and his cheek. Such a tiny thing to douse the fire of Noah's anger and hatred: a cloud lifts; a friendship is restored or at least partly repaired; a reminder that sometimes the smallest things are the biggest.

"Why wouldn't you want us to get together?" Noah asks, less angry but still confused. "What in God's name was the harm in that?"

"They told us that you had some special genius, that I was your guardian. And that Deb'rah was real smart too, but toxic. You were too much in love to see what she was. She was an addict. She hid it pretty well, but you must have known about the pills, the bennies, the hard stuff. It would have dragged you down, 'dimmed your prospects,' they said. You must have seen something."

Noah did know. It was pain meds at the start, the cascade toward addiction later. The addiction that, in his love for her, he buried. The addiction that he knew would take him down one day if he stayed. Instead, he asked, "Who's *they*?"

"Good question, Bud." He almost always called Noah "Bud."

"We just knew them as the Rose School agents at first. Later I learned they were part of a bigger group, the Rose Network. Later still, I heard about another group, something in Europe and the Middle East that was also involved in this, whatever it was, a group called the Astronomers. And something called the Catholic-Muslim Alliance. Whatever. I gave the Rose Network my life, I gave them more than my life, man." And then, using the frail paintbrush of words, he describes it.

"They recruited us early, using the sports model like I said. They treated us to ball games at first, trips out of the city. We could never have afforded any of that, my mom and me. That part's true," he said, looking left, capturing Noah's eyes in his. "And my mom was proud of me and what they done for us," his accent stronger, painting a picture of the poverty, his background.

"And then you know, they got to training us, like what you'd read about for spies. There was this one guy who took an interest in us, was very kind to me and my mom. He made me into Pete, gave me this life story, building it on much of what was true, so it'd be easier for me to blend into college society, to work with you and whoever else the Rose agents would identify. And they taught me how to befriend you. They actually called it 'befriending,' part of our training."

Noah interrupts, "So this was like a game for you, right? Pretending you were my friend? Be-*friending* me?" Another betrayal, maybe bigger than the first one.

He looks across the car at his passenger, his *friend*. Something is in his eyes, sadness, a minor accompaniment to the tear. He nods, "At first, yes. Then later, no. I wasn't faking any of it, the times together, you and me. You were my brother. I was as close to you as I ever been to anybody except my mom." A long pause, a looking away to the lights of an oncoming car, a deep breath. "I loved you. Once, remember once? You and me at a hockey game. We went drinking afterwards? We wound up on M street at a bar? I said I had something to tell you?"

Noah nods, the memory of the noise and crowd on M street bright in front of him.

"I wanted to tell you about me. You knew Pete. I wanted you to know *me*, about DeJohn. But how was I to tell you I been spying on you, that you had been identified as a potential genius needing protection? I couldn't do it."

"I thought you were going to tell me you were gay," Noah laughs a non-laugh, wishing he could recall it.

"Nope, that sure wasn't it," he said, laughing too, a short, ironic sound, too small to hold any humor.

"No shit, Sherlock." Noah almost always called Pete "Sherlock."

The memories are overwhelming, though softening in the dark night. Noah stops listening, unable to hold on to all the facts. Like a patient hearing bad news from a doctor, his mind is full.

"Just give me some time," Noah says.

For many reasons, it's time for a break. Pete says, "I think we're safe to pull over. We can see the road pretty well from here. Besides," as he wipes the tear away with the flat of his palm, "I have to take a leak."

They pull off, snaking their way up a hill sculpted by two or three switchbacks, achieving an elevation high enough that they can watch the curving ribbon of asphalt road below. It's empty. Beyond the road, the great glisten of the Yarra makes a Kincaid painting. The river lies before them, flowing from the hills out to the sea. Like both their lives. A small historic marker waits at the top of the hill, commemorating Dieppe and its deaths, planted like a stone perennial by the fathers of the State of Victoria. Sometimes the details of moments like this burn themselves onto a mental retina. Noah's image will last a long while.

It takes Pete several long minutes to finish his business, leaving Noah to wonder what else is brewing. He checks on Kate in the back seat. "I'm fine," she says, drowsy, her hair messed and her clothes in disarray. He thinks she looks beautiful.

What was Pete doing? Anticipation hangs in the air like ground fog.

"You okay, Noah?" he starts, finally leaning against the hood of the car. "I got something big to tell you." A large sigh.

"Bigger than what you just told me?" Noah asks, not believing. Pete nods, a slow metronome.

Years before, Noah's mother made him sit down to tell him that his father had left. That there was a new woman in his dad's life, a woman he never liked. He knows the numb, mute feeling—and the need to sit. He leans back against the hood of the car, two men side by side, looking out at the distant city and the Yarra River, a story not yet born between them. He places his hands on the hood, splayed out as they were outside the Georgetown house only days before. They're ready to—what?—support him? Propel him away from the car? Punch Pete? The car hood is still warm, the opposite of his insides; they are cold, the temperature of fear.

"It's about Deborah. And me. And you. And the baby," Pete says.

It is bigger.

51

DANDENONG HILLS. VICTORIA. AUSTRALIA.
SUNDAY NIGHT–MONDAY MORNING

A sudden deep in-breath, fueling Pete. He needs courage to open this door. Sympathy, history—and something more—arc like an electric current between them.

"Please Noah, don't think bad of me. All along I did what I thought was right, what they taught us, what the network agents planned. Today, right now, I know how fucked that was, but then I didn't know," his eyes plead. Noah nods, another metronome, steeling himself.

The African American in his speech disappears. What comes next has the feeling of rehearsal, the scene played out in some tiny stage in Pete's head. "Deborah was all over the place after you left. One day she'd talk about suicide; the next day she'd say she was happy with me. It was why they didn't want you to hook up with her in the first place. She was unstable, even at the best of times. The next day, full up with remorse, she'd say she'd beg your forgiveness, but you knew what she was like, right? She'd never do that. And she moved into the harder stuff, less at the beginning, more as time went along. Once in a while she'd have a good day and I'd think maybe we could make a go of it.

"Then came the big news. Maybe two months after you left, she told me she was pregnant. That seemed to straighten her up, you know? She wasn't on pills anymore, no more hard drugs. She was brighter, more optimistic. Those were the best months we had. Then she had the baby. I have to tell you, she had a beautiful baby girl." He looks at Noah for the first time, shuffling his feet, making little tracks in the gravel beside the car.

"It all started to fall apart. We had moved by then, a little apartment in Foggy Bottom. First thing was, she hadn't done any of her master's work assignments. She failed one course, then another, didn't even show for her defense. Then she started really using, was talking about you. I have to tell you something. When you found us together, when we, um, were doing it? She never said my name.

"She only said yours."

The pause hung between them, an almost palpable third presence—like Deborah—if only for the moment.

"After the baby though, when she started acting like that, on pills and shit, I didn't know what to do. If I told my Network manager they'd want to take the baby away, and I couldn't let them do that. I was growing to love her too. She was so smart, so lovable! And then one day I come home and there's no Deborah. She had gone somewhere and left the baby, the one thing I knew for sure she loved. Poor kid was all soiled and hungry, crying so hard her eyes were as red as lipstick. I was scared, man. I was so *scared*. What you going to do? I axed myself." The accent was back, his feelings overwhelming him. Noah feels them too, an invisible magnet.

Pete straightens his back, continues. "What do you do when you have trouble, man? You send for your mother. And I did.

"She said to me, 'You living with that girl and she not right? I'll come down, help look after your baby.' First time it only lasted a day or two until I could find Deborah. And then it was good for a while; she promised to stop. Maybe a month later, she was gone, sleeping with another guy this time, doing crack. Then my mom said she'd move to DC and raise her. She'd had foster kids before; she loved babies. I could pay her rent and kind of child support, be with the baby when I wasn't, um, working. It was the best thing to do, the right thing to do."

The overture had stopped, but something more was coming, hanging in the air between them, crackling.

"You've probably guessed by now, haven't you?" Pete asks, avoiding the words.

Noah shakes his head slowly, still digesting.

"You've met my mother. She's Sharron Johns."

The English have an expression—"The penny dropped"—but this is no penny. This is a wealth of emotional history and baggage, distorting what would be, for any of you, a simple calculation of dates and times. Not for Noah, however.

"DiShannia was your daughter, yours and Deborah's, right?" Noah asked, incredulous, his voice cracking like a fourteen-year old's.

"No. We thought she was. I lied to myself for the first few months, you know checking dates when we were together, looking for my features in her little face? My mother swore she looked like me when I was a baby. Every baby looks the same, though, huh? I sure *wished* she was mine. But every year I saw less of me and more of you. She was lighter, like you, for one thing. But we carried on, my mother and me, as best as we could, pretending like I was her father, protecting her from the network, watching her grow into this beautiful, smart, incredible young woman. I got to visit her pretty regularly, like two-three times a month. Not enough, but I loved her, Noah, and I got to watch her grow.

"And then she got into this Mayan thing. Man, it was so strong in her! My mom said she'd talked to a teacher and they had put her in touch with someone at the Smithsonian, and *they* had put her in touch with some woman at the British Museum. She was like a full-on university researcher. At thirteen. You read about child prodigies, you know, like Beethoven."

The words seem to crush Pete. They make him smaller somehow. Younger.

"All this would have been easier if she had been my daughter, Noah," holding his hands out like he was checking for rain drops, looking for some message from heaven. All *this* of course meaning her life, and her discoveries, and her death, and the role of the agency he worked for. And then Pete says, another deep sign, tears now clearly visible on his face, both cheeks now, and soon on Noah's, "But she was yours. *Your* daughter, Noah."

52

THE DANDENONG HILLS. VICTORIA. AUSTRALIA. MONDAY MORNING

I t's more than possible.

It builds in Noah's unconscious the whole time that Pete talks, like some rapidly-growing pregnancy. He has suppressed much of his own recollections of the time—the fights, the tears, the regrets, the accusations, and finally, one night, an attempt at reconciliation. For Noah the attempt was a bitter act, one part lost love and reclamation of lost territory, like some ancient battle, the victor planting his flag, a strange one at that. Instead of making a path towards reconciliation, they were making a baby.

Not out of love, perhaps from the memory of love.

And then it hits him, a flood of more recent memory. How much Kate said DiShannia reminded her of him. How he liked her instantly. How he had recognized something in her. It's entirely possible that that something was himself.

It is the journey of a life, compressed—in one week he has gone from not being a father, to knowing he has a child, to losing her, a lifetime—into a heartbeat.

The rest of the trip is in silence, each man deep in the mine of his own thoughts. Once, Noah asks what happened to Deborah. "Dead," Pete replies. "Fentanyl." Two words to describe her passing. Fentanyl, the modern day hemlock. Noah has a million other questions, almost all about Shanny, about her growing up, what she was like, what it was like to be with her. They can wait. *There'll be lots of time for those questions*, he thinks.

Time, something you barely understand.

They move quickly on the traffic-free roads, the way lit by a hot moon, clear and almost-full, as big as an approaching sun. They turn off onto a dusty, dry side road. It's so bumpy it almost throws Kate off the back seat but in a few minutes it succeeds in getting them to their destination, a wooden swinging gate. Above it, a sign, advertising the The Eucalyptus Inn in a flowery, feminine script, small birds dotting the sign like confetti. Whatever relaxed, B&B atmosphere the sign and rustic gate convey give way to a tense almost-military presence: two guards, dressed identically in white shirts and black trousers appear simultaneously, swinging the gate open. This is no lovers' resort, no family retreat; this is a debriefing compound.

A simple rutted road cuts through the dried grass, illuminated by moonlight; cottages are strewn at angles along the curve of the road. They are taken to one of them, Kate lifted from the car and taken inside, half-supported, half-walked, with Noah on one side and one of the white-shirts on the other. Dead eucalyptus leaves make fragile crunching noises underfoot, like tough, dried egg shells.

Noah lays her gently on the bed, covers her with a blanket. A kiss finds its way to her forehead. She wakes to ask for water, gets up to use the bathroom with only a little help, and is ready for bed. She has no memory of the last twelve hours. *One good thing*, Noah thinks.

A doctor arrives, a pony-tailed gent of about fifteen to Noah's eyes. He carries an ancient doctor's bag with him, perhaps an effort to make himself look older. Examining Kate, he pronounces her "fit as a fiddle," the word sounding more like "feet" than fit. He defers to Noah as though he knows of his medical background, telling him that it appears to be a simple, mild barbiturate reaction, one that has pretty much worn off. He tells him that her bruising was not internal and that the large bruise on her leg was not a hematoma, a serious, deep bruise, prone to infection. He calls it a *hema-tomato* in that too-cute way of new doctors. Pete and he breathe twin sighs of relief.

He lays down beside Kate, clothes on, too tired and sore to take them off. They feel, for the first since Heidelberg, safe. Or safer perhaps. And, If not free, then protected.

They are neither.

In the morning, despite his aching body, he has one thing on his mind. He wants to run.

It's less the physical act of running that he wants, the limit-pushing of his bruised, still-stiff body, but the freedom from worry and constant tension that have been his companion for the last five days. He wants to *run*, to escape seeing the threat of Kate being molested, the slide towards terror induced by seeing Miriam Al-Ansari plunge to her death in the Underground, the bullet-ridden body of Isaac Zapinsky. Perhaps to absorb the huge, pregnant knowledge that Pete's given him to digest.

He wants to *move,* perhaps find a bike, perhaps ride.

He slips out of the bed at daybreak, slowly pulling on shorts and track shoes intent on heading up the road that had brought them there last night. He gets only to the front gate however when he's met by the same two tall men, virtually identical. The early morning light shines behind them, obscuring their faces. They're Marius and Marcus, products of Bondi Beach or something similar. He would learn their names later. Tanned, muscled, still in black pants and white T's. One of them says, "This is far enough, mate."

Noah is getting used to hearing it as *mite.* He glimpses something parked just inside the gate, hidden in the eucalyptus woods, a white truck marked *Andersen's Food Products.* It's unlikely that it holds food products; the small array of satellite dishes on top of the thing is a giveaway.

Where he *is* allowed to walk is inside the compound, not outside it. The cottages run up the hill like scattered children's blocks, each one charming in its Disney-like fascination with wooden side boards, cedar shingles, white and green painted shutters and extended front porches. The cottages are the unlikely offspring of Martha Stewart and one or more of the seven dwarfs. Their porches are marked by flowerboxes stuffed with a plastic exuberance of geraniums, pansies, marigolds, and enough daisies to fill Mr. Andersen's truck. The largest one is about half way along the laneway.

A grapevine basket holding cut flowers (these at least look real) sits on the big front porch. They're placed beside a century-old milk can painted white, and a wrought iron chair and table. On one of the chairs sits a woman doing something Noah hasn't seen for years, except in movies.

She's smoking.

She stands as she put her cigarette out in a water filled vase. Her voice is deep, close to raspy, "You can't be too careful when the woods are this dry, can you?" From her lips, it sounds ominous.

Iona Campagnola is in her early fifties, strong, taller than Noah. She extends a large right hand, reminding him suddenly of Michelangelo's David. It embraces his in a warm, hard, masculine squeeze. "You're up early, Noah," she says, demonstrating concern and knowledge simultaneously. She is in charge. Italy is echoed in her gently curled black hair, her oval, olive-complected face, and a body toned by exercise. Like her mothers and aunts, she is dressed entirely in black. Perhaps she was widowed at an early age. She clearly hasn't read the Martha Stewart/Disney colorful dress code.

It might look the same from the outside but, inside the spa, Martha's touches are absent, replaced by Early Government/Utilitarian. The Murphy bed has been pushed up into daytime oblivion. The usual cottage fare of wicker tables, loveseats, and chairs has been moved to another room and the now-empty floor is filled with a small-town version of mission control. Even at this early hour, the double flat-screen monitors are in use, computers hum, and people—mostly young—talk in small huddles. There are at least a dozen others present.

"What is this?" Noah asks. "Your headquarters?" She smiles, an indulgence, one that implies, *What do* you *think, Genius?*

"Noah," she says, "this is a small mobile division. We've been following what you might call," her forehead wrinkles slightly, word-searching, "….developments. In particular we've been highly interested in the Clinton-Gates meeting, tracking the movements of the Astronomers, even your movements."

Movement seems to suspend for a moment. The quiet click-click of keyboards slows, a staff member passing papers to another hesitates, stops. *Ominous* hangs in the air, like an odor. Suddenly, Noah's sense of safety—of being in a compound, of being protected—is gone. He is frightened.

He's also puzzled. "You've been tracking all of this? All that *we've* been following?" Disbelief rings bells of doubt, even anger.

"Actually, Noah, we've been on the same path you've been on." She leads him into the room, stepping over the heavy cables, like pythons. They visit several work stations and their staffers, learning a little bit from each one. There are a baker's dozen of them, married to their twin-screen monitors like porn addicts, fingers flying magician-fast, some of them talking into headsets in soft, semi-urgent murmurs, a river of conversation in the otherwise quiet room. A Teddy Roosevelt lookalike mans the first desk, working on, he says, the "Naomi thing." Naomi, they've just learned, is okay. She was in danger from General Wilcox and his crew, but now safe. Noah is happy.

"When did you know about Harry?" Noah asks. He has a thousand more questions in his mind.

"We call him Aabis, Noah. Others call him the Astronomer. His latest attempt has been to coerce scientists world-wide to work on the question of a parallel universe. His funding sources are huge. He's been active in this for a long time, at a pretty high level. Perhaps even the highest level." She changes her tone, pushes her hair back over her ears, "Can we let it ride for a minute? I know you're impatient, and you have a right to hear it all, but in time. We're on the same team here, Noah."

Iona's words offer reassurance. Noah, reluctant, takes it.

That is the pattern of the next few introductions: a quick stop at each desk, a sentence or two about what each is working on and then a step to the next work station. From the Washington desk where Teddy sits, to a table where two Asian girls work on DiShannia's health records and her pseudo-diabetes. To the British desk where a young woman downloads Mayan texts, many already translated. This is Emily, her hair dyed a color of purple that almost blinds. They move to visit someone about the same age as last night's doctor, Bernard, actively scanning the presentations and posters at the Clinton-Gates Conference and its satellite conferences, including one on eschatology—end of world theories—winding up. To twin computer screens in the next workstation, where a tall blond man, mid-30s, unfolds like an accordion from his seat to shake Noah's hand, demonstrating an unusual politeness. He is William. In fact, they all stand when Noah is introduced to them, deferential, respectful.

Unusual traits in Australia, the sunburnt, roughened continent.

Later that morning, in an adjacent room at the spa—a room clearly designed for other purposes—Noah and Kate face Iona, Pete and a host of other people. It feels like something between a job interview and a policeman's third degree. They are grateful, though. Pete and his colleagues have saved them from what

Noah calls *Death on a Wine Barrel*, an attempt (not a very good one, given their response) to lighten the mood.

They've had their breakfast, have caught up on the events of the outer world for the last five days: flooding and record breaking temperatures in Bangladesh; much of the Netherlands and some of the eastern shore of the US almost entirely underwater. More migrants displaced by war, fire, and famine. More political argument. Fear of nuclear and chemical weapons getting into the hands of terrorists. Some uptake of the proceedings of the satellite pre-conference.

Between the morning's short tour of the control center and the sit-down an hour later, fear has seeped into the room like ground fog, slipping through the floorboards, through the lace-covered windows. It overwhelms the ambitions of the creators of the small parade of chintz bed-covers, the painters of pale cream walls, the picklers of pine floors. It swallows the ghosts of honeymooners and other lovers. It overcomes whatever feelings of relief the escape from Harry has crafted.

This is no holiday cottage.

Two love seats, properly overstuffed, paisleyed and pillowed, face each other in front of a stone fireplace. An oval floral rug separates them, bearing more flowers than most gardens. Two chairs face the fireplace, armless and uncomfortably straight backed, upholstered in green and white vertical stripes. Pete takes one of them. Iona conquers a loveseat, arranging her papers, notes and a lap top, spreading them. Her research spills around her, her IPad sits firmly on the tiny ribbon of skirt. She tugs at the skirt hem slightly, pulling it a millimeter towards decency. It's an unconscious gesture; her mind is on other things. Noah and Kate occupy the loveseat opposite her.

Others come and go, using dining room chairs, arranged haphazardly in the room—Teddy Roosevelt, Bernard, purple Emily, William, others. A new player, a priest whose scarred face shows the ravages of an adolescent war with acne; the scars of tiny land mines still crater his face. The two men Noah met outside earlier, muscled and tanned, blatantly Australian, products of testosterone, gyms and the beach. They appear to be mute; the only way their presence is known is when they enter or leave the room, letting the palpable wall of morning heat invade. Pete's protective radar scours the room, reassuring Noah and Kate.

Despite this cast, most of the conversation is clearly between Kate, Noah and Iona. Except for Pete, the rest watch, children looking at fish in a fishbowl. Pete is in and out of the interview, on his cell phone, monitoring other events the fishbowl doesn't hold, just as he's watched over Noah, DiShannia, others. The Rose Network had at least one thing right: Pete is loyal.

Iona is a tightly wound, highly caffeinated woman, in charge of the interview, typing into her iPad with a ferocity of fact-finding. She is pleasant but business-like, marching them through the chronology of the last five days, from DiShannia's death to today. She lifts each stepping stone along the journey, examining it for hidden details. They think of themselves as good reporters but her questions are as pointed as darts. It would not surprise the others in the room to learn that she stood first in her law school.

When was the first they heard of DiShannia? Did she ever reach out apart from the WashPO story? She hadn't. *What did you observe at the school?* Noah recalls the little episode he thought might represent telepathy. She nods, notes it vigorously on her IPad, doesn't comment. *Tell us more about the Dulles homeless camp. Did Noah and Kate think the blockade was purposeful or was it a random act? Did they recognize anyone there?* They thought random; they're not sure about recognizing anyone they'd seen previously. *What about the diabetes expert from Georgetown? Did they think he might be implicated in the plot to kill DiShannia?* They don't think so. *What about Wai-Ching Lam? Was he involved in some way?* Kate is adamant about him, her own loyalty strong despite her own personal feelings. He's an innocent bystander; all his attempts at publication about the Maya have been rejected.

"Did he say who blocked them?" she asks Kate.

"I don't know. Journal editors of course, but I don't know who they might be. We didn't have time to..."

Iona interrupts, leans into the skinny Bluetooth thing in her right ear. "Find out what journals a climate change specialist or an ecologist would submit to. Look up the names of their peer reviewers and match them to the List." The capital "L" in list is audible. It is the first stirring of Noah's questions for Iona. *Just wait, Lady. I have lots.*

There is more of the same, more stepping stones to be examined. *What about Miriam Al-Ansari? Did she recognize the Jamaican Rastafarians in the Museum? Were they the same men who attacked her later in the subway?* Yes. *Were they sure?* Yes again. *What was she doing having you take her picture? What was she pointing at in the picture? Do you still have the picture? What about CERN?*

What? When? Where? Who? The reporter's questions.

And then, suddenly, like a detective examining a suspicious story, there is this: *Tell me about Heidelberg.* Noah begins—his impression of Ingrid, of Dr. Zapinsky, what the professor said, how he died, how Ingrid revealed she was his wife at the end. How Ingrid might have been involved with the man next door. Iona is surprised at this, makes notes, talks to her Bluetooth again. The man is one of theirs; so are many of the homeless, it seems. Kate adds details about reversed red shift, about Zapinsky's estrangement from the scientific community. They had rejected him like some flawed part of a production process, not fitting their specifications. Anna appears less interested in this. She pushes.

"Tell me how you got away from the Heidelberg house." Her tone doesn't change but something in the phrase makes Noah's stomach turn. "When you escaped through the bathroom and down the stairs, did you have the feeling you had been there before?"

Noah wonders how she knows that. His heart skips, like a prisoner locked inside a cell, pounding on the door. Sweat traces its way between his shoulder blades. *Jesus.* A shaky hand reaches for the talisman. His own.

"It's okay," Anna says. Kate takes his hand. Anna's voice crosses the space between them. "We know you were there before, Noah. It'll be okay."

Maybe it is the short skirt and the display of sympathy. They remind Noah of Aija, of the long hours outside Helsinki, of the after-session saunas and the smell of pine logs on his skin. The sessions. The talisman. What happened *before* he got to Helsinki.

"It's time I told you something about yourself, Noah."

53

THE DANDENONG HILLS. VICTORIA. AUSTRALIA.
LATE MONDAY MORNING

Iona the aggressive lawyer/reporter has become Iona the explainer. Noah has paid his debt.

"Earlier you asked some questions—about Aabis, the person you call Harry, and about the search you've been on. Let's start before all that, though. Let's start with you."

Noah is surprised, sits more upright in the loveseat, difficult for someone who's practiced the nonchalance of the slouch all his adult life.

"You're more a part of this than you know, perhaps even more than we know. It begins with the codex." Perhaps everything does.

He is, sufficient to say, all ears, the sweat drying up, his heart settling.

"Miriam explained it to you?" He nods. "That it was written over a thousand years ago in Palenque? That we're unsure about who wrote it, but since it documents changes in the planets over a several decade period, we think there was more than one author."

She takes a deep breath. The priest, Father Pugliese, uninterested until now, pulls his chair into the circle. He has been sitting at a small wicker table, a charming object if it were anywhere else. His voice conjures images of Cambria and Sicily; consonants followed by invisible but audible vowels.

"You know most of this, I am sure." He takes out a white handkerchief, surprising against the backdrop of his black suit, wiping the sweat from his bald head. Even there, acne has planted its battle scars. He reminds them, needlessly, of deLanda, the overzealous Spanish archbishop of the sixteenth century.

"It wasn't the codices he was destroying; it was their message. The collapse of the planets implied three things about God: that He was imperfect; that He care nothing for the human race He had created; and that He was a destroyer, not a Creator. The message frightened the Holy Father enough that he founded the *Astronomi* and commissioned the building of the first Observatory at the Vatican and then another in *Castel St'Angelo*. The two locations were kilometers apart to study the movements of the planets. And then the Muslim world also became interested in astronomy."

Iona continues the story. "Not all the Muslim world, just segments, and in particular a group called the 'Tahl-ibh-an,' the Taliban. It appears as though they are much more ancient than we think and that they wanted *you* when you were in Afghanistan. The young man who led you into the trap wasn't interested in the rest of the troop; they were simply innocent bystanders. The Taliban wanted....well..." she says, her eyes fixed on Noah, "your genius, it appears."

Noah is stunned. "Why me? What could I possibly know?" he asks, the fear from that day and this uniting. "What information could I have had that would be of use to them?" It's the same question he had in the winery. His head aches, a small companion to the pain from yesterday's beating. Pete leaves the room, talking loudly into his cell phone, another interruption.

Iona ignores him, "We have our own theories, Noah. We think they were after your extraordinary mathematical and your problem-solving ability— something I don't think you know you have—and they wanted to capture you and use your knowledge to fix the collapse somehow."

Noah has trouble finding the next words. Kate fills the quiet with a question of her own, asking "What about the codex?"

Iona says, "We aren't entirely sure. It appears it was discovered by a graduate student after the tomb of Pakal was opened. It was hidden in a strange place, deep *under* his sarcophagus, as though they were afraid to destroy it but equally afraid to let it see the light of day. He or she sold it to the Smithsonian which sent it to the British Museum. The story, *your story,* Noah, gets interesting here. Someone named Mary Catherine O'Rourke brought it back with her to the Museum where she was a researcher. It appears that she met Alan Turing on the Queen Mary on her return, beginning their work deciphering the codex, and also, beginning their love affair."

They are puzzled. Father Pugliese nods, joining in, "It is commonly believed he was gay, but love is a strange thing is it not?" This, from a priest. "Together, they deciphered the symbols. He was a genius, you know, possibly the inventor of the computer, the person who saved the world from Hitler."

Someone, possibly Marcus, chooses this minute for an interruption of his own. As he enters the room, he lets in a wave of heat so strong that their breaths are held prisoner for a moment. Marcus has brought a tray of glasses filled with ice tea, one for each of them, lemon and mint-flavored, giving new meaning to the word, "refreshing." Iona takes a deep breath, downing it in almost one go. Equally parched from the heat and the anxiety, Noah also drinks it, putting his glass down empty. The loud *hummm* of the air conditioner kicks in. The *ear-con,* he remembers.

Marcus picks up Noah's glass with a napkin.

In just three days, Noah has been called a genius three times—by Ivaan Horkonen, by Pete and now by Iona. Instead of calming him, it adds to the burden of learning that he was DiShannia's father, learning that Pete was *watching* him, learning about this group and others, the deaths surrounding him. Too much.

"So what do we *have* here, exactly, Iona?" Noah raises his voice over the air conditioner, over his frustration. It surprises Kate. It doesn't surprise Iona. She reassures him, moving to the middle of the love seat, putting some of her papers away. Shuffling them, buying time, allowing him to digest the facts. There is more to come.

"I know, Noah, I know. You're feeling much as we felt when we first began exploring this. There are so many players." She stands, walking around the room, trying to clear her head, trying to find the right words among a million.

"Right through the war and afterwards," she says, "the Palenque Codex was housed in England, deciphered bit by bit by Turing and O'Rourke. There was a problem though: Turing was talkative, spoke about their findings—and the collapse—repeatedly. As a result, the British government created a task force to deal with him called 'Operation Hemlock,' which eventually killed him, making the murder look like a suicide."

"What about Mary Catherine?" asks Kate.

Iona is only half finished. "She was pregnant, frightened, and fled Britain, strongly suspecting that the government was behind his death." There is no shock in this room; death hardly rattles anyone.

"In the seventies, the Astronomers learned about the birth of the Rose School Network in North America. They had developed as separate organizations, but there was considerable overlap in their goals—to find those who knew the secret of the collapse, to ensure their silence, and—at least in the case of the Rose Schools, to try to grow a student body to study space travel. Whatever collaborations there were, they were loose at first, tighter as time went by.

"But there was a problem." She put her iPad down, looked directly at Noah and Kate. "Their methods, those of the Rose Network, and those of the Catholic-Muslim Alliance, were increasingly violent. Witness what they did to your young woman," she checked her notes. "Your DiShannia. Look at how they killed Miriam Al-Ansari, the graduate student in Toronto. There are dozens of such examples. We—your friend Pete, our DeJohn, myself, Marius and Marcus, all of us here, and others you will meet later—have come to the conclusion that this must end."

Noah lets his frustration show, like the bruise on his neck. "So. Let me get this straight. There's a group in the US called the Rose Schools, sort of a Network. There is some kind of Arab–Catholic alliance, and a Catholic group affiliated with the Vatican, the Astronomers. And now there's your group, yours and Pete's. Who are the bad guys? Who are the good guys?"

She smiles, possibly the first time in the hours of questions. To be fair, a Mona Lisa smile, not what you'd call overly generous.

"You know," she says, the smile broadening a bit, kindly, "For a WashPO reporter, you're pretty naïve. Oh yes, and a doctor, at that!" She laughs, a first. "Good guys, bad guys. Yes, pretty naïve. I'll leave the description of the Alliance and the Network until after lunch wzhen my boss arrives. My bosses, actually." The smile grows, more open, kinder. "We're called the Society, by the way. But there's another much more *interesting* phenomenon here to describe." The word takes on new meaning.

Iona continues, "Mary Catherine and Turing had a child, surprising, since Turing was openly gay. Homosexuality was a crime in those days: he was arrested, incarcerated, then treated as though it were a disease, by chemical castration of all things. Whatever effect on him appeared to be minimal however and we have every cause to believe that, just before he was killed, Mary Catherine became pregnant by him. Mary Catherine herself was lost to us for a long while, but we do know that she immigrated to the US, most likely to the northeast, given her connections to the Smithsonian. We have strong evidence that she raised her child. A daughter."

Iona looks around the room, engaging each of them. *Are they following?* Noah concentrates on his breathing. Something is sucking the oxygen from the room.

"We found her, partly by luck, partly by DNA testing. Mary Catherine used another name—Mathison—and stayed successfully below the radar, working in odd jobs that she got through the museum. She was a good mother, gave the little girl every advantage. She in, turn—the daughter that is—did very well. She became a clinical epidemiologist, working for the NIH for years. She died of breast cancer."

Kate, bereft of grandparents herself, sees it right away, reaches for Noah's hand, understanding, wide eyed.

Unable to grasp the obvious, Noah thinks, *My mother would have known her.* His mother was also an epidemiologist, also worked at the NIH. It takes several minutes for Iona's further description—that the daughter lived near the zoo in Washington, that she was married but divorced, that she raised a son—to sink in. A son who had taken a unique career path, graduating medicine, working internationally, finally becoming a reporter for WashPO. Like a mother feeds a child, Iona provided Noah one fact at a time, allowing him time and space to realize his heritage. Time and space, bless her.

I am Alan Turing and Mary Catherine's grandson, he thinks, finally. The thought floats at the very top of his consciousness, barely penetrating, like leaves on a pond.

The penetration comes later.

54

THE DANDENONG HILLS. VICTORIA. AUSTRALIA. MONDAY AFTERNOON

Like sifting through a thousand old pictures, Noah processes Iona's news about his mother, his grandmother, his grandfather. Pete's news about his daughter. It's still a superficial process, like reading the obituaries of distant relatives.

The heat doesn't help; he feels it inside his body as well as outside. Marius brings in lunch along with the heat, helped by Marcus, carrying the trays like they were tiny saucers. Marius and Marcus are followed by two women well past middle age. They resemble each other—both with short, dirty blond hair, oval, pale faces, broad-beamed noses and identical glasses. The dirty blonde slides towards gray, another color shift in their world. They are clearly sisters, perhaps even twins, their identical nature marred by one sister's deformed neck, twisting her head sideways and into her chest cavity. They all stand when the new women walk in, shaking their hands.

They introduce themselves as Kym and Karla Mandelson, a trace of West Virginia still in their vowels, but business and precision in their manner. The irony of two sets of twins in one room is lost on them; too many other worries press in on them.

They stop for lunch: sandwiches made somewhere else; fruit with an awful aboriginal name but welcome. In fifteen minutes, they are back at it. A million questions. About two dozen answers.

Kym and Karla have taken over the loveseat from Iona. It's like watching a tennis match. Together, in the stereo of twins, they lead the conversation into current matters. Beyond the history of the Maya, beyond the story of Alan Turing and Mary Catherine, beyond even the most recent events, DiShannia's death. These are all behind them, their implications to be explored later. If there's time.

Time.

Karla begins, "We come from the Society, the reform movement," she says, shifting the unmovable granite of her upper body to look at Noah and Kate. "We were hired by Vice President Cheney and put in charge of the Rose School Network, but we found many disturbing things, many, um, practices that we could not condone. So, for the last few years, school by school, step by step, we've focused our efforts on finding answers, not keeping secrets, not harming students. Eastern Market School for example, was infiltrated by the Astronomers. Along with the Swiss Guard, they are implicated in the death of DiShannia; she simply knew too much, was about to communicate it widely. *Like her great grandfather,* words not said in the room.

"Overall though, the Society has been successful, recruiting Pete for example." She nods towards the porch where Pete is talking on his cell. Noah will always remember him that way.

DiShannia's name prompts Karla to add, "We are sorry for your loss," swivelling, looking directly at Noah. *It's Pete's loss too,* Noah thinks. There is a deep sadness in the twinned thought, the losses to both biological and adoptive fathers.

"We've been following the Astronomers as they've orchestrated the satellite meeting you attended. We think they were going to harm the scientists there, but the plan fell through. They've tried very hard to bring together anyone who's touched the Palenque Codex and its secret—you've met a sample of them. We believe that the Astronomers don't intend to advance science, but to kill whatever story or news the events creates, probably by killing *them.*"

Karla bends, as much as bending is possible, to her laptop, an almost reverent gesture. Kym takes over, "They've proven this time and time again. We have reason to believe they murdered JFK." Like Noah's news minutes before, the information barely penetrates.

Kym takes a deep breath, "It is the most widespread and horrendous plot or series of plots in the modern world, perhaps in the history of the world. They're highly lethal and ruthless, murdering at the drop of a hat–DiShannia, for example. And," she pauses, "they are truly, powerfully connected. We know the Rose Network and the schools were funded by Wall Street, but the *Astronomers,*" she says as though there were something distasteful in her mouth, "have enormous resources, from the Vatican, even from the Islamic world."

Karla, looking up from her laptop, adds, "The Society, we, have something different driving us. The Astronomers have had one goal, to prevent the spreading of the truth about the Palenque Codex. That was their primary motive five hundred years ago; it's virtually their only driving force today. Look at us." She makes a point of scanning the room, pivoting her body, "We're about the solution."

More stereo from Kym. "We've gotten smarter about our efforts to embed ourselves in the Astronomers' ranks, to learn their plans. And now CERN is on board. And we think we're ready. We have the perfect scenario."

Nothing could be perfect here, Noah thinks, but doesn't say it, his mind still processing the news of the Astronomers, the Taliban, of his heritage, of DiShannia, his daughter. Processing his future, his and Kate's.

A larger audience gathers from the next room where the computer screens are left abandoned and unmonitored. Close to thirty people, the same size as the Monday morning WashPO scrum that met—how long ago?—A month? A year? A week? A *katun?*

They pull in chairs, sit on the floor, filling the Martha Stewart room. They watch Karla begin the presentation, flipping material from her laptop to a large, movable flat screen. It's awkward for her to stand, point at the screen and talk, but she manages, bending stiffly to show them a map of the world. Strands of graying-blonde hair block her view. She brushes them away, a small annoyance.

"Let's start with the trap. Here's what we've learned. Several weeks ago, as the conference center was beginning to get ready for the Clinton Gates meeting, the Astronomers managed to have several external panels fall onto the pavement below. It appeared spontaneous, but the 'accidents' continued, injuring a tourist, and the city fathers—well, fathers and mothers—decided to investigate. Look at this," she says, pulling up a picture from a battery of little thumbnails at the bottom of the screen. It's a shot of the conference center covered almost completely by an exoskeleton of scaffolding. Other pictures show where the windows have been removed, displaying ducts and pipes.

She continues, "Late last week, we learned that two of the workers were Astronomer agents, installing *new* ducts and cylinders, here and here…" she swings her arm awkwardly to indicate several points on the picture. There is a pause in the room, a collective breath-holding. Kym takes over, standing on the other side of the flat screen. "Last week we managed to have several of the panels removed." Her left hand finds a small thumb nail, bringing it into view. It's a picture of a cylinder, now thankfully freed from the duct work. It's marked *Freon: for A/C used only* in white, but, just below it, a small word can just be made out, its covering label removed.

Sarin.

Noah has a sudden memory of his first assignment with Reporters without Borders: stumbling into a Syrian village where chemical weapons had been used; bloated bodies and stomachs, mocking pregnancy; the children—seven of them, he said something over each one; the arched backs, urine and worse trickling between their legs, fouling them. Small traces of foam on their lips. Eyes wide open, as though death had come suddenly, freezing them, making it impossible to stop watching the horror.

Sarin.

Karla interrupts his thoughts. "You can see what we're up against. This time though, I think we can outwit them. We've searched every panel. We think we've blocked this plot."

Think is not a very reassuring word. Noah looks around the room for Pete, searching for reassurance. But he can't find him; he's been driven outside by his phone and its messages.

Kym expands on their plans, "We've also replaced the two canisters with lookalikes. They won't release anything, but we've attached remote GPS locators on their release mechanisms. When they set them, it'll lead us to the Astronomers. It's why we couldn't take Harry when he visited you in the winery. We have a perfect opportunity here, a window, in which to finally produce an open, honest, full disclosure of all the facts—to reveal the truth about the Astronomers and their unholy Alliance, about the old Rose School Network, about the murders. We can build on the huge international interest in this story, so closely tied to global warming, and the fact that many of the globe's major scientists are here.

"We intend to host a major press conference to stop this once and for all."

55

THE DANDENONG HILLS. VICTORIA. AUSTRALIA.
EARLY MONDAY EVENING

Ordering pizza in the middle of nowhere is an almost-magic act, an attempt at normalcy in a world that is far from normal. They have an hour before it arrives driven by a *Pizza Pizza* guy or the Australian equivalent. They are miles from nowhere, but close enough to get delivery. *Probably*, Noah thinks, *the moons have pizzerias.*

In the early evening the temperature is now a more comfortable ninety-five, not the unbearable low hundreds that the day held; a brief afternoon rain has helped. Pete finds them on the little porch in front of their cottage, the vessels of their brains full, overflowing. He wants to talk to them, but they react differently to the day. Kate decides a nap might still the voices in her mind. She touches Noah's back as she leaves the porch. It is hard, like the cement of Karla's neck.

Pete suggests a walk. They head up the road to the main cottage, talking about the Alliance, the Society, about Harry-Aabis, about the codex and what it means. About the sarin plot. They kick stones. They avoid touching on DiShannia or Deborah, their shared past. Those topics, mother and daughter, generate feelings.

Pete spots it first—a long bike rack beside the main cottage, with men's bikes in blue, women's bikes in a shade of pink meant to cause blindness. They have identical thoughts. Pete adopts a serious, almost crippling stare as though he is angry, then breaks into a grin.

"Race you for the bikes," then, after a slight hesitation, "Chickenshit."

The rutted gravel roadway leads them high above the compound to a hill overlooking a little river. It's like their view the night before, but broader, more open, more settled after the rain. In daylight, it's breathtaking. They're only at the bottom of another, higher hill.

"Race you to the top!" Noah yells, words of a twelve year-old. He wins the race but only because Pete has let him; he stopped a few meters from the top. The gesture robs Noah of the chance to brag. So has Pete's better physical shape, maybe the only benefit of a lifetime as an agent.

"What's wrong? You cop out?"

"Nope," Pete says, "Just wanted to see if you still had it." He gets off his bike, tossing its thirty pounds aside like it's made of tissue paper. In five steps he is beside Noah.

They hug.

Noah is still on his bike, his right leg on the ground, uncomfortably stretched, his knee twisted, his sore left hip now probed by the sharp bike mirror, his groin uncomfortably wedged against the bike's bar. The position is ungainly in the extreme. It's also one of the nicest things that has ever happened to either of them. Men's feelings are like icebergs—huge, solitary and for the most part invisible. This is as close to their expression as Pete and Noah will come.

"You up for some more?" asks Pete. He'll always be Pete to Noah. Never De-John. *DeJean. Whatever,* he thinks.

"What, more bike riding? Yeah. Of course. I'm in great shape. We got hours, nothing else to do."

"No," Pete says "I have something more to tell you."

Noah's stomach knots quickly. He joins Pete at the crest of the hill, discarding his bike. They sit together, their feet dangling over the ledge, their view of the spectacular Yarra Valley spread like burnt butter below them. What Noah is about to hear is as dangerous as the hundred foot fall that looms in front of them. He feigns nonchalance, picking at weeds at his feet. He fools no one.

Pete starts, "I want you and Kate to know what you're facing tomorrow. I don't mean the press conference so much; you'll ace it. It is a big deal, but it's not...." he searches for the word, picking at a little weed, "dangerous. But, for your protection, you need to know everything."

It occurs to Noah that Pete has always protected him.

"Kym and Karla and them, they all think we should keep you in the dark. We should get you two to the press conference, use you as a lure to attract Aabis and the Astronomers. I, um, differ." More weed-pulling, this time by Pete, buying time. Noah thinks, *This little hillside'll be pristine by the time we're done.*

"First, what Karla was talking about today, the sarin gas canisters? She's right. You're safe there. I went over the specs last night, looking at the spread sheet of every single panel removed and replaced. There were only two canisters. We got 'em both. And we have the ability to trace whoever has the remote. She was being up front about that. But not," another pause, another three weeds, "about this."

It is absolutely silent at the top of the hill. Clouds move low in front of them in the hot air, chasing each other, like doubts.

Pete begins, short staccato sentences laying out a huge problem, as large as the space in front of them. "A few weeks ago, Aabis, your friend Harry, met a woman, another Astronomer, in San Francisco, in some Starbuck's. We got lucky. We had a tip and put one of our agents in as a barista that morning. She brought a little listening device with her. It picked up their whole conversation, well, *almost* their whole conversation. Much of it was about the sarin plot, but we were already on that. There was something at the end of the recording that escaped us; something is garbled at the end. We think it's another operation, possibly *another* plot to sabotage this conference—like a Plan B in case the sarin plot fails? We did pick up one word, something like *Headrick.*"

Noah has no idea what that means. Pete continues, "We're digging in every record we have, in every text from Aabis, every communication. We even broke into your app. Don't ask me how. We think it has something to do with a shipment of a parcel from Russia. So here's my question: Are you comfortable going into the press conference tomorrow, knowing that there might still be an attack of some kind?"

There are no more weeds to pull. Noah rubs his talisman unconsciously. "You know if it was just me, I'd say yes. It'll attract those guys like a magnet. We have to get them, especially Harry. But there's Kate —she has to be told." There's a loose stone at his feet. He pitches it over the edge, watching gravity take over, part of dark matter. Finally, "Why don't we sleep on it tonight? You'll maybe know more tomorrow. If you don't, we can pull the plug on us attending. If you do and we're safe, we'll go for it. We'll tell Kate everything."

"My thoughts exactly," Pete says. "We will know more. The guys in Europe are working on the package angle. There's somebody in Russia we're talking to first thing tomorrow morning—that's tonight here. We've got all night, and we've got time on the drive in to Melbourne tomorrow. We can always pull the plug like you say. Get you out of there, safely."

Reassuring words, as substantial as the clouds.

56

THE DANDENONG HILLS. VICTORIA. AUSTRALIA.
TUESDAY EARLY MORNING

Dreams invade Noah.

In the middle of the night, he cries out, frightening Kate. She wraps her arms around him, an attempt at providing comfort, but the demons are inside him, not outside. She cannot help.

In one of the dreams he meets his grandparents on a porch. It's the house in Georgetown that the three of them—Pete, Deborah, him—lived in. He goes to the front door, rings the bell and his grandparents open it to greet him. But they're old, appear only mildly interested in him, confused by his visit. The grandmother looks like the woman in the zoo. She holds a little baby girl. The child is black. He reaches to hold her, but they push him away. From that dream he wakes crying like a ten year old, but there are no tears. It is a dream of crying. And from that dream, thankfully, little memory.

He has other similar dreams, dreams of rejection and betrayal. By the middle of the night—the darkest, neediest part of the sun's absence from earth—he is afraid to sleep. He's not alone. Harboring the dangers that Pete and Noah shared with her that evening, Kate too is afraid. They reach for each other, are soon naked and inside each other. She occupies a space inside him that no one else has filled, even Deborah-of-his-dreams, now Deborah-of-his-past. It's mirrored by her feelings. No man has ever come this close to her; she is sure, for whatever time they have together, that he is her future.

For him, it is more than his erection inside her.

It's his life.

He sleeps afterwards, exhausted. Kate lies in the safe crook of his arm, another illusion.

He remembers one last chapter in this night's book of dreams. This time he is in a zoo, searching for his grandmother. He finds her in the faux-farm at the end of the long downward path, paved with endless hexagonal orange-brown tiles. She is younger, beautiful and she's with a man—tallish, thin, deep-set eyes, and black hair that falls over his eyes. The man says, "*I hear you're my grandson.*" Noah runs to hug him but wakens, hugging his pillow. In the curious parallel universe of dreams, he thinks it's the trunk of an elephant.

The elephant's sadness creeps into Noah, takes minutes to drain away. One conscious thought pulls at his naked body, *I am their grandson.*

He has questions of course. *Do they have proof?* Yes, DNA testing has confirmed the relationship—it runs from his grandparents, Mary Catherine and Alan Turing, the man she referred to as Mathison, through his mother, to him, and, perhaps most sadly, to DiShannia. But a million other questions remain: *What happened to my grandmother? What am I to make of this?*

If this is his past, what is his future?

There are other pressures on them that day, however.

In the morning, sitting on the edge of the bed, thinking about the press conference and worrying the question of how much he should say, Kate kneels behind him, her nipples teasing his back. She hugs his neck, reaching around. *Time,* he thinks to himself, the tide of arousal rising in him, *I wish there were more time.*

"Can I ask a favor?" she says, whispering into his left ear, knowing the answer would probably always be "Yes." "You know, when you're on top?" she asks shyly, only partly playfully.

"I have a vague recollection of that," he says. It was three hours ago. "Oh, you mean, when I am plunging my huge, manly member into your moist..." he channels his inner porn star. She slaps him on the side of his head, not hard, a playful gesture. "Don't be rude!" she says, trying not to laugh. "No, I mean yes. When you're like that, your talisman swings, you know, and it hits my face. It's not a big thing, but I was wondering..."

"I'll take it off," he says, reaching back to untie the little leather strap.

"No, no. I like it. I like how it makes you look. I think it's..." a small pause, a little shyness between them, the wanton couple of only hours before, "sexy. Especially when it's the only thing you have on. I'll just take the strap and make it shorter."

It takes her a minute to untie the tightly wound knot of sweat and leather and shorten it. Raised higher on his neck it looks cool, he thinks, up there keeping Adam and his apple company. She reaches around him, her breasts more fully in view, and kisses the new place where it lives.

They're interrupted. Pete reminds them they have to be at the press conference, his voice muffled by the closed Martha Stewart door. *Pete the Pest,* Noah thinks, but it's playful, like Kate's slap. Pete wants them to eat, wants to make sure that they understand the risks involved in conference and whatever else "Headrick" implies. They have a long drive into the city, have to be prepped for the press conference this morning. The voice-behind-the-door finally stops with, "I'll see you in fifteen minutes!"

Noah goes to the upscale Walt and Martha bathroom to shave. This bath has a tub with lion's paw legs and a little high-end shaving mirror that would set him back a week's salary. But this is a day on camera, so he spends an extra minute shaving using the mirror. The little talisman, its edges rounded by years of rubbing and by age, is now magnified, in plain if reversed view. He sees its dots and ridges forming a pattern. Like a blind person seeing Braille for the first time.

Interesting he thinks, but Pete's banging on the door interrupts the thought.

Car doors slam. They're on their way to a destiny none of them could have imagined only a week ago. They are in the same Honda that brought them there, almost out of the hills, almost onto the brave, flat, *hot* plain that leads to Melbourne.

Iona is driving, hands Noah and Kate one-pagers that she calls "Talking Points," making Noah think of politicians, not with any fondness. Kate and Noah skim them: *express sympathy for the lives lost over many years; describe all events in general terms (the death of a teenager, your pursuit of clues about her killers, her broad research interests); outline your kidnapers' affiliations in general terms; express gratitude for the attention brought to the issue of global warming; state your support for the work of the Clinton-Gates Foundation; ALWAYS refer to the solar or universal collapse in general terms, without specifics, implying these phenomena are remote, of no immediate concern.*

Noah's inner teenager rebels. He has the strong desire to sit there, tear up the talking points and tell them precisely about the collapsing universe, the years of denial and conspiracy on the part of the Catholic Church and the Catholic-Muslim Alliance. To tell them about the cover-ups, the dealings of the Rose School Network—the murders of young people for starters. To tell them the truth, the reporter's only currency.

Instead, he lets he lets Iona push them into an alien land—an excursion from South Korea into North, from the South to the North in Civil War times. Into hostile territory.

Pete is alternately with them, encouraging them, and turned away, bothered by his Bluetooth, his phone, and the voices that live there. At one point they hear him say to Iona,

"Pull over at the side of the road. *Now*, now please!" And to the person in his ear, "*What?* What did you say?" his face intent. He turns to the back of the car, telling them in a stage whisper, "We've had a complication. It's not safe to go into Melbourne. We'll know in a minute."

57

THE 9:37 TO MELBOURNE. TUESDAY MORNING

It's an odd thing, being a commuter train. One might suppose it to be a boring and repetitious life, like the 9:37 from Stony Point to Melbourne. *Boring and repetitious* do not describe today's ride.

Perhaps it's the gentleman in the third-to-last last car. He looks similar to all the other businessmen—gray pants, a worn dark blue jacket, a maroon tie with tiny crests of a local university, smiling at others but preoccupied by a large real estate deal, possibly. Perhaps it's the heavy, extra-large aluminum briefcase that he carries with him, holding what exactly? Samples of window treatments? Of hardware?

The man double-checks the signs, boards the third-to-last last car. It's already made one trip into the city, full, has returned almost empty and now waits for its return to downtown Melbourne. It's the same train he took yesterday on a practice run, something his over-achieving bosses said he must do. He sits in the same place, the briefcase tucked into the same tiny space under his seat. And smiles, just like yesterday, thinking of what is to come.

This time he does something different. He releases tiny clips at the four corners of the brief case, places it into the narrow space under the steps in front of him. He turns the brief case so that the marked side faces the tiny wall. He adjusts the mechanism to begin its countdown.

The train starts. The legend over the car doors says the journey takes them from Stony Point, to Crib Point, to the awkwardly-named Morradoo, to a handful of other places, finally to Melbourne.

It fails to mention hell; hell has, until now, not been on the schedule.

He waits, his job finished. He has precisely seven stops before he gets off, long before the last one. He looks out the window, seeing graffiti illuminating the concrete tunnels and passageways, rapid movie-screen images of trees, towns, cars, telephone poles, burned-out houses and derelict apartments, the scorched countryside. He sees the un-recycled detritus of the homeless—plastic water bottles, beer cans, food wrappers, newspapers—in a camp, less than a thousand feet from an upscale mall. He listens to the train's wheels as they rocket over the rail breaks, hearing the swelling and diminishing sounds of Herr Doppler as another train passes, sucking the air out of his car, shaking the doors.

It's difficult to say who sees who first, the man with the cumbersome briefcase and the maroon tie, or the two men that Pete has sent to find him. Whoever it is, maroon-tie whispers into his Blue Tooth, "They've made me!!" He hears in reply, "Abort! Reach into the little space, take the brief case and leave. *GO!!*"

He is suddenly energized, moves quickly to the exit door, hustling down the too-small concrete steps that separate the two levels of the commuter train, trying to get to the exit just as it opens. His timing is perfect. He hears, "*Please stand clear of the doors!*" and two tiny *dings*. He bursts through the door, surprising the incoming passengers. He sprints to the exit stairs that take him below track level, through two tunnels and—he hopes—to the car the tiny voice in his ear has told him will be there.

Two men burst out of the same car doors five seconds later. While they're dressed casually, there's nothing relaxed in their adrenalized chase of the first man, ahead of them by a hundred yards. They take off after him, vaulting over the railing, running down the stairs two at a time, holding on to the sides as they swing round to the next landing, pell-mell into the tunnels. Anxiety and desperation fuel every step.

Maroon-tie charges ahead, thinking to take the escalator, managing two steps at once. Yesterday at this time it was heading up. He believes—perhaps *hopes* is a better word—that this would give him just the advantage that he needs, leveraged by the up-moving stair. His plan is to hit the button at the top and reverse it just in time to cause the two, now gaining on him, some pain and frustration. He could escape.

His mistake is fatal: the stairs have yet to be reversed. He's forced to run up the down-escalator. Surprised, he trips and falls, striking his head, almost comically. He's momentarily senseless. The escalator delivers him directly into the arms of his two captors. Breathless, one of them wrestles the briefcase from him while the other wraps duct-tape around the man's arms. They decide not to open the briefcase, wisely. Instead, in a few minutes, they use a tiny Geiger counter on it, registering radioactivity.

"We got it!" says one of them, winded but relieved, into his phone.

"Check the train anyway!" Pete orders, his cell phone pressed close to his black ear.

They stop the train at the next station. Pete's men search it thoroughly, looking for another briefcase. Armed with a perfect description and Geiger counters, Aussie security guards and Pete's team scan the cars, the seats, the storage spaces, in the train and under it. They find nothing. One little space under the stairs is entirely unoccupied to their eyes, its olive green walls are as clean as a whistle.

One of the agents, an Australian, communicates with Pete, "I've the situation in hand, mate!"

They have unfortunately not noted that one small space in the third-to-last car has been made smaller by two inches, its tiny wall now occupied by the other half of the brief case, perfectly airtight. Perfectly radiation-tight.

The situation is not in hand.

58

EN ROUTE TO MELBOURNE. TUESDAY MORNING

Ten minutes later, relief in his voice, Pete takes several calls. They hear him say, "You're *sure*? You've combed through the train? There's nothing left?" Reassured and reassuring them, he tells Iona to proceed.

Federation Square is the aluminum, angular heart of Melbourne, perched on a giant shelf above the city's major transport hub, Jolimont Railway Yards. It's part icon, part convention center, part village square. It draws people like a magnet, hosting fall and spring fairs, rock concerts, celebrity visits. Weddings. Festivals. Last month, a nude biking event attracted several thousand brave Melbourne residents.

The press conference is held in the main floor conference room of Federation Square, the site of the just-finishing Clinton-Gates conference.

Reporters from all over the planet fill the seats, the aisles, standing at the back of the auditorium, jostling, using their iPhones as cameras.

In the last few days, since the death of Dr. Zapinsky, Kate and Noah have become famous, instant celebrities of Facebook or Twitter, of the twenty-four hour news cycle. A fate which provides them with a podium to tell it all, revealing what they know about multiple deaths across many countries and over many centuries, about the collusion between the Muslim world and the Catholic Church, about the collapse. A fate which provides them with the platform of an international, live-broadcast press conference. A fate that the Astronomers cannot abide.

They're unaware that the news about their journey has penetrated social media, like the story of some space-age Bonnie and Clyde. The collapse of WashPO has helped fuel the story, as have fantastic stories about Catholic conspiracies and end-of-world theories. Today, billed as *Reporters Reveal Their Story,* the press conference has attracted over a thousand people to the square, holding signs that read *End of the World, The Fiery End,* and others. In some ways they resemble the homeless camp outside Dulles Airport. How they could stand the 120 degree heat that day on the hot pavement is beyond Noah. Ovens are cooler.

The four of them enter the rear delivery entrance—a little cooler, a lot less crowded—and are joined by Marius and Marcus. They enter through a garage door, its hinges squealing, warning them but of what is uncertain. They proceed down long white hallways, reminding Kate of WashPO, with doors marked *Storage, Recycling, Electrical.* Up a rear concrete stairway and into a long hall marked by angular glass panels and more doors, ending in a "T," or as close to it as the angular building will allow. A sign looms in front of them. Pointing to the left, it says, *Restrooms, Federation Plaza, Amphitheatre, Conference Rooms.* To the right are *Management Offices, Conference Planning, Helipad Access, Development Office.*

Pete stops suddenly, for once not grabbing his Bluetooth or his phone. He puts out his hand to stop the five hurrying behind him.

"We're still trying to arrange enough security," Pete says, absorbing a message inside himself, his eyes growing wider.

It has occurred to him that it is not *Headrick* that they heard in Aabis' conversation with Anna. His hockey days in Detroit have come back to him in a rush. It's not *Headrick;* it's *Hat Trick.* The new knowledge is more forceful than if he were hit by a puck, the hockey game of memory playing out in his mind.

In light of the events that follow, the next few minutes are sculpted in their minds, even heroic. Pete takes Noah aside, their faces only inches apart, a hot black line between them like a tightrope. On it balance enormous burdens, perhaps gifts. Friendship. The shared battleground of Deborah. Loyalty. Pete's years of protecting Noah.

It's decided in twenty seconds: Noah, Kate, Marcus and Marius turn right; Iona and Pete turn left. Pete has a trick of his own up his sleeve. He also looks back at them. In that moment, Kate sees a small tear in Pete's eye, identical to its predecessor two nights ago.

59

LARGE CONFERENCE ROOM, FEDERATION SQUARE CONFERENCE CENTER, MELBOURNE, TUESDAY MORNING

The hour-plus passes quickly; there is so much to do, to arrange, to prevent.

The conference room was most recently occupied by Clinton-Gates participants, steeped in matters of science and the spaces between its disciplines. They've left disappointed—the funding announcement by the distinguished visitor has been delayed even further.

A raised platform sits at the front of the room. A table perches on it, draped with a white cloth as tightly tucked in as a hospital bed. A bank of oversized flat screens occupy the center of the platform, behind the table, allowing speakers not in the room to be almost-present. Cameras are aimed at both the panelists and the audience. One wall is marked by a jumble of windows—irregular angles and edges, like the chaos immersing them, like a bath of ice cubes in boiling water. Pete, Karla, Iona and Kym occupy chairs on the podium, slightly offset from the center where Noah and Kate are the central stars. The room is crowded with reporters, sitting, standing, security guards now lining the door to let no one else in. If anything, the slight delay has crowded the room even more.

Iona introduces herself, then Pete, Kym and Karla, Noah and Kate. Noah takes a deep breath, a look at his notes, and starts. He pulls the skinny microphone towards himself and spins fifteen minutes of prepared remarks like a well-scripted politician, using pictures shown on the flat screen to illustrate their journey. He shows the Temple of Inscriptions, the Palenque Codex, the Eastern Market Rose School, the Vatican Observatories. He does not know about a Russian Monastery where a nuclear bomb changed hands. It's a pity; it would have made a good picture.

The entire time Noah thinks how superficial this is, how much it follows the bland language of bureaucratic talking points. He skims over the less-than-detailed descriptions of the allies and forces, of the agents and agencies, of the theories.

There are lots of questions, some of them shouted, some of them delivered in obnoxious, belligerent tones. *Was I ever like that?* Noah wonders. "Who are the Astronomers?" "Who founded the Rose Schools?" And many more. Finally, a woman in the front row grabs one of the few microphones moving haphazardly in the room, an aggressive gesture. She is artificially blonde, her long hair perfectly arranged. "Dr. Scott, we've really talked *around* the main issue here. If the solar system is collapsing, is the universe as well? If so, how much time do we have?"

The small buzz in the room stops. These are *the* questions, aren't they? Noah has given general, ten thousand foot answers to almost everything, satisfying some of the audience but not himself and clearly not some of them. This question has no talking point.

It starts.

He is comfortable in front of people, even on camera, has given front-line reports in Afghanistan, in Syria. He has no doubt he can handle the questioning until this moment. His heart races, his brow begins to sweat. He has the vain thought, *This will look like hell on TV tonight*. The sweat begins to run down his back, his hands feel like ice cubes. He reaches for his talisman, as though pausing to choose his words carefully, like a man lighting his pipe to gain time before he answers a question. It's in its new location.

And then it comes to him—what the marks on the little pendant are, even reversed by the mirror that morning.

It also comes to him that the room in front of him and its human contents have disappeared, as though a signal has been lost. A solar flare, perhaps. As though a sign might appear on a screen saying, *Signal lost temporarily.*

60

THE HUBBLE TELESCOPE. TUESDAY MORNING

I t's a blessing that Hubble is, for all intents and purposes, deaf.

At least deaf in the way that humans are deaf. It can't hear the sudden but short-lived cries of children, the shouts and expletives of adults, the horror expressed by those a hundred miles and more away, of the shrieks of those who watch. It can't hear the cries of humanity.

It cannot hear the nuclear wind as it sears and scours the suburbs of Melbourne, as it has already leveled the Central Business District, as it......... No, at 380 miles above the earth's surface, nothing disturbs what I've called the silent, siren song of space.

Hubble is also thankfully blind to earth, turning its face perpetually outward to the universe.

And so it cannot see—another blessing—the huge, sudden, powerful ejaculation of earth and man-made structures below it, vaporized in an instant, erased by forces of nuclear origin. It cannot see the Yarra River turn to steam or

Port Philip Bay boil. It cannot see the huge cavity that was once downtown Melbourne, carved out like a hollow pumpkin, by the small but oh-so-deadly—and oh-so-dirty—nuclear explosion.

It cannot see the mushroom cloud, earth's carcinoma, rise above the city in triumph, the face of evil written in each rolling, unfolding wave of gray, dead-but-alive debris.

It can only see *out* to where the sun grows warmer, looms closer, perhaps less to the naked eye, more to Hubble's. To where the stars grow closer, the moons, the planets. To the edge, the beginning, of the universe. Where I live.

Where I shed tears, too; this universe held so much promise.

SECTION V

NOT WITH A BANG
"THE HOLLOW MEN." BY T S ELIOT

61

AUSTRALIAN BROADCAST STUDIOS. CANBERRA. TUESDAY MORNING

A   *Hat Trick*—in hockey, a game in which three goals are scored by one player.

For the Astronomers and Harry-Aabis, it is no game. It's a triple threat, a potential sarin attack, and two bombs cleverly hidden in one fat aluminum briefcase. One of the bombs is disguised so cleverly that it matches the color and size of a small space under commuter train stairs, painted a pale olive gray-green, and protected by a lead skin of the sort that no radiation can penetrate. Three plans, two redundancies—the children of malicious overachievement.

For most of the residents of Melbourne, among the planet's great cities, it is virtual, immediate annihilation. The area between the central business district on the north and Port Phillip basin to its south is reduced to a giant nuclear cavity. Its contents, including the human ones, are vaporized in an instant. Its outskirts, the dozens of outlying neighborhoods, are shredded to bits by a giant nuclear tornado, the radioactive wind leaving shells of unrecognizable structures, leaving a periphery where humans are too near death to be counted as survivors. And later, leaving scores scorched, burned, wasted and anemic, envying the dead. Later still, thousands of children born with terrible birth defects, and—even if normal at birth—prone to thyroid and other malignancies. Truly a giant cancer on the earth.

Except with its emotional and human fingers, it does not touch Noah and Kate.

They are safe. Shocked, horrified, moved beyond belief in the small broadcast room, hundreds of miles away, in tears, but safe.

They have been saved by Pete's decision to send them in one direction down the long white hallway to the heliport where he arranged for a quick flight to Canberra. He of course went in the other direction, to possible, then probable, now certain, death. Noah and Kate, along with Marcus and Marius, were flown to a small broadcast center owned by the Australian Broadcast System participating in the press conference by videoconference. Pete, staying in Melbourne, sat to the side during the press conference, aware that nothing he could do could save them or Melbourne. Or himself for that matter. Praying that his team would find the bomb. And then knowing, in a nuclear instant, that they had failed.

62

THE AIRLY WHITE HOUSE. AIRLY. VIRGINIA. ONE WEEK LATER

It's the view of the Rose Garden that gives it away.

The rest is the same you've seen in pictures. The central oval rug, the eagle and his arrows still ensconced in the middle. The two cream-colored chesterfields facing each other. The period coffee table between them, with cups and saucers laid out expectantly, bearing little emblems of the White House. The picture of Saint Abraham. The famous Kennedy desk where John Junior played. The Federalist Grandfather clock; the clock never chimes; it has no hands.

What's not right is the view of the Rose Garden, somehow two-dimensional and artificial, like the pictures of Noah and Kate seen at last week's press conference. It's a picture on a flat screen. This is the Airly White House, in Virginia, on land owned by the FBI, buried seventy feet underground, an almost perfect replica of the original, and a welcome escape from the hot pavement of

Pennsylvania Avenue. The other White House is used for official business, but at night—when safety is less than certain, when the terrorist hot lines hum with threat and when the homeless camps are most restless—it's inhabited only by guards.

As they enter, POTUS is on the phone. Sofia Esqualita Lopez Black, mother of two, divorced and remarried, her father African-American, her mother Hispanic. Former mayor of Pittsburgh, Pennsylvania, then junior senator from that state, then governor. For ten months, the president of the United States of America.

Despite this pedigree, she is not at all impressive physically. Short, on the far side of stocky. A round face that, even in its youth on her wedding days, only her husbands and mother would have said was beautiful. Her face a perfect, mocha-colored, intelligent convexity, framed in a halo of grey-brown curls. Her handshake is exceptionally firm. Her voice is as deep and rich as her culture and heritage. A lover of single malt scotch, almost her only vice. But there is this an aura about her that is simultaneously appealing and intimidating.

She holds up a surprisingly long index finger indicating, *a moment please.* It's a famous finger. Over a year ago, in a final debate with her too-scripted opponent, she pointed at him. "You wouldn't know to take the garbage out without someone telling you to do it!" The women of the country resonated with the comment, voting for her in droves. Time Magazine put her hand on its cover, *The Finger That Became President,* the caption said.

She replaces the phone, pauses slightly, "My apologies. I've been trying to call the families of the Americans killed in Melbourne. Nearly five hundred names in just over a week. Hard to fit them in between meetings and other calls, but it's important to me. All those people—children, servicemen, tourists. It's so sad."

She greets them and within minutes she exhibits her other famous traits, inviting them to sit, hugging them, offering her sympathy on their loss. Ordering coffee, giving them an hour, an enormous amount of time in the schedule of a POTUS. Putting them at ease. She tells them what they know about "Hat Trick"—the sarin gas canister stolen from its Level Four storage facility in Missouri, twin nuclear bombs stolen by Chechens conveyed from a Moscow monastery to Melbourne by the Astronomers.

"They did a pretty good job don't you think? Duplicating the oval office?" a non-question question. "When my first husband and I separated thirty years ago we determined that our kids' lives would be as dislocated as little as possible. And so we built, well, not identical houses, but similar enough; the kids' rooms were almost the same."

She pours their coffee, prelude to thanking Noah and Kate for their work, to explaining. Noah and Kate nod. Words seem so tiny in the vast space of their loss, the earth's loss, a handful of rain drops in an immense hot desert. Apart from the thanks and support, apart from the human touch that she knows she must apply like a salve, she has other agenda items.

She begins with the updates, using her index finger.

"One. We think we have the Astronomers identified and controlled at least in the US, but it's their world-wide presence that alarms us. The Church, or at least the Vatican, has been deeply involved in this for years, at the highest level, it seems. So have certain Arab groups, mainly the Taliban. We've considered sanctions, but that may be too hot politically to tackle." *Politics,* Noah thinks.

She places her thumb and second finger together, a reminder of someone else from the White House, years before. "That brings me to the second topic, your former employer." Two sets of eyebrows raise. "It looks like the workings of the Rose Network involved the board of WashPO, filtering down to several of your co-workers. Sydney is in jail. She was behind the attack on Noah that almost killed him at the start of this. Gerry Weiss is also being investigated. He had word of the nuclear risk weeks before, but said nothing. Naomi is less clear; her disappearance while you were in Europe is deeply disturbing. Erich is more complex, but is most likely innocent—too busy with the politics of Washington to be aware of what people around him were thinking or doing. Overall, it's clear to me at least that they subverted much of the goals of the press—generating *truth.*" She is adamant about the Fourth Amendment.

"Third," the president says, her middle finger and thumb meeting, "The connection with the US Army. We also know that at least one of WashPO's board members is involved—General Wilcox." Noah has a recollection of seeing his name badge the night when he was almost pushed off the roof at Bezos 1. "Wilcox diverted funds for research on parallel universes, was involved up to his neck in the Rose School business and a shell organization called Poseidon. The Rose Schools were like a laboratory for them, finding and testing things like telepathy. There's also a strong connection between the network and the Kaiser Health team that looked after DiShannia's so-called diabetes. They were making her too sick to function." Her face radiates disgust.

Kate asks something that's been on her mind for days. "Madam President, we ran into several homeless individuals who resemble each other, maybe even we think we've seen the *same* man on several occasions, in different locations, in DC, in Europe. Is that possible?"

The ring finger and thumb meet. "That's a good intro to the fourth item I wanted to raise. I do know that some of our agents—that is, those of the Society, which we've funded—were disguised as homeless people. I don't know anything about the homeless man you refer to, but there's a lot we don't know here. I do know this: the Army, probably as early as the Cheney days, has undertaken highly secret work on parallel universes, maybe even building another Large Hedron Collider somewhere." She leans forward, confiding, "Here's something right out of science fiction: one of the key scientists in the Army's project on parallel universes was on that Malaysian airline flight years ago, the one that we've never found."

They are amazed by it all—the depth to which the Astronomers penetrated WashPO, the murderous elements of the Rose School Network, its ties to the Army, CERN's experiments with particles so small that we cannot conceive of them, with implications as big as the universe. Amazed at the *science*, no longer the science fiction.

The updates out of the way, she gets to the main agenda Item, her thumb and baby finger making a perfect circle.

"You're not safe."

Surprise is only one of the feelings Kate and Noah experience; it is the easiest to register.

"I don't believe you know how valuable you are, Noah. It was *you* that the Taliban was after years ago; they wanted to kidnap you. They were part of the Catholic-Muslim Alliance. In the end, knowing the troop they sent to kill you was gone, they elected to give you the talisman. They believed you would figure out what to do with it. They must have discovered who you were, traced you when you visited your grandmother. You do know she was Mary Catherine O'Rourke, am I right? She used the zoo to visit you?"

Noah nods, a slow metronome.

"And then after the Taliban incident, some members of the Army under Cheney's control virtually kidnapped and interrogated you, drugged you, then released you and put you in treatment. We think they learned nothing. Noah, you are very important to us, to the future of this world. You have a genius in you, an analytic ability inherited from your grandfather and possibly your grandmother. And you are in danger, we believe. Your Harry, our Aabis, is still out there."

Almost simultaneously, Noah and Kate have the same question, "Who is Harry?"

"We know a bit about him. He was apparently born a Muslim in India and raised there until his parents' death when he was young. He was then adopted by an English family, converted to Catholicism, and identified early on as a young man of considerable potential. He was recruited into the priesthood. We're uncertain about the details from that point, but it appears as though he was selected as an Astronomer and quickly rose to becoming one of their key figures. His last few years have been carefully crafted to find and use Noah. He is, if nothing else, a master planner, an expert at building in redundancies."

President Lopez-Black continues, touching Kate's arm as reassurance, simultaneously a large and small gesture. "That really brings me to this last point: to protect you fully we need to remove you from your daily lives, to change your identities."

"Like in a witness protection program?" Kate asks.

"Exactly, we could also accommodate family members, a small number at least, but at all costs, we must protect *you*." She looks at Noah. "Forgive me Kate, it's not that we don't value you, but it's Noah that we need."

He says only, "Where I go, Kate goes," taking her hand. The president's words, intended to support and congratulate, weigh him down with expectation. He is beginning to learn what his so-called genius is required to do. He touches the talisman, unconscious of the action, unconscious of its importance.

There is a quiet in the room in which only the hum of the hard-working air conditioner makes any noise.

Suddenly, the president startles them. "I almost resigned, you know," her voice as rich as chocolate, the color of her skin, "...when I learned of the collapse. And then I expect I went through the stages of grief that others describe—the anger, the denial, the depression or sadness at least. Then, now, today, acceptance. I do believe there is a way forward. I believe Noah can help us get there."

Other elements enter their conversation, logistical intruders. Where they might like to live, who they might want to take with them. The hour goes quickly. They find they like her immensely, the true source of her power. Finally, shaking hands at the door, Noah asks,

"So this," pointing back into the room as though their conversation still existed there, like a ghost, "...was all concocted to protect a theory that said our universe was expanding, right? Instead of which it's contracting, meaning, what, that we'd have a sort of big collapse millions of years away, right, Madam President?"

Kate is surprised; Noah's tone is more confrontational than one would expect with a Commander-in-Chief. The president is unmoved however. She knows this isn't anger; this is his sadness, his fear. She knows that this is love for Kate.

"Are you worried about what the end will be like? The scientists say that the collapse is logarithmic, that is, it is very slow at the start, then speeds up dramatically at the end. The end will be very quick."

Noah and Kate are blank; this is not what they asked.

"Forgive me," POTUS laughs. "It's a politician's curse. Ask us a direct question we don't want to answer and we answer one you didn't ask! You want to know *when* of course."

The long finger touches her cheek and stays there. "The collapse will come within our lifetimes, our children's at the most. It's possible I may even be the last president of the United States."

63

PORTMEIRION. WALES. UNITED KINGDOM. CURRENT DAY

ortmeirion lives its life out of time.

It's a small village in Gwynedd, North Wales, near Anglesey and its estuary, still a piece of the ever-shrinking United Kingdom. It's the nineteenth century child of a Scottish architect, Sir Clough Williams-Ellis, who imported Italian buildings, sculptures and artwork into quintessential British countryside. It's a living example of genius, another illustration of work out of time.

If the UK is no longer as united, nor the kingdom as royal, Portmeirion is still the typical British village. There is an open market Tuesdays and Saturdays; farmers bring their locally grown produce and wares (honey is featured this week); women hang their washing outside Monday mornings; children play soccer and cricket in the central open space.

Noah and Kate have moved into a low, tan Tudor building of a dozen apartments, a pitched roof curved at the edges to mimic thatching, its casement windows leaded. Converted to condominium living, it's home to several couples and families. Their apartment overlooks an arm of the Welsh Ocean, an estuary which glistens, moistened by the sea on its moon-drawn wanderings. It's home to Kate and Noah's new marriage, to their few possessions.

It's also home to Noah's depression.

Kate has moved more quickly through the stages of grief. While the earth is hot, and the news of floods, the other disasters, and of the growing homeless camps disturb her, she has learned to accept their fate, to live one day at a time. Her parents have been moved to a small apartment nearby. Sharron Johns was invited to join them but refused; she is more comfortable in her own surroundings, "Waitin' for the end," she tells them, helping the poor souls that occupy the *Eastenders* one room apartments. Kate is able to visit her parents every day, to support her mother. She has a purpose. Noah, however, despite the call of genius, has none. He is stuck.

The future, at least for Noah, holds an incredible weight. It burdens him. It buries his ambitions and dreams in layers of gray. It takes him beyond the immediate aftermath of the statement, "I may be the last president of the United States," into days where the words haunt him. It drops him into a well of depression as deep, if not as catatonic, as the one he suffered in Afghanistan. And it lasts for nearly a month. He goes through the motions—making coffee in the morning, but not tasting it; picking up the paper but not really reading it; checking his emails and texts with listless fingers and a numb mind. He has ceased to be the Noah Kate fell in love with.

It is not the physical journey that disturbs him—from Melbourne, to Washington, to Wales and his new marriage. It's the mental voyage that eats away at him—the movement from denial (the universe is collapsing but not for billions of years) to realization (the billions of years have shrunk incredibly to a handful), to depression (what's the use?) Cancer patients know this journey well. Scores of Mayans and possibly Arabs knew it generations—*katuns*—ago. More often however they end in a different place than depression; they end at acceptance and some form of peace. Not Noah at this point. For Kate, the more optimistic of the two, it is a shorter journey from denial to acceptance.

Finally, at the end of the third week of what she calls his exile, she's had enough. "You're just going through the motions, aren't you?" she asks, with less kindness than usual. It's early one morning, the sun just coming in their glazed, mullioned windows—the hot, hot sun. She carries her coffee in one hand, her breasts struggling against the thin cloth of her nightshirt.

She chooses to start with a businesslike checklist. "We've got to register our new names at the town hall (they have become Mr. and Mrs. Tomas McIntyre). I'm the only one with a driver's license; you have to get yours. There are boxes, in case you haven't noticed, in the bedroom and beside the fridge. And Ivaan Horkonen has been trying to get you for days."

Kate's become the scolding housewife, much different than who she wants to be. He looks past her, so much like pictures of his grandfather they've both seen.

She tries another tack. "It's a beautiful day, cooler you know. We could go for a walk, visit my parents. We've hardly even begun to explore the area. We *chose* this place because of the countryside, remember? You know, we've hardly even made lo…"

Her words are tiny Davids against the Goliath of his self-pity. Words may be the reporter's currency, but this reporting, the waiting and watching, are not life. She makes a decision, only partly consciously.

She puts her coffee down, copying the intense heated look he's taught her so well. She is a good student. She moves towards him, raising her long T-shirt, straddling him, settling on his lap. She breathes in the rumpled, early-morning smell of him. Her breasts push outward, rebelling against the thin cloth. She settles on him, rubbing his palm against her right nipple, hardening in the early morning light. She takes his other pity-me hand, and presses the palm against her left breast, rubbing it, slowly, just the palm. Her nipples rise to meet his hand.

They are not the only things hardening in the room.

She slides back slightly, enough to examine what she has created. It rises to meet her hand. As she grasps it, a tiny viscous dot of fluid emerges, glistening in the morning sun. It sits atop the hard, strong thing rising between her legs. It is as though she has created a miracle.

She has. It is the miracle of life.

There is urgency in the room now as she raises the night shirt over her head, freeing her breasts. She takes his T-shirt off; his pajama bottoms follow. She kisses his talisman, the only thing that either of them are now wearing. Briefly she thinks, *He needs to eat more, I can see his ribs.* But it's only a short-lived thought, soon overwhelmed by her desire to have him *occupy* her.

She moves quickly then, settling on his lap and the warm, stone-hard thing that fills her. Both move quickly, abandoning all thought. It is soon over, but it is only the first wave. After a minute or two, fueled by a heat neither of them has experienced before, the pent-up, stored hunger for life emerges. It's slower this time, the movements of her hips less primitive, more calculating. His thrusts are deeper, his lips and tongue never leaving her. When it is finished this time, with sounds that they think that Welshmen in the next town must hear, she has arrested his depression. She has grabbed vitality, just as she has grabbed his erection, like some throttle, pulling him back into life.

The moist, curative machinery of lovemaking.

He has learned the lesson that she has known all along: if there is nothing in tomorrow, there can be a world in today.

64

PORTMEIRION. WALES. UNITED KINGDOM. CURRENT DAY

louds scud in front of a growing moon.

The disease that almost claimed Noah has a name, possibly several. Hopelessness. Depression. Despair. Regret. Whatever its name, its effects are legion. He is not the first to feel its cold, gray fingers around his mind; he needn't be ashamed that he, temporarily at least, has succumbed to its call. It is fueled by a feeling of uselessness and loss of control, of sadness at the death of Pete and many others, of the guilt of surviving.

But it is short lived. With her help and his own sizable reserves, he recovers, becomes himself again. Her husband. The helpful son-in-law. The reporter. The genius. Her lover.

Small things help. That afternoon they visit her parents, settling surprisingly well in their new apartment, just across the central greenspace in the village. Her mother says, "So long as he has his own chair and the same food, he's fine."

They go for a walk, and after that, drive into a neighboring village. They are both learning to write *neighbouring*. They visit a small country market. They clip a rose from just outside the front door from a bush he had never noticed. Late that night, they make love again.

A world in a day.

Larger things, things of the universe, help as well.

A long Skype call with Ivaan begins a regular morning routine. Eight a.m. in Wales is seven a.m. in Munich. Some calls last a few minutes; some last for a morning. It has the feeling of a tutorial, though the roles of tutor and student are fluid. At the outset, the student is Noah, but his reading is intense and voracious; notepads fill with ideas and equations. Kate hears words like *String Theory, quarks, leptons, muons*—a strange new language that holds no meaning for her. Within days however, Noah has his own ideas, is questioning theories, helping, then it seems to her, even instructing Ivaan, building on the notion that they might create a Higgs Accelerator, able to transport—what? Electrons? Worlds? People?—across the incredible barrier of time and space.

And there is an urgency to their work. While the general population has only hints that something is wrong with the solar system and their planet—the too-bright sun, the rising oceans, the record high temperatures—Ivaan and his team know the truth about the universe. That the collapse, thought to be generations away, is accelerating. That the "clock is ticking," as Ivaan says.

In spite of, or perhaps because of the pressure, Ivaan, his team and Noah make headway. The progress is fueled by a fantastic idea. One day, Kate is in the kitchen looking over Noah's shoulder while he Skypes with Ivaan. His visits are two dimensional, but familiar, like that of a neighbor.

"Kate, did you ever see same homeless man in unusual places?" It's the question raised in the faux White House weeks before.

"Yes," she says, remembering him at the top of the Dupont Circle Metro, on the way to the Eastern Market School. In Dulles and England.

Ivaan reports even more strangeness—the appearance and disappearance of particles that they cannot explain, not appearing to come from outer space or from Earth. They come to share a dream that transmission of particles across the divide is possible. Their dream is limited by a huge knowledge gap.

Noah tries to explain it to Kate one night, in bed. "We're stuck," he says, not the first time he's described Ivaan's and his work as dual. "I mean, we can get the tiniest sub-particles to transmit, or at least we believe they transmit, the muons and the bosons and such; we've even made progress transmitting several at a time like a scatter gun. But we can't get to the next level, to the larger ones, to the particles themselves. Ivaan's theory is if we could do that, we could move quickly to protons and electrons, then to higher order structures like crystals—tangible objects—perhaps even living matter."

Kate can't even comprehend what he's talking about. *Send them where?* she wonders. *To some universe that doesn't exist? To one with an even hotter destiny than this one?* She's not alone.

"I wonder sometimes," he says, those black eyes receding, "whether a parallel universe even exists. Ivaan's convinced. I'm not." The challenges keep Noah awake at night, not the insomnia of depression and regret, but the insomnia of ideas. Progress in any sense of the word.

There is also progress also in the business of living day by day, a challenge for persons living in this new, hotter world, perhaps for all of you.

One day, Kate decides that the kitchen is the wrong color.

"How can a color be wrong, hon?" Noah asks, a question with no good answer. He has just finished reading the results of Ivaan's last experiment. Other than more reading, there's nothing to do until the next test results come in the following morning.

Kate has an answer. "The yellow is too bright, Noah. The kitchen's already hot when the sun hits those windows; that yellow just makes it worse. Why don't we try a pale blue or something?"

It appears that "or something" has already been decided. In the way of wives, Kate reaches into her enormous purse and pulls out a small color palate, an array of blues that look identical to Noah. The local hardware store has a paint sale— "20% off on all Williams-Sherman products," the little flyer says—and by the end of the day, the painting has begun.

The fridge has been pulled out from the wall and a step ladder now leans against the door frame between their bedroom and the kitchen. A box, stashed for weeks beside the fridge, the only one still unpacked from their move, has found its way onto the kitchen table. Newspapers and an old sheet line much of the floor. Noah, in his oldest jeans and T-shirt, is on the third rung of the ladder, rolling a pale blue color over—he has to admit—an obnoxious and steamy yellow, temporarily acting the family man. He's glad to have a distraction from considering the fate of muons and bosons.

He's also displayed a touch of OCD by carefully rolling out meters of greenish painters' tape to protect the ceiling and trim. Kate, similarly dressed for domestic combat, is moving furniture around, covering the stove with an old bath towel, laying down more paper.

Kate's local mobile phone rings, the third time today. Its ringtone, almost the only one she ever hears, is her mother saying that her dad needs help getting ready for bed. "Could you come, darling? I hate to bother you tonight but I think it won't take a minute or two. I just need help getting his pajamas on."

Kate agrees, thinking she'll be gone for only a short while. Noah knows it will take longer than that; it always does. He hopes he'll be finished the first coat by the time she gets back.

Both are wrong.

When she returns three hours later, somewhat rattled by a prolonged battle of wills with her confused and restless father, Kate finds something entirely unexpected.

If somewhat disrupted before she left, the kitchen is now in total chaos.

She stands, mesmerized, at the door. The kitchen is hot, registering over ninety degrees; the air conditioner has been turned off. The paint roller has been left on the top rung of the ladder, a few drops of latex paint slowly dripping onto old newspapers lining the floor. The paint can lid, still open, begs for someone to step on it. The printer-scanner now sits on the stove top, plugged in, spewing out paper copies of something that looks like night skies, some of them negative images. No cooling pale blue surface greets her, instead dozens of documents line the walls pinned to the wall by fragments of green painter's tape—pictures of a Mayan sarcophagus lid, copies of dots and lines, photographs from Miriam Al-Ansari's book, a crumpled page now straightened, marked by three bloody fingermarks.

It's a reminder of the team room many weeks before, possibly the little paper napkins in their room in Geneva. But that's not what shakes her to her core.

It's the image of Noah, his shirt off, sweaty, the hot dew of discovery glistening on his skin. Using his new UK mobile, he appears to be taking pictures of photos almost entirely covering the kitchen cupboards that line one wall. She is glad to see his excitement; it's something else that bothers her. His black eyes, always deep, are almost hidden from her. He looks through her momentarily, frightening her, leaving her to wonder if he's relapsed into the depression of a few weeks ago. He looks through her—to the other room, to the future, to another universe, she cannot tell.

It is an attack, but one of his genius, nothing more.

"Darling," she says, thinking this is the easiest question to answer, "Why is the AC off?"

"The fan was blowing the pages," he says, waving vaguely at the giant old AC-fan unit in the kitchen window, as though anyone could see the problem.

"It's like a giant jigsaw puzzle," he says without any preamble, finally engaging her with those black eyes. He comes close to her, takes her by her shoulders, his grip almost too strong. "I was on the ladder, painting and I noticed the box."

It is the cardboard liquor box that he brought from his favorite wine store, the Calvert-Woodley, marked with the single letter "D." She was never sure if it was the fourth box he packed, or that it was meant for a den, or that the letter stood for something. She only knew he had stashed it beside the fridge after their move and never opened it.

"I decide to open it finally and look at it," he says. "It's about DiShannia," his face reflects the sadness that her name evokes. "It's all I have of her really. It's the work she scanned and sent to Miriam Ansari, the photos and pages in the envelope, other material we collected at Zap's house. My old phone and its photos. All I have of her," he repeats.

"I've put it off, you know, but I thought tonight, with you out of the house, I'd do it."

The sadness passes from his face like a cloud crosses the sun; he is eager to show her the jigsaw. He takes her hand, leads her to the first of the dozens of drawings now lining the walls, the kitchen cupboards, hanging on the refrigerator.

"There are three or four main pieces," he says, taking her to photos and text pinned on the side of pulled-out fridge.

"First, remember I said I was worried that there *is* no parallel universe?" She does. "The Mayans also thought about this, strange as it may seem. Just look at Pakal's sarcophagus cover," he says, showing her pictures from the book Miriam gave them and from DiShannia's notes. They are taped to the fridge like some pre-schooler's art collection.

"The sarcophagus lid is pretty famous. It shows the king lying on a sort of palette or bed looking up, maybe being re-born. Some have said he's in a kind of rocket ship heading out to space, but DiShannia thought it was even more bizarre than that. Here," he points to a drawing that Shanny made, with her notes surrounding the lid, marked, "Two heavens, not the same," "Seven Gods," "Venus," "Tree of Life?"

"I wondered about the 'Tree of Life', what she meant." He points to a photo from the coffee table book—a Mayan ceiba tree. "The tree is meant to describe the branching nature of the world, how one action can develop into two or more, each split representing an alternative existence. *That's* what Pakal is looking at as he reclines; he's looking at two worlds, somewhat the same but different. Don't you see?"

At times, Noah's genius doesn't extend to understanding the shortcomings of others. This is one of those times. Kate doesn't see.

"They're describing parallel universes!

"And not just the Mayans. I came across the page that Ingrid tore from the book when Dr. Zap was shot." He points to the page, the three bloody finger marks now browned, re-copied on cleaner paper.

"It isn't at all what I thought, you know—I thought it'd be about red shift—but it's an essay on parallel worlds written from two aspects, the Arabic view and the Mayan, both views stressing heaven as the place where the parallel worlds live, just like on Pakal's sarcophagus lid.

"But *where* in the heavens would a parallel universe live?" he asks. "That's the second puzzle piece." He turns her slightly so that she can see the wall, now partly painted, beside the fridge. It's a horrible blend of the calm blue and assertive, too-bright yellow, thankfully covered by a dozen or more pictures of the night sky.

"I took these from the codex, from Miriam's book, even from the photos I shot in Shanny's room, remember?" Kate does recall him asking Sharron if he could take pictures.

"How does the night sky—the heavens—point the way to a parallel universe? DiShannia knew. Look at the sketch she made of the sarcophagus. She's circled the bar along the top, marking it 'Seven Gods.' And here…"

He shows her his old iPhone, now safely unhinged from the wireless universe. He thumbs through photos he's taken—some of Kate sleeping, a selfie of the two of them in Heidelberg in the *Schloss*, several of DiShannia's posters, some pictures of Palenque's Temple of inscriptions, and finally one of Miriam standing beside a mural in the Tottenham Court Underground. Even in its diagrammatic form, it's clear that it represents the sarcophagus.

"Miriam is pointing to the same 'Seven Gods!'"

He moves her to standing in front of the pantry cupboards, now lined with blown-up pictures from the envelope that Miriam gave them—pictures of the Palenque Codex, Shanny's sketches.

"The Seven Gods are a definite place in the night sky, a constellation, sort of recalling the Mayan creation story. We call it the Pleiades or the Seven Sisters. It appears in the northern sky, generally in the fall, in the early morning. Venus crosses it every year: it's the timing of that crossing that made their astronomers aware that the universe was contracting. Venus seems to be pointing to the constellation.

"Of all the pictures of the night sky, it's this tiny section that's most important. I'll show you why." He takes her hand, leads her to the final trove of pictures, taped over the kitchen table. Some of them are reversed, negatives of the night sky, black marks against an all-white background.

"What do you see?" he asks her.

Frankly, she sees nothing of significance, but she tries. "Dots and lines," she says, a beginning question raises her voice.

"Exactly! It's a QR code. There are lots of pictures of them in the Codex, but only these," he points to some of DiShannia's original sketches hanging beside the pulled-out refrigerator, "match the area in the night sky that the Mayans, Shanny and Miriam tried to point out. That's the breakthrough!"

"Do you mean the code was *in* the sky?" Kate asks, incredulous.

"Exactly right!"

"How did you figure this out, all of this?" Kate stops, uncertain about what to call "all of this," the disbelief still in her voice.

"I had help, Kate. I had Shanny's translations and Miriam's work, and once I had *them*, the rest just came into focus. The hints of a parallel universe, the particular piece of the night sky that holds the clue to this, whatever, this QR code."

Kate's mind is a blur, just able to cope with today, let alone yesterday or even tomorrow for that matter. Tomorrow presses in on her.

"Does it work, the code?" she asks.

"It's what I was doing when you came in the room, testing it." He's using his recently-purchased UK mobile.

"But it only works so far, then stops." It reaches a blank screen. There is no doubt that he's reached a website, just an empty one.

"It's incomplete," they both say simultaneously.

It is incomplete. Small squares occupy three of the four corners of the page, and dots and dashes occupy the space between them, except for a small area in the middle, disappointingly void of any markings. Noah continues to try to use the code-scanner on his phone, stewing over the pictures of the code, adjusting the focus each time, fiddling with the angle, increasingly frustrated. The fussing lasts for an hour, an hour in which she takes down the pictures beside the fridge, stacks them, finishes painting one wall, cleans up the kitchen, moves the fridge back on its rollers, urges him verbally to come to bed. She has lost her father; she will *not,* she determines, lose her husband.

She gives up on the use of verbal persuasion and finally, purposefully, comes to his side, turns him to face her and presses into his hot body. His lower body warms as well, insistent, expressing its own urgency, a different and more comfortable immediacy than that of an imploding universe.

"Come to bed," she says, "please, get some rest. You'll solve it, I know, just, come to bed."

It is not to rest that he comes to bed. It is the parallel world, the physical, not the mental, that calls him.

When they are finished, as she drifts off to sleep, glad to have her husband back, glad that the evening with her father is behind her, Kate holds the talisman in her hand, rubbing it with her thumb. She feels its ridges. "Thanks for moving it," she says, referring to its new higher position on his neck. It's the only thing that either of them are wearing. A post-coital drowsiness envelops them both.

"No problem," he says, smiling at her. "Nooo problem."

But her comment stimulates a thought in him, a recollection. It percolates through his dreams.

Later that night, at its deepest hour, at a time perhaps that Venus might choose to cross the path of the Pleiades, his eyes suddenly open. His parallel brain has been busy searching its files like a computer, asleep but not sleeping. He disentangles himself from Kate, not wishing to wake her, and rushes to the bathroom where they've—in the new spirit of home-making—have purchased a shaving mirror for him, not as expensive as the one in the Eucalyptus Inn, but "a nice touch," Kate says.

He turns on its soft circular light, undoes the talisman from around his neck and places it into the arc of the mirror's soft light, adjusting it. It shows exactly what he saw weeks before—the rough outline of a QR code, tiny squares occupying three of the four corners of the thumb-sized pendant. In the mirror, the three squares are aligned correctly—two tiny squares at the top of the tiny stone rectangle, one square at the bottom left—but reversed on the stone image itself.

And at its center are six tiny dots and dashes, the remainder of the QR code, carved by a skilled hand a millennium and a half ago. We know the name of the talented stone carver—A'Ciliz—though Noah does not.

Later, Kate reaches for him, awakened by the sound of the copier, its soft whirring the only noise in the quiet apartment.

She finds him in the kitchen in reality but in a deeper reach of time and space in his mind. She finds him sitting at the kitchen table in his undershorts, multiple photocopies of a QR code spread around him like Iona's several weeks before, like some derelict back yard.

"Look! Look at this!" he says, excited. She is happy to see his enthusiasm, but like last night he looks right through her, into outer space, into the inner reaches of particles.

"You know last night when you mentioned the talisman? This morning, I remembered where I saw it, I mean really saw it, for the first time. In the Eucalyptus place, before the, well, before." He cannot make himself form the words, "press conference." Its consequences, the huge mushroom cloud of loss and Pete's death are still too great.

"It's hard to see, you know, it's so tiny, but the talisman has the same markings as these," he shows her the other drawings still pinned to the wall. "Except that it contains the dots and dashes in the center that the others were missing! It's amazing, amazing…"

It doesn't take very long for them to finish photocopying, enlarging and then adding this image to the others. Not long when you consider the giant distances involved. Not long when you consider the enormous time that has passed, like some ancient geological force, since its creation. Finally, his hand shaking, he scans the newly formed, now complete code, and watches while his phone takes them to a website that they have never seen before.

To a website the world, this world at least, has never seen before.

65

PORTMEIRION, NORTH WALES, UNITED KINGDOM, CURRENT DAY

He has solved it.

The giant puzzle pieces—hints of a parallel world described by the universal concept of a Tree of Life, a planet crossing a constellation slightly earlier each year, the unobserved but important links between the worlds of the west and east—have come together.

"Amazing," Ivaan says, his round face almost filling the small Skype screen. It is hard to say what he means, the website, or the discovery, or them.

Kate and Noah are sitting in their newly (if still only partly) painted kitchen, now showered, dressed and ready for the day. They sent the link to Ivaan just before dawn, his beard white in the Skype picture, like snow. There is no snow anymore on Earth.

"It's *so* interesting. Is unique. Here's what we have so far." His usual northern European reserve replaced by enthusiasm, Ivaan has turned his CERN team working on the new website as an answer to their quest for a portal from one universe to another.

"First, is not flat website, is three dimensional. It has multiple layers. You can push through the text and images like a CT scan! It's as though you are floating above massive country of text and graphics and you can zoom in on any one of them. Next, text is also unique."

He tugs at his beard, moves away from the screen, sends them an image.

"I will give you sample. We thought it was foreign language, just one unknown to us. A friend of mine, a professor of linguistics, he has run text through a search program, looking for root words or symbols that ancient languages. There are none. He thinks it has origins not of Earth, or at least, from *this* Earth. With one exception, I should say. There are few symbols that look like early Mayan, like Olmec." They are not surprised.

"Last, it has no URL."

Kate does not understand.

Ivaan explains, "When you are on a website, Kate, along the top bar you see its address. It shows you the server where that website exists. On this website, is no address, is no code. Is nothing."

A dam has burst.

Within hours, Ivaan has begun to organize the largest network of scientists in the history of the world, dwarfing the Manhattan Project. They come from dozens of disciplines, some of whom Kate and Noah have never heard of. Astrophysicists and cosmologists. Theoretical physicists and cognitive scientists. Semioticians. Mathematicians and proteomics experts. Within days, the team is networked by email and social media and is able to work on documents and theories in a secure cloud of information. Ivaan need not assemble them in a physical sense; this will be a virtual team. Huge, interconnected, dynamic, but virtual.

Their meetings take on a life of their own, a whirlwind of conference and Skype calls, of multiple voices and accents using English, and a language with words that Kate has heard but still does not understand—muons and bosons, String Theory and transmission to parallel universes. There is something else she does not understand.

"I don't get it," she says one evening after supper, after an unusually long and heated Skype call for Noah, and another trying day for her, one of many, with her father. The remains of a leftover meatloaf occupy some of the kitchen table. "The way the codex, the sarcophagus lid, the Seven Gods constellation, and the talisman are all linked. And Miriam's pointing at the mural in the Underground? I don't get that either."

"Took me a long time too, hon," Noah responds, glad to have something more tangible than particle physics to understand and explain. In addition to his new-found knowledge in the realm of the atom, he's been doing some on-line reading about Mayan, Arab and Spanish civilizations.

"The Palenque Codex is the key. It was created in the seventh century A.D., most likely discovered by the Spanish in the 1500s. There's no doubt they tried to destroy it—they certainly tried to destroy its message—but somehow it made its way to the Smithsonian and then to the British Museum. Mary Catherine, my grandmother, worked on it with Alan Turing—deciphering its symbols and its message. After he was killed, work on the codex ceased for years, then was restarted decades later by Miriam herself, and even Shanny. Weird, huh? How Mary Catherine's and Alan's obsession was picked up by their great granddaughter? They had done much of the work; all I had to do was put it together." He doesn't mention his own provenance—that of grandson and father—in the mix. Or his genius.

Her questions are still there. "What about the talisman?" she asks, not satisfied. "How did a little stone pendant, one that held the final clue, find its way to you?"

He fingers it, his saviour so often in the past. "I don't know the details, but it looks old. It's probably the same age as the codex and most likely moved along the same Spanish-Arab route that the codex—or at least its message—took. Somehow the Taliban, the part of the Arab world that carried this secret, knew what the stone held. They wanted me to have it." This piece of information still astounds him.

She's not done. "Why would Miriam stand in the Underground like that and point at a mural?"

"It's in the envelope of pictures and documents that she gave us. Most were pictures of the codex, you know, the writing and her interpretation. Some were pictures of the sarcophagus and Shanny's attempts to translate it. But one was an old newspaper clipping."

He reaches over the last of the meatloaf and finds the envelope, extracting a yellowed, fragile piece of newsprint, an ancient artifact, now encased in plastic. It shows a picture of a reopening of the Tottenham Court Underground in 1960: a group of distinguished-looking gentlemen, sporting vests, watch fobs. One of them wielded an unusually large pair of scissors, cutting a ribbon in front of the murals. The caption reads, "The Lord Mayor of London, Sir Bernard Waley-Cohen, First Baronet, left, and the Executive Director of the Underground Corporation, Sir Henry Cappleton, right, cut the ribbon to re-open the Tottenham Road Underground Station. Closed for renovations for over a year, its position near the British Museum is reflected in new murals lining the walls of its major platforms. They were designed by the museum staff, led by Miss Mary Catherine O'Rourke, Director of Community Relations."

Kate slides the plastic covered newspaper clipping back into the envelope, notices one more picture.

She asks, "And the Pleiades? What are they? I still can't believe that they provide a clue to this, this…"she has no word for the new world that occupy Noah and Ivaan and their team. She points to Noah's laptop, where pictures of the new website have lived, danced and led them for days.

"Ivaan's asked one of his team, an astronomer, to research it. She says it's almost unique among the constellations. Most of the others are just random collections of stars that our imagination has made into pictures, like Orion for example. But the Pleiades or the Seven Gods are really a natural cluster of stars—there's many more than seven by the way—spinoffs of a sort of mega-star. They'd appear as a constellation no matter which way you looked at them. She also said it's got nothing to do with Venus; the planet just acted as a pointer to the importance of the constellation, like Miriam's finger in a way. And she has no explanation for why it—or at least its negative—forms a QR code. The astronomer thinks the constellation might be the creation of an alien civilization, maybe a portal to another world. Who knows?"

There's that lack of imagination again. Even astronomers and Noah suffer from it.

Despite this interest in the past, the forward-looking work of Ivaan and his team has an urgency allowing little time to explore questions not related to a parallel universe. Those questions can wait. The ones that can't wait have to do with the future. They raise questions that not even Ivaan and his team can answer. And he needs Noah there to help answer them.

Ivaan, to whom the term *stubborn* hardly does justice, is serious that Noah join him. "There is only so much we can accomplish at distance," he says. "We have too much problems to solve. I need you here. Can you join me?" The refrain is persistent, and it stays in Noah's brain long after the Skype calls, an annoying chorus.

Noah is reluctant at first; Kate even more so. The weight of argument tells him he should not leave Portmeirion. They have had the fear of discovery drilled into them. They have lost friends. Their guardians, Marcus and Marius, are particularly adamant that he not go. They know that Melbourne and its surrounding suburbs a good section of a continent is now uninhabitable. They do not know where Harry is, or really, who he is. All arguments against leaving.

On the other hand, there is Ivaan. In the end, he and the siren call of another universe win.

To satisfy Kate, also stubborn, Noah tries to change his appearance. His straight black hair is curled, lightened, not quite Aryan blonde, but close. He is able to grow a beard, an impressive, close-cropped bush that covers his face, alters him to many observers. Glasses help. In a light-hearted mood, he says, "I could be a spy, huh? Like some intriguing dude you'd find under a lamppost wearing a trench coat?" She laughs, but is mostly unimpressed, hiding her fear. He hides it, too.

His trip to Geneva and CERN is uneventful, but not without observation.

Other than his own security network, Noah is watched by other eyes. Someone who has, let us say, borrowed the world's security cameras, someone whose facial recognition software is of the latest technology, someone who, hours later, recognizes the deep-set eyes, the wide forehead, the look of Turing. Someone whom we know by at least a couple of names—Harry. Aabis.

Some might even say Death.

66

CERN. MEYERIN. FRANCE. CURRENT DAY

The next two weeks speed by them in literal and figurative ways.

It is the most intense time, intellectually at least, that Noah has ever experienced, like the heat of a furnace. It builds on the work that Ivaan and he have started by Skype over the preceding weeks. Pat finds a small room for him, decorates it with a touch that long preceded her transition to Patricia. They find a rollaway bed, making CERN his home. Ivaan commutes from Geneva daily but the days are so long that his wife suggests, in somewhat unfriendly terms, that he sleep at CERN. Pat finds a room for him, too, thinking, *Well,* this *wasn't in the job description!*

They start by naming the mysterious on-line blueprint that they work from, calling it the Palenque-II Codex. They struggle with the name of their work itself but finally, bowing to Noah's lineage, call it the Turing Project.

They meet almost constantly, pouring over the text and graphs, the symbols, the equations. The mysteries. One by one, they fall to Noah's understanding, his parallel thinking, his problem-solving. And they fall to knowledge gained from the hidden website, the one with no home in this universe. Ivaan is the more methodical, both helped and burdened by his deep knowledge of particle physics, of the universe. Noah's approach is less burdened by detail and fact; he is more intuitive. They discover equations within the website's text, apply them to their development of the understanding of the Higgs boson and other particles. They build a theory slowly, brick by brick, of parallel universes and the means to traverse them, building new magic into what was the Large Hedron Collider.

In something less than ten, twenty-four hour days, they convert the giant collider into a Higgs Accelerator, something with a purpose greater than studying and understanding the universe. It is the impossible, insurmountable challenge of crossing into another universe, with purpose and intent. Now made surmountable.

Finally, early on the day before Christmas, they're ready. Noah takes him aside. They're having lunch, using the plates that Pat has brought to them, the plates that demonstrated parallel universes only a few months ago. In some ways, those months feel like years; in other ways, like hours. The malleability of time.

"Ivaan," Noah says, spearing a piece of lettuce on the plate, rushing through what he has to tell him. "I'm going to fly home this afternoon. It's Christmas after all. You don't need me for the practical part of this. It's not fair to Kate to spend our first Christmas alone. I'll stay in touch of course, even tomorrow if you need me, but I have to be home."

Ivaan nods slowly, thinking that at many levels Noah is right: that the mechanics of the experiment do not require Noah, that his contributions are much more conceptual. But he has come to depend on Noah's intuition, and is afraid that, at a distance, the spark that has made their discoveries unique might disappear. He argues against the plan, but only weakly.

And there is something more—something that Noah has suggested that he might try this week, an experiment much larger and more ambitious than the ones that Ivaan, the more cautious of the two, has proposed. If it's successful, it will be a sort of Christmas gift for Noah. They have, not to put too fine a point on it, become friends.

67

PORTMEIRION. WALES. UNITED KINGDOM. CHRISTMAS EVE

Kate doesn't know about Noah's surprise.

In the evening, she has supper with her parents as she has for every one of the long days that Noah has been gone. They seem endless. His absence has been like a physical ache, more than just an empty bed at night. She's taken to sleeping in the living room on the couch. But she's kept busy, and decides tonight she'll go alone to the Christmas Eve Church service in the village. Her mother would like to attend but her father requires almost constant attention, especially in the evening, the sundown of Alzheimer's.

For his part, Noah is intent on surprising her. He arrives just in time for the service to start. He walks across the commons to the tiny, ancient Anglican Church, hears the music and the choir. "Joy to the World" drifts like a cloud across the small space. The church will be packed. In fact, every church, every synagogue, every mosque, every temple has been a magnet in the last few weeks, overflowing with worshippers, frightened by the sight of a nuclear holocaust, afraid of rumors of a planetary collapse, fearful of a growing sun.

Many or most have turned to their vision of God. Foolish, of course, but understandable.

Added to this call, at least for Christians, it's Christmas Eve.

In a tribute to the upside down world of global climate change, a light snowfall has whitened the commons, the thatched roofs, the tree tops. And made them quiet, as though a blanket covers the village. In the midst of this, after the hymn has ended, Noah hears—in a town where the farms lie over a mile away—cattle, possibly sheep.

The church vestibule is full of animals. He has forgotten that this is the Christmas pageant when local farmers donate their sheep to inject reality into the manger scene. Mary and Joseph are at the front of the church, holding what appears to be a sleeping newborn, one of only a handful in Wales.

From the back of the church, standing awkwardly beside two sheep, Noah sees his Kate. She is midway between him and the sleeping Jesus, on an aisle. Without knowing that he will return this evening, she's kept a space for him. One of the sheep butts him gently, bumps him again, seeming to nudge him into the church. He isn't ready to go yet.

One minute more, he thinks. *I just want to look at her.* For a minute his heart fills, a vessel almost overflowing.

POSTLOGUE

L et me share a final note with you, the end of the tale.

Ivaan's experiments have seen electrons disappear to a parallel universe, he believes. He's seen protons and other particles appear as though from nowhere. Today's experiment will attempt to transmit digitized data across what Noah has come to express as the parallel divide using the Higgs accelerator. There are some big ifs here: if they can transmit small particles, then they should be able to transmit data, and if data, then perhaps molecules, cells or at least blueprints for them. Perhaps one day even humans. Today's experiment is limited to data.

Ivaan is optimistic.

They've thought of attempting to transmit the Palenque Codex itself but consider it too cumbersome, the graphics too challenging, even in its new translated and digitized form. They have talked about transmitting pages of the ghost website, but consider that too dangerous; its most likely source is another universe, a parallel one.

Instead they fix on this: transmitting this text as an experiment. "Too long!" Ivaan says gruffly when Noah first suggests it, like an ancient editor. "We need to use something much smaller." Noah is persuasive however and their friendship has made the decision easier.

You might ask, *This text?*

Yes. *This* text. The story of a young girl who discovers a secret held by the Maya, is awarded the President's National Science Award at fourteen. The story of her murder. Of the deaths of a Mayan scholar at the British Museum, of a famous astrophysicist, of others. A story in which Brad Pitt gets to star in *Titanic,* Richard Nixon has three daughters and the times zones between Wales and France are reversed. A world in which the Second World War was fought against the Russians and the Kennedy assassination occurred in Houston. The story of a journey of a doctor-turned-reporter from Afghanistan to Washington to Wales. The story of the nuclear demise of a city. The story of a discovery, of its translation. The story of a collapse. The story of friendship. Of love, perhaps the biggest story of all.

A story of the Potter with a capital "P." My story, one of many.

Today, Christmas Day, Ivaan will try, though of course he has a question, *How will we know the transmission is successful?*

You'll know, won't you? You exist in a different universe from Kate and Noah, much as the recipient of Alexander Graham Bell's first phone call was in another room. A universe with many similarities to your own. There is one sizable difference however: yours is still full of promise.

You will write the end to your own tale. Please don't disappoint me.

www.ingramcontent.com/pod-product-compliance
Lightning Source LLC
Chambersburg PA
CBHW051945240626
47153CB00005B/1639